The Toybox

Charly Cox was born in the South, raised in the Midwest, and now resides in the Southwest United States. She enjoys jigsaw and crossword puzzles, hanging out with her husband and her spoiled Siberian husky, visiting her son in Arizona, and traveling.

T0002262

Also by Charly Cox

Detective Alyssa Wyatt

THE
TOYBOX

CANELO
US

San Diego, California

Canelo US
An imprint of Printers Row Publishing Group
9717 Pacific Heights Blvd, San Diego, CA 92121
www.canelobooksus.com

Printers Row Publishing Group is a division of Readerlink Distribution Services, LLC. Canelo US is a registered trademark of Readerlink Distribution Services, LLC.

First published in the United Kingdom in 2020 by Hera. This edition originally published in the United Kingdom in 2021 by Hera Books.

Published in partnership with Canelo.

Correspondence regarding the content of this book should be sent to Canelo US, Editorial Department, at the above address. Author inquiries should be sent to Canelo, Unit 9, 5th Floor, Cargo Works, 1–2 Hatfields, London SE1 9PG, United Kingdom, www.canelo.co.

Publisher: Peter Norton • Associate Publisher: Ana Parker
Art Director: Charles McStravick
Senior Developmental Editor: April Graham
Editor: Julie Chapa
Production Team: Beno Chan, Julie Greene

Design: Brianna Lewis

Library of Congress Control Number: 2022947083

ISBN: 978-1-6672-0530-4

Printed in India

MIX
Paper from responsible sources
FSC
www.fsc.org   FSC® C010615

27 26 25 24 23   2 3 4 5 6

For Mary McAfee – one of the strongest, bravest, most giving women I've ever known.

And

For Kerrie and Victoria – for everything.

Chapter One

Saturday, May 18

The thumping bass from the stereo reverberated through Rachel's body and drove nails through her temple, and no matter where she moved in the house, the bass followed her. Having just reached the tail end of a nasty cold, she hadn't really wanted to hit the frat party where the booze flowed freely, and for some, so did the drugs, but her friend Anna insisted she attend this epic celebration. Marking the end of finals, the end of her freshman year of college, and the beginning of summer break, it was the most anticipated bash of the year. How Anna had heard about the party before her was a mystery since she didn't even attend the University of New Mexico. In the end it hadn't taken much to convince Rachel since she wouldn't normally have hesitated if she hadn't been feeling under the weather.

Following Anna's advice, she donned her shortest skirt – which was still two inches longer than the one Anna wore – and her new crimson halter top with the sparkly embroidered stars strategically placed to cover her breasts. She swiped on fire engine red lipstick, threw on a couple of coats of mascara, and dabbed her favorite perfume behind her ears and on her cleavage before determining she was ready. She didn't need the full-length mirror to tell her she was walking sex in heels. Her family had hit the beauty jackpot, so she was used to – and sometimes craved – the appreciative stares from the men and envious ones from the women.

Within minutes of walking through the door, Anna ditched Rachel in favor of flirting with some pop star wannabe who looked to be stuck in the eighties with his bleached blond mullet, flipped-up collar, and scratched penny loafers. Rachel shook her head. Maybe Anna could convince the guy to fast forward to the new millennium at least. Sticking to the edges of the room, she sipped from the beer placed in her hand the second she'd hit the front door and headed to the only group of girls she recognized – even though she didn't know a single one of them by name – but before she could reach them, they disappeared into the thick of the crowd. An hour later, she lost track of Anna completely. The last she'd seen her she'd been sneaking up the stairs with some guy who wasn't the pop star wannabe.

–

Rachel lifted the blue plastic cup to her lips, trying to figure out when she'd gotten another beer. She vaguely recalled some guy wearing a wife-beater removing her empty cup. Maybe he'd handed her another? A sudden throbbing pain in her right temple coupled with an increasing heaviness in her limbs forced her to lean against a wall for balance. She was beginning to fear she'd been overly optimistic about being at the end of her cold. Clearly, coming to this party hadn't been the greatest idea after all.

As soon as she was certain she wouldn't topple over, she set her sights on the couch a few feet away, wanting nothing more than to collapse onto it and give in to this crushing fatigue. A warning buzzed in the back of her mind reminding her that falling asleep at a party was risky and never a good idea, but she really just needed to close her eyes for a minute. Then she'd go find Anna and convince her it was time to leave.

Inches from the couch, someone bumped into her, sloshing her with what reeked of whiskey. 'Oops.' A sandy-haired guy latched onto her elbow while simultaneously stepping further into her personal space.

She tipped her head back so she wouldn't be staring at his pectorals, regretting it when the room began spinning. When it finally stopped, she narrowed her eyes in an effort to focus. He wasn't someone she recognized or even someone she'd normally enjoy flirting with. She just wasn't into guys who bathed in cheap cologne, athletes, or guys who wore jeans so tight they might as well be denim-painted skin. Nor was she impressed with the way he rolled up the sleeves of his red t-shirt sporting a white Lobos logo to emphasize his biceps. In her experience, he was the type of person who thought a cute smile would land him anyone he chose.

A point he proved when he smirked and lowered his head, making clear his intention. She jerked her head to the side, so instead of her mouth, his lips grazed her cheeks – and so did his tongue. A chill raced over her skin, making her shiver. She simply wasn't in the mood to fend off his unwanted advances.

'I have to go find my friend.' *When had her tongue grown to twice its size?* Mixing alcohol with the cold medicine she'd taken as a precaution before leaving must be screwing with her more than she thought. Nothing about this felt right.

Athlete Guy raked his eyes down her body and back up, pausing the longest on her chest, head cocked to the side as his tongue snaked out and swiped across his bottom lip. 'I can be your friend, baby. I can be your *real good* friend.' Amusement gave his voice an almost lyrical quality. Keeping his grip tight on her arm, he took three steps back and collapsed onto the couch, tugging so that she toppled onto the cushion beside him. He forced her back, crushing her between his chest and the arm of the sofa.

Anger and panic wormed its way through the fuzz in her head as he swatted away her efforts to shove him away. A cold sweat broke out over her skin, and tears sprang to her eyes when his calloused palm snaked up her thigh, shoving her skirt higher as he did.

3

She swallowed and concentrated on making her mouth form the word *stop* as he traced his lips along her neck and over the shell of her ear, his alcohol and pot-fueled breath hitting her face and sending a wave of nausea through her. Heart hammering, she jerked her head away, causing the headache sitting just behind her eyes to send a slashing pain through her skull.

'Let go of me right now, or I'll scream.' She barely managed to move the threat past her frozen throat.

With a sound of contempt, the guy shoved her away and stood, towering over her. Eyes narrowed, he made a point of slowly taking in every inch of her bared skin. 'A bit of advice, babe: if you're not willing to sell it, don't advertise.' He threw a final glare over his shoulder before he disappeared into the crowd.

Rachel pressed the heel of her hand against her chest, convinced her heart was trying to escape. She really wished she'd stayed home instead of listening to Anna. Which reminded her… she still had to find her friend if she was ever going to get out of this place.

She swiveled her head to the stairs. Was it her imagination, or had the distance increased since she'd last seen them? With an effort, and after two tries, she managed to push herself up from the couch, but as she forced her way through the throng of bodies and loud voices, she found herself turned around and in the kitchen. Since it wasn't as crowded in here, she took a second to take a full breath that didn't include inhaling copious amounts of cheap cologne and flowery perfume.

Exhaling slowly, she rested her head against the wall. She hadn't been this miserable at the height of her cold. It didn't make sense that two beers had made her feel this out of it. Hell, that rarely even gave her a good buzz. And standing here wasn't getting her any closer to home, so she forced her feet to move.

Keeping her eyes on the open doorway and one hand on whatever it could find, she was halfway across the kitchen when a tall guy with a massive chest bumped into her, almost knocking her down as well as blocking her path.

Out of necessity she gripped his upper arms to avoid falling, a sense of déjà vu washing over her. She really hated this party. She tilted her head back and glared up at him.

He returned her glare with a leer, placed one hand against the wall beside her head, and leaned in. 'Hoping for some action, babe?' She would've rolled her eyes if she could've mustered the energy. 'You're blocking my way.' She forced the words over her thick tongue and past her dry mouth as she tried to move around him. He stopped her by pressing up against her.

His hot breath washed over her cheek as he leaned down to whisper. 'What's the big hurry? Why don't we go somewhere and' – he winked – 'get to know each other better?' He trailed one finger up her neck.

A quiver started in her stomach and worked its way up, and once again she found herself trying to form words, but before she could, a very drunk couple groping each other knocked into his back, leaving just enough room for her to wriggle around him. As she made her escape, she heard him grunt and mutter, 'You probably suck in the sack anyway.'

Shaken and annoyed from both encounters now, her eyes flickered to the stairs, and for a few precious seconds, she considered leaving without Anna. After all, if it hadn't been for her insistence, she wouldn't even be here right now, dealing with these asshats. But she knew she wouldn't leave her friend behind, so instead of heading back to her dorm, she headed to the second floor.

What felt like a lifetime later, she was finally at the top of the stairs. As she paused to catch her breath, she counted at least a dozen rooms with closed doors. Apparently, locating Anna wasn't going to be as easy as she'd hoped. Her mood turned as dark as night, and she leaned against the nearest wall and closed her eyes – which added the highly unbeneficial effect of making the room spin like a merry-go-round. She was never mixing cold medicine with alcohol again. No, she was never *drinking* again. Ever.

Once her equilibrium was somewhat restored, she sucked in several gulps of air. Then, using the wall for support, she made her way to the first door, knocked, and pushed it open without waiting for an answer, interrupting the occupants and continuing until, finally, near the end of the long hall, with only three rooms left, she found Anna lying on a bed with her skirt shoved to her waist and her shirt opened, exposing a flat stomach and a belly button ring. A shirtless guy stood next to the bed fumbling with his pants. She recognized him – he had handed them a beer when they arrived – and he was not the same man Anna had headed upstairs with.

What was his name? Charles? Chase? And then she didn't care because the first words out of his mouth when he turned to see who had interrupted were, 'Come to join the party? I always say, the more the merrier.'

Seriously? As of right this second, she was swearing off frat parties, too.

Anna snickered and lifted one hand to wiggle her fingers in what could've meant *hello* or *come here*. Either way, it was time to get her out.

Grateful for a door to hold onto, Rachel ignored the guy still struggling with his zipper and said, 'Lezzgo.' She swallowed and tried again, this time enunciating each word like she was learning a new language. 'Let's. Go.'

To her surprise and delight, Anna agreed. ''Kay,' she giggled. 'Help m'yup.' Her words slurred together in two smooth syllables.

And while Rachel wasn't convinced she'd be much help, she was willing to try, so she stumbled forward with an unsteady gait, made all the more unsteady because of her high heels, and headed to the bed where she reached out a hand to help her friend up.

But instead of pulling her up, Anna dragged her down, laughing.

6

The bed was softer than she'd expected and closing her eyes felt like the best idea in the whole world. 'Need to leave,' she muttered, trying to resist sinking further into the inviting mattress, but kind of forgetting why she needed to resist at all.

–

It was the last thing Rachel remembered before waking with the hounds of hell trying to claw their way out of her skull. Not to mention that her mouth felt like a sock had been stuffed inside it. Garnering what little moisture she could, she ran her tongue over teeth that felt like the fuzzy outside of a peach.

Every inch of her body hurt, and she groaned, one hand reaching up to cup her sore, scratchy throat. She shifted in an effort to ease the aches, realizing as she did that the bed had seemed far plusher and more comfortable last night – not so scratchy and worn or… foul-smelling.

A chill in the air caused goosebumps to dot her arms and legs, making them feel like the gravelly road to her grandpa's house. Someone must've cranked the air conditioner to its maximum. Maybe Anna could convince the guy from last night to turn it off. And grab her a warmer blanket.

Hushed, frantic whispers she couldn't quite make out forced her to crack one eye halfway open. The gloom of a dimly lit room greeted her, so she willed the other eye to join its partner, which it did, but with an effort.

Ignoring the needling pain shooting through her temples, she shook her head at the unfamiliar surroundings… and the four shocked faces staring back at her – none of whom were Anna.

Chapter Two

It had been a long, exhausting weekend – in fact, it had been a long, exhausting six weeks for Detective Alyssa Wyatt, so she was more than just a little ready to dive headfirst back into work. Not that she was excited about the possibility of another missing person, but at least it gave her mind something else to focus on besides her last case.

Climbing out of her car, she spotted her partner Cord Roberts standing at the precinct door, politely holding it open for her. Ever the gentleman. 'How did it go?' he asked as soon as she was within hearing distance.

Her jaw clenched. *It* was referring to her quick weekend trip to Indiana where she had buried the cremains of her deceased brother, Timmy, who had been kidnapped when he was only four years old. For the past three and a half decades, she had believed him dead, only to discover that not only was he very much alive, but he was in fact the serial killer responsible for the string of gruesome, torturous murders of several young women that she had been investigating. After discovering his true identity, Timmy, known then as Evan Bishop, devised a plan to exact revenge on Alyssa and her family for what he perceived as Alyssa's failure to save him as a child. The first part of that plan came in the form of Bishop impersonating an officer, telling her son she'd been badly injured in an accident and he was there to rush Isaac to the hospital, and kidnapping him when Isaac climbed into the car.

'It went.'

'Fair enough.' He fell into step behind her.

'Morning, Ruby,' Alyssa said to the department secretary as she passed by the front desk.

Instead of a return greeting, the older woman peered over the top of her spectacles and in her usual, disgruntled tone, said, 'Captain Hammond needs to speak with both of you in his office. Right away.' She gave Alyssa a knowing look, then dismissed the two of them by returning to whatever she'd been doing before they'd walked in.

Cord rapped the top of the counter with his knuckles. 'Thanks, Ruby.' He winked at Alyssa when the older woman grunted in what passed for only Ruby knew what.

As she navigated her way to the captain's office, Alyssa allowed the familiar chaotic noises of a busy precinct to calm and help her get her mind back in the game where it belonged, where she liked it.

Steps away from knocking on Hammond's door, Hal Callum, one of her favorite go-to guys on her team and one of the best researchers in all of the Albuquerque Police Department, blocked her path when he rolled up, his old-fashioned wheelchair emitting a low squeak as the wheels turned. Alyssa shook her head at the unusual frown covering Hal's face. 'You know they have motorized chairs now?'

His answer was a growl. 'Don't you start with me, too.'

Years ago, Hal had been shot in the line of duty, paralyzing him from the waist down. For a time, he'd seriously contemplated suicide, but in the end decided he had far too much to live for, namely his wife and children.

For as long as Alyssa could remember, he'd refused to consider a motorized chair, insisting the manual ones helped keep his upper body strength in good condition. Problem was, in the past month, his old chair had begun showing its age.

'How did things go in Indiana?'

She should've known that was why he'd intercepted her. Biting back an irritated sigh, she gave the same response she'd

9

given Cord. 'It went.' Though she knew they cared, sooner or later – preferably sooner – they'd have to realize this was a conversation she'd like to avoid. She maneuvered around the wheelchair and knocked on the captain's door, ignoring Cord's shrug when Hal crinkled his forehead in concern.

At his gruff command to enter, Alyssa turned the knob and walked in. Captain Guthrie Hammond was the kind of man who wore a permanent scowl and could make a large room feel tiny with his bulk. He grabbed a pink slip of paper and extended it her way, focusing his laser-like stare at her as he did. 'How'd it go?'

Third time's a charm. 'It went.' She tilted her head to the piece of paper. 'That have anything to do with why you needed to see us this morning?'

He frowned at her dismissive response, but he handed over the paper. 'This Angela Kazminski called to report that her roommate might be missing.'

'Might be?'

'That's what she said. Roommate's name is Rachel Otis. She attended a frat party Saturday night and never returned to the dorm. Ms. Kazminski's been trying to reach Rachel's parents, but has thus far been unsuccessful.'

'If she went missing Saturday, why wait until today to report it?'

'You'll have to ask her that when you interview her. Get back to me as soon as you have some answers.' His eyes shifted back to his computer, which was their cue to leave.

Alyssa closed Hammond's door behind her before turning to Cord. 'I just need to drop something off first.' She didn't wait for his response before weaving her way around cubicles and desks and making a beeline for the office, which was actually an ancient supply room, barely larger than a walk-in closet, that she and Cord had repurposed as their own personal workspace. It was a tight fit, but they didn't complain. It was an improvement over the cubicles that most of the detectives were still forced to use in this cold, industrial building that housed some of the city's finest.

They had been given permission to use the space after the news broke detailing the true identity of Evan Bishop. The chaos and chatter it had created within the department forced a rare act of mercy from the captain who was not well-known for his generous, understanding nature – he wasn't nicknamed Captain Hothead for nothing – and he'd allowed Alyssa and Cord to use the derelict space as their own.

In their office, she pulled out her rolling chair that had nowhere to roll and leaned down to unlock her bottom desk drawer. From the inside pocket of her jacket, she removed a copy of the authorization she'd signed for Timothy Archer's organs to be donated to science, dropped it inside, and then closed and locked the drawer once more. 'Ready,' she said, pretending not to notice the question in her partner's gaze.

–

Thirty minutes later, Alyssa parked her government-issued Chevy Tahoe in one of the few available spaces not designated for residents outside the apartment complex where Angela Kazminski lived with her parents when she wasn't staying in the dormitories of the University of New Mexico.

Alyssa stepped out of the vehicle into the heat of what was promising to be another scorching day and glanced around. 'Which building?'

Without looking at his notebook, Cord pointed to the third building on the right. 'C. Number 1102.'

Being on the ground floor, the apartment was easy to find. At the door, Alyssa knocked, setting off a thunderstorm of angry, excited barking by what sounded like very large dogs, followed by a woman's irritated voice. 'Shut the hell up! Sit!' Two seconds later, a dark-haired woman in her late forties or early fifties, who had to be ready to top six feet tall in her bare feet, opened the door, an unlit cigarette dangling from her fingertips. When she realized it was there, she pushed it behind her ear. 'Sorry. I just quit. Sometimes it helps if I'm just holding it.' Her eyes dropped to the badges clipped to their hips. 'Are you here to speak to my daughter about Rachel's disappearance?'

The mouthwatering aroma of roasted green chiles and tamales drifted out the door and filled every part of Alyssa's olfactory sense, causing her stomach to growl. Another low grumble – this time not coming from her stomach – had her eyes shifting from the woman's face to the dogs who sat obediently behind her, their bodies taut with barely restrained eagerness, ready to pounce at the slightest invitation. 'Are those dogs or miniature horses?'

The woman laughed, taking her comment in stride. 'They are humongous, aren't they?' Bending slightly, she reached back and patted the top of one dog's head before repeating the motion with the other. 'Despite what their size implies, they're actually quite friendly. Unless you're a bad guy; in which case, I've seen them nearly rip a leash in half to get to someone they don't trust.'

'Good to know. Yes, we're here to speak to Angela. Is she home?'

'She is. Why don't you come in while I get her? My name's Gabriella, by the way.' She reached out slender fingers to shake their hands. 'I'll be right back.' Turning to the dogs, she pointed. 'Stay.'

The dogs followed their mistress with their heads until she was out of sight, and then they turned their attention back to the detectives as they entered the apartment, the dogs' tongues lolling out the sides of their mouths, tails thwapping against the floor in a rhythmic beat. Less than a minute later, Gabriella returned with her daughter in tow.

Angela Kazminski wore a pair of leopard print yoga pants with a yellow blouse that hit mid-thigh. Shorter than her mother, she was also more robust, but in a healthy way, as if she wasn't afraid to eat something besides salad. And if her mother's cooking tasted as heavenly as it smelled, Alyssa didn't blame her for wanting to devour more than green leaves and power foods. The expression on the girl's face as she approached the living room was a cross between fear, hope, and nerves.

'Angela?' Alyssa asked.

'Yes, ma'am. Thank you for coming.'

She made it sound as if it had been an invitation of some sort.

'I'm Detective Wyatt. And this is my partner, Detective Roberts. We'd like to ask you a few questions regarding your dormmate.'

Angela pointed to an oversized couch that seemed entirely too large for the space it was in. 'Do you mind if we sit?' She laughed, a self-deprecating sound, and said, 'I'm nervous, and I'd hate to faint on you or something.'

'No need to be nervous. We just need to clear up a few things so we know where to direct our focus,' Cord said, following her as she led the way to the living room.

Choosing the recliner closest to the television, Angela wrapped her legs beneath her, smiling when both dogs sidled up to either side and plopped themselves down in a semi-circle of protection around her. Keeping a careful eye on the newcomers, they rested their heads on their paws.

'We understand you think Rachel went missing sometime Saturday night. Why did you wait until this morning to report it?'

Angela sucked her bottom lip between her teeth and brought her hands together, clasping and unclasping them. When she realized what she was doing, she slid them under her thighs. 'I wasn't really sure she was missing.' She cleared her throat and bounced her gaze between Cord and Alyssa. 'I was packing because we were supposed to be clearing out of the dorms for summer, so I'm ashamed to admit I didn't even realize right away she hadn't come back yet. It wasn't until I had to move

13

some of her things to get to mine that it hit me she wasn't back and that I hadn't seen anything on any of her social media sites.' She pulled her hands from beneath her legs and twisted the ring encircling her pointer finger. 'And then I was afraid of calling Rachel's parents because I didn't want to get her in trouble, you know?'

'Get her in trouble how?'

'Drinking. But, it's not only that.' Angela shifted in her seat. 'Excuse me for saying this, but Rachel's mom can be one cold bitch, and if she – Rachel – was just off on a bender, I didn't want to get her into unnecessary trouble with her parents.'

As a mother to both an eighteen and fourteen-year-old, Alyssa wasn't sure underage drinking should be considered 'unnecessary trouble,' but she kept that opinion to herself. 'Did you try calling her?'

Angela nodded. 'Yes, of course, but she didn't respond to any of my texts, and when I called, it went straight to voicemail.'

'You said you were supposed to be clearing out of the dorms for the summer. Is it possible Rachel simply went home?'

Angela laughed. 'No way. She was dreading it as it was. Not a chance she would've gone any sooner than she had to.'

'What are their names, Rachel's parents?' Cord asked.

Face tinged pink, Angela admitted, 'I don't know their first names. "Mr. and Mrs. Otis" were the only names I'd ever known them by. According to Rachel, her dad is some kind of specialized heart surgeon, and her mother is an interior decorator turned professional nuisance.' She plucked absently at the dog hairs decorating her clothes. 'I only met them twice, and they were, um, obviously out of my league of players, you know?'

'How do you mean?' Alyssa asked.

Angela waved her hand around the apartment. 'This place could fit inside their house, like, twenty times.'

'Tell us about the last time you saw Rachel. Did she seem nervous or distracted, excited to meet someone at the party, maybe?'

'No, nothing out of the ordinary. I mean, she wasn't even planning on going at first because she was just getting over a cold. But since it was *the* end-of-semester frat party, another friend convinced her to go.'

'And what is that friend's name?'

Another flush of color raced into Angela's cheeks. 'I think it was Anna, or something like that. I don't really remember, and I never knew her last name. I'm sorry. I'm not much help, am I?'

Cord smiled. 'You're doing fine. So, this Anna, you weren't friends with her?'

Angela shook her head. 'Rachel only just met her recently, like within a few weeks, right around finals, maybe? Rachel said she didn't go to UNM but didn't say where she did go. Or if she did, I don't remember. Honestly, I was so focused on studying for my tests – I can't afford to lose my scholarship – that I wasn't paying close attention.'

'Do you think you could give us a description?'

'I only got a glimpse of her a couple times when she and Rachel were heading out somewhere, but she had medium-length hair, kind of a reddish blonde, about my height. Skinnier, though.'

'What can you tell us about the party Rachel attended?'

Angela raised both hands, palms up. 'Really, not much. I mean, I wasn't invited – not that I probably would've gone even if I had been. I don't even know which frat house hosted the party.'

Cord glanced down at his notebook and circled something. 'Okay, so aside from Rachel being inactive on social media, what makes you think she's missing instead of just sleeping off a hard night of partying? After all, some of these parties can go into the wee hours of the next morning.'

'Rachel posts about *everything*– mostly pics and selfies – but other than when she first arrived at the party, there was nothing. Sometimes if she parties too hard, she'll just hang somewhere and sleep off her hangover like you said, and at first, I thought maybe that's what she was doing. But when she didn't come home last night either, and I still didn't see any posts, I told my mom about it, and we decided if I still hadn't seen anything or heard from her by this morning, I needed to call.' She chewed on a hangnail sticking out of her thumb. When she spoke again, her voice cracked. 'What if something's happened to her, and I've waited too long?'

'We don't know what happened, so let's not jump to any conclusions.' Alyssa did her best to reassure the girl. But *if* something had indeed happened to Rachel Otis, they needed to get moving on it soon because they'd already lost those first precious twenty-four hours. 'I know you said you weren't invited to the party, but do you know anyone else who might've gone?'

'Chance Williams.' She rolled her eyes as she said his name. 'He's um, a bit of a player. He posted *tons* of pictures on his Insta from Saturday. He's with a different girl in every one. He fancies himself a real Lothario.' She shot a sideways glance toward Cord before concentrating again on Alyssa. 'He's hot, and he knows it. It's like he gets a thrill out of knowing everyone wants him, and he can pick and choose the ones he wants.' A small smile lifted the corners of her eyes. 'Well, almost.'

'I take it you turned him down, and he didn't appreciate it?' Alyssa clarified.

'Something like that. He never said anything. I just stopped getting invited to the parties.' One shoulder lifted and dropped. 'No biggie. They weren't really my scene anyway. I know as a college student, I'm supposed to be all about the parties, getting drunk and all, but like I said, I can't afford to lose my scholarship, so…'

'Chance Williams,' Cord wrote as he spoke. 'Any idea how to contact him?'

Angela nodded even as her phone magically appeared in her hand. 'Yep. I've got his number right here.' A few seconds later, she held her phone out for Cord so he could write it down.

'How about an address? I don't suppose you have one of those for him, do you?'

'Not really. But once, at a different party, I heard him telling a group of girls his family lives around the university area. Maybe around Ridgecrest? He could've just been lying, so who knows if that's really true anyway?'

'Since you've got your phone out, would you mind showing us a picture of Rachel?'

'Sure. I can even send you a screenshot, if you'd like.'

'That would be great, thanks.' Alyssa pulled a business card out of her pocket and handed it over, as did Cord, and then she stood. 'If you think of anything else, even if you don't think it's important, please call. It doesn't matter what time it is.'

As they stepped outside, Angela placed a hand on Alyssa's arm. 'You'll let me know if...' She swallowed and tried again. 'You'll be able to let me know if she's okay... or not, right? Like, I know I'm not family or anything, but...'

Alyssa patted the young girl's hand. 'I'll tell you what I can when we find something out. In the meantime, please remember to call if you think of anything else, or if you hear from Rachel.'

'I will, and thanks.' Angela closed the door behind them, shutting off all those amazing smells coming from the kitchen.

'I want Casa Benavidez for lunch,' Cord said as soon as he slid into the passenger seat.

'Took the words right out of my mouth.'

'It was all I could do not to salivate all over myself.'

Alyssa laughed because it really had smelled that good.

As they pulled out of the apartment complex, Alyssa realized it had been a while since she'd felt like this – in her element, doing her job. She was glad Indiana was behind her so she could concentrate on what was in front of her. And right now, that entailed tracking down a bunch of college-aged kids to try to convince them they needed to talk to the police about a frat party where a missing girl was last seen.

Chapter Three

Beau Cambridge and Jersey Andrews leaned against the living room wall, kissing – the sloppy kind – as Holly Wyatt, Sophie Quill, her best friend since sixth grade, and Leigh Ann Wolfe counted cracks in the wooden beams on the ceiling, studied pedicures, examined split ends, or pretty much anything else to avoid seeing what they could unfortunately hear. The sickening sound of smacking lips and groans from the two lovebirds – at least 'lovebirds' for the past fifteen minutes; give it twenty, and they'd likely be back at each other's throats – was almost enough for Holly to lose her appetite… and everything else she'd consumed that day.

'When I told Jersey to *embrace the suck* earlier, I didn't expect her to take it quite so literally,' Sophie deadpanned, not bothering to keep her voice low.

Holly would've laughed, but she was far too irritated. Instead, she raised her voice and addressed the make-out queen. 'Jersey, my stomach is currently gnawing on my spine I'm so hungry, so we're heading to Saggio's *now*. Are you coming with us or not?'

'Hear, hear!' Sophie clapped, her head bobbing vigorously as she leaped to her feet and headed toward the door.

Leigh Ann remained quiet as she watched the couple like she might a movie that wasn't good enough to continue but not bad enough to turn off. Then she, too, uncurled her frame from the couch and followed Sophie.

As Holly had expected, Jersey's arms dropped from around her boyfriend's neck as she lowered herself from standing on her tippy toes, as was required by her petite five-foot-one-inch frame compared to his towering six-foot-three.

But when her friend tried to take a step back, Beau's fingers gripped harder at her hips to hold her in place, his lips and tongue all over her face (God, how could she stand that?). Then, he opened his dark eyes, stared directly at Holly and licked his lips as if he'd just polished off a juicy steak.

It was akin to being injected with live insects, and Holly fought the urge to scratch at her arms. She glared back before turning away just in time to see Sophie's eyes nearly roll to the back of her head.

Beau made a last grab at Jersey between her legs, winking at the others as he did, finally ending the semi-public display of affection. 'Walk me out, baby. I still need to talk to you about something.' In his typical caveman fashion, he dragged his girlfriend behind him to the door. He skewered Holly with his eyes when he passed her, clearly blaming her for prematurely ending his make-out session.

Good. Holly hoped he was pissed. The way he treated her friend like she was his property made him one of her least favorite people. She didn't know what Jersey saw in him, but it wasn't for her to decide who Sophie's cousin dated. Not that she'd listen anyway. Jersey had never been great at taking advice, at least not since Holly had known her, when they'd become friends at the age of twelve.

Before the front door closed, Sophie said, 'God, I hate him. Seriously. It's like watching a tiger stalking its prey. Creepy AF, I'm telling you. Oh, and did I mention I hate him?'

'You say that every time he's around.' Leigh Ann stared outside where Beau's hands now roamed inside Jersey's unbuttoned shirt as he ground his hips against her in a way that appeared painful.

'I do,' Sophie agreed. 'And I mean it every time. He's a pig. We all see it. Why can't she?'

Leigh Ann shrugged. 'Yeah, well, she did say bacon is one of her favorite things, right?' Her head tilted to the side. 'What are they doing now?' Jersey's palms were flat against Beau's chest, and her head was averted.

Holly snorted. 'Come on, let's go find out.'

They didn't have to go far because the moment they stepped onto the porch, it was clear Beau and Jersey – now in tears – were fighting. What could've possibly gone down in the thirty seconds it had taken them to join the two outside? Holly had never met anyone who could pinball between emotions so quickly.

Less than a minute later, Beau, his face turning a crazy shade of crimson as Jersey shook her head emphatically and tried pulling away from him, shoved his girlfriend hard enough that she stumbled, barely catching herself on a tree before she tumbled to the ground. Calling her worthless and pathetic, he stormed over to his souped-up four-wheel-drive, hopped in, and then peeled away from the curb in a spray of rock and gravel, flipping them off as he squealed down the road.

'Mature,' Holly muttered. She draped an arm around her friend's shoulder, squeezing her slightly as she guided her toward her car. 'Are you okay?'

Jersey nodded slowly, trembling as she watched Beau's Jeep disappear.

'Come on. Let's go eat.'

Jersey sniffled and pulled a crumpled tissue from the pocket of her short shorts, wiped her eyes, and blew her nose. 'Shotgun,' she announced, dropping the tissue to the ground, causing Holly to cringe.

'You're kidding, right?' Sophie snapped. 'We waited freaking forever for your live soft porn show to end. You think you deserve *shotgun* after that? I hardly think so. Besides, I already called it.'

She didn't, but Holly didn't contradict her. Not just because she was starving and didn't care who sat up front since she was in the driver's seat, but because for as long as they'd been driving, the unspoken seating arrangement had been Holly and Sophie up front, passengers in the back. Because she had surpassed hungry and dipped into hangry, she said, 'I don't care who sits where, but anyone not in my vehicle when I turn the key in the ignition gets left behind.'

When she moved around to the driver's side and opened the door, the others scrambled in. And to Sophie's supreme satisfaction, judging by the look on her face, Jersey buckled herself into the backseat behind Holly, muttering under her breath about Sophie's spoiled selfishness.

The drive was short, only fifteen minutes, but the grumbling from Jersey made it feel three times longer, made even worse when they spent another twenty minutes searching for a parking spot that didn't require walking two miles to the restaurant.

Ten minutes later, the four of them were settled at a table in the back of the crowded Italian restaurant that was a favorite of the university crowd. To Holly's relief, their talk centered around an upcoming concert until their food arrived, but five bites in, Leigh Ann asked Jersey if she was ready to talk about whatever it was that had set Beau off.

Their friend swallowed the bite in her mouth and washed it down with a drink of unsweetened tea. Blushing, she glanced all around her, then leaned in closer. What came out of her mouth was not at all what Holly expected, and her reaction showed it.

'He wants a threesome.' She gulped down another drink as tears pooled in her eyes. 'But not with him. He wants to watch me have sex – with two other guys. He got super mad when I told him no.' She shook her head. 'Maybe I overreacted. Maybe I should've at least considered it or listened to him anyway. I was just feeling a little hurt and shocked.' Jersey grabbed her phone, and Sophie slapped it out of her hand.

'For God's sake, are you seriously going to text that jerk now? What is wrong with you?'

Holly stepped in before things could get heated. 'Jersey, what Sophie is trying to say is that you did *not* overreact. At all. If it's something *you* want, then fine. But I don't think it is. And if you give in to this, what's going to stop him from pushing you into doing other things you're not comfortable with?' She placed her hand over Jersey's and gave it a squeeze. 'Honey, you have every right to say no and mean it.'

'And not to be pressured, and especially not *bullied* into a yes,' Leigh Ann added.

Jersey rubbed the base of her neck, her body seeming to shrink in front of them. 'Maybe I just need to hear him out. Maybe he was just embarrassed to ask and got mad when I didn't listen.'

'Oh, for God's sake, Jersey. Has the way your father treats your mother taught you nothing about guys? Beau. Is. An. Ass. Accept it and move on. Or keep denying it, but stop whining when he treats you like a piece of meat.'

Sophie's words were harsh, and both Holly and Leigh Ann sucked in their breath, anticipating a dramatic explosion.

Jersey shoved her plate away and slammed her hand down, almost knocking her drink over. 'Why are you *always* so mean to me?' Crimson crawled up her neck and into her cheeks while fat teardrops spilled down her face.

'How exactly am I being mean to you, dear cousin? By speaking the truth?'

'You don't understand what I'm going through! First my grandma dies, then Mom and Dad announce they're divorcing after thirty years! All I have is Beau!'

'What do you mean *all you have is Beau*?' Pointing, Sophie waved her arm in a circle around the table. 'What about us?'

'What Sophie means—' Leigh Ann began.

'What *Sophie* means,' she snarled, 'is that it is insulting for *Jersey* to tell us all she has is *Beau* when not only are we sitting right here in front of her, but we, *not* Beau, are always there for her – me, since we were children, Holly since we were twelve,

and Leigh Ann since mid-freshman year. On the other hand,'
– by now, flames were shooting from Sophie's eyes – 'Beau has
"been there" only as a condescending jerk for about six months.
So, yeah, what Sophie means is that that was a crappy thing for
Jersey to say.'

Holly stretched her neck left and right to help ease the
ache in her head and the tension in her muscles. As she did,
she noticed they were beginning to attract an audience. She
groaned – on the inside, but still. She caught the waitress's eye,
raised four fingers, and mouthed, 'Boxes, please,' relieved when
the woman nodded. She was probably as glad to be rid of them
as Holly was to be gone.

–

Several minutes later, their bill paid, the four of them weaved
their way through the maze of tables and bodies until they were
finally outside with Sophie marching ahead of Jersey.

Jersey cried as Leigh Ann did her best to soothe her. The
most patient and comforting of the girls, Leigh Ann had what
Holly and Sophie joked was the *magic touch*. Which was kind
of ironic, considering she'd just joined their little group in the
last four years.

Wishing their girls' night out had gone better was a waste of
time, so as they made their way to her car, Holly looked at the
bright side of their evening ending earlier than planned. Her
parents had gotten back from Indiana late this afternoon, and
she hadn't yet had a chance to see them. They would be out
to dinner with Isaac, but now she would be home when they
got back. She wanted to make sure her mom was doing okay.
Ever since she'd realized the serial killer she'd been hunting was
also the brother she'd always believed had been murdered when
he was four, her mom had done her best to hide the emotional
turmoil and impact it was having on her.

Her mind whirling with thoughts of her mom, it took Holly a second to realize Jersey had stopped just steps away from the car.

'You know what? I think I'm going to hang back, go for a walk and clear my head.' She wrung her hands together, avoiding all their gazes.

'What? Why?' Holly asked. A quick glance at Leigh Ann told her she was just as surprised. Sophie's face registered more impatience than anything else.

'I need some fresh air is all, so I'm going to head over to the duck pond for a bit.' Jersey tipped her head in the direction of the university.

Not feeling comfortable leaving her friend alone and without a car, especially since daylight was fading, Holly tried to get Jersey to reconsider. 'It's going to be dark soon, so why don't you just come with us, and I'll drop you off first, okay?'

Jersey shook her head and turned to stare at the windows of a nearby retro clothing shop, her pretty features reflected back at her from the double-pane glass. She chewed on her bottom lip before a sad smile turned down the corners of her mouth. 'I'm sorry for being such a downer. I know this was supposed to be our fun night. And this isn't the first time my parents have threatened divorce, but since Dad's already in another country with his nearly-my-age girlfriend, I'm pretty sure it's for real this time.' She lowered her voice, still not looking at her friends. 'Don't worry, I'll be okay. I won't be long, and when I'm ready to head home, I'll call an Uber.'

Considering that it had been less than two months since Evan Bishop had been targeting young women, Holly couldn't, in good conscience, allow her friend to go off on her own. If anything happened, well... she didn't even want to *consider* something like that. 'We'll all go with you, then. We'll even hang back, if you want, so it'll be like we're not even there.' She widened her eyes at Sophie and Leigh Ann and tipped her head toward Jersey.

Grudgingly, Sophie agreed. 'Right, like we're not even there. See, zipping my mouth, throwing away the key starting now.' She may have rolled her eyes as she made the offer, but at least Jersey didn't see it.

Leigh Ann hooked her arm through Jersey's and with forced cheer, said, 'We'll be like ghosts. Invisible. So, lead the way.'

A haunted look passed over Jersey's face as more tears gathered in the corners of her eyes. Then she untangled her arm from Leigh Ann's. 'Thanks anyway.'

Holly frowned. 'I really don't like this, Jersey. At least text me when you get home, okay?'

'Maybe. Look, don't worry about me. I really just need to be alone to think about – everything.' And then she walked to the corner where she waited for the light to change so she could cross the street onto the grounds of the university.

'Did she just pass up an opportunity to share all that drama?'

Leigh Ann shot Sophie a dirty look. 'She's obviously got a lot on her mind. And you refusing to understand isn't the most helpful.'

Sophie shrugged, unbothered by the chastisement. 'Her dad's a sleaze, and his mom's death was just the green light he needed to dive into his midlife crisis. Everyone in my family hates him because he's such a dirtbag. Probably why she latches onto Beau; it's a daddy issue. And you know she's going to call or text him as soon as we're out of her sight. It's ridiculous.' Then flipping her perfectly straight, long black hair, she opened the passenger door, slid in, and slammed it shut, cutting off Leigh Ann's reply.

Twenty minutes after she dropped off her friends, Holly flopped down on her bed and sent a text to Jersey reminding her to call if she needed or wanted to talk, then she donned a pair of headphones, swiped through to her favorite playlist, and closed her eyes as she waited for her family to return home from dinner.

She hadn't realized she'd fallen asleep until the door banged downstairs, startling her awake. She bolted upright, her heart jackhammering in her chest as she slowly became aware of her surroundings.

At the sound of her mom's and Isaac's voices, she smiled. Her family was home. She shut off her music, threw her headphones to the bed, and went to welcome her parents back.

Chapter Four

'Wh – where am I?' Rachel choked out. Along with the four other occupants of the room, she was confined in what strongly resembled a jail cell with its thick metal bars stretching from floor to ceiling. Lining each wall with about twelve inches between them, were ten cots, the kind she'd seen used in military shows in makeshift hospitals.

Off to the side was an open doorway with no door; inside it was a toilet, a shower stall with no curtain, and a pedestal sink.

One rectangular window rested so high up on the wall, all she could see were the tree trunks that filled its glass frame. Outside the caged-in area was what appeared to be a finished basement, though it was currently bare of furniture.

A tall brunette wearing a red silk robe that stopped just shy of mid-thigh stopped chewing her bottom lip long enough to answer. 'We're not sure. I'm Becca, by the way.'

Rachel was still trying to process that when a groan as creepy as it was unexpected had her head snapping to the right, causing a lightning flash of pain to shoot through her skull. After the dizziness wore off, she noticed a girl who could've been fourteen or forty covering her mouth as she whimpered, her glassy eyes wide as she rocked back and forth, hard tremors knocking her body against the painted cinderblock wall. She, too, wore a silk robe, only hers was royal blue.

'That's Cheyenne,' Becca whispered softly, sadly. Then she tilted her head to what probably used to be a stunning redhead but whose face and arms were now covered in scars, red scratches, bruises, and open wounds. The girl, dressed in a yellow silk robe, lay in a fetal position, mewling sounds that resembled a cornered cat emerging every few seconds, hollow eyes staring at nothing as she scraped at her skin. 'And that's Meghan.'

'Wh – what's wrong with her?' Rachel asked, aware she didn't really want to know the answer.

'She's been like that since yesterday, ever since they brought her back downstairs.'

Who was they? Nausea twisted her stomach into little knots. 'Where's Anna?' Her lips quivering, she reached down to straighten her skirt only to realize in horror that her clothes had been replaced by one of the silky robes the other girls wore. Hers was a deep burgundy. Her skin crawled as questions screamed in her brain. *Who had undressed her? Why?*

As if her thoughts had been spoken aloud, she received her answer from somewhere behind her and to her right when yet another girl snorted, and a voice as cold as the other's had been warm said, 'Welcome to the sex trade, where unwilling participants are sold for sex to the highest bidder – or bidders. And the more terror you show, the more they want you. And unless *you're* Anna, no one knows who the hell she is.'

'Christ, Faye! What's wrong with you!'

Rachel moaned, the contents of her stomach churning and threatening to revolt. She clapped her hands over her ears. 'No, no, no, no, no!' Sold for sex? Things like that happened only in the movies or on the news, but certainly not to her. Her mind numb with horror, she listened as the girl called Becca berated the other.

'What? You think she's not going to figure it out soon enough, just like the rest of us did?' The girl called Faye waved her purple silk-encased arm around their cell.

As if she were a balloon that had been pricked with a needle, Becca deflated. 'Still, you don't have to be such a bitch about it,' she insisted, though the fight had already gone out of her voice.

'Well, what would you do? Wait until they've come to drag her upstairs and let her figure it out then?'

Afraid if she started screaming, she wouldn't be able to stop, Rachel pressed her fist so tightly against her lips that her teeth cut into both, trying to concentrate her focus on that pain in an effort to hold herself together. She'd woken to a nightmare, she thought, glancing around the cell as muffled whimpers escaped around the space between her mouth and hand.

A tan arm reached over and rubbed her shoulder in a weak attempt to comfort. Becca.

'Faye shouldn't have dropped that on you like that.' There was no censure in the girl's voice, just a sad sort of resignation or even acceptance.

Bile burned the back of Rachel's throat as each of the girls in the room came into focus, each wearing their silk robe as if they were at some kind of high-end slumber party. Shaking her head from side to side, she squeezed her eyes shut. If she didn't listen, didn't look, she could pretend this wasn't happening. Her brother often accused her of ignoring the elephant in the room, and for once, he'd be right.

At the thought of Nick, a flash of something like hope shot through her – he'd be looking for her – but as quickly as it was there, it was gone. Knowing Angela, she'd be oblivious to the fact that Rachel hadn't returned after the party, so no one would even know she was missing, much less be trying to find her.

Wrapping her arms around her stomach as she tried to hold her pieces together, Rachel glanced over to the girl called Faye. In a purple silk robe that reminded her of royalty sat a stunning girl with milky skin and deep brown eyes. Even in this dimly lit prison, Rachel could see the girl was beyond beautiful – she was exotic.

Faye held her stare, unblinking and unapologetic, until Rachel shot up, moving frantically around the room and into the tiny bathroom area, searching high and low, running her hands up and down the walls and along the floorboards as she searched for… anything – a hole that could be made larger, a weapon to use, anything. She had to get out of here. Now.

It took less than a minute to come to the realization there was no escape, yet she couldn't stop. She even tested her strength trying to push the metal bars apart, straining until she collapsed to the floor, beating her hands against the cage that imprisoned her and the others.

She had no idea how much time passed before she felt two pairs of arms lift her from the floor and move her back over to the bed. The two girls then sat on either side of her as they offered her… what? Comfort? Friendship? Rachel shivered, and Becca scooted closer in an effort to offer whatever warmth she could.

'Can't we escape?'

This made Faye snort in a way that Rachel's mother would describe as 'unladylike.' 'How could we escape? We're kept in this God-forsaken cage like wild animals. What are we going to do? Gnaw through the bars?' The next words out of her mouth were a splash of cold reality that Rachel could've gone on denying for a while longer. 'You know, we wouldn't really be doing you any favors by sheltering you from the hard facts. Instead of trying to give you false hope, it would be better if we taught you how to survive.'

Chapter Five

Monday, May 20

Before leaving Angela's neighborhood, Cord had called to ask Hal to run a search on Mr. and Mrs. Otis, and within minutes, he had an entire history in front of him, including an address and cell phone numbers. Sometimes it was easier to find facts on people who had money.

Since Rachel's parents weren't answering their phones, Alyssa and Cord decided to take their chances at catching them at their residence in the hope that Angela was wrong, and Rachel had indeed decided to return home early without telling her friend. They'd been driving in silence for a few minutes as Alyssa processed the million thoughts vying for first place in her head, not the least of which was Rachel. That another girl could be missing so soon after closing the serial killer case ratcheted up the tension for her, especially as Bishop had targeted young women for nearly two decades. She couldn't help but fear a copycat killer.

'It's not going to be easy getting a bunch of underage-drinking college kids to admit to being at a frat party, much less give up helpful information,' she told Cord.

He nodded his agreement. 'Yeah, but if we can get some of them to come into the precinct, I'll bet Hal can make them talk.'

It was true. Alyssa had never seen a man so capable of getting suspects, victims, or anyone else to relax and spill everything, whether it was relevant to a case or not. He always joked that it

31

was because everyone trusts a man in a wheelchair, but Alyssa knew it was more than that… there was just something in his demeanor and personality that relaxed people, that told them he was safe. And she'd seen it long before his life had taken the turn that landed him in the chair.

Traffic was lighter than usual, so it wasn't long before Alyssa flipped on her blinker and slowed for the turn onto Rio Grande, arguably one of the most scenic drives in the city. And the twenty-five mile per hour speed limit allowed travelers to admire the combination of old farm homes interspersed with ultramodern ones, different in their architectural style but all enjoying huge, spacious plots.

Six minutes later and after passing the house twice, they finally located the address and pulled up to a huge black wrought-iron gate. Alyssa and Cord both let out a low whistle. 'Angela wasn't kidding, was she?' The house behind the gate looked like it could house a family of fifteen without the inhabitants ever running into each other.

'Tell me again what Hal found on the parents.'

'Mister was born wealthy and inherited money from his parents. That, coupled with his being a very specialized heart surgeon – whatever that means – gives them a very bloated financial statement. Like Angela said, the missus was an interior decorator/designer before marrying, and according to some social article in *Albuquerque, The Magazine*, the two met when he hired her to decorate his home in the foothills. And then they moved here.'

A crackling sound startled Alyssa until she realized it was coming from a cleverly hidden speaker nestled inside the hedge outside the gate.

'Can I help you?' a disembodied voice asked.

'Detectives Wyatt and Roberts with the Albuquerque Police Department. We need to speak to Mr. and Mrs. Otis.' Alyssa tapped her fingers on the steering wheel when there was no response. With each passing second, her tapping became harder and more insistent until Cord reached over and placed a hand over hers to stop the incessant noise.

'Impatient, much?' He removed his hand. 'Patience really isn't your strong suit, is it?'

'And after five years of being my partner, this surprises you how?'

Five long minutes later, just as Alyssa was reaching out to jab the intercom button, the voice returned. 'Please pull in.' Before she could thank the invisible person, the gate rolled open, and she drove through.

Weeping willows, cottonwoods, and maple trees lined what appeared to be a private forest on either side of the winding driveway. The Otises lived in luxury most people only dreamed of. Surrounded by such lush greenery, Alyssa had to remind herself they were still in the metropolitan area. 'It must take a small army to keep this yard up.' As they neared the house, a maze of hydrangeas hugging a monstrous marble birdbath arose, shielding nothing of what had to be a ten-thousand-square-foot house – which didn't include the attached six-car garage. 'I could fit almost five of my house into this one,' Alyssa muttered just as another thought occurred to her. 'If they have all this money, why is their daughter attending a local, public university?'

Cord shrugged. 'Good question. You should ask.'

She'd barely turned the ignition off when a heavy oak door opened to reveal a woman wearing tailored blue slacks and a matching silk blouse, large diamonds dangling from her ears, and a pearl necklace draped around her neck. Behind her and slightly to the left stood a man who maybe wasn't quite as impeccably dressed, but his clothes still shouted *expensive*. The expression on his face could've been either boredom or irritation, Alyssa couldn't tell which, or maybe it was a little of both, at this unexpected visit.

'What? No butler?' Alyssa mumbled as she opened her car door, only half kidding.

Cord chuckled. 'Must be his day off.'

As soon as their feet hit the paved drive, they both patted their pants to make sure their gold shields were still clipped to their clothes and visible to the people they were approaching. When they were close enough, Alyssa extended her arm and introduced herself. 'Detective Wyatt. This is my partner, Detective Roberts. Mr. and Mrs. Otis?'

Was it her imagination, or did Mrs. Otis curl her lip into a sneer before finally accepting the handshake? A visceral chord of dislike ran through Alyssa, but she shoved it aside. She didn't have to like or admire people in order to do her job. If she did, she would've had to quit ages ago.

Unlike his wife, Mr. Otis accepted the detectives' handshakes with a firm grip of his own. 'Please come in,' he said, turning and leading the way through a foyer and an open living area into an equally open kitchen that was home to not one, but two enormous granite-topped islands. Modern, dark-stained wood cabinets lined the walls. But what really made Alyssa's mouth water were the three ovens situated around the room. She blinked, then counted them again. Yep. Three. How many guests did one invite to warrant that many ovens?

'How exactly can we help you, Detectives?' Though there was a definite chill in Mrs. Otis's voice, there was still an appreciative glint in her eyes as she directed her question to Cord.

Alyssa mentally shook her head. Women had a tendency to gawk at her partner – who was rather handsome with his dark hair and piercing blue eyes tinged with ridiculously long lashes many women would pay a pretty penny for – though perhaps not as openly in front of their husbands.

The attention often made him uncomfortable, but he used it to his advantage when necessary. He smiled his million-watt smile. 'Firstly, thank you for seeing us like this. We tried calling, but when no one answered, we decided to try our luck at catching you at home. We spoke to your daughter's roommate this morning. Angela Kazminski?'

An angry frown turned down the corners of Mrs. Otis's mouth, and Alyssa was certain the woman's face was going to freeze into an icicle as any hint of warmth drained from her expression. 'Yes, Angela called us a while ago. Is this going to take long, Detectives? I do have things on my agenda for today and can't be held up.'

The woman's attitude and behavior stunned Alyssa. How could she not be worried about her daughter possibly having gone missing? Through gritted teeth, she said, 'Things that are more important than your missing daughter?' Alyssa now understood Angela's reaction when she'd asked if it was possible Rachel had just gone home to her parents' house. Mrs. Otis's coldness made it clear to her why Rachel had definitely not chosen to come home after attending the frat party, just as her roommate had insisted.

Rachel's mother didn't exactly roll her eyes, but it was close. 'As I explained to Angela' – the way she said the girl's name made it sound like Rachel's roommate was slightly above the status of a rodent – 'I... we... don't believe our daughter is missing. She's simply run away for the time being. Isn't that right, dear?'

Alyssa didn't wait for Mr. Otis to respond, nor did she try to temper her disgust as she compared her own reaction when she had realized her son was missing, only to discover he'd been kidnapped by a serial killer. 'First, let me be the first to point out that your daughter is nineteen years old, in college, and *technically* can't be a runaway. And what makes you think she's simply chosen to randomly disappear? Has she ever done something like that before?'

Mrs. Otis made a derisive sound and waved off Alyssa's suggestion. 'Of course not.'

'Then, if she's never pulled something like this before, what makes you think she has this time? In fact, let's take it one step further... what if you're wrong?'

Before Mrs. Otis could respond, the alarm over the front door emitted a long, loud beep, the sound followed by a bellowing, 'Mother? Father?'

Mr. Otis yelled back. 'In the kitchen.'

Heavy footsteps fell across the tiled floor, muffled only when they hit carpet. A brown-haired, brown-eyed young man, tall with what Alyssa liked to think of as a tennis player's build, and a charming smile rounded the corner, hesitating only a fraction of a second before walking up first to Alyssa, then Cord, shaking their hands in turn.

'You must be the detectives searching for my sister. Angela called me after she spoke to my parents.' His lips tightened before he continued. 'I'm Nick. Rachel's older by four minutes and thirty-three seconds brother.'

A disgusted 'hmmph' burst from Mrs. Otis's mouth, causing her son's smile to widen as he explained. 'Mother here simply *despises* it when I introduce myself as Nick. She prefers Nicholas, as it sounds so much more distinguished and snobby, much more befitting of her social circle.' Despite the smile, his eyes were full of concern.

Alyssa liked the young man already. 'Nice to meet you, Nick,' she said, intentionally using the nickname his mother apparently loathed. His grin told her he approved.

Almost immediately though, the smile fell from his face as he reached up to rub two fingers over his eyebrows before catching himself and dropping his hand back down to his side. 'Thank you,' Nick said now. 'But to be perfectly frank, I wish I wasn't meeting you, or at least not needing to.' Then he shot a narrow-eyed glare over his shoulder as he said, 'If I'd known Rachel hadn't been seen since Saturday night...' He let the rest of the sentence trail off before saying, 'As it is, I had to find out from my sister's roommate.'

Alyssa didn't miss the blush that ran up Mr. Otis's neck and burned into his cheeks, nor the pursed lips indicating Mrs. Otis's displeasure at her son's irritation. Guessing she'd get more information from Rachel's brother, Alyssa focused her attention on him instead. 'Nick, your parents seem to think your sister isn't missing, that she's merely taken off. Do you share that view?'

She ignored the disgruntled huff coming from his mother, and so did he. His thumb and forefinger traced over an invisible goatee as he considered how to respond. 'Well, now, to be fair, I wouldn't put it past Rach to take off for a few days, especially if she'd done something stupid.' When his mother muttered something that sounded like *I told you so*, Nick clenched his jaw and flicked his wrist as if trying to swat away an irritating bug. In this case, his own parent. Alyssa liked him more with each passing second.

'However, she would never voluntarily be gone this long without posting something on her Instagram or Snapchat accounts or answering her phone – it's gone straight to voice-mail every time I've called which means Rach let her phone die, or she turned it off, something she never does. To be frank, Detectives, I love my twin, but anyone can recognize she's an attention-whore.'

This time, Mrs. Otis couldn't be ignored. 'Nicholas Owen Otis! That is hardly an appropriate way to speak of your sister. We are *Christians*,' she hissed.

Nick twisted so his body was angled toward her. 'Are we though, Mother?'

An outraged gasp preceded her glare as she repeated, 'It is inappropriate, and I won't tolerate you speaking this way!'

Nick matched her cold glare with one of his own. 'Nor is it *appropriate*, Mother, to pretend your daughter isn't missing, merely for the sake of having to set aside some of your social activities or because it might look bad among your peers! What? Do your *friends* – and I use that term loosely – think running away is more au courant somehow?'

'Well, I never!' Mrs. Otis dramatically slapped her hand over her heart – if she even had one – as if her son had physically broken it, and then wheeled around to snap at her husband. 'Roger, are you going to allow our son to speak to me in this manner?'

Alyssa turned her attention to Mr. Otis who, so far, seemed more like an embarrassed spectator than an active or willing participant in his wife and son's exchange. With all eyes on him, the renowned surgeon shrugged. 'Nicholas, please refrain from speaking to your mother in such a way. It's impolite and disrespectful.'

Instead of sounding like he meant it, he sounded like someone used to reciting his lines, willing only to do his part, or the part delegated to him. The man may have been born with the proverbial silver spoon, but that sure hadn't bought him a backbone.

Nick's head tilted back as his eyes lifted to the ceiling, and then he turned his back to both parents, addressing Alyssa and Cord once more. 'I *don't* think my sister ran off. She was never much for the technicalities of school, but since Mom and Dad told her they'd cut off her allowance if she didn't attend college, she went. I talked to her after her last final, and she was relieved her freshman year was out the window and she could focus on enjoying her summer break. That doesn't really sound like someone who was secretly about to take off for places unknown. I don't know *what's* happened to her, but I'm willing to answer whatever questions you have so we can figure it out and find her.'

'We appreciate that, Nick.' Alyssa turned her attention back to Mr. and Mrs. Otis. 'Do you mind if we take a look at Rachel's room?'

Mrs. Otis narrowed her lips into a thin line. 'Very well. Come along. Though I don't know what you're hoping to find.'

Turning on her expensive high heels, Mrs. Otis led the way to Rachel's room. At the bedroom door, with her hand on the knob, she turned to Alyssa and Cord. 'Please touch nothing.' The way she said it made it sound as if she expected them to abscond with half their daughter's belongings tucked beneath their shirts.

It was impossible not to notice the woman was far more concerned with her daughter's belongings possibly disappearing than she was with the daughter herself. If Rachel had to come home to this for an entire summer, maybe she had run off. Alyssa couldn't say she'd blame her. She didn't try to hide her sarcasm when she responded. 'We'll try not to.'

Opening the door, Mrs. Otis ushered the detectives in with a wave of her arm. 'My husband will attend you here. I'll be downstairs.' And then she was gone, leaving Cord and Alyssa to explore the room under the eagle-eyed glower of Mr. Otis and the anxious eyes of Nick.

She wasn't sure what she expected, but what Alyssa found was nothing short of a typical young female's room. Clothes, pricier than the ones her own daughter had, hung in an over-sized closet; both framed and loose photos, mostly from her high school days, adorned the walls, shelves, and corkboards; and expensive knickknacks from all over the globe were on display in a rather large, ornate curio cabinet. Aside from that, there was nothing that offered any clues as to where Rachel may have gone, or with whom.

'Angela mentioned something about a new friend Rachel had begun hanging out with. You wouldn't happen to know who that person is, would you?' Alyssa directed the question to Nick but darted her eyes to Mr. Otis for his reaction. Aside from reaching up to rub his chin, his face remained blank, and he too glanced at his son to hear his response.

'Come to think of it, she did mention meeting someone not too long ago. Not really sure of the timing, to be honest. Anna somebody or another.' Like Angela, Nick turned a light shade of pink as he admitted he'd been distracted. 'Rachel was in one of her moods where she just rambled on and on, and since I was the one who answered my phone...' He let his sentence trail off, slowly shaking his head. 'I guess I should've paid closer attention.'

And then, as if something had just occurred to him, he jerked his head up. 'Wait, do you think this friend might know something? Maybe I could ask around.'

The last thing Alyssa needed was a civilian scaring off potential witnesses by hammering them with questions. No, she'd rather find this mysterious friend and question her herself. 'Actually, what would be helpful is if you could give us a list of friends your sister usually hung out with. Do you think you could do that?'

Nick was already pulling out his phone, and then he walked over to his sister's desk, opened a drawer, pulled out a sheet of paper and a pen, and began scribbling names and numbers down.

While he was busy doing that, Alyssa asked another question. 'Do you know if Rachel had a boyfriend, or were there any guys she might've been interested in?'

Nick continued jotting down phone numbers but shook his head. 'No. Rach never really talked about guys she was interested in. Not even in high school.' He stopped writing, hanging his head for a second before turning worried eyes to Alyssa. 'I wish now that I'd asked about those things, but we just never had that type of relationship.'

'What you're doing' – Alyssa tipped her head toward the paper in Nick's hand – 'will be very helpful. Now, before we go, I have one more question for you. Does your sister have any tattoos, piercings, or other distinguishing features?'

Nick's face paled, and his hands began to shake. Cord stepped in to reassure him. 'It helps to know when we're asking others if they've seen her.'

Color returned to his face, but his tremors remained. 'No, Rach didn't have any noticeable scars, no tattoos, but she has six piercings, three in each ear. That I know of anyway, and *that*, I believe, is something she'd definitely tell me.' He shifted his eyes toward his father who still stood in the doorway of the bedroom. 'I think if she'd gotten a tattoo or something, she would've called because that's exactly the kind of secret she'd share with me.'

Chapter Six

Jersey's brain was fuzzy as she swam through a sea of darkness trying to rouse herself from one of those terrifying dreams where everything felt real. But when she opened her eyes this time, nothing but blackness greeted her, not even a shadow.

She blinked, hoping her eyes would adjust.

A sudden jolt knocked her sideways, and she realized she was in a moving vehicle. But whose, and why, and why was it so dark? She squeezed her eyes shut as a wave of dizziness washed over her, and then immediately reopened them, heart galloping as if it was trying to win a race, as the last thing she remembered before waking hit her.

She'd been walking towards home after leaving her friends and the duck pond, contemplating the current suckiness of her life.

Anger. At Beau. Her parents. Her friends. The world.

Then...

Nerves tingling as footsteps thudded behind her and wishing she hadn't insisted on being alone to clear her head, wishing she hadn't stayed to watch the ducks as long as she had. She knew the dangers in being a young female walking alone at night. But there had been a cute college-aged boy who'd kept watching her, and then he'd moved closer, flirting with her a little until he finally had to go. The attention had been nice on her bruised ego, and so she'd stayed for another hour, until the sky blotted out the rest of the sunset, replacing it with stars.

The steps behind her had quieted, becoming only a whisper of movement as they slowed.

And she'd relaxed, even laughed a little at her paranoia. She didn't own the park. It made sense someone else would be out walking. It was a perfect night for it, still just cool enough for a sweatshirt, despite the heat of the day. She'd pulled out her phone to call an Uber after all.

Then, out of nowhere, she felt a presence next to her. She turned...

And was slammed to the ground, the air knocked out of her. She tried to suck in oxygen, to scream, but her face was being ground into the dirt. She remembered something jabbing her in the neck, remembered struggling as she tried to lift her head, panicking when she realized she couldn't because every part of her was paralyzed – her feet, her hands, everything. All she could feel was... heaviness.

Then came the whisper, 'Nighty-night.'

I know that voice, she thought as the darkness closed in around her.

Sometime later she woke in an unfamiliar room, a seedy hotel by the look of it, but before she could think much about why she was there, she was out again, but not before that familiar voice penetrated through the fog as it told someone, 'She's here and ready for transport.'

Chapter Seven

After being inside the nice air-conditioned house of Mr. and Mrs. Otis, stepping outside into the heat and wind was almost like stepping into another country. People might call Chicago the Windy City, but Albuquerque could give it a strong run for its money – even if it was true that the 'windy' in Chicago's nickname stemmed not from the cold breezes that came off Lake Michigan but from politicians who were full of hot air.

As soon as Alyssa and Cord were back in the car, buckled in with the air blasting, Cord said, 'Angela Kazminski called that, didn't she? Mrs. Otis is one cold individual.'

It was unlike her partner to make such comments, so Alyssa shot a quick peek at his profile where she could see there was something more on his mind than the nastiness of Rachel Otis's mother. For a brief moment, she considered asking what it was, but knowing how much she hated being asked that question herself, she opted to let him tell her when he was ready. Instead, she agreed with him. 'Took the words right out of my mouth.'

As she headed for the open wrought-iron gate, she spotted Nick in her rearview mirror, standing on the porch, hands pushed deep into his pockets, staring off into the trees beside the house. It seemed like he was the only one in his family concerned for his sister's welfare, the only one who thought something was off, that Rachel's disappearance could be a foreboding of danger. Alyssa usually had what her team liked to call a sixth sense about these things, but after visiting the Otises, she didn't have a gut feeling that leaned strongly one way or the other. In Rachel's shoes, she'd be tempted to run away, too.

But based on Nick's and Angela's reactions, she'd gather her team and proceed by treating this as a mysterious disappearance. There was no evidence of foul play, but that didn't mean none existed. 'Why don't you call Hal and have him contact Joe and Tony? Maybe they can get started on checking security cameras in the area while we check out some of the names on that list.' With luck, Officers Joe Roe and Tony White, two more members on their team, would find something on the cameras that might point them in the right direction.

Before Cord could answer, Holly's ringtone blared through the car. Alyssa tapped the Bluetooth screen. 'Hi, sweetie. I'm driving, so you're on speaker.' She was greeted by dead air, and for a second, her heart threatened to bolt from her chest. Finally, Holly said, 'Hi, Cord.'

'Hey.'

Alyssa heard her daughter's lips flutter as she drew in a deep breath and released it. 'Is this a bad time, Mom? I could call back if it is.'

Hearing the worry in her daughter's voice, Alyssa's shoulders tensed, her mind immediately conjuring up Isaac's face; specifically, the image she had of him when he'd escaped his kidnapper six weeks ago. 'Nope, not a bad time. Like I said, I'm driving, so go ahead. As long as you don't mind Cord hearing whatever it is you have to say.' She forced a cheery tone into her voice, though the nerves in her stomach were doing a great impersonation of an unraveling ball of yarn.

'Okay, so I could be wrong, but I think Jersey's missing. Her mom called Sophie a little bit ago to ask if she'd seen her because Jersey didn't come home last night.'

'Why do you think she's missing?' From the corner of her eye, she noticed Cord remove his notebook, pen poised to jot down the information. Two possible missing girls? Once again, Alyssa couldn't help but be reminded of Evan Bishop's desire for torturing young women.

'Remember how I told you last night that Jersey was really upset about her parents divorcing and her grandma dying?'

'I remember.' Though Jersey and Holly were friends, Alyssa mainly knew her as Sophie's cousin. And rarely did Sophie seem pleased when the other girl tagged along. When Alyssa had asked about it, all her daughter had said was, 'Jersey can be a bit much.'

But when Leigh Ann started hanging out with the girls a few years ago, the tension between the two cousins seemed to wane a little. When Alyssa had pointed it out, Holly had laughed, attributing it to Leigh Ann's magical touch.

'Well, I left out the part about her and her boyfriend fighting before we left for dinner.' There was a lengthy pause, and when Holly spoke again, it was through gritted teeth. 'I didn't actually hear what they were fighting about, but I saw him shove her, then he called her pathetic and worthless before he stormed off. At dinner Leigh Ann asked if she wanted to talk about it, and Jersey admitted Beau was trying…' – she cleared her throat before continuing – 'to pressure her into a threesome, but with him as an observer, and her with two other guys.' The choked tone of Holly's voice conveyed her embarrassment.

Cord's head snapped up, and Alyssa turned to look at him, shocked to see the ticcing in his clenched jaw.

'That doesn't tell me why you think she's missing.' Alyssa divided her attention between watching the traffic around her and sneaking peeks at her partner. His left hand squeezed the pen so tightly, she was certain it would snap in two. What was going on in his head?

'Well, while Jersey was telling us what happened, she decided she might've overreacted and picked up her phone to text Beau, and Sophie snapped at her. Jersey started going on about us not understanding what she was going through, and that Beau was all she had. One thing led to another, and before I knew it, they were yelling at each other, and by the time we got out of there and reached my car, Jersey decided she wanted to be alone, to get fresh air, she said.'

Holly's voice wobbled. 'It was starting to get dark, and I didn't want her to go off by herself, especially after what happened with Callie McCormick and those other women.'

Callie was Evan Bishop's final victim, and after she died from the torture he'd inflicted, her husband had taken matters into his own hands by killing Bishop on the courthouse steps.

'I don't blame you for being concerned,' Alyssa said.

'We offered to go with her... well, I did anyway, but Sophie and Leigh Ann were on board, but Jersey insisted she wanted to be alone to think. I asked her to text or call me when she got home or if she wanted to talk, but she never did, so I assumed she still needed some alone time.'

'Is it possible she's with Beau?' Alyssa's scalp tingled. The duck pond. The university. Near the same area where Rachel Otis was last seen before mysteriously disappearing. In the passenger seat, Cord scribbled furiously in the notebook. Her eyes flickered down long enough to see he'd scrawled *Rachel Otis/Jersey/UNM* and surrounded it with several black circles — apparently sharing the same thought that had crossed her mind.

A frustrated grunt echoed through the car. 'No. I called him before calling you. To be honest, I'm surprised he answered. Anyway, when I asked if he'd seen Jersey, he laughed and said, and I quote here, "If you haven't heard from her, I wouldn't worry about it. This is her thing. She disappears for a day or two to make me worry, then waltzes back in. She thinks she's punishing me, but I really don't give a shit." Then he asked if that's why Jersey's mom had been trying to reach him that morning.'

'Sounds like a stand-up character,' Cord muttered under his breath. 'What's this Beau's last name?'

'Cambridge. I can text Mom his number and address when I hang up, and Jersey's mom's, too,' Holly offered.

'That'd be great,' Alyssa said. 'Her dad's, too, if you have that.'

Holly snorted, disgusted. 'Her dad's currently somewhere in Europe or Asia or hell, I don't even know. I just remember

Jersey telling us he was gallivanting around somewhere with his new twenty-something girlfriend, so I don't think anyone's contacted him yet because it's not like he could tell us where she is, so…'

Alyssa didn't want to ask the next question, but she knew she had to. 'Do you think there's any credibility to what Beau said?'

'No. Jersey is full of drama and likes to be the center of attention, usually in any way she can get it. But that's precisely *why* this doesn't feel right. She wouldn't go *quiet;* she'd want everyone around her to know how miserable she was. I mean, even Sophie is starting to worry. Besides, Jersey sucks at ignoring her phone, so she either doesn't have it, the battery died, she turned it off… all of which I highly doubt,' she hesitated, 'or something… else… has happened.'

Holly's breath hitched, echoing through the car's speakers. 'I should've tried harder to convince her to let me take her home… or at least insisted on going with her to the duck pond. I could've even followed her without telling her. Mom, if anything—'

Alyssa cut her off. Holly was blaming herself, a trait she likely inherited from her. 'Stop. First of all, we don't know if something's happened. Try not to create scary scenarios where we don't know any exist, okay?'

She could swear she heard her daughter's eyes doing a three-sixty in her head. 'Right. Don't create scary scenarios. I don't know if you're cognizant of this one small fact, but my mother happens to be a detective who *investigates* scary scenarios and sketchy people all the time, and so she's taught me to trust my instincts.'

Alyssa smiled. 'Fair enough. Tell you what, why don't you send us that information, and Cord and I will look into it after we finish what we're doing, and then we'll get back with you in a little bit, okay?'

'Mom, I'm scared,' Holly whispered.

'I know, but try to let us do our jobs before jumping to conclusions and staying there, okay?'

'Thanks, Mom, Cord.'

'Anytime, you know that. I'd tell you not to worry, but since I already know that's pointless, my advice instead is to make yourself busy so you don't lose your mind waiting for answers.' Cord's soothing voice was completely at odds with his flared nostrils and the pulsing vein in his temple.

After Holly hung up, Alyssa took a minute to gather her thoughts. 'Don't you think it's a little odd and a tad too coincidental that two girls around the same age in the same city near the same area would go missing within a day of each other?' Her eyes wandered to the file holding the missing person report for Rachel Otis. Whereas earlier she hadn't had a gut feeling leaning one way or the other, her instincts were screaming at her now that something sinister was afoot.

Cord's fist tapped against his thigh. 'It's not out of the realm of possibility that Jersey called her boyfriend while she was out on her walk, begged him to forgive her and pick her up. He picks her up, thinking she's going to give in to his demands, and when she doesn't, he snaps, they fight again, and then…'

His carefully controlled voice trailed off, and again Alyssa couldn't help but wonder what her partner was thinking. He was always so calm and collected that his reaction to the situation went beyond merely unnatural. She decided to be direct. 'Want to tell me what you're thinking?'

'I'm thinking we need to locate this Beau Cambridge and find out what he knows.'

Alyssa noted his choice of words: Find out *what* he knows, not *if* he knows anything.

Chapter Eight

While Alyssa drove in the general direction of the university, Cord called Hal and asked if he could track down Chance Williams's address.

'This is what I'm thinking. Pay a visit to this Chance fellow, and then we'll—' She was interrupted by the ringing of her phone. 'I seem to be popular today.' She didn't recognize the number that popped up on her screen. 'Alyssa Wyatt speaking.'

A woman's hoarse, wobbly voice came on the line. '*Detective* Alyssa Wyatt?'

'Yes. Who is this?'

'My name is Natalia Andrews. I'm Jersey's mom. I understand Holly already told you we fear my daughter may be missing?'

'Yes, she did. Has Jersey come home?'

'No, I'm afraid not. I, um, just wasn't certain if I needed to call you and officially ask for a missing person's report to be filed.' A choked sound escaped as if Jersey's mom was fighting back tears. 'This isn't the first time my daughter's taken off, but it is the first time she hasn't let me know she's okay, and after everything that happened recently with that serial killer...' She cleared her throat. 'Her father is out of the country for the time being, but I have left a message for him to contact me.'

'When's the last time you spoke to your daughter, Mrs. Andrews?'

'Yesterday afternoon. I was enjoying a pampering day. You know, spa, nails, massage.' Alyssa didn't know, but she listened as Mrs. Andrews continued. 'I'd invited Jersey to come along, make it a girls' day, but she said she'd already made plans with Holly, Sophie, and Leigh Ann.'

'Was her boyfriend there at the time?'

'No, ma'am. He showed up sometime after I left. In fact, if Holly hadn't told me about their fight, I would never have known he'd been at the house. Jersey knows I'm not his biggest fan. As it is, I tried contacting him, several times in fact, but he never answered my calls.' This time her voice was brittle, angry. 'Holly told me what he said. It's probably my fault Jersey stays with him at all. After all, she's learned from a pro how to stay with someone who's toxic to be around. I should've left her father ages ago, but I thought staying together for Jersey's sake was better, healthier somehow. I realize now that was a mistake.'

Unfortunately, Alyssa saw that same reasoning time and time again during her investigations involving domestic clashes. 'When did you notice Jersey wasn't home, Mrs. Andrews?'

'This morning around nine. I knocked on her bedroom door to ask how her evening went and see if she wanted to go to breakfast. When she didn't answer, I opened her door and found her bed unslept in. My first thought was that the girls had been having so much fun they must've slept at one of their houses. I admit I was a little upset she hadn't let me know. And then she didn't answer her phone when I called, so I thought I'd try Sophie. But then Sophie told me she hadn't seen her since dinner last night, and offered to ask Holly and Leigh Ann. When she called back, she said none of them knew where she was, so I thought maybe she'd spent the night with Beau.' The way his name came out strangled, it sounded more like a curse word.

'Detective, I don't know where my daughter is, and I'm worried. Yes, she can be a bit spoiled and dramatic, but this goes beyond even her wildest stunt. So, I'd like to know what I need to do to officially file a missing person's report.'

'Consider it official. Thank you for calling. We'll let you know as soon as we find anything out. And please do the same. If you hear from her, or if she comes home, do give me a call.'

As soon as she hung up, Alyssa changed lanes so she could make a U-turn. 'Since we haven't heard back from Hal yet on that address for Chance Williams, let's go have a chat with Beau Cambridge.'

Cord's face could've been carved from stone the way it hardened. Without responding, he tapped the navigation screen and entered the Cambridge family's address.

It took less than ten minutes to reach Tanoan East, the gated community situated around one of Albuquerque's golf courses. The Cambridge residence was in the center of the subdivision, and it boasted oversized windows which allowed passers-by to glance into and through their home to the Sandia mountains nestled behind them.

In the driveway sat a souped-up four-wheel-drive Rubicon that Alyssa knew from Holly belonged to Jersey's boyfriend. Next to it was a newer model BMW convertible with buttery yellow leather seats that looked like they hugged the bodies of its passengers. Situated on two pillars in front of the house were two humongous brass lions.

'Apparently, I missed the memo that all our interviewees today were going to be swimming in currency.'

'You're telling me.' Cord's head swiveled as he took in the surrounding area. 'But next to the Otis residence, this one kind of looks shabby, don't you think?' Though his words held a note of humor, there was none to be found in his gaze. She wondered when or even if he'd share what was eating away at him.

Shoving her partner's frame of mind aside, Alyssa led the way up the walkway and through the courtyard to the front door. Pressing her finger on the white button, she rang the bell, listening to the chime echo throughout the house. Seconds later, the clickety-clack of high heels across tiled floor reverberated as someone hurried to see who was calling.

They heard the sounds of an alarm being disarmed, a series of rattles from a chain lock being removed, and the clap of a deadbolt turning before the door opened to reveal a woman in her early to mid-fifties who appeared to be trying her best to look at least a decade younger. From a distance she probably pulled it off. Up close, however, the stretched look from Botox injections told a different story. Her blonde hair was perfectly styled, make-up airbrushed into perfection so that it gave her face the appearance of a porcelain doll. Large sparkly sapphires dangled from her ears, completing the look.

'Mrs. Cambridge?' Alyssa asked.

The woman's gaze flickered between Cord and Alyssa, and she sucked her bottom lip between her teeth, worrying it before she finally answered. 'Yes. Who's asking?'

'I'm Detective Wyatt from the Albuquerque Police Department, and this is my partner, Detective Roberts.' Twisting her torso toward the driveway, she pointed. 'Does that Jeep belong to your son, Beau?'

'Yes.'

'Is he home then? We'd like to ask him a few questions regarding his girlfriend, Jersey Andrews.'

At the mention of Jersey's name, Mrs. Cambridge dropped her gaze to the floor but not before Alyssa glimpsed a shadow pass over the woman's face. And then, with a carefully schooled expression that had Alyssa's instincts screaming, Mrs. Cambridge said, 'Beau *is* home, but I'm afraid he can't be interrupted right now. He and his father are planning' – she waved her hand in the air – 'whatever they plan.' In the blink of an eye, she'd gone from timid and nervous to self-assured and forceful, if not quite assertive.

Alyssa studied the woman in front of her. 'I wonder if he would mind being interrupted if he knew the other option would be for us to take him downtown for questioning.'

Mrs. Cambridge paled under her perfectly applied make-up, and she swayed just the tiniest bit. 'Let me just… let me… I'm sure he won't mind speaking with you for just a few moments.' And then she closed the door in their faces as they listened to the receding sounds of her heels traversing back the way they'd come.

'Who's she afraid of, do you think? Her husband, son, or both?' Alyssa kept her eye trained on the door while Cord moved to the left, openly staring into the house through the window.

'I bet we're going to find out in a minute.'

Except two minutes, then three passed, and Alyssa was considering ringing the doorbell again when an angry voice and heavy footsteps preceded the door swinging open to reveal a middle-aged man dressed in golf attire, gray peppering the edges of his dark hair. Behind him, with a cocky grin on his face, was a boy of about eighteen or nineteen who she assumed was Beau Cambridge.

Mr. Cambridge puffed his chest out and stepped into Alyssa's personal space, instantly putting her back up as her hand moved to her hip where it hovered above her gun. From the corner of her eye, she noticed Cord tense as he moved in closer to her, his palm resting on his weapon.

'What's this about the police threatening to haul my boy downtown for questioning?'

If the man's booming voice was intended to be threatening, it had the opposite effect, proving instead to piss Alyssa off, especially combined with the way he continued to press forward. 'I've been warning Beau he needed to get rid of that little tart because she was only good for bitching and blow jobs, and he can get that anywhere.'

A horrified gasp escaped from Mrs. Cambridge a second before she clapped her hand over her mouth. The gleam in her husband's eyes told Alyssa the man was pleased with his wife's reaction.

Eyes blazing and temper beginning to simmer, Alyssa said, 'First off, sir, you're going to want to take a healthy step back and

54

get the hell out of my face.' At five-three her height might be diminutive, but her temper was not. She didn't miss the defiant expression that flashed briefly across the man's face, making it obvious that women didn't often challenge him. But she wasn't most women, and he was about to discover that fast if he didn't back up. After all, he certainly wasn't the first male chauvinist she'd encountered in her career or her lifetime, and sadly, he wouldn't be the last.

Without moving, Mr. Cambridge curled his lip and shot a disgusted sneer Cord's way, as if judging him to be inadequate for his inability to keep his *female* partner in line. When he stared back down at her, his eyes narrowed to a razor edge. 'This is my house. Who's going to make me step back? You?'

Alyssa didn't blink, didn't telegraph her intent in any way before she moved in, crowding him now. 'Yeah, me. Would you like to test that fact?'

Even though she had to tilt her head back to see his face as he towered above her − Mr. Cambridge was taller even than Cord − she knew by the shadows that passed over his face that he was considering how far he could, or should, push her. The wrong choice would find him on the ground in nothing flat, bested by a woman a foot shorter than him. If nothing else did, that would certainly get his attention.

Finally, his face flushed a mottled red, he took two steps backwards into the foyer. His wife stood to the side, eyes wide, lips trembling, hands twisting an enormous sapphire ring around and around on her finger. Near her in an open archway, Beau Cambridge stood with his legs spread and arms crossed over his beefy chest, an amused smile on his face. Alyssa could understand why neither Mrs. Andrews nor Jersey's friends liked him. Without ever having heard him speak, she found him highly unlikeable.

'You have five minutes, Detective, and then you need to leave. And if any of your questions seem accusatory, I'll have you fired for harassment.' Mr. Cambridge adopted his son's posture and crossed his arms over his chest as his eyes shot daggers through her.

Alyssa didn't bother to hide the fact that she was rolling her eyes at his dramatics. *You can try*, she thought, but refrained from stoking that fire. Instead she raised her steady gaze to his and countered with, 'If your son has nothing to hide, then he has no reason to fear any of the questions we choose to ask.' She let her stare carry over to Beau. 'Beau Cambridge?'

His eyes shifted toward his father's before he dropped his head in a brief nod.

'What happened to your face?' Two red scratches zigzagged across his right cheek and stretched down his neck where they disappeared beneath his shirt collar.

Again, his gaze flickered toward his father. 'Why? What's it to you?'

Before Alyssa could respond, Beau turned to his mother and snapped out an order, punctuating it with a pointed finger. 'Go get me a Coke.'

She half expected a military salute before Mrs. Cambridge immediately retreated to obey, and it took yet another layer of Alyssa's willpower not to stop her and demand the spoiled brat get his own damn drink. *Forcing him to show a little respect is not why you're here.*

As soon as Mrs. Cambridge was out of sight, Cord pushed further into the foyer, edging closer to the two men, his stance indicating a hyper sense of awareness, the expression on his face unfamiliar to her. His nostrils flared, and the tendons in his neck stood out, as he leveled both men with a fiery stare.

'What it is to me,' Alyssa enunciated clearly, 'is that your girlfriend hasn't been seen since leaving the restaurant where she and her friends had dinner. And I'm wondering if those scratches could have anything to do with her disappearance. So, I'll ask again. What happened to your face?'

That cocky, arrogant smile spread across his face once more, and he leaned back against the wall, one heel resting on it as he crossed his arms in a way that showcased his gym-made muscles. He and his father shared a smirk before he focused his gaze on Alyssa. 'A cat scratched me. And Jersey's not my girlfriend anymore. You heard my dad. She was only good for two things. And she wasn't much good at one of those. I'll let you guess which one.'

The way Cord's body tensed, as if he was a snake coiled to strike, had Alyssa on edge. She tried to catch his eye, to convey to him that he needed to calm down, but his narrow-eyed gaze remained steadfast on Beau's.

She refocused her attention back on Jersey's boyfriend – or ex – if what he claimed was true. 'But you were with Jersey yesterday, is that correct?'

Beau flicked an imaginary piece of lint from his jeans, turning as his mother returned with a glass filled with ice and Coke for him, and a smaller one filled with what appeared to be whiskey for her husband. *Great. Handing hard liquor to a man who was already an ass was a tremendous idea.*

Only after chugging half the drink did Beau answer. 'Yeah. I was with her at her house, but I broke up with her before I left.'

'But she was still your girlfriend when you suggested the threesome she declined?'

Beau's eyes shot up before he relaxed, shrugged, and presented a bored face. 'I don't know what you're talking about.'

'I'm talking about your suggestion that your girlfriend have sex with two men at the same time while you watched.' Alyssa didn't miss the small grin on Mr. Cambridge's face, nor the smirk on Beau's.

'I don't know who told you that, but it's a lie.'

Whatever Alyssa would've said next was interrupted when Cord stepped forward. 'Why don't you show me your hands?' He may have posed it as a question, but his tone made clear that this was an order.

Beau stiffened. 'What for?'

'Let's just call it curiosity. Worried I'll see something you don't want me to see?'

After shooting a nervous glance his father's way, Beau held his hands out, first palms down, then flipping them up, before shoving them back into his armpits.

Alyssa noted another scratch on the outside of his left hand. 'From the cat?' she asked, allowing the sarcasm to drip through.

'Yeah.'

'Whose cat?'

'What?'

She shrugged. 'Whose cat? Yours?'

'No, a buddy's.'

'You don't mind if we have a look at your room and in your vehicle, do you?' Cord asked.

Beau shoved himself off the wall, his arms dropping to his sides, his gaze flitting to his father. 'What the hell for?' Was it panic or something else that caused his face to flush pink?

At the same time, Mr. Cambridge said, 'Not without a search warrant you won't!'

Alyssa shrugged, not surprised by the response. 'No problem. We can do that. Maybe even impound it if we feel it was used in connection with a crime.'

Between her steady gaze and Cord's, Beau began shuffling his feet, but all he said was, 'I didn't commit no crime.'

'What did you do, and who were you with after you left Ms. Andrews?' Cord asked.

The way he perked up, preening at Cord's question told Alyssa what Beau was going to say before it ever left his mouth. He was with another girl.

'I had company. Here. All night. In my room. Do you want pictures?'

The glow from Mr. Cambridge's face was bright enough to guide a ship home. Unfortunately, he was the wrong port. On the other side of the room, Mrs. Cambridge blushed.

'We don't need pictures, thank you,' Alyssa said, pretending she'd taken his question at face value. 'However, we will need the girl's name and contact information.'

Another smirk crossed his face, and this time, Alyssa's palm itched to slap it off.

'I don't have her contact info,' Beau said now. 'She wasn't good enough for me to get it.' He chuckled as his dad snickered, and Alyssa felt the temper that had been simmering just below the surface begin to boil.

Beau continued. 'This bitch was hitting on me, and when she told me what she wanted to do, I had her follow me home. We didn't exchange names.'

'What time did she leave?' Cord asked, controlled fury in his voice.

Beau's shoulders lifted and dropped. 'Maybe two, three in the morning. When we finished, she didn't seem to want to hang around, and I didn't ask her to. Already got what I wanted and didn't need a repeat. Like I said, she wasn't all that good, and definitely not worth more of my time.' He actually winked at Cord, and Mr. Cambridge laughed out loud, laughing harder as Mrs. Cambridge finally decided she'd heard enough, turning on her expensive high heels and stalking out of the room and down the hall, where a door closed loudly enough to indicate anger and disgust, but not so much that it would be considered to be slammed.

A second later Cord decided he was done playing nice.

To Alyssa's shock, her partner lost his composure, and in two quick steps, he was across the floor and in Beau's face, and when Mr. Cambridge moved to intercept him, Cord's right hand shot out to stop him in his tracks. Never taking his eyes from the boy in front of him, he growled between gritted teeth. 'If you did something to Ms. Andrews, we *will* find out, and when we do, we'll see how arrogant you are when we toss you in jail. Maybe see how you like being someone else's b—'

Alyssa stepped in and laid a hand on her partner's arm, stopping him from saying what was on the tip of his tongue, not only because it was condescending and sexist in its own right, but because she was afraid he might actually punch Beau in the face. Not that he didn't deserve it.

She knew it was only because Cord allowed it that she was able to draw him back. Seething, he turned his barely contained fury on Beau's father.

Mr. Cambridge's frame shook as the color in his face surpassed red and morphed into purple. 'You don't know who you're dealing with or the people I know. My lawyer will be contacting your boss *and* the mayor. You'll be out of a job before you can leave this neighborhood.'

Cord's head fell back in unamused laughter before his neck snapped up, and he stepped closer to Beau's father, lowering his voice to just above a whisper. '*You* don't know *who* I know, either, man. Should we place bets on whose threat's going to hold more water? Because if you're smart, you'll bet on me.'

And with that her partner stormed out. Unlike Mrs. Cambridge a few moments earlier, Cord made certain he slammed the door hard enough to rattle the windows, and Alyssa had to fight back a cringe, hoping they didn't shatter. Not once in five years had she ever witnessed him lose his composure, not even when he interviewed hardened criminals. In fact, he was often the calming force that kept *her* from exploding.

Before following him out, she removed a business card and placed it on the small table near the door. 'You'll call if you think of anything you might've *forgotten* to mention,' she said, making it a demand instead of a request. Back outside she made her way to the curb where Cord stood facing away from the house, the muscles in his back vibrating.

She pushed the key fob to unlock the car, and without turning around, Cord yanked open the passenger door and slid inside. After she buckled herself in, Alyssa turned the ignition, peeked at her partner's profile, then slowly pulled away from the curb. 'Want to tell me where all that came from?'

She glanced over in time to see his fingers squeezing his thighs as he breathed slowly in and out through gritted teeth. The ticcing in his jaw grew more pronounced as her question lingered in the air, the weight of it heavy in the space between them. Just when she was sure he wasn't going to respond, he finally spoke.

Chapter Nine

Heavy footsteps above their heads drew the girls' attention, and they all looked up, necks craning. And as if some evil fairy had sprinkled silent dust over them, they fell eerily quiet, the sounds of their breathing hushed, barely audible wisps of air.

A key jiggled in a lock just before the door opened and a bright overhead light flipped on, burning Rachel's retinas as she reached up to shield her eyes from the brutal glare. Still, she focused on two stocky men as they made their way down the stairs, stepping into the center of the room outside the metal enclosure. No words passed between them as they slowly shifted their gazes from left to right, their intense concentration seeming to undress and inspect each of the girls in turn, and Rachel chomped down on her cheek to keep her teeth from chattering against each other. The urge to close her eyes battled against her will to watch their every movement.

'Christ Almighty! Would you shut that one up already?' The taller of the two men suddenly bit out, anger flushing his face a deep red.

That's when the noise filtered through to Rachel, and she realized Cheyenne or Meghan – she couldn't remember which was which – had begun shaking back and forth as her fingers gripped her mattress, undecipherable words and spittle flying from her mouth in a chorus of high-pitched wails.

Tendrils of dread worked their way up her spine as she watched the girl's reaction to seeing the men. And then her gaze flew away as Tall Guy announced, 'That one.' When Rachel saw he was pointing at her, her eyes shot around the room, searching for a place to run, to hide, to escape. And then the man produced another key and unlocked their enclosure. As he stepped inside, she noticed a third man standing just off to the side, holding what appeared to be a weapon of some sort. A gun? Taser? She couldn't tell.

And then it didn't matter because the three men ordered the other girls to stay put as they moved toward her with purpose. Rachel scrambled to get away though there was nowhere to go... except out there. The door was open, and without thinking about the consequences, she bolted between the men and was brought roughly to a halt when one of them reached out and wrapped a handful of her hair around his fist, yanking her to the ground.

Ignoring the pain shooting through her skull, Rachel jerked her head forward trying to escape the man's grip, relieved when his hold on her hair released. Taking advantage of being loose, she shuffled backwards and huddled into the corner of the enclosure, pulling her knees in as tightly as she could, wrapping her arms around them, violently shaking her head back and forth, barely recognizing the sounds coming from deep inside her.

Stopping at her feet, the imposing figure of one of the men asked, 'You going to cooperate, or do we do this the hard way?'

Rachel didn't have time to wonder what the hard way was because Faye answered for her, in a voice much softer and gentler now than the one she'd used before. 'She'll cooperate. She's just scared. You don't have to... she'll cooperate.'

Hysteria bubbled up inside, threatening to erupt. *Scared?* She wasn't scared; she was freaking terrified. And despite her efforts to make herself invisible, rough hands reached down and dragged her out of her corner. Immediately, and regardless of Faye's promise of cooperation, Rachel struggled, clawing her nails down the face of one of the men, eliciting an outraged

63

howl of pain. Even as the men tried to control her flailing limbs, she kicked out at anything she could. It was only when the cold barrel of a gun pressed into her temple that the fight drained out of her, and her body went limp as Tall Guy and his partner gripped her arms and hauled her upstairs while the third man relocked the cell.

After winding their way through a series of hallways, they entered a large room where two well-dressed men in business suits sat perched on the edge of a red velvet sofa, their bodies relaxed as they watched her being brought in, eyes gleaming with malicious interest. One of the men licked his lips as he inspected her from her highlighted hair to her painted toenails.

Both men rose to their feet. 'She'll do nicely.' They each pulled out a wad of bills which they thrust out towards Tall Guy. He grabbed the money and handed it to his partner behind him who slowly counted it. When he stuffed it into his pocket and nodded, Tall Guy shoved her forward.

Right into the waiting arms of the two businessmen who latched onto her upper arms. Ignoring her pleas and the tears that fell in torrents down her face, they marched her down yet another hallway, this time ending at a closed door labeled '*The Toybox*.'

When they led her through the doorway, and Rachel saw what was inside, her knees buckled, and only the force of their grip kept her on her feet.

Chapter Ten

The fingers gripping Cord's thighs turned white, and after he inhaled slowly through his nose and exhaled through his mouth, he began. 'There's something...'

He shook his head the way Alyssa did when she was trying to dislodge a memory she didn't want, then tried again. 'There's something I've never told you. It's not because I don't trust you; it's because I don't talk about it with anyone. Not even Sara – well, not anymore anyway.' He sucked in an audible breath and expelled it in a rush. This time when he spoke, his words were quieter, not quite a whisper, but uttered almost reverently, and Alyssa found herself straining to hear.

'My little sister was seventeen, on the dance team, happy, kind – really, I'm not just saying that because I'm the big brother. *Everybody* loved her. And she was *smart*.' The way he gnashed his teeth made it sound like he was angry about it.

At a stoplight, Alyssa angled her body toward him in time to witness the tortured look on his face, the way his mouth trembled just enough for her to notice. It made her want to reach over and remind him where he was. Instead, she made a right turn and drove a block until she reached a park where she pulled in but left the car idling. It was quiet here with only a handful of mothers and their toddlers running around in the sand. She kept her focus on them while Cord composed himself.

'She was sharp as a whip. Except when it came to boys.' He reached out and cranked the air conditioner to high, and

Alyssa got the impression it had more to do with the fact that he needed to do something with his shaking hands than it did with the temperature inside the vehicle. Careful not to distract him, she pointed her vent away from her face.

'Her senior year, she was dating some football jock who was possessive and abusive. I was off at college when I got the first phone call from my mom. Shelley came home after one of the games, her arms covered in red scratches which she attributed to mosquitoes. Of course, there were no bites, which my mother pointed out. Shelley became defensive and angry – something she never did – she was just never that kind of teenager – so Mom let it go until the next morning when she noticed something even worse than the scratches.'

The tic in Cord's jaw sped up as he stared out the windshield, and Alyssa's galloping heart caused the blood to pulse in her ears, making it more difficult to hear or concentrate because she was suddenly sure she knew where this story would end, and she wasn't certain she wanted to know this anymore. Sometimes ignorance really was bliss, and there was a reason her partner said he never spoke about it anymore.

Memories stormed across his face. 'Shelley's throat was red, with strange lines circling her neck, like someone had been squeezing it. And when she spoke, her voice was hoarse and raspy. She tried telling our parents it was nothing but a cold and a sore throat from yelling. But if it came from yelling, it wasn't from the cheering kind. Anyway, Mom pulled out her old Polaroid camera, and when Shelley went to lay down for a nap later that afternoon, she snuck into her room. That's when she saw some of the old bruises that dotted her stomach. She snapped as many pictures as she could before my sister woke up. She wanted to have evidence.'

'Cord, I'm so sorry,' Alyssa said. 'You don't have to say anymore. I understand.'

He continued as if he hadn't heard her, his voice lower still, filled with strangled anguish. 'I talked to Shelley, and then Mom and Dad made her break up with him, but three months later, towards the end of the school year, in May, Bradley Morrison and one of his buddies talked her into going to Morrison's parents' cabin where he beat and raped her. Repeatedly.' A single tear rolled down his left cheek as he choked on the words.

'My parents thought she was with some of her girlfriends, so when Shelley missed her curfew, they didn't worry right away. After all, she wasn't with Bradley anymore, and they didn't want to overreact. But when she wasn't home by three that morning, Mom knew something was wrong and called the police, then me. Shortly after they made the report, a jogger came across Shelley lying in some trees, barely alive, "painted in blood," that's how the witness described it. When he first spotted her feet sticking out, he almost ran by, thinking she was just some drunk sleeping it off. But the closer he got, the more evident it was... that it was... more than that.'

The emotions played across Cord's face – anger to helplessness to heartbreak and back again – as he returned to that dark time in his life.

'She was rushed to the hospital and kept in a medical coma for two days. When she woke, she told us what had happened.' A harsh sound came from deep inside Cord's chest as he bent forward slightly, almost as if he was reliving his own physical pain from what had happened to his sister.

'Of course, Morrison and his buddy denied it all, said that she'd begged to go with them, and that she'd been the one to initiate... everything.' His palm tapped against the dash. 'He said she'd confessed it was her secret desire to be taken forcefully like that.' A choked sound fell flat as he said, 'As if that's every young girl's dream. To be raped and brutalized.

'And his parents weren't any better, brushing off their son's involvement entirely, insisting Shelley was the only one to blame because she kept throwing herself at Bradley, was practically stalking him.' He removed the hand that had been on the dash and wiped it down his face. 'A few days after she was released from the hospital… Mom found her in the bathroom. She'd hanged herself.'

His voice cracked, and he swallowed several times, and while Alyssa wanted to tell him 'no more,' she knew he needed to finish.

'She left a note saying she was sorry but that she couldn't deal with the stares and whispers, people wondering if any part of what Morrison and his parents said was true. Couldn't handle people she thought were her friends turning their backs on her in support of him.'

The fracture in Alyssa's heart spread. Slowly, she reached out her hand and covered Cord's arm. 'I'm so sorry. I should never have asked.'

'In exchange for a lighter sentence, his buddy gave a different version of events and turned state's evidence, but of course, by then, at least for Shelley and my family, it was too late. That was twelve years ago this week.'

When he turned his head toward her, the impact of his haunted past slammed into her with the force of a tropical storm.

'That's when I changed my degree. At first I thought I wanted to be a prosecutor, to put scum like them away for good. But it didn't take long for me to realize what I really wanted was to capture them myself.' His attention was drawn to two little children fighting over an action figure while their mothers tried to diffuse the situation before it turned into a full-blown tantrum. 'So, I became a police officer and worked my way up the ranks to detective. When my folks died, Sara and I decided to pack up and start fresh here in New Mexico.'

Alyssa had known he'd moved to Albuquerque from Seattle, but she didn't know if that was where he was raised. 'Was Seattle where Shelley…?' Even though she investigated these types of crimes all the time, she still couldn't bring herself to finish the question. For some reason, in this setting, with her partner's soul exposed, it seemed too invasive.

'Portland, Oregon. Mom and Dad couldn't stay in the house after Shelley died, and since I was attending university in Seattle, they moved up there. Seven years ago, Dad had his stroke and died, and eighteen months after that, Mom lost her battle against breast cancer. Too many sad memories permeated the entire Pacific Northwest, and I wanted out.'

Something akin to guilt passed over his features. 'I'm not proud of it, but I was the biggest asshole around and did my best to push Sara away – both after what happened to Shelley and when my parents died. But my Sara's pretty tenacious in her own right – she was like that in high school, too, which is why I fell for her our freshman year. Anyway, she wouldn't let me shake her. Thank God.' A sad smile lifted one corner of his mouth. 'Do you know, what happened to Shelley is why Sara became a nurse? She just wanted to help heal other girls who'd... who'd had that happen... to remind them they *could* heal.'

Alyssa had always liked and admired Cord's wife, but a new respect filled her for the woman who seemed to have saved Cord from himself. The silence that filled the car was crushing as Alyssa allowed this glimpse into her partner's past to swill around in her head. She knew she should say something, but what?

Cord finally turned to look at her, dark circles shadowing his red eyes, 'Remember three years ago when I suddenly had something come up and had to leave for Washington?'

Alyssa nodded. 'I remember.'

'An old college buddy of mine called to let me know Morrison had been killed in the prison yard. Cliché as hell. But if rumor is true, he'd been bragging to a new guy about Shelley, trying to puff himself up to look like a badass. Turns out the guy he was spouting off to had a little sister who'd been raped and murdered. In fact, that's why he was in prison, for taking the law into his own hands. I'll spare you the details, but let's just say the only reason the person who'd killed his sister was able to be identified was because his face was left intact. Unlike the rest of him.'

Cord's face hardened, turned cold. 'Ronald Erickson didn't have the same weapons at his disposal inside prison, but he made do with what he had. Bradley Morrison's face didn't fare so well.' He turned his head to stare out the passenger window. 'I know we've dealt with cases like this in the past' – he rubbed the back of his neck – 'but it's the anniversary of Shelley's suicide, and Beau Cambridge and his father brought it all rushing back, their attitudes.' He released a huff of sound and glanced at Alyssa. 'I let it get the better of me, and I'm sorry. I should've had better control.'

The grief in his eyes matched the grief in Alyssa's heart. 'Now I understand why we make such a good team. We're connected by tragedies that brought us to this profession so we could try to make a change, no matter how small. And we're making it work.'

'Damn straight we are,' he said at the same time his phone rang. 'Talk about timing.' His chuckle was forced but there.

'Hey, Hal, do you have that address for us?'

Aside from a slight trembling in his hand, Alyssa never would've guessed that just moments earlier, he'd been relaying the most tragic event of his life. Now she had to wonder how interviewing Chance Williams might affect him, especially if he was the player Angela Kazminski made him out to be. Would it be another Beau Cambridge all over again?

'1901 Valley Crest Drive. The roommate was close. Ridge-crest is just a block north.' Cord tapped in the address and asked Alyssa if there was anything else she needed Hal to do.

'Actually, yes, he can call Tony and Joe and let them know we need them to help us round up and question potential witnesses to Rachel Otis's disappearance.'

'Hal says "Consider it done." Anything else?'

'Nope. Thanks, Hal.'

Cord relayed the message and then put his phone away.

Silence filled the cab of the Tahoe before Alyssa finally dove in. 'Do you think you're ready to interview Mr. Williams with me? Because I'm sure I can get Joe or Tony if you need some time.'

'I can do my job...' Cord held his palm up when she opened her mouth to explain she hadn't meant to imply he couldn't. 'I know I let things get to me with Cambridge, but aside from that slip-up, have I ever given you reason to doubt I'm capable of maintaining my professionalism?'

'No, you haven't. But that's not what I—'

He cut her off. 'That's because I learned a long time ago to compartmentalize when it comes to things like that. I already apologized and said it won't happen again. And it won't. So, you can relax, and let's get this done.' He ended the conversation by settling back and buckling his seatbelt.

Alyssa removed her hand from the gear shifter and touched Cord's shoulder, waiting for his eyes to meet hers. 'Thank you for trusting me with Shelley's story. Trust me' – a short, humorless laugh pushed past her lips – 'I know more than some exactly how difficult that can be. We can agree on that, right?'

Cord's eyes glassed over with moisture, and his Adam's apple bobbed as he swallowed. 'Right.'

'So, for the record, I wasn't asking for another apology. Nor was I doubting your ability to perform your job because I have absolute faith in you when it comes to that. I asked if you were ready to conduct this interview as your friend, not your co-worker. Okay?'

One knuckle brushed away a stray tear as he shot her a watery smile. 'I appreciate that. And thank you. But I can do this.'

Chapter Eleven

Twenty-two minutes later, Alyssa and Cord pulled up to the Williams' residence. She allowed herself a moment to glance around the property before getting out of the car. Surrounded on all sides by spongy grass, the house was a patchwork of wood, reminding her of the one in the Hansel and Gretel story she'd grown up hearing and then had shared with Holly and Isaac before they'd learned to read themselves. The green roof sloped over the frame of the house in a rounded dome, and the blazing red door was the exact same shade as the one on the dollhouse she'd once begged her parents for just before they learned her mother was pregnant with Timmy.

In the passenger seat, one hand perched on the door handle, Cord, too, observed the house. 'Reminds me of the witch's house when she invited Hansel and Gretel in for candy.' Alyssa chuckled since it was exactly what she'd been thinking. It was funny – and sometimes a little unsettling – how often the two of them were on the same wavelength.

Two young men perched on the front porch, legs propped up on the wooden railing which was in bad need of a fresh paint job. They eyed Alyssa and Cord as they stepped out of the vehicle and onto the sidewalk, and when they were within feet of the front porch, the guy on the right lifted a can of a popular energy drink to his mouth and guzzled, wiping his hand across his mouth when he finished. Then holding her gaze, he let out a loud belch.

If his intent was to get a reaction, he would have to try harder than that. At the top of the steps, the shorter of the two guys flickered his eyes from his friend to the badge resting at her hip to the car parked in the street before finally landing back on her, his mouth opening and closing comically as if he was practicing for the part of a fish in a play. She was going to go out on a limb and guess that, based merely on Angela Kazminski's personality description, this guy was not the one they were here to talk to.

Alyssa planted herself in front of the guys while Cord took up residence to the right of her, the two of them effectively blocking off the stairs. The shorter guy's eyes refused to hold still as they bounced from the badges back to his friend who reclined with his chair tipped back, legs crossed at the ankles on the railing. Suddenly, the short, nervous one shot to his feet as if his chair had been set on fire, and Alyssa's arm immediately snaked out, prepared to stop him if he tried to bolt.

In contrast, the other guy yawned then shook his head as he studied Alyssa and Cord with bored indifference, or at least that's what he wanted it to look like, but the way his eyes shifted ever so slightly to the badges, as well, told her he wasn't as unaffected by their presence as he pretended to be. He tugged a piece of string from the holes in his jeans. 'Can I help you, officers?'

'Chance Williams?'

Nervous Guy's head wobbled on his neck as he shook his head no, reminding Alyssa of a Parkinson's patient she'd once met on a domestic disturbance call when she was still in a patrol car. 'Naw, man, I'm Darnell.' He shot a sideways glance toward his friend who'd let his chair plop down on all fours as he planted his flip-flopped feet on the porch.

'Yeah, I'm Chance.' In a move that was disgusting and, she was sure, meant to throw her off, he let his gaze rove over her body, lifting his eyebrows and whistling in appreciation. Beside her, Cord stiffened. 'Something I can help you with?' If his tone didn't imply that he thought he was cute and sexy, the way he narrowed his eyes and licked his lips sure did.

73

The one named Darnell cleared his throat. 'Uh, I think I'm gonna bounce, man.'

Cord's stare drilled into the kid. 'How about you wait a few more minutes and answer a few questions for us first? Start with where you were this past Saturday.'

Darnell's head flopped back and forth, hair flying into his face like he was a live Bobble Head, except instead of being perched on someone's dash, he was stuck on this porch. 'Uh, I live down in Hobbs, man. I just came up last night to visit my cousin here. I was heading back today. Gotta work, you know.' His left eye twitched, either because he was lying or nervous – or both.

'What's your last name?' Alyssa asked.

'Williams?' He posed his response as a question.

'Are you asking me? You don't know what your own last name is?'

Bright red circles stained both cheeks as he stammered, 'Naw, man, I know. Williams.' He nodded his head as if he was still trying to convince himself.

Alyssa's stare caused him to shuffle his feet back and forth. 'Who can verify you were in Hobbs Saturday?'

'My boss. I was working, so yeah.'

'You always work on Saturday?'

Another quick jerk of the neck. 'Yeah. I'm off Sundays and Mondays.'

'Where do you work?' Alyssa's eyes held steady even as Darnell's landed anywhere except on her or Cord.

'Dawson Construction. I'm learning to be an electrician. We worked until five, then a group of us hit up a bar.' He fumbled in his back pocket before producing his license. 'Uh, do you need to see my ID?' Alyssa almost laughed.

Instead she grabbed the license and handed it behind her to Cord so he could jot down the information. 'Is the address on your license current?'

Darnell's head jerked forward. 'Yes, ma'am.'

'We're also going to need a phone number in case we need to contact you later, along with your boss's name and number as well as the boys you hit the bar with.'

'Wh–wh –why do you need to get ahold of them?' His eyes darted to the driveway where, Alyssa assumed, one of the cars there belonged to him.

'To verify you were where you said.'

'Oh, right. Sure, sure.' Rubbing at his nose, Darnell pulled his phone from his pocket and opened his contacts. A minute later he rambled off the names and numbers of his boss and the three guys he claimed to have been with Saturday night, and the second Alyssa told him he was free to go, he wasted no time skirting past them as he scampered over to his car.

Alyssa watched him back out of the drive before she turned back to Chance, who watched his cousin disappear around the corner. When he brought his gaze back around, he skipped over Cord to land on Alyssa, a smirk replacing the indiscernible expression he'd been wearing. Leaning back once more in his metal chair, he rested his left ankle on his right knee, the stress on his jeans causing the tattered holes to rip further. 'If you're here about that frat party, I didn't see nothing or no one.' He cleared his throat and then spit off the porch.

'Nothing or no one, hmm?' Alyssa said.

'Nope.'

'What makes you think we're here about a frat party?'

'You asked Darnell where he was Saturday night, so two and two together...'

'Let me get this straight. You're adding two and two together to reach the assumption that we're here because of a frat party. Yet, you're saying you saw "nothing or no one." Is that about right?'

One shoulder lifted and dropped.

'Interesting.' Without taking her eyes off the boy in front of her, Alyssa stretched her hand over to Cord. When she felt his phone in the palm of her hand, she glanced down at the public profile of Chance Williams's Instagram account. Her fingernail clicked against the screen as she read: '*Dude, you know it's a bitchin' party when you gotta boot and rally*.' As a parent to two teenagers, Alyssa understood a lot of teenage slang, so she knew that 'boot and rally' meant vomiting before continuing to party. She flipped the phone around. 'This is your Instagram, right, and that's you in the photo above the caption?'

Another shrug accompanied his 'Maybe.'

'So, what you're telling us is you attended a "bitchin' party," and you expect us to believe you don't remember a single person who was there? Not even those girls you've got your arms draped over in this photo?'

Cord cocked his head to the side. 'College parties I attended were full of alcohol, too, but no matter how much I drank, I always managed to remember at least the girls. But hey, maybe you're just not all that memorable, so those girls didn't even bother to give you their names.' He smiled like he'd solved the world's most difficult puzzle. 'That it?'

He'd hit the machismo nerve in Chance Williams that Alyssa had known he would.

'Man, you don't know what you're saying.' He snorted. 'I was with a lot of girls. You expect me to remember all their names? Things got a little blurry around the edges, if you know what I mean.'

'Well, if things are blurry around the edges, what about the middle? That blurry, too?' Alyssa asked.

'It's all blurry, lady. When's the last time you hit up a party?'

'A frat party? It's been awhile. But one thing I do remember from those days was that there were a lot of underage drinkers. You have many of those there Saturday night?'

Chance flew out of his chair. 'I never said that. You can't go putting words in my mouth. Isn't that like entrapment or something?'

Even though he did his best to stare her down, Alyssa won out when he shifted his gaze away. 'What exactly do you think we're trying to trap you into?'

'Contributing to the delinquency of minors!'

'Oh, are you twenty-one?' she countered. She knew he was because Hal had pulled a copy of his license. He'd hit the legal drinking age a month before Saturday's frat party.

She knew she'd trapped him then, so she turned the heat up. 'Listen, Chance, I don't really want to launch an investigation into your fraternity party, round up a bunch of college kids for releasing a little stress. But if I did, I wonder what else I'd find?'

Color drained from his face. 'Man, why you trying to bust my balls like that?'

'Truth be told, Chance, I don't want to bust your balls at all. I have more important things to do, and right now, you're wasting my time by forcing me to spin my wheels. So, you can either talk, or we can go about getting the information another way. Your choice, but you'd better choose fast before my patience runs the rest of the way out.'

'What do you want to know?'

'One of the girls who was there Saturday night, Rachel Otis, never returned home from that party. What can you tell us about that?'

In an instant, his smirk returned. 'I don't know a Rachel Otis.'

'Are you sure about that?'

'Couldn't say. I was with lots of girls that night, and other nights, too. Can't remember them all.'

Maybe it was because she'd had to deal with Beau Cambridge and his father's similar cocky attitude toward the female population, or maybe it was because she now knew about Cord's sister, Shelley, but whatever it was, Alyssa was finding it more difficult to keep her patience in check.

Within seconds, Cord produced the picture on his phone that Angela Kazminski had sent them and held it in front of Chance's face. 'Rachel Otis.'

A count of ten passed before he said, 'Yeah, come to think of it, I might've seen her. She barged in on me and her friend just as we were about to get it on.' He gauged Alyssa's reaction to his comment, but she kept her expression flat.

'What was her friend's name?'

'Didn't catch it.'

'What happened when Rachel "barged in"?' Cord asked. 'Did that make you mad? Throw things off? Give the friend time to change her mind and back out?'

Chance threw his head back and laughed. 'Dude, two hot girls in the same bedroom with me? Naw, man, that didn't make me mad. I invited her to join us.' After another shrug he admitted, 'She declined, then laid down on the bed with her friend, and they passed out. I left them there to sleep it off and hooked up with someone else.' He threw a pointed stare Cord's way. 'And before you ask, no, I didn't catch her name, either.'

'Listen, Chance, a girl is missing, could possibly be in danger, so if you know anything about that, you need to start talking now.'

'I told you, lady, I don't know what happened to her. She passed out. I left. End of story.'

'What about the other people who were at the party that night? The least of my concerns is whether or not a group of university kids too young to be drinking were celebrating the end of the semester,' she reminded him. 'Unless, of course, you refuse to cooperate, in which case I can make that someone else's focus. So, before you decide to claim temporary amnesia, I want the address of the frat house, and then you can start naming names before the rest of my patience disappears into the wind.'

Whether it was the tone of her voice or the way she stepped into his personal space, it worked. Fifteen minutes later, they had a list of ten names, four phone numbers, and two addresses. As they pulled away from the curb, Cord called Hal and rattled off the information Darnell Williams had shared, asking him to run a background check and verify the alibi he'd given. Then he called Joe and Tony, and after divvying up the names Chance had offered up, Alyssa plugged the first address into the GPS, and a minute later, they were on their way.

Chapter Twelve

Monday, May 20

Quick, shallow breaths were all Rachel allowed herself to take because anything deeper sent excruciating waves of pain coursing through every nerve ending in her body. Her throat burned, and her voice was hoarse from the screams that had served only to further fuel the men's twisted excitement as they abused her in ways she didn't know were possible.

Her wide eyes strayed to the closet they stood near as they cleaned themselves off with the stack of towels nearby. Sweat trailed like miniature rivers down their bodies, dripping onto the floor and leaving small puddles of wetness beneath their feet.

Rachel's gaze followed the blond-haired man whose muscles rippled as he pulled his shirt over his head. A shiver raced down her spine, and she swallowed convulsively against the bile that rose up her throat at the image of those flexing biceps holding her immobile while his partner attached hot metal clips... She squeezed her eyes shut, willing the memory to leave her alone, but it continued to flash through her, and the only thing that stopped her from vomiting was the fear of drawing their attention back to her, having them decide they weren't really done with her after all.

Several minutes ticked by as the men, heavy breaths heaving in and out from exertion, joked back and forth, much of it having to do with what they'd try *next time*. At their words, Rachel turned her head and pressed her mouth against her shoulder in an effort to stifle her whimpers. But when a knock sounded at the door, a muffled, scratchy cry rumbled up through her chest before she could stop it.

When they'd dragged her in here, she'd begged: *please, don't do this.* Then, she'd prayed: *please, no more.* Though to whom she issued that prayer she was unsure, as the second she'd been tethered to this contraption, she'd stopped believing in any supreme being, much less the God her parents pretended to worship because it made them look better if they attended church services.

A key jiggled in the lock, and the door opened to reveal a woman in her mid-forties, wearing her gray-streaked hair pulled back in a severe bun and dressed like she was ready for a night at the opera instead of entering a room where it was obvious a girl had been brutally and repeatedly victimized. The woman spared a brief glance at Rachel before addressing the men.

'From the looks of things, the product meets with your satisfaction.' Her voice was much softer than seemed right or natural in this setting, especially given that her cold gaze had once again returned to Rachel as her critical eyes swept over her body, as if she was mentally checking off items on her list. Suddenly, she snapped her fingers, the sound echoing in the room, and immediately two girls appeared.

'Get her cleaned up and back downstairs,' she ordered. To the men she said, 'After today's event, you'll have to give her a day or two to recuperate.' Both men argued, but the smile she bestowed on them halted their rush of words. 'You don't want her to wear out too soon now, do you? Not like the last one.' She swept her eyes around the room before settling them back on the men. 'From the looks of it, she's going to be a favorite request for a while.'

Tears leaked from the corners of Rachel's eyes, surprising her because she didn't think she had any left. Her stomach twisted in on itself when one of the men laughed. 'Oh, you can bet on that.'

The man who'd placed the metal clips on her stepped forward. Re-dressed in his business attire, he looked like someone leaving an important board meeting instead of someone who had just brutally physically violated a young girl. He issued a quick look at Blond Muscle Guy before speaking. 'We're willing to double the fee if you keep her on call for us.' There was a grating, edgy, anxious sound to his voice, and Rachel knew she'd never forget it as long as she lived, even if she lived to be a hundred.

Though the woman laughed, it was lightyears from friendly. 'Gentlemen, even if you offered to triple or quadruple the fee, you'd still fall far short of the profit I plan to make on this cute little number.' Then she turned and walked back to the door where she once again addressed the girls who now stood on either side of Rachel. 'I thought I told you to get her cleaned up.' Then she disappeared down the hall with the two men following on her heels as they continued to argue terms.

Rachel swayed, stopped from falling only by the padded wristbands that held her chained and suspended with only the balls of her feet touching the floor. On the verge of hyperventilating, her breaths heaving faster and spots flashing in front of her eyes, she reeled from the woman's words which played on a loop in her mind until she felt the pressure on her wrists release, and she slumped to the floor in a heap.

When she didn't move, a hard, loud slap snapped her neck to the side. 'Don't make us carry you,' hissed one of the girls. Up close, Rachel thought she couldn't be more than seventeen or eighteen. But she didn't have time to wonder about it because a second later she was yanked up roughly by her arms and shoved forward and out into the hall where she was paraded naked until they reached a lavish restroom where the other girl, the one who had yet to speak, proceeded to run a bath.

While they waited for the tub to fill, Rude Girl opened a cabinet and grabbed different items before placing them on a low shelf on the wall. Then she opened a door that revealed dozens of silk robes in various sizes and colors. Choosing one at random, this time a deep coral, she closed the door, tested the water, and then both girls helped her inside, but instead of allowing her to soak her pain away – or better yet, allowing her to drown herself – they each grabbed loofah sponges and roughly scrubbed her tender body from head to toe, not bothering to be gentle. Hoarse howls of pain, rage, and humiliation exploded from her, and if she'd been able to think about it at all, Rachel would've been surprised the two girls allowed it to continue.

When they finished, they pulled her up as water cascaded down her body, wrapped a towel around her, and dried her off because Rachel's body trembled violently, her muscles too weak to complete the job on her own. Her throat was on fire from screaming, and she felt that if someone stabbed her right now with a blinding white-hot knife, it couldn't be nearly as painful as the way the rest of her felt. As the girls slipped her arms into the robe, all she wanted was to die.

There. She'd thought it. Never in her life had she ever considered death as an enviable option. And yet she knew that if someone handed her a gun right this second, she'd shove it in her mouth and pull the trigger without a moment's hesitation.

…*Unless she killed those bastards first.* The thought came out of nowhere, and she realized her eyes were searching for… anything: pills, a knife, hell a razorblade she could steal.

The quiet girl moved in front of her clinching the belt at Rachel's waist, bringing a crashing halt to her fantasy. She tried to get the girl to look at her so she could ask her the questions burning the back of her throat, but the girl's eyes strayed from focusing on any one thing for more than a second. Rachel thought she detected a bit of regret and sorrow in the girl's gaze. Who was she? How long had she been here? Had this been her life first? Was she herself destined to become a slave to washing the other captives?

The gurgling swirl of the last of the water rushing down the drain turned Rachel's attention to the tub. Watching, she bit down hard on her lip to hold back her hysteria.

It didn't matter how much they bathed her – she'd never be clean again.

Chapter Thirteen

It was nearing quarter to eight Monday night when Alyssa arrived home, exhausted and frustrated because few of the individuals she and Cord or Joe and Tony had spoken to claimed to know or remember much. Of the ones who weren't suddenly struck with amnesia, three had admitted to seeing Rachel, but none seemed to know anything about this mysterious new friend, though two of them recalled seeing Rachel arrive with another girl. And now Alyssa was concerned that they might not have one missing girl, but two – three, if she included Anna.

Because Jersey, Rachel, and Anna were on her mind when she walked into the kitchen, she was only mildly surprised to see Holly and her friends seated around the kitchen table, waiting to hear what she'd learned. Mabel, her mother-in-law, stood at the counter wrapping up the leftovers from the dinner she'd offered to make when Alyssa had called her husband to let him know she'd be late getting home. All four of them twisted their heads in her direction as she put her weapon in the gun safe.

Tears formed in Holly's eyes when Alyssa came into the kitchen and kissed the top of her daughter's head. 'Did you learn anything?' The tone of her voice clearly showed she wasn't expecting good news.

'No, honey, not really. I'm sorry. I wish I could give you better news.'

'Aunt Natalia told my mom this afternoon that Jersey's dad returned her call.' The lines around Sophie's lips and eyes tightened. 'He didn't seem overly concerned, saying she'd come home when she was ready, that she was probably just out "sowing her wild oats."' She snorted as Leigh Ann covered Sophie's hand with her own. 'I think he's mistaken his daughter for himself.'

Just then Brock came downstairs, fresh from a shower. His smile lit up when he saw Alyssa. 'Hi, babe. Do you want me to heat up a plate of food for you? It shouldn't take too long. We actually just finished about half an hour ago.'

'Oh, I can get it,' Mabel offered, already moving back to the refrigerator.

'Thanks anyway, but Cord and I grabbed a bite to eat about an hour ago.' She walked over and standing on her tiptoes, kissed her husband. 'I'm going to sit with the girls for a bit, and then I'll be in to talk to you, okay?'

Brock's eyes darted in Holly's direction before flitting back to Alyssa. 'Sounds good.' He leaned down to give her a peck on the forehead before turning to his mother. 'Care to join me in the living room? I'll even let you pick what we watch – as long as it's not one of those hand-someone-a-rose shows you like.' He shook his head and shuddered.

'Sure.' Mabel removed the apron she'd borrowed and draped it over the oven handle, then followed her son into the other room. As she passed Holly, she ran her arthritic hand down her granddaughter's hair before giving her shoulder a gentle squeeze.

Holly watched her dad and grandma leave before voicing what she was thinking. 'Isn't it a bit unfair for us to be going through this again? I mean, isn't it someone else's turn?' The second the words left her mouth, her face flushed. 'I'm sorry. I didn't mean that. What I meant is enough is enough. No one should have to endure this ever, but certainly, no one should have to go through it *twice*.' Her face paled as she snapped her neck in Alyssa's direction. 'Oh my gosh, I can't stop putting my foot in my mouth.'

Alyssa placed her hand on Holly's cheek and forced her daughter to look at her. 'It's okay, sweetie. You're worried about

Jersey. I know where your heart is.' Since it had been just last month when Isaac was kidnapped, it was still a fresh wound, and Jersey's disappearance only aggravated it.

Holly's shoulders sagged. 'God, Mom, how do you do *this* day in and day out? I mean, you're *always* searching for someone. It's your job.'

'Because I will always try to help families have a happier ending than my family did.'

Minutes ticked by as the four of them sat around the table, each lost in her own thoughts. The weight of silence lifted as soon as Isaac slid into the kitchen, drawing up short when he realized his sister's friends were still there. His eyes darted around the room, landing first on Holly, then his mom, the refrigerator, and back to Holly.

'Still nothing on Jersey, huh?'

Though his voice was steady, Alyssa recognized the spark of fear as he recalled his own experience. To keep herself from standing and wrapping him in a hug, her hands moved from the table to grip the sides of her chair.

'Still nothing.'

Isaac rubbed at his neck and bounced on the balls of his feet. When he finally opened his mouth to speak, nothing came out. Instead, he grabbed a drink from the fridge, and after guzzling half the bottle he wiped his mouth and turned to his mom. 'Hey, if you have a second when you're done here, I need to talk to you and Dad about something.' His eyes fell on Sophie and Leigh Ann, his forehead creased. 'If that's okay.'

'Alright. I'll knock on your door in a bit.' In the back of her mind, she wondered if it had anything to do with seeing his therapist this afternoon. Brock had taken him this time, and even though it was only Isaac's fourth visit, to her relief, they seemed to be helping. He no longer left his bedroom door ajar, but she knew he still slept with his bathroom light on. Baby steps, perhaps, but at least they were steps forward and not back.

Before heading back upstairs, Isaac snagged a strawberry Pop-Tart, which caused his sister's mouth to drop open. 'Where

87

does he put it all? He *has* to have a hollow leg. I mean, he had three plates of fettuccini alfredo at dinner,' she muttered.

'I'm a growing boy,' he yelled over his shoulder.

Both Holly and Sophie watched as Isaac disappeared around the corner, their eyes lighting with love and concern for the teenager they both called 'little brother.' Leigh Ann hadn't known him for as long, so she didn't have the same relationship with him that Sophie did.

Once Isaac's bedroom door closed, another round of silence fell on the kitchen. Sophie was the first to break it. Voice cracking, she asked what all of them had to be thinking. 'What if something bad has happened to her? I'll never forgive myself.' A single tear rolled down her cheek and splashed on the table, darkening the light wood.

Leigh Ann placed her hands over Sophie's. 'We don't know if anything's happened. It's still possible she's just trying to teach us all a lesson for not caring enough about what she was going through. I mean, really, we could all just be overreacting here.'

Sophie snorted and yanked her hand from beneath Leigh Ann's. 'You mean, teach *me* a lesson for not caring? And how is worrying about her *over*reacting?'

Leigh Ann blanched under the anger in Sophie's voice. 'That's not what I meant, and you should know that.'

Holly twisted her hands together. 'Listen, we all know Jersey can be dramatic, and maybe we could've been more under-standing, but we can't focus on that right now. All we can do is apologize when she comes home *safe* and promise to do better next time.'

Suddenly, Leigh Ann straightened up, excitement in her eyes and voice. 'What about the Find-A-Friend app? Could we locate her that way? I can't believe we didn't think about that already!' Her excitement was short-lived because Sophie knocked the idea out of play.

'She doesn't have it anymore. She deleted it when she discovered Beau was tracking her every movement. She w he always seemed to know where

ong until he left his phone out one day

er location blipping on the screen. She

downloaded the app onto her phone.'

keep her expression neutral. If Jersey's

y been at the top of her list, this infor-

kyrocketed him there. 'How long ago

the sharp look Holly shot her way. It

when she accused Alyssa of using her

the question. 'A month ago maybe?

more or less. I don't really remember.'

ders dropped. 'Why didn't Holly and I

t… *did* you know?'

ead. 'I didn't know, either.'

flyers like we did for Isaac?' Color rushed

Alyssa was sure she hated bringing up the

at idea,' she told her.

o the window, and her shoulders

for them to do any good tonight.

gh Ann can come by my

some out and start

worked out the details, Alyssa moved into

she stood, she spotted Isaac standing in the

hen again, the same odd expression on his

there earlier – thoughtful and curious at the

hing on your mind, sweetie?' she asked as

se enough to whisper.

her way as if he hadn't noticed her standing

lyssa knew he'd become hyper aware of his

didn't think that was what had startled him.

ead then smiled at her. 'No. I'm good. Is now

k to you and Dad?'

'Sure.'

with him

moved ov

vision. 'O

Brock d

about som

Like he

feet, one o

her racing

hand in her

'So, Tre

his family th

said I could

Alyssa's st

had been set

betray her f

weekend, sh

Not hear i

excitement.

'Isn't there

Isaac rolle

actually made

that showed h

already know

graders gradua

seniors go bac

It was a fai

years earlier.

'So, can I?'

What Alyss

in the mountai

were kidnappe

husband's gaze,

that made her f

The next w

'Janelle said she

uldn't understand how he always seemed to know where
e'd been and for how long until he left his phone out one day
ith the app open and her location blipping on the screen. She
dn't even know he'd downloaded the app onto her phone.'

Alyssa was careful to keep her expression neutral. If Jersey's
oyfriend hadn't already been at the top of her list, this infor-
ation would've just skyrocketed him there. 'How long ago
as that?' She ignored the sharp look Holly shot her way. It
as the look she wore when she accused Alyssa of using her
Detective-Mom' tone.

Sophie considered the question. 'A month ago maybe?
uld've been a little more or less. I don't really remember.'

igh Ann's shoulders dropped. 'Why didn't Holly and I
out this? Wait... *did* you know?'

shook her head. 'I didn't know, either.'

we put up flyers like we did for Isaac?' Color rushed
and Alyssa was sure she hated bringing up the

at idea,' she told her.

the window, and her shoulders
or them to do any good tonight.
igh Ann can come by my
some out and start

ed out the details, Alyssa moved into
she stood, she spotted Isaac standing in the
hen again, the same odd expression on his
there earlier – thoughtful and curious at the
ething on your mind, sweetie?' she asked as
close enough to whisper.

ed her way as if he hadn't noticed her standing
Alyssa knew he'd become hyper aware of his
e didn't think that was what had startled him.
s head then smiled at her. 'No. I'm good. Is now
talk to you and Dad?'

'Sure.' Alyssa hooked her arm through her son's and walke[d] with him into the living room where she released him an[d] moved over to sit next to her husband, who muted the tel[e]vision. 'Okay, what's up?'

Brock didn't seem surprised that Isaac wanted to talk to the[m] about something, so he must've already known.

Like he had earlier, Isaac began bouncing on the balls of h[is] feet, one of his tells that he was nervous. Alyssa tried to cal[m] her racing heart by reaching over and clasping her husban[d's] hand in her own.

'So, Trevor asked if I wanted to go camping with him an[d] his family this weekend for Memorial Day. His parents alre[ady] said I could. In fact, it was their idea.'

Alyssa's stomach plummeted, and her nerves felt like [a] had been set to them. When she was certain her voice betray her fear of letting him go away without [her for a] weekend, she asked, 'When are they leaving?'

Not hearing an outright 'no,' Isaac's voi[ce rose with] excitement. 'Well, we'd leave Friday, earl[y]'

'Isn't there school on Friday?'

Isaac rolled his eyes, and wh[at he said next] actually made Alyssa smi[le], [a sign] that showed he was [already know it's nothing] graders graduate Thursday evening. It's stu[pid that the] seniors go back to school *after* they're han[ded their diplomas.']

It was a fair argument and one h[e'd made] years earlier.

'So, can I?'

What Alyssa wanted [to say was: you]
in the mountains, in the woods, [where you] were kidnapped.' Instead, she lifted [her head to meet her] husband's gaze, knowing his fear wa[s] similar t[o hers, and] that made her feel better, though she wasn't sur[e why.]

The next words out of Isaac's mouth clinc[hed it.] 'Janelle said she thought it would be a good thi[ng]

90

do if I felt comfortable with Trevor's family.' Then he stared directly at Alyssa. 'I agree. I think I *need* to do this, Mom. I can't be afraid forever.'

Something ballooned inside her, making Alyssa's heart feel too large for her chest. She trusted Isaac's therapist because she'd made such strides with him in a relatively small amount of time. When she caught Brock's eye again, she saw the acquiescence in his expression. He squeezed her hand tighter, and she turned to Isaac.

'You can go—'

Isaac whooped loudly, pumping his fist in the air.

'—but I want to speak to Trevor's mom before you leave.'

'Thanks M and D!' He swung around and raced to the stairs to let Trevor know, but stopped at the bottom step and whirled back around, a mischievous glint in his eye. 'You know what else Janelle recommended? Getting a dog. Very therapeutic, she said.'

Alyssa and Brock both chuckled. 'Don't push it, mister.' As soon as he disappeared upstairs, the echo of his slamming door reverberating through the rest of the house, she tilted her head up to Brock. 'How much do you want to bet we hit a rescue shelter sometime after he gets back?'

Her husband's response was to smile, shake his head, run his fingers over his face, and mutter, 'Nothing. I want to bet nothing because that would be a sucker bet.'

When Mabel cleared her throat, Alyssa realized she'd forgotten her mother-in-law was still there. Her eyes swung in Mabel's direction in time to see her wipe her eyes with one of the ever-present tissues she kept stuffed in her smocks. 'He's going to be okay, our boy.' Her words were whispered so low that Alyssa wasn't certain if her mother-in-law was speaking to them or herself.

'Yes, he is.'

Shortly after that, Holly walked Sophie and Leigh Ann to the front door, all of them promising to call immediately if they heard a hint of anything at all. After waving them goodbye, she joined her parents. 'What was Isaac so excited about?'

'He's going camping with Trevor and his family this weekend.' A shadow fell across Holly's face, and Alyssa was quick to reassure her. 'He's going to be okay. Besides, he can't stay a prisoner in the house forever. He needs to get back to doing the things he loves.' Even as she spoke, she didn't know if she was trying to convince herself or her daughter.

Tears filled Holly's eyes. 'I know. We definitely have to start treating him like he's going to get past this, otherwise it'll just take him that much longer to heal.' She angled her head toward the stairs. 'I'm going to head up to my room. I really hope Jersey's out there somewhere just trying to punish us for not being sympathetic and understanding enough.'

'Me, too, sweetie.'

The sudden disappearance of both Rachel and Jersey – and possibly Anna, though they still didn't have much information on Rachel's new friend – was another reason Alyssa wasn't entirely comfortable with one of her children being out of her sight for several days. But she knew she couldn't afford to live – or allow her family to live – in that type of fear. If they did, none of them would ever leave the house again.

Chapter Fourteen

The darkness of this living nightmare gripped Jersey in its relentless grasp, refusing to release her into unconsciousness. Instead, every movement, every breath sent arrows of burning pain shooting along her nerve endings. Wincing, she touched her side. Of course, she couldn't be sure, but she suspected her ribs were bruised from the beating she'd received when she refused to obey the lady's commands. And because she bruised so easily, her legs were already covered in various shades of green, yellow, and purple where she'd been restrained by powerful arms.

From the trunk of the car she'd been transported in, she'd been escorted – actually, *dragged* was more accurate – inside this house and taken down into a basement where she was thrown into a cell with several other girls, all of them dressed in colorful silk robes. Pretending a boldness she didn't feel, she'd swung around to demand to know what was going on, but the metal door had clanged shut, barely missing her face.

Shaking, she'd turned around to find several sets of eyes staring back at her with varying degrees of disbelief and pity on their faces. When the cell door reopened behind her, her heart had leaped, taking up residence in her throat, only to plummet when she watched in horror as two men roughly escorted another girl – this one dressed in coral – down the steps. One of the men unlocked the cage and shoved the girl inside, sending her sprawling onto the floor. Jersey stared as the lingering disbelief that she'd been kidnapped began to sink in. The attractive girl in the coral robe had brown hair streaked with strands of gold, but it was the raw, red marks scattered along her skin, and the way that she curled herself into the fetal position, even as full body tremors shook her violently against the floor, that Jersey hadn't been able to tear her eyes from. She'd wanted to ask what had happened but didn't really want to know the answer. Mewling whimpers of pain had escaped the girl as, silently, two others moved to her side, helping her stand so they could lie her gently down on one of the mattresses dotting the cell.

'What is happening here?' Jersey's voice was brittle and high-pitched as she'd forced the question out. A subarctic chill penetrated her as every dead-voiced, numb answer chipped away another part of her soul. Words like *forced sex, beatings, The Toybox*, and *pleasure in pain* ricocheted around in her head. Somehow, she had fallen into the blackest of all rabbit holes. Never in her life, not even when Beau had convinced her to go through the state's self-proclaimed scariest Haunted House of Horrors, had she experienced such mind-numbing terror.

That was, until in the twilight hours of a new day, when their prison door had once again opened. Only this time it was she who'd been dragged upstairs to be delivered to one of the most frightening men she'd ever laid eyes on. Even through her rising hysteria, she'd refused to strip naked, unable to release the image of the battered girl in the coral robe. The lady with the severe bun had given her a choice: disrobe or be disrobed forcefully.

Jersey had never been one to be brave, not like Sophie, whose courage and tenacity she secretly admired. She'd never stood up to bullies – she'd never really had any reason to.

But this time? This time she'd had no choice. Even when the lady slapped her face so hard it snapped her head back, even as the tears streamed down her cheek, she was brave. It wasn't until the two men stepped forward again that her courage had begun to falter.

Still, her need for self-preservation wasn't quite ready to release its grip, and her flight instinct – something she wasn't even aware she had – had kicked in. Her eyes had darted to the door. She wasn't even aware of her feet moving in that direction until someone had a fistful of her hair, yanking her to a stop. The men had each grabbed hold of either side of her, imprisoning her as the woman produced a pair of scissors and methodically sliced Jersey's clothes until they fell off her in ribbons of cloth, leaving her naked, on show for the man whose face finally emitted a reaction.

Excitement.

If only it had ended there. She had been marched down the hall to a darkened room, backlit with an ominous blue light that cast eerie shadows on the walls and ceiling. 'She's all yours,' one of the men had said before shoving her into the room, sending her tumbling, her arms coming up a split second before her face slammed into the floor. As she'd pushed herself to her knees, she'd barely recognized the horrified screams that were coming from her. She'd almost crawled to the corner when a pointed boot had nailed her side, sending her reeling back down, gasping for breath.

Still she hadn't stopped. She'd known her life depended on her getting away, so using her elbows, she'd inched forward on her stomach only to have two strong, smooth hands grip her feet and flip her onto her back. The man with black, soulless eyes stood with his legs on either side of her hips, smiling down at her as he lifted his booted foot and slammed it down into her stomach.

Sixty of the longest minutes of her life later, he was done. She knew how long it had been because someone had knocked on the door seconds before a booming but disembodied voice announced the man's hour was up.

Had it really only been Sunday when she'd been whining to her friends about problems that weren't really problems at all? The finality of the door clanging shut behind her as she was tossed back into the cell with the other girls barely penetrated through the fog of agony. She was somewhat aware of gentle hands easing her onto the nearest mattress, where she curled herself into as tight a ball as she could. As she lay there sobbing, gasping for breath, the memory of the voice from that night, the one who'd whispered *nighty-night* just before her world had blacked out, slammed into her.

It had to have been her mind playing tricks on her. No way could the person she knew be involved in something like this.

She refused to believe it.

Chapter Fifteen

Tuesday, May 21

Burned trees and shrubbery blocked Alyssa's view as she forced her feet to move faster. She ignored the melodious songs of the birds and the mocking caws of the crows as she extended her arms in an attempt to save Isaac. Urgency filled her as he slipped out of her grasp, his body conforming to the shapes of the trees which suddenly became Timmy's arms. Cymbals clanged in the distance, and then she lurched awake, disoriented, eyes stinging and blurred. It was the same nightmare she'd had for the past six weeks.

'You going to answer that?' Brock mumbled.

Mind still warped from the dream, it took a second for Alyssa to realize her phone was ringing. She checked the time. Four-sixteen in the morning. Voice thick with sleep and nerves, she jerked her phone off her nightstand. 'Hello?'

'Detective Wyatt? This is Officer Vogler. Captain Hammond asked me to call you.'

Alyssa shook her head to clear it, trying to catch up. 'Asked you to call me about what?'

'We've got a dead body down on Central and Louisiana.'

Her stomach muscles tensed, and she gripped her phone tighter. 'Female?' It had to be, otherwise the captain wouldn't have found it necessary to drag her out of bed at four in the morning. Images of Rachel Otis and Jersey Andrews ran like a reel through her foggy brain.

'Female. Appears to be fairly young, but it's hard to say with the condition she's in. I'll let you take a look for yourself.'

'I'll be there as soon as I can. Thanks for the call.' She leaned down to kiss Brock, whose eyes were now open and trained on her. 'Someone found a deceased female near downtown, so I've got to go. Try to go back to sleep.'

'I will.' He gripped her hand tightly in his, holding her in place when she tried to stand. She turned back to him, eyebrows lifted. 'Call or text as soon as you know who it is – or isn't.'

She pulled her hand from his grip and cupped the side of his face. 'I will. But if it is, we'll tell her together.' She sent a silent prayer to anyone listening that it wasn't either of her missing girls.

Twelve minutes later, she was in her Tahoe and on the road, and thirteen minutes after that, she pulled up behind Cord's vehicle just as he was climbing out of it. Unlike her, he'd answered his phone on the first ring when she'd called.

She joined him on the sidewalk as together they headed toward the abandoned, half-finished construction of what was supposed to have been a restaurant when it was completed. 'You know, even if there wasn't crime scene tape and police lights blazing, I would've known where to go. All I'd need to guide me is the large gathering of looky-loos trying to get a glimpse of someone's corpse.' She growled at a few individuals who held their phones high above their heads in an effort to snap photos to post on their social media sites. 'Why are there so many people even out at this hour?'

When a short, balding man wearing a Dunkin Donuts uniform blocked her path in his attempt to get a better shot, Alyssa snapped. 'Have a little respect, people!' She pushed the man aside, whipping her head around to bark at it him when he protested. 'Isn't it time for you to make the doughnuts?'

As she forced her way through the throng of bodies, she felt her patience fray. 'Get the hell out of my way!' Heads turned, but other than that, her words had no effect as the people continued blocking her path. 'If any of you here without a badge are still in my way in two seconds, I'm slapping cuffs on you!' Whether it was her threat or the fact that Cord had planted himself in front of her as he elbowed the remaining people out of the way, she didn't know and didn't care.

Each step closer to the perimeter set up by the first responders increased the heavy scent of death that lingered in the air. Mixed with that was the unmistakable odor of unbathed bodies. It was a sad fact that a large number of homeless individuals congregated in this area despite the various nearby shelters. Alyssa did her best to breathe through her mouth and not her nose.

She ducked under the crime scene tape into the building. Being careful where she stepped, she moved over to the body, trying not to feel guilty at the relief that flooded her when she realized it was neither Rachel Otis nor Jersey Andrews. Still, the girl was someone's daughter, sister, aunt, and the sadness of that registered heavy in Alyssa's heart.

The red-headed girl on the ground wasn't nude, but she might as well have been for what she was wearing. A pair of burgundy short shorts that would have barely covered her buttocks were ripped open, exposing her pubis area, and revealing she wore nothing beneath them. The top she wore was a see-through mesh material and exposed more than a bikini top would. As Officer Vogler had indicated, the girl was young, but since she was covered all over in deep scratches and open wounds, it was difficult to gauge her actual age.

Her open eyes stared vacantly at the building across the street to the north. Strange ligature marks around the girl's ankles and wrists had Alyssa squatting down for a closer look. Almost immediately she noted an odd mark on the girl's left hip. 'What's that?' Without taking her eyes off the body, she asked, 'Anyone have a light?' Immediately, four hands holding flashlight apps on their phones extended her way. She grabbed the one closest to her, shaking her head. She could've used her own phone. Whatever happened to a good old-fashioned flashlight?

She shined the light over the area on the girl's hip, a memory tickling the back of her mind. Something about that mark was familiar. She twisted her neck to ask Cord what he thought, but as she did, her eyes landed on the girl's hands. 'Holy Christ! What the hell happened to her fingers?' Where there should've been fingernails, the tips of the victim's fingers revealed only red and raw skin.

Very little shocked Alyssa anymore, but somehow this atrocity managed to. Standing, she handed the borrowed phone to Cord so he could take a look himself, but he waved it away, using his own instead. Like her, he squatted down and leaned in for a better look. His head shook back and forth twice, and then he brought himself back up to his full height. 'Hard to say what that marking is.' Something in his voice made Alyssa tilt her head up to study her partner's face, but his expression was closed-off.

An officer, about five-foot-seven with pitch black hair, walked up. 'I'm Officer Vogler. I called you.' He tipped his head forward. 'Are you finished with my phone?'

'Oh, yes. Thanks.' She handed it back and asked him to fill her in on what he knew.

'Not a lot right now, I'm afraid. Dispatch received a call about three-thirty this morning. The name she gave was Naomi Kenney, but since she was hesitant to give that much information, we're not sure it's the caller's real name. Anyway, she said she was searching for a place to sleep when she spotted a flashy red car – make and model unknown – and something about the way the driver was acting made him seem suspicious.'

Cord interrupted. 'What time was that?'

Vogler shook his head. 'No way she could tell the time, but she said she'd waited awhile before using that payphone next to Route 66 Motel.' All three of them turned to the ramshackle, rundown motel that had once been glorious in its day but now housed more mice than people. Since the city had condemned it, the motel had become a nest for drug exchanges or strung-out individuals looking for a place to rest their head before searching for their next fix. It was heartbreaking to see.

'Back to what I was saying — Ms. Kenney said she spotted this car driving around, and when Dispatch asked her to explain what the driver was doing that made her suspicious, she stated that the car drove around the block five or six times, like the driver was either looking for someone or making sure no one else was around. When the driver suddenly stopped in front of the building here, Ms. Kenney said she became nervous and ducked behind a dumpster.' He twisted around and pointed. 'I'm guessing that's the one she was referring to since it's the closest one.

'She watched the driver get out of the car, describing him as an average-sized male in a rumpled suit with a scratch down his face, which she noticed when he stepped underneath the streetlight. Another indication that the dumpster she hid behind was that one. She said the driver popped the trunk and removed what appeared to be something heavy, walked into this building and returned empty-handed to his car a few minutes later. Dispatch asked her if she went inside to see what the man left behind, but Ms. Kenney became agitated and hung up. A few of us wondered if she was lingering out there' — he tipped his head toward the gathering of the curious — 'but if she is, she's not coming forward or admitting to it.'

Cord ran his hand over his head. 'Any other witnesses or people you've talked to?'

A frown turned down the corners of Vogler's lips as he lifted his chin towards the ever-growing mob standing on the sidewalk. 'They might gather out of morbid curiosity, but they scatter like birdshot when it comes to procuring witness statements.'

Alyssa and Cord both nodded. 'Unfortunately, it seems very few people feel compelled to step forward when it comes to matters of speaking to or assisting the police.' Before she could thank Officer Vogler, a commotion behind them grabbed her attention.

Lynn Sharp, the medical examiner, had arrived and was making her way through the crowd. Alyssa's mind flashed back to the last conversation she'd had with the woman, the one where Lynn had informed her that Evan Bishop's DNA indicated he was Alyssa's sibling.

'Damn vultures. They're lucky I'm not holding my scalpel,' Lynn groused as soon as she reached Alyssa's side.

Alyssa chuckled. Despite the fact that the doctor was indirectly threatening mutilation, she was actually one of the gentlest women she'd ever met. And maybe that was because she had to be, especially when she was the one present for grieving individuals brought in to identify their loved ones.

'Alright then, lead the way so I can make sure they're preserving evidence the way they should be.' As gentle as she may be, it was no secret that no one wanted to be on the receiving end of Lynn Sharp's wrath if a deceased person's body wasn't handled the proper way – and by proper, she meant *her* way.

As Lynn snapped pictures, Alyssa pointed to the mark on the young girl's hip. 'Does that look familiar to you? I've seen it somewhere, but I can't think of where.'

Lynn spared a glance before directing someone to place protective bags over the girl's hands. 'Off the top of my head, I can't say. But once I get her on the table, I'll have more time to check it out, and then I can let you know what I think. For now – based on the rigor mortis – I'd guess she's been deceased between twenty-four and forty-eight hours.' Gently, she placed a gloved finger on the girl's chin. 'Unfortunately, from the damage to her face, I don't feel comfortable yet even guessing at an age range.'

By the time the young girl's body was escorted to the morgue hours later, the sun was blazing high in the sky, making Alyssa hot and sticky. And irritable, because the heat and the scent of death were attracting flies and other critters she loathed. She moved over to Cord who was busy scribbling something in his notebook. He glanced up when she approached.

'You've been quieter than usual. You okay?'

He went back to writing. 'I'm fine. Aside from the obvious.' He waved his hand around the abandoned building.

She wasn't convinced, but she let it go. She waited for him to finish jotting down his thoughts then sucked in a deep breath before lobbing her verbal grenade. 'Did that mark look like a branding to you?'

'I'm not sure what I think yet.'

It wasn't the answer – or lack of one – that concerned Alyssa; it was the delivery. Since it was the anniversary week of his sister's suicide, she wondered if she needed to talk to him about stepping back from this case, as well as Rachel and Jersey's, maybe even taking a little time off. Normally she wouldn't even consider it, but this situation was different. Watching for his reaction, she said, 'If it *is*, I can only think of a few reasons for those. Pimps marking their prostitutes or, worse, sex traffickers branding their product.'

Cord's jaw clenched and he wiped a hand down his face before shoving his fingers through his hair. 'The thought crossed my mind, too.' Then he swung around, catching her staring at him. 'I know what you're thinking, but I'm fine. I wouldn't risk jeopardizing a case because of… what happened to Shelley. I can handle it. So, please do me a favor and stop looking at me like I'm going to fly off the handle any second. Allow me the same courtesy I gave you when you found out Evan Bishop was actually Timmy. Now, I think it'll help if we can figure out where we've seen that symbol before.'

Alyssa nodded. He was right; he'd never treated her like she would break when the Bishop case became far too personal, and she owed him that same respect.

Chapter Sixteen

Tuesday afternoon, a bleary-eyed Alyssa unlocked the conference room and set her items on the long table before moving to the wall so she could flip on the lights. A too-early call-out and lack of sleep were biting at her heels.

Be that as it may, the issue of at least two missing girls, one of whom was her daughter's friend, and another involving the Jane Doe who was now lying in the morgue awaiting Lynn Sharp to perform the autopsy dictated that sleep deprivation was the least of her concerns.

As she waited for the rest of her team, she thumbed through several of the witness statements Officer Vogler and the others *had* managed to get. Cord walked in as she was reading one from a guy with no known physical address who claimed the girl was in the line of fire from a gang fight. He swore he'd watched her be gunned down. Since there were no bullet holes in the deceased's body, they could safely toss this one aside.

Alyssa waved her hand over the statements. 'From these, it would seem that right now our best lead appears to be Naomi Kenney.' Randomly, she grabbed one of the papers and read from it. '*I watched the chick and her dog trying to rob a guy, and so he stabbed her and took off.*' Her eyes lifted to her partner's. 'I didn't see stab wounds. Did you see stab wounds?'

'None that I saw. Hal's checking to see if we can locate this Naomi, right? If nothing else, maybe she's got family who would know where she is. And if that doesn't pan out, we can always send Tony or Joe out to patrol that area, see if she shows up again. Who knows? Maybe that's where she regularly lays her head at night.'

Alyssa agreed. 'Worth checking out.'

Just then Hal rolled in with a stack of folders in his lap and his phone and laptop in the large pocket on the side. 'Morning Alyssa, Cord. Sure would be nice if Liz was back. We could get her to do a sketch of this mystery male – if we locate Ms. Kenney – and we could even show the composite to the homeless shelters in the area, see if anyone else recognizes him.'

Liz Waterson, Alyssa's favorite forensic sketch artist and member of her team was in North Carolina visiting her parents. She wouldn't be back until after Memorial Day weekend, so not for another week. 'Her help would be nice, but we'll have to make do without her until she returns,' she said.

'Have you heard from her, heard how her mom's doing?' Hal asked.

After Liz's sister was murdered by an ex-boyfriend, their mother's health had slowly declined over the years, which had prompted this latest visit. 'I didn't talk to her, but she did send a text letting me know it was definitely a heart attack but that her mom was stable and resting comfortably. The prognosis was good, she thought.'

Joe and Tony walked in just then, and of the two, Tony appeared far more chipper.

Joe, on the other hand, was scowling at something Tony said.

'Hailee's still colicky, huh?' Alyssa asked. Ever since his baby was born in March, Joe often came in looking either ready to drop or snap someone's head off. Frequently both.

'I'm beginning to think she'll be colicky until she's a teenager.' He rubbed one fist into his tired eyes.

Tony patted Joe's back. 'Hate to tell you, partner, but when Hailee's a teenager, you'll be wishing it was only colic giving you sleepless nights.' He merely grinned at Joe's frown.

Hal popped open his laptop and projected the screen onto the wall for everyone to see, effectively moving the topic back to work. He clicked the downloaded images from the crime scene then, splitting the screen, opened a blank document where he typed *Rachel Otis* and *Jersey Andrews* in bold and underlined text. In red, he added *Jane Doe*.

Alyssa walked over to the crime scene photos, specifically studying the mark on Jane Doe's hip as she spoke. 'Okay, we don't know that these cases are related. So far all we have in common is the young age of at least Jersey and Rachel.' An image of the battered body of Callie McCormick, Bishop's last victim, popped into her head, and she shut it down. People, including young girls, went missing every single day for various reasons. It didn't mean there was another serial killer in their midst. She couldn't – wouldn't – allow her last case to cloud her mind or hinder her ability to do her job. Like every case, she'd methodically move the pieces of the puzzle around until they began to connect.

'I'll check the cameras in the Central/Louisiana area, though I doubt we'll have much luck since the city got tired of replacing and repairing them every single time they got vandalized,' Hal offered.

As frustrating as it was not to have working cameras, it was also frustrating watching public funding funneled into constantly replacing them. 'While you're at it, check the Missing Person's database to see if our Jane Doe matches any of the profiles. Without knowing her age, it might be more difficult, but it's a place to start. Okay, moving onto Rachel Otis.' She peeked at her notes. 'We still need to locate Calvin McDougal. He lives at the frat house where the party was held, and according to several of the individuals we interviewed yesterday, he was seen hitting on her and didn't take too kindly to being rejected. One of the witnesses claimed to overhear him accuse her of "false advertising" before storming away.'

Joe's eyebrows scrunched together, and he held his hand up for Alyssa to stop. 'False advertising? What the hell does that mean?'

Cord answered, speaking through clenched teeth. 'It means she was wearing something that McDougal took as an invitation and an automatic yes to sex and didn't appreciate being told no. *Allegedly*.' His eyes were full of anger as he tacked on the word, sneering as he did.

Alyssa wondered if anyone else heard the mental ledge Cord teetered on.

'Anyway, no one could tell us when he left the party, and no one admitted to knowing his whereabouts yesterday, so Cord and I will try again today.'

Hal picked up from there. 'I contacted Dawson Construction like you asked. Darnell Williams's alibi checked out. He was at work, and when I contacted the bar where he said they headed afterward, the bartender was able to verify everything he said.'

The team spent a few more minutes discussing Rachel's case before moving onto Jersey's. Pushing her personal feelings aside, Alyssa focused on what they knew while Hal typed it into his computer under Jersey's name. The most glaring similarity between the two cases, aside from their youthful ages, was the location of each of their disappearances. The duck pond was within a quarter mile of the frat house where Rachel had last been seen less than twenty-four hours before Jersey had gone missing.

'Hal, what did you find on Hugh or Beau Cambridge?' The only indication of the rage Alyssa knew Cord felt regarding the Cambridge men was the way his fingers clenched on his pen. Again, she wondered if anyone else noticed.

'Hugh Cambridge is the chief financial officer of Harrison Motor Company and has been for the past thirty years. Married for twenty-six. One kid – Beau – football player, piss-poor grades that should've had him kicked off the team at least half a dozen times. According to his social media accounts, he and Jersey met at a party about six months ago and "hooked up." I cross-referenced her accounts, and they said basically the same thing. It didn't take much scrolling through either of their accounts to recognize they liked to air their fights or disagreements or whatever online, and from their feeds, they've had a pretty tumultuous, on-again, off-again relationship. I'll keep digging.'

Alyssa exchanged glances with Cord. 'What do you mean by tumultuous? How so?'

The corners of Hal's mouth tipped down, and he snorted as he tapped a few keys on his keyboard. 'Allow me to show you this example from two months ago.' He cleared his throat and began reading.

When you walk in and find your boyfriend's tongue shoved down some skank's throat…

If you don't want me to shove my tongue down someone else's throat, don't be such a prude. BTW, don't you ever embarrass me like that again.

Or you'll do what?

You don't want to find out…

Alyssa cut her eyes toward Cord. The tendons in his neck bulged, his nose flared, and his fingers gripped the edges of the table. 'Print that out for me, Hal, and any others that seem to implicitly threaten violence. And see if you can find a way to verify Beau's whereabouts for Sunday night, specifically between the hours of seven-thirty to let's say, six the next morning. Those posts don't paint him in the most favorable light.'

'You bet.'

'Now, what about cameras in the university area that could help tell us what happened to either girl. Did they leave alone or with someone? Did they walk, drive, or Uber? See if we can find any witnesses that place Beau Cambridge near either girl before she disappeared. We already know he was with Jersey earlier in the day, so I'm talking about later that evening.' She tapped Jane Doe's image. 'And let's find these girls before we have two more deaths on our conscience.' She squashed down the voice that said they already might.

108

Chapter Seventeen

Tuesday, May 21

Throughout the night, Rachel's nightmares kept jerking her back to wakefulness, only to remember that she was still in one, images of *The Toybox* flashing behind her eyes seared into memories she'd never be able to rid herself of. And each time her eyes drifted closed again, a fuzzy Anna stood with her arms outstretched, just out of Rachel's reach, yelling something to her. This time when she woke, panting, bathed in sweat, wincing at pain the likes of which she'd never before experienced, she was mildly surprised to find her face wet from tears.

Anna. Where was she? Had a fate worse than her own befallen her friend? Was death really worse anyway? Had whoever drugged her – and she was sure now she'd been drugged at the frat party – done the same to her friend? Had she somehow managed to escape? For a second Rachel allowed herself the fantasy of imagining Anna heading up a search party and leading the cavalry to their rescue.

Carefully, slowly, she rolled to her side, her eyes landing on the new girl with the petite frame. Some part of her brain had processed the new girl's arrival, but when she'd been brought back downstairs, she'd been in too much pain and was far too traumatized to care about anything except death or escaping this nightmare – whichever came first, she'd take it. The dim light from the bathroom cast a shadow over the fair-skinned girl, and a feeling of guilty relief combined with the suffocating weight of shame flooded her system. Maybe the new girl would be more to the liking of the men who'd purchased her. From the deep purple and blue marks on the girl's body, she appeared to bruise easily, something the men seemed to enjoy.

Part of a conversation her subconscious had picked up when the girl had been tossed in the cell played in her mind. Becca had said something about being forced into prostitution.

'Prostitutes get paid in something other than beatings, bites, and bruises. You can't make this anything other than what it is – slavery – Becca, so stop trying.'

Faye's words rang in her head even as Rachel's mind caught up to the fact that the newcomer was staring back at her, the dull, dead look in her eyes mirroring that of her own. 'What's your name?' Her voice was hoarse, raspy, and her throat burned as if molten liquid had been poured down it.

Before the girl could respond, a high-pitched scratching sound invaded the cell, and Rachel jerked her hands up to cover her ears as, heart pounding, she tried to locate the source of the noise. Her eyes swung to the window in time to see a broken-off branch scratching across the glass as if it were trying to etch a picture into it.

With trembling hands, she pressed both fists tight against her chest, twisting her knuckles into her sternum in an effort to calm her thundering heart. Similarly, the new girl's hands gripped the light sheet each girl was allotted.

'I'm Rachel,' she whispered. But the new girl wasn't listening. Her eyes had already strayed, so Rachel trained her gaze in the same direction, a low moan escaping her as she did.

Faye's robe was opened, her body on display. Visible in the barely-there light were fresh cuts sliced into her skin, her left eye was swollen shut, and blood seeped around the crust that had formed around her nose. Rachel shoved her hand against her mouth and swallowed back the nausea. *When had that – what had happened?*

Faye's eyes were empty, devoid of even tears, as if her spirit had died and her entire being along with it. Staring at her,

Rachel felt her resolve disintegrate. She hadn't even grasped onto the understanding that she'd been holding onto a tiny beacon of hope in this dark tunnel of her existence until now. Sure, Becca was kinder and gentler, despite what they were all going through, but Faye was a fighter, and that was where the hope had come in.

The new girl's sobs finally broke through the barrier of Rachel's numbness. Without realizing she was doing it, she found herself moving over to Faye's mattress, offering her what strength she had, though it was little. She sensed movement behind her, and turning her head, she saw Becca drawing up next to the new girl, running her hands down the girl's hair as her broken cries became muffled by Becca's shoulder. Faye didn't so much as turn her head in the girl's direction or acknowledge Rachel's presence. A shadow fell across the mattress, and Rachel twisted around to see Cheyenne's hand hovering in the air, as if she wasn't sure what she should be doing. It was at that moment that Rachel realized Meghan was missing, and she tried to recall the last time she'd seen her.

And then she stopped thinking about anything because the door at the top of the steps clanged open, and all their heads – except for Faye's – snapped in that direction. One of the men was carting yet another girl down the stairs in a fireman carry while another led the way, gun out, key in hand. *God, not another one!*

With the cell door opened, the man stepped in and dropped the unconscious girl on the closest mattress before turning around and leaving. Rachel's stomach churned, and shock slammed into her when she noticed how young this one was. There was no chance this tiny sprite of a thing could ever survive *The Toybox* and its many instruments of torture.

Suddenly, Faye was back and moving. She eased between the mattresses where she knelt next to the new arrival, gently tugging the girl's t-shirt back into place before stretching out next to her and wrapping an arm around the girl's waist, as if by doing so, she could shield her from what she would encounter when she woke.

When Faye's shattered, broken cry rippled through the cell, Rachel's gaze rose to the small two by three-foot window, wishing for all the world that she could follow her soul through the lightly frosted glass.

Chapter Eighteen

Tuesday, May 21

The light from the window shifted, trailing up the table, and Alyssa glanced up before checking the time on her phone. Six-thirty. Her team had gone non-stop for nearly fifteen hours after receiving the call this morning, so she'd sent everyone home because she needed them to be rested – at least as much as they could be – and focused, so they could find the missing girls, as well as dig into what had happened to the murdered girl found in the abandoned restaurant.

Cord had offered to stay and wade through the mountains of pages of interviews with her, but she insisted he leave with the others. With all that was on his mind already with the anniversary of Shelley's suicide and his unexpected, out-of-character reaction to Beau Cambridge, she had to admit she was afraid that adding exhaustion to the mix may be the final straw before he snapped. It had taken some convincing, but he'd finally, reluctantly agreed.

She tapped the yellow highlighter against her teeth as she read over Calvin McDougal's statement. They'd caught him just as he'd been about to leave. Alyssa recalled how he'd arrogantly swaggered out onto the front porch of the frat house, fingers tucked into his front pocket, a smirk playing around his lips throughout the entire interview as he clearly showcased his feeling of superiority over authority figures.

Cord had opened the questioning by showing McDougal a picture of Rachel. 'Did you see this girl at the party?'

Calvin shrugged. 'Sure.'

'Did you talk to her?'

'Sure.'

College sure wasn't teaching him a fine repertoire of vocabulary.

'And…?'

'And what? She made it clear she wasn't interested, so I turned my attention elsewhere. Plenty of chicks there. No need to waste anybody's time with one who was offering nothing but false advertising.'

Beside her, Cord stiffened, and for a second, Alyssa was afraid of a repeat of the Cambridge scenario, but to his credit and her relief, he maintained his composure.

'That's not what we heard,' Cord said. 'Lots of people told us you didn't take it too well when Rachel turned you down, said you got pretty riled up about it.'

Calvin snorted, but both his posture and eyes shifted. 'Whatever. Those people are wrong. Like I said, she said no, and I moved on. Last I saw her, she was still sitting on the couch where I left her.'

Immediately recognizing the similarity in their responses, Alyssa asked, 'Do you happen to know Chance Williams?'

'Yeah, I know Chance. We don't hang, but he's usually here, even though he's not a member of the house. It's all good because he usually has a nice posse of chicks who show up with him.' He actually winked. 'Brings variety, you know.'

Had times really changed that much? During her college days, she couldn't remember anyone being so brazenly disrespectful to the cops. Or maybe that was just the circles she ran in.

Alyssa couldn't decide if it was the guy's attitude – his words and his lack of interest in the fact that a young college girl he'd admitted to hitting on had gone missing – that ate at her, making her distrust everything that came out of his mouth. If she could figure it out, maybe she'd have a large enough piece of the puzzle to make the other pieces fall into place.

She was still thinking about that when a shadow filled the doorway, reluctantly drawing her away from the interview transcript. A scowl on her face, she turned to snap at the person unfortunate enough to interrupt her concentration, but when she saw the lines around Captain Hammond's eyes, his face drawn tight and looking like he'd aged another five years in the past five days, all that flew out of her mind.

'What?'

'I'd ask why you're still here when the rest of your team's gone, but it doesn't matter because you're needed.' Even his voice was gruffer than usual.

Alyssa's stomach plummeted. 'What's happened?'

Hammond sagged against the doorjamb, one hand reaching up to rub his temple. 'I have to tell you, Detective, I don't know how much longer I want to do this job in the world we live in today.' He straightened, his stare drilling into her. 'Dispatch just received a call about another missing girl. Katelyn Phillipson never came home from school this afternoon. It's been just over three hours, but she's only thirteen years old. I need you and Roberts to head over. We already have two – possibly three – missing girls and one dead one in a remarkably short amount of time, and we can't afford to risk waiting another second. As of right now, I want you, your team, and the department on high alert.' He twisted until he was staring out the window. 'Our city's still reeling from realizing we had a serial killer walking amongst us for the past two decades.' The sound of defeat practically vibrated across the room as it poured off her captain in waves.

For a moment the weight of Evan Bishop's reign of terror settled onto her shoulders, but then she shook it off, knowing there was no way to undo the past. Right now, she needed to focus on the case in front of her. At least three missing girls in a span of three days? Add a deceased female into the mix, and Alyssa's instincts shouted that there was no room left to doubt these cases were somehow connected. It was far too much of a coincidence – something she rarely believed in. 'Address?'

'I have it right here.' He stopped her with a hand on her arm as she snatched the paper he'd extended her way. 'I expect an update the second you have a chance; I don't care what time it is. I don't like what my sixth sense is telling me about this disappearance.'

Some people swore the eyes were windows to the soul, and with the shadows filling Hammond's eyes, Alyssa believed it. 'I don't like what it's telling me, either.' She flung her bag over her shoulder and pushed past him.

Unable to stop them, memories of Jane Doe's then Callie McCormick's battered bodies haunted her as she raced to her car. She shook her head. This couldn't be happening again. She wouldn't let it.

Her nerves singed with a renewed sense of urgency, she tossed her bag into the passenger seat. The second the ignition caught, she ordered her Bluetooth to call Cord. Just as she was about to join the traffic, a group of kids on bikes executing complicated wheelies and other tricks passed in front of her, forcing her to wait instead of punching the gas and speeding to Katelyn Phillipson's home.

'Hello?'

'We've got another one. Thirteen years old, didn't return home from school.' The days of terror following Isaac's kidnapping, of realizing he wasn't home, tried to drag her under, but she shut it down.

'Um, Lys, this is Sara. Cord's in the shower. If you want I can drag him out, or I can have him call you right back.'

Already overwhelmed with the pressing need to find Katelyn, Alyssa didn't have time to be embarrassed that she hadn't realized she was speaking to Cord's wife and not him. 'Yes, please have him call me back immediately.'

'You know what, I just heard the water shut off. I'll just go let him know now.'

Muffled words whispered through her speakers, and then Cord was on the phone, his voice tight and controlled, something she still wasn't used to hearing from his normal laid-back personality. 'Lys, what's going on? Sara said something about another missing girl?'

'Katelyn Phillipson, thirteen years old, never returned home after school. That's all Hammond gave me. I'll be driving near your neck of the woods, so I'll swing by and pick you up.' Her gaze swung from the time displayed on her dash to the red lights of stopped traffic in front of her. Damn construction. 'I'll be there in more than five, less than ten.'

'I'll be outside waiting.'

And then he was gone.

—

Less than twenty minutes later, Alyssa pulled up to the residence on Glendale Avenue in Northeast Albuquerque Acres where many homes went for at least half a million. This one probably soared closer to the million-dollar range. Like Rachel Otis and Jersey Andrews, Katelyn Phillipson came from wealth.

Cord released his seat belt, fingers on the door handle. 'Ready?'

'Not even a little,' Alyssa answered truthfully. She took a calming breath, then climbed out of her SUV. They'd barely cleared the courtyard when the front door opened, revealing a tired-looking man in his late forties wearing rumpled clothes. His thinning hair stuck out in tufts where he'd run his fingers through it. Fear and frustration rolled off him in waves, something Alyssa was all too familiar with because it had been her and her family just six weeks ago.

'Mr. Phillipson?'

'Ye…yes.' Jason Phillipson cleared his throat and wiped a hand over his haggard face. 'Follow me,' he said as he stepped to the side and ushered the two indoors.

It wasn't the massive, expensive paintings that decorated the small foyer or the crystal chandelier hanging from the high-vaulted ceiling that immediately snagged Alyssa's attention. It was what could only be described as a shrine to their daughter that did it. One four-tiered shelf held a multitude of silver soccer trophies, a couple of swimming medals, and what appeared to be dance or cheerleading accolades. On either side of the shelf were nearly wall-to-ceiling photographs of a smiling and quite petite Katelyn in various poses and throughout various stages of her life from infancy to her eighth-grade dance, which if it was anything like Isaac's school, would have been held just two weeks ago.

Despite the obvious wealth, it was equally obvious that the Phillipsons cared more about showcasing their pride in their daughter than interior decoration. The differences between them and the Otises were glaring.

Alyssa moved closer to the pictures. Without fail, in every single photo, whether by herself or posing with her friends, family, or with a myriad of different animals ranging from a leashed rat to a kangaroo and everything in between, Katelyn Phillipson wore an ear-to-ear smile, the kind that worked itself up all the way into her eyes. It didn't take detectives of Alyssa and Cord's caliber to realize the missing teen was not only a happy girl, she was adored by her parents; the wall collage just proved it.

As Katelyn's father led the way into the family room, he said, 'My wife will be out in a moment. She's just getting off the phone with her mother back in New York.'

While this room wasn't a continuation of the absolute adoration found in the other one, evidence of the love and pride they had in their daughter still decorated several spaces.

'She's a straight-A student,' a voice said from behind Alyssa, and she turned her neck to see Mrs. Phillipson exit from a home office and cross over to the brown leather sofa, stopping to stare at the wall where yet another photograph of their daughter hung. Then, as if her legs could no longer support her weight, she sank into the sofa. 'She's not only smart, but she's kind and respectful.' She turned her teary, fear-filled eyes to Alyssa. 'Please, you have to find her.' She held out her arm, her hand gripping a stack of photographs which she offered to Alyssa.

'I promise you she didn't run away, Detectives. That's not like our Katelyn. She was so looking forward to her last summer before high school, and with only two and a half days left, she'd already made plans for most of it.'

Katelyn's mother rambled, but neither Alyssa nor Cord stopped her. Sometimes they learned more that way, things that would assist in finding their daughter.

'She's a good girl,' Mrs. Phillipson whispered. 'She was already planning on helping me out at The Rescue Center downtown where I volunteer. *That's* the kind of teenager she is, the kind who helps feed the homeless on her first day of summer break.' Her voice cracked, and Mr. Phillipson moved in closer to his wife, placing a comforting hand on her shoulder. She reached up and squeezed his fingers. 'Jason and I wanted Katelyn to realize that, while she had a good life here, there are many out there who don't. We tried to teach her that money doesn't bring a person respect. Kindness and your actions do.'

The Cambridge and Otis families could take some pointers.

Mrs. Phillipson pressed the heels of her hands into her red, swollen eyes.

Alyssa moved so she could sit across from Katelyn's parents. 'Mrs. Phillipson...'

'Please, call me Mary,' she said, looking up again, her voice thick.

Maybe it was because Katelyn Phillipson was so close in age to Isaac, or perhaps because her own experience so closely mirrored Mary's, but Alyssa found it increasingly difficult not to reach over and clasp the woman's hands between her own and promise her everything would be okay.

Cord took a place beside Alyssa and leaned forward, his elbows on his knees. 'Mary, Jason, we know this isn't easy, but why don't you start from the beginning? We need to try to retrace your daughter's steps so we can find her and bring her back home to you.'

Mr. Phillipson dropped his head forward in wordless assent and settled himself next to his wife, pulling her in so she was nestled next to his side, offering what little comfort and security he could.

Alyssa's eyes strayed to an ornate grandfather clock nestled into the corner of the room. Seven-fifteen. Four hours had passed since school let out. 'Let's start with what Katelyn was wearing today. Do either of you remember?'

Mary nodded. 'Kate was wearing a pair of faded denim jeans, salmon-colored flats, and an Imagine Dragons t-shirt her best friend gave her as an early birthday gift. Her birthday's in just a few weeks,' she choked out. 'We knew she was going to Stephanie's house right after school let out, but she was supposed to be home by four-fifteen because she was going to help me bake cupcakes for my book club meeting tomorrow evening.'

Alyssa interrupted. 'Stephanie is the friend you mentioned?'

'Yes. Those two practically became best friends in utero. When Katelyn still wasn't home by four-thirty – she's never once been late without letting one of us know – and she didn't answer her phone, I called Steph. She said Kate left her house at quarter to four. I wanted to call the police straight away, but Jason told me not to overreact.'

At this, Mr. Phillipson dropped his arm from around his wife's shoulder and hung his head, his body shaking with silent sobs.

Mrs. Phillipson reached over and gripped his hand tightly in her own, tugging until he brought his gaze back up to hers. 'I'm not blaming you. You shouldn't be blaming yourself, either.' She turned back to Alyssa and Cord. 'A few weeks ago, Katelyn and I had a bit of an argument when I refused to allow her to attend a friend's party – this friend's parents are notorious for ignoring the goings-on of the kids. She accused me of overreacting and said that I should trust her to do the right thing.

'So, when I wanted to call the police, Jason told me I should first ask Steph to help me contact the rest of Katelyn's friends while he drove around and checked the parks and neighbor-hoods. Just in case. After all, even though she's never done anything like this before, she is still a teenager who will be going into high school, and boundaries are bound to be pushed... Jason was right. I didn't want to overreact and set the tone for the future. Especially after our little spat. We've always assured Katelyn that no matter what she's done, she should always know she can come to us. Anyway, that's why we waited two hours after she was supposed to be home before contacting the police.' The pooling moisture in her eyes spilled over, streaking the blush on her cheeks.

More than anything, Alyssa wanted to believe that Katelyn Phillipson was doing nothing more than pushing teenage boundaries. 'How long did Katelyn stay mad about the party?'

'My goodness, not long at all. She was over it before the night was out. Katelyn's not very good at hiding her true feelings, so if she'd still been angry, I'm sure we would've known.'

'Mr. and Mrs. Phillipson, we'd like to speak to Stephanie. Can you get us her phone number and address? In fact, if you could jot down the contact information for any of her friends whose home you think she might've gone to if she needed to, that would be helpful.'

'Yes, yes, of course,' Mary said.

Mr. Phillipson pushed to his feet and paced the length of the room, waving his hands in the air as he did. 'But we told you, we've *already* checked with all her friends. No one's seen her. Retracing our steps is only wasting time better spent on finding my daughter!'

Mary pressed one palm to her stomach. 'Jason, please...'

Mr. Phillipson whirled around, his face turning red as tears slipped down his cheeks. 'No, Mary.' He pointed to Alyssa and Cord. 'They're supposed to *find* her, not just do the same things we already did.' He choked on the final words, collapsing into his wife as she stood and cupped her husband's face in her palms.

'I know. But we have to allow them to do their job the best way they know how.'

Jason's eyes bored into Cord's first, then Alyssa's. 'Please, you have to find her.'

'That's exactly what we'd like to do, so the sooner you get us those contacts, the sooner we can get started on that.' Alyssa's tone was gentle but firm.

Ten minutes later, list in hand, Mary walked them to the door but stopped Alyssa with a surprisingly strong grip on her forearm. 'Detective, I know it's human nature for parents to believe their children are innocent of getting themselves into trouble. But—' Her words fell out in a strangled sob, and she struggled to get the rest out. 'Please, just bring us back our little girl.'

'I promise we'll do all we can to bring your Katelyn home.'

Back in the car, Alyssa called the captain to request an Amber Alert be issued while Cord plugged Stephanie's address into the navigation system. She didn't wait to finish her call with Hammond before heading over to speak to Katelyn's friend, Stephanie. As she drove, something niggled at the back of her mind, and she shifted her eyes left and right trying to figure out what it was about the area that was bothering her.

Chapter Nineteen

Stephanie's house, a short five-minute drive away, while still beautiful, came nowhere close to matching the grandeur of Katelyn's home. Alyssa's gaze swept up and down the street, turning only when the door behind her opened. A young girl with rainbow-colored hair and wearing a summer dress and flip-flops stood in the doorway, eyes wide and tear-filled. Her hands shook, as did her voice. 'Are you the detectives looking for Kate? I'm Stephanie. Kate's my best friend. Mary called to say you were on your way.'

'Hi, Stephanie. I'm Detective Wyatt, and this is Detective Roberts. Can we speak to you for a few minutes?'

Movements jerky, the young girl stepped back as she waved Alyssa and Cord inside.

'Are your parents home?'

'No, ma'am. They were having dinner with friends in Santa Fe. But I just called my mom a few minutes ago to tell her what was going on, and she said they would leave right away. Do they have to be here before you can talk to me? Because I can call my mom back again, and she'll tell you it's okay. She'd want me to do what I can to help.'

Alyssa smiled softly. 'If it would make you feel better to have your mom on speaker while we ask you a few questions, that's fine, but we just want to try to get an idea of what happened between the time Katelyn left your house to us getting the call that she hadn't returned home.'

Stephanie's index finger, already red and bleeding, went to her mouth. Moisture spilled from the young girl's eyes, and her shoulders shook as she began gasping for air. 'I don't know what hap… happened to her. She left here at… at three forty-five, and then her mom called at four-thirty saying she hadn't come home yet and that she wasn't answering her phone, and then I tried to call her, but she didn't answer my call either, and so I sent her a text, but she didn't respond to that, and so I tried…'

Seconds before the young girl crashed to the floor, Alyssa caught her, easing her over to the stairs right behind her. She threw a glance behind her to Cord. 'Water.'

He nodded and disappeared around the corner where she heard cabinets opening and closing, and then a minute later, he returned. She took the plastic cup from him and held it up to Stephanie's lips.

'Here. I want you to take a drink, okay?'

Even when the young girl's hands reached out to take the cup, Alyssa kept hold of it, not trusting that it wouldn't fall from her grasp. After three small sips, Stephanie twisted her head away and wiped at her eyes. 'I'm sorry. I'm just scared.'

'That's okay, it's understandable. Do you think you can answer a few questions now?'

Stephanie nodded. 'Yes, ma'am. I can try.'

'Are you okay sitting here on the stairs, or would you feel more comfortable in the living room?'

'I'm okay.'

'All right, Stephanie. Mrs. Phillipson said Katelyn walked home with you after school today. Did you come straight here, or did you stop somewhere along the way?'

'Straight here because Kate didn't have long before she needed to be home to help her mom, and she was excited to see the dress I got for our eighth-grade promotion.' Her voice choked. 'It's Thursday. We're supposed to go together.'

'Okay, so you got home and showed her the dress. What else did you do?'

Cord produced a tissue from a packet he kept in his pocket and handed it to Stephanie when her nose began to drip. She thanked him and wiped her nose before answering. 'We talked about how we'd wear our hair and then watched a couple YouTube videos to get some ideas.' One shoulder lifted in a shrug as she whispered. 'That's all. She told me she'd text me tonight after she was finished helping her mom bake, and that was the last...' Her words trailed off as another bout of frightened tears fell.

Alyssa gave her a minute before proceeding. 'Stephanie, can you tell us the route Kate would normally take to get home?'

'She usually cuts across the street to the park. Most of the time she takes the bike path, but if there're too many people, she'll walk down the arroyo, head up Eagle Rock to Ventura to Glendale.'

'Does she ever go another way that you know of?'

'Not when she's just going home, which she was.'

'Would she tell you if she was going to stop somewhere else?'

Stephanie's head snapped back like she thought the question was absurd. 'Of course.'

They asked a few more questions, verified what Katelyn had been wearing and that she had a pink bag with black polka dots, and then waited while Stephanie answered her mom's call before leaving to retrace Katelyn's steps. At the park, Alyssa parked next to the curb.

'I'm going to update Hammond. Why don't you get ahold of Tony and Joe, have them meet us here? They can start knocking on doors in the area while we search the park. It would be nice if the city could get closed-circuit cameras everywhere, but until then, maybe someone's Ring doorbell or security camera captured something that'll help.'

Calls made, Alyssa automatically checked the time. Eight-fifteen. The sun had set only moments ago, taking the last remnants of light and replacing it with deepening shadows. She reached over, unlocked her glove box, and retrieved two flashlights, handing one to Cord before closing it again.

The park was a narrow one with only a couple of trees, one picnic table, and a bike or walking path on one side. An arroyo snaked down the middle, and that's where Alyssa headed first while Cord took the bike path. As she passed under one of the only trees, a reflection coming from above made her glance up, searching for whatever object had caught her attention. And when she saw it, the last hope she'd had that Katelyn had simply wandered off to another friend's house vanished. Caught in the branches of the tree rested the pink and black polka-dotted bag Stephanie described, a mirror dangling from the zipper catching the moon's reflection, which is what made Alyssa look up. A few feet away, near the stucco wall separating the park from the neighborhood, lay an abandoned phone, face up, a faint, flashing blue light beckoning her.

'Cord,' she yelled. 'I've got something.'

Chapter Twenty

Wednesday, May 22

Jersey lay in a crumpled heap in the center of the bed that was shoved up against one wall of the room called The Toybox. It hadn't taken long at all to break her down. To muffle the sobs that shook her body, she burrowed her head into the pillow, doing her best to ignore the pain from the bruise she felt blooming on her thigh.

An image of Beau flashed through her mind, the argument they'd been having just before she and her friends had gone to dinner. Given what had been happening to her the past few days, it was ironic really that she'd been so angry and devastated at the suggestion that she play out his twisted sexual fantasies, ones in which he wasn't even a participant but an observer. Her fingers curled into her palms, the jagged edges of what was left of her fingernails driving deep. Every bit of the pain and degradation, every endless second of it that she'd endured since she'd been dragged here was because of him.

At the sound of a key turning in the lock, Jersey's muscles tensed as her teeth bit into her lower lip hard enough to draw blood. When the door opened revealing the already all-too-familiar face, her tremors morphed into full body shakes, a scream clawing at her throat as it begged to be released.

His eyes steady and cold, the man quietly closed the door, locking it behind him gently as if what they were going to do was nothing more than an intimate interlude that he didn't want to have interrupted. Only when he slid open the wardrobe closet simply labeled '*The Toolbox*' did his eyes stray from Jersey to the items organized neatly on hooks before bouncing back to her as if weighing which would be the most painful, the most degrading. His choice finally made, he set the item off to the side and slowly removed his clothes, folding each item carefully before placing it on a chair perched in a corner. As he did, he watched her watch him, ignoring both her whimpers as well as the tears that leaked from the corners of her eyes, further soaking the pillow beneath her head.

Then, fully nude, fully aroused, eyes gleaming with pure evil, he approached the bed, his right hand gripping the wardrobe item. And though she knew it was a useless effort, Jersey forced her arms and legs to move, to scramble as far away as possible. If there'd been a window, she would've found a way to jump through it, even if it meant leaping to her death.

She made it less than a foot before the snapping sound whistled through the air a split second before the burning sting of leather struck her soft flesh, and this time she did nothing to hold back the agonized howl, allowing it to grow louder as the man roughly grabbed her already bruised body and flipped her onto her back, a sickening grin covering his face.

Jersey squeezed her eyes closed against the nightmare that wouldn't end and did something she hadn't done since she was nine years old. She prayed. Prayed for death to come this instant and carry her far, far away. Even hell had to be better than this.

And then she found herself praying for something else, something more.

Revenge.

Chapter Twenty-One

Shortly after five-thirty the next morning, a mere five hours after getting home, Alyssa walked back into the precinct, sleep-deprived and weary, yet full of adrenaline and drive to find Rachel, Jersey, and now Katelyn. The disappearances were connected; they had to be. And she was determined to hunt down that connection. Her gut told her if she found that link, it would also lead to Jane Doe's killer.

She set her stuff down and booted up the computer before grabbing a stack of multi-colored sticky notes, a black marker, and a plastic cup of pushpins. She was standing by the enlarged map of Albuquerque when the conference room door banged open against the wall, the scent of coffee filling the room. She spared a quick glance over her shoulder. Cord juggled a four-pack container of take-out coffee with a fifth cup perched precariously in the crook of his elbow.

'Thought you might need this this morning. Black and strong, just the way you like it. Where is everyone else?' He carefully set everything down before handing her one of the cups and then heading over to the white board writing: *Rachel Otis, Jersey Andrews, Katelyn Phillipson*. Beside each name he wrote the date each had disappeared. Then he wrote *Jane Doe* and listed the date her body had been discovered in the abandoned restaurant.

Leaving him to do what he was doing, Alyssa returned to her own task, but before she could get started, Hal rolled in, speaking over the squeak of his wheelchair. 'Tony sent a text to say he's five minutes out. Construction slowed him down. Joe is parking his car.'

'Nope, Joe has finished parking his car and is present and accounted for.' With his foot, Joe pulled out the chair closest to him and dropped into it, pointing to the coffee. 'One of those for me?' He didn't wait for an answer before grabbing one of the take-out cups and taking a careful sip. 'You know, it's a sad thing when the workings of a police station are far less grating than the nonstop cries of an infant who can't be soothed.' He leaned his head back and closed his eyes for a second. 'Okay, have I missed anything yet?'

'Nope. We're still waiting for Tony,' Hal answered.

'Wait's over.' Tony walked through the door, a sub sandwich and a bag of salt and vinegar chips in hand. 'What? I didn't get a chance to eat it last night, so I brought it for breakfast this morning,' he said when Hal's eyebrows shot up to his hairline. He tore open the bag of chips and dumped them onto a napkin, offering them to the rest of the team.

No thanks echoed around the room before Alyssa moved everyone back to the missing girls.

'Now that we're all here, let's get started. Someone out there has to *know* something; *someone* had to have seen something. The idea that these girls simply went *poof* into thin air – one minute there, gone the next – is absurd.' She took a step back, forehead furrowed in concentration. She tapped Rachel's name. 'Rachel Otis attended a frat party with a friend who we only know as "Anna." No one seems to know who she is, and so we can't locate her. What happened to this girl? Are she and Rachel together somewhere? Has anyone reported a missing girl of eighteen or nineteen that fits her general description?' Despite already knowing the answer, her gaze swept around the room, waiting for everyone to shake their heads in the negative. If any of them had heard of a report, she would've been the next to know.

'Both Rachel Otis and Jersey Andrews disappeared in the UNM area' – she tapped the map – 'here and here. Katelyn Phillipson's items were located in Noreste Park here.' She angled her body away from the map so everyone could see. Then, using a different color sticky note for each girl, she tacked the names onto the spot where each girl lived, including Rachel's dorm as well as her home on Rio Grande. As she pushed Jersey's name into place, she swore. 'Damn it!' This was the something that had been bothering her last night as she drove from Katelyn's home to Stephanie's.

She grabbed a highlighter and drew four circles, connecting them with lines. 'This is the Phillipson home, Katelyn's best friend's home, the place Katelyn's belongings were discovered, and this is where Jersey Andrews lives, half a mile away.' A sinking feeling in the pit of her stomach made her lightheaded, but she pushed it aside. Keeping her voice steady, she turned to Hal. 'Let's check the registered sex offenders in the area, see if any of them have a residence nearby.'

'I'll check into that as soon as we finish up in here. And before I forget, Channel 13 is running the sketch of our Jane Doe like we discussed last night. She may or may not be related to these other disappearances, but with a little luck, someone will recognize her and give us a call.'

Cord jumped in. 'Either way, we need to find out who she is and what happened to her. Someone out there has to be missing her, and they're going to need closure of some kind, even if it's knowing they no longer have to search for her.' There was an unnatural gravelly tone to his voice, and Hal, Tony, and Joe darted curious looks his way.

'Along those same lines...' Alyssa exchanged her yellow highlighter for a neon pink one. 'Like Hal said, we don't know if our Jane Doe case is related, but here's the frat house where Rachel was last seen; within a quarter mile is the duck pond.' As she spoke, she circled the locations. 'And here,' she added another circle, 'less than a mile and a half away is where our

Jane Doe was discovered.' She caught the eyes of everyone in the room. 'That's a little too close for me to take as coincidental. Add in the proximity of two of the girls… I don't like what my instincts are screaming at me.' She forced herself to say the rest. 'Especially in light of the fact that just last month, we were on the hunt for a serial killer who targeted young women.'

'Okay, I get what you're saying, but as big as Albuquerque is, it's not *that* big, and Katelyn Phillipson's things were discovered nine miles away in the Northeast Heights,' Joe interjected.

Alyssa sighed. 'True. Yet, there *is* still a connection. Rachel Otis, Jersey Andrews, and Katelyn Phillipson all hail from wealthy, financially stable backgrounds. As tenuous a link as it may be, it's still a link. It could mean nothing, or it could be the one thing that opens this case up.' She concentrated her focus on Hal. 'You're the best at digging up dirt, so I need you to check into financials for all these families. While you're at it, let's see if any of them have any common interests, maybe belong to the same church, gym, whatever, anything that might tie them together somehow.'

At the mention of the gym, a thunderous expression flashed across Cord's face, there and gone in an instant, and she knew Beau Cambridge was the reason why. He was still high on her list of persons of interest but being an asshole didn't automatically make him guilty. Still, it sure as hell made his actions suspicious. So far, they'd been unable to verify his alibi, and knowing he'd been at Jersey's house the day she'd disappeared placed him in the same area as Katelyn Phillipson's house. Maybe he'd seen her out walking with Stephanie, maybe…

'Cell phone records. Joe, why don't you check on those? See who each person last called or texted, see if we can ping that location. Of course, with Katelyn Phillipson, we already have this information since we have her phone. The last text she sent was to her friend Stephanie, telling her to meet her in the atrium after school. At three-fifty an incomplete and unsent text to her mother simply read "On my," so assuming she was letting Mrs.

Phillipson know she was on her way home. Every incoming call and text after that is from Stephanie or her parents.' Alyssa glanced at Cord before once more addressing Joe. 'Check Beau Cambridge's records, too. If we have to subpoena them, we will, but let's see what we can find out first.'

Tony opened his mouth to speak, but Alyssa's ringing phone cut him off. She pulled her phone out of her pocket and glanced down. 'It's Lynn. I'm going to take this.'

'Dr. Sharp, you're up early. What've you got?'

'Couldn't sleep this morning,' the medical examiner said around a yawn. 'So, I came in to work on our Jane Doe. And before you ask, no, I don't have an identification on her. But I wanted to fill you in on a few things in case they can help with what you've already got.'

'Yeah, well, that's not much, so I'm ready for anything I can get. I'm going to put you on speaker so everyone can hear you.' She tapped the screen and leaned the phone against the whiteboard. 'Okay, go ahead.'

'First off, based on several factors, I'm placing Jane Doe anywhere from fourteen to eighteen years of age. Second, the ligature marks around her wrists and ankles are consistent with both manacles and some type of rope. Based on the markings and scarring, my professional opinion is that those were inflicted during separate incidents.'

'What about the girl's fingers?'

'Are you referring to the fingernail avulsion?'

'Fingernail what?'

'Fingernail avulsion… complete removal of the finger or toenail… I've never experienced it, but as a form of torture, this could be quite effective, which is why it's used, I imagine. Which, I suppose, is my answer to your question. Anyway, back to the ligature marks, I was able to pull a small bit of fiber from a couple of the wounds, and I'll get those sent off to the lab asap. Later today, I'll be running a toxicology report, and I'll get back with you as soon as the results are in. I was also able to retrieve several hair follicles in the folds of Jane Doe's neck. I hate to use this phrase, but we're in luck because it appears the root is attached, which of course means we have a much higher likelihood of retrieving DNA.'

'Thanks for this, Lynn. I appreciate it.'

'There's more. Alyssa,' Lynn's lips vibrated noisily as she exhaled through her mouth, 'I discovered probably ten bite marks, and I don't mean gentle love nips, either. I'm talking chomping down, breaking through skin and tissue bites. In addition, there are a number of small puncture wounds consistent with an ice pick or something of a similar nature on Jane Doe's backside, around her buttocks, thighs, and lower back.'

All color slipped from Cord's face, and his head snapped back as if he'd been slapped. Shoving back from the table, he paced back and forth between the door and the table. By the third trip, the veins in his temple bulged, and a dangerous shade of red had returned to his face.

Anger turned Alyssa's vision into a blurry haze. 'Christ.' She'd once read a forensic study about how some killers subdued their victims by utilizing ice picks to control them. The wounds would be extremely painful, but not necessarily deadly, though of course, they could be. Her gaze followed her team's reaction to this news. Hal sagged deeper into his chair, and Joe ran fingers through his hair, shaking his head, doing his best, she imagined, to rid himself of the image placed there by Lynn Sharp's description. Tony wiped both hands down the front of his face, muttering the same thing Alyssa had.

'I'm fairly certain Christ had nothing to do with this,' Lynn remarked, reminding Alyssa the woman was a devout agnostic.

'Thank you, Lynn,' she said. 'I appreciate you taking the time to call us with this.'

'Good luck, Detective.'

The room was unnaturally quiet, save for the deeply controlled breaths of everyone present as they each processed the news in their own heads. A few seconds after the call ended, a light tap at the door preceded Ruby poking her head in, her eyes sweeping across the room until she spotted Alyssa.

'There's a Sergeant Boudreaux from Santa Fe on line two. He says he thinks he recognizes your Jane Doe.'

Alyssa thanked Ruby as she rushed over to the blinking light and pressed the button, once again placing the person on the other end on speaker as the entire team moved in closer to the phone. 'This is Detective Wyatt.'

'Detective, this is Sergeant Boudreaux from the SFPD. I saw the composite sketch of your Jane Doe on the news this morning. I think she could be fourteen-year-old Meghan Jessup who went missing up here in late April. Her family thought she'd run away after a row when they put their foot down about her dating some senior. According to her dad, she got pretty upset, and the next day, she never came home from school.'

'Has her family seen the news?'

'When I spoke to them, they hadn't, and as they're headed straight here, I doubt they will. When they arrive, I'll drive them to Albuquerque to see about making a positive ID. We should be there in less than two hours. I'll let you know when we hit the city limits, so you can meet us at the coroner's office.'

'I appreciate it, Sergeant.'

Hal caught Alyssa's eyes. 'Sergeant Boudreaux, this is Hal Callum. Out of curiosity, where do the Jessups live?'

'Off the top of my head, I don't have their address, but I can get it if you need it.'

'Just the general area for now, if you don't mind.'

'Well, I can tell you the Jessup residence is in one of the pricier communities up here. Do you mind if I ask why?'

The team exchanged glances, and Hal lifted one brow in question, deferring to Alyssa, but she nodded, encouraging him to continue. 'We have a bit of something going on down here. Three girls aged thirteen to nineteen have up and disappeared in the last few days. And while it may be nothing, especially in connection with your case, we've noticed an unusual financial

135

link threaded through these cases. It may be in no way related, but then again, I don't want to discount anything at this point.'

'I understand. Detective Wyatt, can I get your digits so I can contact you directly when we arrive?'

'Absolutely.' They exchanged numbers, Alyssa thanked him again, and then she ended the call, unsure whether her nerves wanted her to move about or simply fall back into the chair as the fear of another serial killer out there gripped her. How would Holly deal with that? How would *she*?

Alyssa shook the thought off. She couldn't think that way. They had to focus on what they knew, not what they feared. She pushed herself to her feet and headed for the door. 'I'm going to give Hammond an update.' She motioned for Cord to follow. 'You coming?'

Before she'd even finished her sentence, Cord was by her side. 'Let's do it.'

Chapter Twenty-Two

Wednesday, May 22

Police are asking residents and businesses in the area to check their security systems and to contact authorities if there is anything that could assist them in safely locating these missing girls. Details are listed on your screen beneath the girls' images. Again, please...

Holly hit the button on the remote, freezing the pictures of Rachel Otis, Jersey, and Katelyn Phillipson on the television. Beside her, Sophie rested her hands on her knees and leaned forward as if by getting closer to the screen, she'd somehow be closer to her cousin.

'You know what's really sad? That complete strangers are more concerned than her own father that something may have happened to her.'

Holly didn't know what to say because her best friend was right. Just last night, Sophie and her mom had been with her Aunt Natalia when she'd called Jersey's dad to give him an update, and all he'd had to say was, 'Listen, I'm sure she's fine. She's probably just doing what I'm doing, dropping off the grid and kicking back with some friends. If she's not back by the time I return in a couple of weeks...'

Jersey's mom had cut him off. 'I highly doubt your daughter has flown the coop with her half-her-age girlfriend. You disgust me. This is a new low, even for you. You'd rather get laid in some exotic location than come home and help search for your missing daughter. But that's fine. At least we know now to stop wasting our energy on keeping you in the loop.'

Enraged, Sophie had climbed into her car and driven straight to Holly's where she'd ended up sleeping over since her mother had been staying with Aunt Natalia since Monday night. According to Sophie, Natalia was too afraid to leave the house in case Jersey came home or the police came calling. Sophie had planned on staying with her as well but hadn't been able to deal with Aunt Natalia's constant pacing up and down the halls or opening and closing Jersey's door every fifteen minutes as if she expected her daughter had somehow slipped in without her noticing.

This morning, Holly and Sophie sent a text to Leigh Ann asking if she wanted to come over and help them put up more flyers around town. The three of them had already posted them all around the university, including the student union building and all the restaurants and businesses in the area. They'd been discussing where they wanted to focus next when the news had captured their attention.

Just as Holly finished dividing the colorful flyers into stacks of three, the doorbell rang, and all three girls jerked their heads in the direction of the front door. Holly threw a puzzled look at her friends before moving to peer through the peephole in the door. Beau Cambridge, the last person she would've expected to be standing on her front porch, twisted the enormous class ring on his finger, his head turned to one side, staring at something only he could see as he waited for someone to answer the door.

'What the hell is he doing here?'

'Who is it?' Sophie asked even as she peeked through the window to find out for herself. 'What the hell!' She released the wooden blinds so quickly, they slapped against the window hard, the blast of sound like a small explosion in the room.

Face flushed, Holly disengaged the locks and threw open the door, startling Beau. He swung around, eyes widening the second he spotted Sophie and Leigh Ann behind her. He angled his body away from them and back towards his Jeep, glancing at it before turning back to Holly. 'Um, this was a bad idea. I probably shouldn't have come.'

'No, you *definitely* shouldn't have,' Sophie bit out, shoving her way in front of Holly. 'So, why did you? Not getting enough sympathy posts from your adoring fan club on Instagram?'

A curtain closed over his expression, but he was saved from answering when Leigh Ann maneuvered in front of both Sophie and Holly, latching onto Beau's arm so she could tug him inside. 'If you're worried about Jersey, then this is where you belong, with her friends.' She turned her gaze on them, silently begging them to be understanding. 'Right?'

A fine red haze passed over Holly's eyes at Leigh Ann's gall. She didn't even know how to respond, and then Beau spoke, and the red haze turned into a dark storm.

Standing in the foyer, one hand cupping the back of his neck, he smiled down at Leigh Ann. 'Thanks. I didn't know where else to go. A couple of detectives came by the other day, busting my balls, accusing me of knowing where Jersey was, implying I'd done something to her even. Dude, that lady detective needed to get laid; she was a flat-out bitch. And I thought the man was going to punch me when I told them I didn't know where Jersey was.'

'Oh, you mean Holly's mom? That bitch detective? Short, auburn hair, tough as nails attitude – or apparently what you would call "bitchy"? Partner is a tall, good-looking guy? *That's* who needs to get laid?' Sophie jabbed her pointer finger toward a family picture on the opposite wall.

Beau followed her finger, his jaw falling open as if someone had dropped a heavy weight inside it. A vein near his temple pulsed in rhythm with his breathing, and for the first time Holly could remember, Jersey's jerk of a boyfriend was rendered speechless, if only temporarily.

When he swung back in her direction, she crossed her arms, her own expression chiseled from stone in a quiet challenge to say something else about her mom. '*Wyatt*. I didn't make the conn…' Whether out of self-preservation or because he actually did have a few intelligent brain cells, he snapped his mouth shut with an audible clack.

'Speaking of getting laid, maybe if *you* hadn't gotten so angry when Jersey declined your *suggestion*, if you'd respected *her* wishes, then none of us would even be standing here right now because Jersey wouldn't have gone off on her own. You ever stop to think this is your fault to begin with?' Twin red spots bloomed, staining Sophie's cheeks as she shouted at Beau, standing nearly toe to toe with him.

Rage flushed Beau's face, and he spoke through gritted teeth as if he'd already forgotten he was playing Charades: Concerned Boyfriend Edition. 'I wasn't going to force her to do something she didn't want to do. Sometimes girls just need to be convinced of what they want.'

Leigh Ann waved her hand between all of them, trying to stop the speeding train wreck in front of her. Neither Holly nor Sophie paid the least bit attention.

'Yeah, and sometimes girls just mean no when they say no. Ever consider that?' Holly shoved her clenched fists into the pocket of her jumper, slightly afraid she might actually punch Beau. Would her mom be able to get the charges dropped if she did?

Just as quickly as his temper had blown up, his shoulders sagged, and Beau, looking to Leigh Ann for support, which she gave by stepping in closer to him, lowered his voice to a whisper. 'Look, I know none of you like me, but Jersey was – *is* – my girlfriend, and I'm worried about her, too. I guess I thought you, of all people, would get that.' He turned to leave, but Leigh Ann stopped him by gripping his hand and closing the door behind him, her eyes pleading once more for Holly and Sophie to understand.

'We're all worried about her, and we do understand. We're all scared, so our tempers are a little close to the surface. We know that just because you and Jersey were fighting doesn't mean you two didn't love each other.'

Holly's mouth dropped open in stunned disbelief while Sophie exploded, planting herself in front of Leigh Ann this time. 'Are you out of your freaking mind? You can speak for yourself, but I, for one, and I know, Holly, for two, don't want this snake here. Furthermore, I don't believe for one second he's sorry about a damn thing.' She jabbed a finger into Beau's chest. 'I don't know what game you're playing, and despite what our *friend* here says – You. Are. Not. Welcome. So, get out.' And then she shoved herself between Leigh Ann and Beau and pushed open the screen door, her body vibrating in tightly controlled fury.

Holly half expected him to refuse to leave – and half expected Leigh Ann to leave with him so she could console his poor battered ego. So, she was mildly surprised to see him step back outside only to stop and turn around, his eyes searching the ground. When he spoke, he mumbled, and she barely caught his words.

'I don't know where she is. She's never been gone this long. She probably doesn't even care how much I'm worried about her.' He wiped a finger beneath his eye as if removing evidence of tears, then walked to the street where he'd parked his four-wheel drive.

'If only he hadn't just made Jersey's disappearance about him, he might've had a bright future in an acting career,' Holly bit out.

The second his Jeep was out of sight, Sophie turned her wrath on Leigh Ann. 'What in God's name are you thinking? This isn't *your* house, so you had no right to invite him in!' Without waiting for a response, she whirled away and stormed into the kitchen where she jerked open a cupboard, yanked a cup out, filled it with water, and gulped it down without taking a breath. When the cup was drained, she slammed it down on the counter and rested her head in her hands.

Leigh Ann stood in the middle of the kitchen, head swinging back and forth between her friends. 'Listen, I'm sorry, okay. I just think it's better if we...'

Whatever she said after that was drowned out by Sophie wrenching open the dishwasher and slamming anything plastic down as hard as she could.

The corners of Leigh Ann's mouth turned down. 'I guess that's my cue to leave.'

'What's Sophie doing? And who's the beefsteak dude that just squealed away from the house?' Isaac's voice startled Holly, and she shrieked, her hand raised to her heart as she tried to calm the galloping muscle.

'I didn't hear you come in.' Holly watched Isaac's gaze switch from Leigh Ann to Sophie who'd swung around, a spatula raised in the air like a weapon she was about to wield.

Leigh Ann forced a smile to her face. 'Hey, Isaac. Are you excited for your eighth-grade promotion tomorrow?'

He shrugged. 'Not going. It would've been stupid and boring anyway.'

Holly was taken aback not so much by his words but by the heat in them when he addressed Leigh Ann. But if her friend noticed, she didn't let on.

Leigh Ann turned towards Sophie and gave her a half-smile. 'I'll talk to you later, okay. And I'm sorry. Again.' Then she turned to Isaac. 'It's nice to see you. You're looking good.'

'Yeah, thanks.' Isaac's response was lukewarm, at best.

As soon as the front door clicked, Holly tilted her head to the side. 'Why the attitude toward Leigh Ann?'

For a minute, Isaac didn't answer. Instead he grabbed an apple out of the bowl, chomped into it, and around a mouthful of food, mumbled, 'I don't know. I've just never liked her. Why are you acting surprised? It's not like you didn't already know that.'

'Yeah, but you've never been quite so rude before, either.'

Isaac shrugged. 'I don't know. She just bugs.'

At this, Sophie joined the conversation. 'You're not wrong, bro. I'm right there with you, Zic.' She used the nickname she'd given him ages ago, mostly to annoy him, but over the years, it had kind of stuck.

'You guys need help putting up flyers today?'

With her foot, Sophie closed the dishwasher, and then moved over to Isaac, draping an arm around his shoulder. 'We would, but um, quick question, why are you home at noon, huh?'

Holly hadn't even thought of that, and she watched her brother's face pinken as he turned to her. 'Don't tell Mom or Dad, okay? Our teachers told us they're not even taking attendance, so if we're not there, no one will know. All we're doing is watching lame movies, helping them clean their rooms, or returning textbooks to the library. I thought my time was better spent helping you guys.'

'You didn't even know we were here,' Holly countered.

'Please, sis.'

She relented because he was right; the last few days of school were nothing more than teachers babysitting bored teenagers. Plus, now that Leigh Ann had abandoned ship, she and Sophie really could use the help. 'Go grab the flyers; they're on the coffee table. But just so you know, if you get busted, I'm not lying for you.'

'The only way I'll get busted is if you cop out and snitch.'

A few minutes later, the three of them were out the door, a plan in place.

Chapter Twenty-Three

It was almost noon when Sergeant Boudreaux finally called.

'Detective Wyatt speaking.'

'Detective, this is Sergeant Boudreaux. We, or rather Mr. and Mrs. Jessup, ran into a problem when a city worker parked his construction truck in front of their drive, blocking them in. It took us longer than it should've to track the guy down after he left with a co-worker for another site. Claims he couldn't tell it was a private road; thought it was an old trail no one used anymore. I was heading to pick them up myself when the city got ahold of him to move it. Anyway, we're in Albuquerque now. We'll be at the morgue in about fifteen minutes. Still care to meet us there?'

'Absolutely. I'll see you in a few minutes.'

Twelve minutes later, she pulled into the parking lot of the County Morgue, having phoned ahead to alert Lynn Sharp that the possible family of their Jane Doe had arrived. She waited in her car until she saw an SUV emblazoned with Santa Fe PD on the side before she climbed out.

Sergeant Boudreaux unfolded his long form from the driver's seat and opened the back door. Mrs. Jessup stepped out of the vehicle, leaning against it as she waited for her husband to come around. Her hair was unkempt, as if she'd been running her fingers through it, and her face was pale. Mr. Jessup was slightly taller than his wife, and his eyes bounced continuously from Sergeant Boudreaux's SUV to the front doors of the morgue.

Even from across the parking lot, Alyssa could see they stood on wobbly legs.

'Sergeant Boudreaux?' Alyssa asked as she approached.

The Santa Fe officer extended his hand. 'Detective Wyatt? Thanks for meeting us here. This is Mr. and Mrs. Jessup.'

'Hello. I'm sorry we have to meet like this. Tell me when you're ready, and we'll head inside.'

Mr. and Mrs. Jessup glanced at each other before turning back to her. In a strangled voice, Mr. Jessup answered for both of them. 'Is anyone ever ready for something like this?'

'No, I suppose not.' Alyssa inhaled deeply and then led the way inside.

Lynn Sharp greeted them in the entrance, leading them into her office before taking them to see Jane Doe's body.

'Sergeant Boudreaux, Mr. and Mrs. Jessup, thank you for coming. Before I take you back, I want to prepare you, even if it turns out not to be your daughter.' Her words were solemn and full of compassion, and Alyssa saw how much it pained the woman to do this part of her job.

As Lynn continued to explain what they should expect, Alyssa tempered her impatience for answers by perusing the office and the numerous degrees and accolades framed on the walls. They were impressive. Finally, Lynn rose and escorted the four of them down a series of hallways before stopping at a set of double doors. 'Please wait here. I'll come get you in a minute.'

They watched through the window as Lynn rolled Jane Doe out on a cart into the middle of a gray, sterile, depressing room, and then, as promised, she invited them inside. 'Take your time, and tell me when you're ready,' she said softly, speaking to the parents.

Mr. and Mrs. Jessup stepped closer to the table on the opposite side to Lynn, while Sergeant Boudreaux and Alyssa positioned themselves near the head and foot of the medical slab, respectively. Mr. Jessup tightened his hold around his wife's shoulder, and then gave a curt nod. 'We're ready,' he whispered, his words coming out as a croak.

Alyssa found herself holding her breath and watching their expressions as Lynn gently pulled down the sheet covering Jane Doe's face, careful to keep the rest of her body hidden in an effort to shield the Jessups as much as possible from having to see the extent to which their daughter – if that's who she turned out to be – had been abused.

A wail escaped Mrs. Jessup as her knees gave way, and she collapsed toward the floor, held from crashing all the way down by Mr. Jessup's grip and the fast reaction of Sergeant Boudreaux who'd jumped over to assist as soon as he'd seen the tormented expression on her face.

'Oh God, Oh God, Oh God, Nooooo… Meghan, please God, No, don't let it be. Noooo.' Her moans echoed throughout the room, bouncing off the walls and shooting like arrows straight into Alyssa's heart. She fought the temptation to close her eyes and ears against the anguish permeating every inch of this suddenly very tiny space.

Lynn gently pulled the sheet back over Meghan Jessup's face, and as Mrs. Jessup sobbed into her husband's chest, clutching at his arms as if he were the only lifeline holding her to shore, she stepped to the side of the room, where she would be as unobtrusive as possible. And only when the hysterical sobs subsided into tormented, strangled cries did she offer to give them a few minutes of privacy in her office, if they needed it.

Eyes red, wet, and already swelling, Mr. Jessup peered first at Lynn, then Sergeant Boudreaux, before finally settling on Alyssa. 'Do you know—?' His words were choked off with an anguished howl, and he had to start over as his wife began to screech again with the pain erupting inside her. 'What happened to her?'

Alyssa deferred to Lynn in this case, and the medical exam-iner explained only what she knew, offering the words as plainly

146

as possible while omitting some of the more painful details because there was simply no way of softening the blow. And with every word out of Lynn's mouth, more of Mrs. Jessup's soul fell from her eyes. In that moment, all Alyssa could see was her own mother and father as they discovered that their son had been murdered. If only they'd known the truth.

After Lynn finished, she tried guiding the Jessups out, but Mrs. Jessup refused to leave her daughter's body. It took several minutes before Mr. Jessup was able to convince her to go. Alyssa's heart fractured as she watched Reed Jessup guide his wife out the door, even as her arms stretched back as if she could take her daughter with her.

After the five adults shuffled into a conference room down the hall, Alyssa knew she had to begin asking the tough questions, though it was never easy to intrude on a family's devastating loss.

'Mr. Jessup, Mrs. Jessup, I understand you and your daughter had an argument over her dating an older boy. Can you tell me about that incident?'

Instantly, Mr. Jessup's face turned into stone, and it took him several moments before he could speak. When he did, it wasn't what Alyssa expected him to say. 'This is his fault. He killed her.'

Alyssa shot a sideways look at Sergeant Boudreaux to gain his reaction, and by the way his posture stiffened, she knew it was the same as her own. 'Why do you say that?'

'Because if he hadn't been trying to convince a fourteen-year-old to have sex with him, then we never would've fought. What kind of sick eighteen-year-old kid wants to date someone four years younger than he is? A future pedophile, that's who.' Venomous anger punctuated every word.

Alyssa didn't necessarily agree that it proved the young man would turn into a sexual deviant sometime down the road, but that wasn't the most important matter at hand. 'Can you tell us this individual's name?'

Mrs. Jessup's shoulders shook as she admitted they didn't know. 'She refused to tell us his name because she was frightened we'd press charges if they ever… ever…' *Had sex.* 'I don't think he even lived in the area. We only found out about him at all because Reed and I were out enjoying Sunday brunch when we saw her with the boy. Neither of us recognized him.'

'Can you describe him for me?'

Chilly goosebumps peppered her skin at Mr. Jessup's response. 'He was quite a bit taller than I am. Big guy, about six-two, six-three, muscular, linebacker build. Short brown hair. I don't mind saying he looked like a real ass.'

Beau Cambridge. Mr. Jessup had just described Jersey's boyfriend.

'Can we take our daughter's belongings, her clothing with us?' Mrs. Jessup directed her question to Lynn, her words sounding tortured as she gripped her husband tighter.

Lynn's eyes swung to Alyssa, passing the question on to her. 'We'll need to hold onto them a little longer, see if our technicians can pull any forensic evidence. I'm sure you understand that every bit of information we can obtain gets us one step closer to finding who did this to your daughter.'

As if Alyssa's words were the final weight her body could handle, Mrs. Jessup's legs turned liquid as she fell into her husband, allowing his strength to support the both of them. Over her head, Mr. Jessup said, 'The sweater she was wearing was a gift from her mother, so when will we be able to get it back?'

Careful to keep her expression neutral, Alyssa said, 'I'm sorry, but Meghan wasn't wearing a sweater when we found her.' She gave a slight nod to Lynn, indicating that she should bring the bagged clothing in. Lynn disappeared briefly, and when she returned, she handed the bag of clothing to her. Alyssa held the items up for Mr. and Mrs. Jessup's inspection. Mr. Jessup's forehead crinkled, and he frowned. 'Those don't belong to Meghan. I've never seen those.' Then tilting his head down, he addressed his wife. 'Do you recognize them?'

Mrs. Jessup's eyes widened as she shook her head. 'No.'

'Is it possible she had a change of clothing she kept at school? Or maybe even a friend's house?'

'Of course, it's possible...' Mr. Jessup hedged. 'But to be honest, those are nothing like my daughter's style.' His gaze never wavered from the shorts and top in the plastic bag. 'Those don't even resemble the clothes we've refused to allow her to purchase in the past.'

Alyssa caught Lynn's, then Sergeant Boudreaux's, eye. If they truly didn't belong to Meghan Jessup, then who *did* they belong to?

Before leaving the medical examiner's office, she and Sergeant Boudreaux agreed to stay in touch. In the car, she allowed herself a moment, closing her eyes, sending up a silent thank you that she and Brock hadn't been faced with the same pain the Jessups were now experiencing. Isaac had escaped; Meghan had not. Witnessing their agonized realization that their entire lives as they'd known had been completely destroyed by their daughter's death brought Alyssa a new determined resolve to bring justice to the Jessup family.

As she turned the key in the ignition, she prayed she and her team would find Rachel, Jersey, and Katelyn before they met the same fate as Meghan. *If they haven't already*. She shushed the voice by calling Cord to fill him in so he could let Hal, Tony, and Joe know.

Chapter Twenty-Four

Like hot tar on pavement, apprehension clung to Rachel's insides. At nineteen, she wondered how *she* could endure this torture day in and day out, let alone how someone as young and innocent as the new girl would survive. She didn't see how it was possible.

Rachel's eyes drifted around the room, landing on each of the girls garbed in a rainbow of color that seemed incongruous with their surroundings, and once again she wondered what had happened to Meghan. But, like the others, she didn't ask. Because, though unspoken, there was a reason they didn't discuss their ordeals. What transpired upstairs in The Toybox was too horrific to relive, even if it was with others who experienced the same nightmare. Tears trailed both sides of her face as she rested her gaze on the young girl's prone form. When she'd finally woken, it had taken quite some time before she'd been able to tell them her name. Katelyn Phillipson.

What would be worse – Katelyn surviving – or dying right away? Again, Rachel wondered if Meghan's sudden disappearance meant she was dead. Was that the end they all faced? Is that what she wanted? When she was in The Toybox, she thought yes, death was enviable. But down here with the others… she found herself hoping they could all find a way to survive this.

What sounded like furniture being moved overhead stole Rachel's attention away from her fear for the new girl. None of them could guess what was happening upstairs, but what they did know was that it had been several hours – from dusk to daylight and back to darkness – since the noises had begun, and in that time, none of them had been requested. At this point she wasn't sure which was the most prominent feeling: relief that they'd been left alone... or vomit-inducing dread that she should be mentally preparing for horrors even more unimaginable than what they were already forced to endure.

She couldn't even take a modicum of comfort in the fact that, so far, after Jersey had been tossed back in the cell with them, the only person who'd been downstairs since Katelyn's arrival was the lady of the house – no one knew her name, nor had they heard anyone allude to it. She'd descended the steps in a royal purple evening gown, a silk shawl trailing down her back like she was some kind of princess waiting for her prince to arrive and ordered them all to shower before disappearing upstairs again. No one had asked why; they'd just blindly obeyed. It was during that time the shuffling sounds of furniture began.

And since then, they'd waited. And waited some more. Each scraping sound, each grunt that traveled down the vents, each second of silence in between the sounds was excruciating, like fingernails on a chalkboard. At some point, the lady, still in her gown, had returned with their meal – a platter of fruit, various cheeses, and some type of bland cracker, along with uncapped bottles of water.

She'd unlocked the cell, set everything inside on the floor and then, after ensuring everyone had complied with her earlier command, left without a word, the metallic clang of the cell door slamming closed resonating through Rachel's very bones.

'Why are the bottles always uncapped?' Even as it left her mouth, she knew this wasn't the question that needed to be asked – not the discussion they should be having.

Apparently, Faye's thoughts ran along the same lines because she snorted. 'Uncapped water bottles – that's what you're most worried about right now? Not wondering what fresh new hell is being prepared for us?'

'I tried to swallow the caps once.' Cheyenne's voice was rough and scratchy, like she had a severe case of laryngitis. One shoulder lifted in weak resignation, her gaze unwavering. 'I thought I could choke to death on them. It damaged my throat. That pain couldn't be worse than the pain from *that*.' Her eyes lifted upward, and a sad laugh escaped. 'I paid the price twice for that failure.'

Rachel realized that this was one of the first times she'd actually heard Cheyenne speak, and now she understood why.

'I didn't know about that, Cheyenne. Saying "I'm sorry" seems so – I don't know, out of place considering our situation – but I am.'

Cheyenne released a steady breath but refused to make eye contact with anyone as her fingers toyed with the seam of the robe. 'It was just after Meghan arrived – we were the only two here until you were brought in.' She glanced briefly at Becca before once again looking away. Her voice was shaky as she added, 'I don't know how long I'd been here when Meghan came, but I remember being relieved I wasn't alone.' She wiped furiously at the tears streaming down her cheeks. 'And then when I saw what they did to her that first time… that's when I tried to swallow the bottle caps. I just couldn't watch another person experience the same torture. I didn't even think about the fact I'd be leaving her here all alone, like I had been.'

Rachel was used to Faye's bold directness that sometimes seemed to border on cruel honesty, so she was surprised when she angled her body toward Cheyenne and spoke softly. 'You shouldn't feel guilty about that. And no one here blames you.'

The silence that fell after Cheyenne's admission and Faye's proclamation was heavy with fear and more dread of the unknown.

Becca bit down on her bottom lip and shifted on her mattress, being the first to break into the sudden hushed quiet of their enclosure. 'What's the last thing you remember before—' Her gaze focused on the cell door as if afraid the upstairs occupants would hear.

152

The question hung in the air, the weight of it heavier the longer it went unanswered. Finally, Jersey spoke. 'I'd gone for a walk to clear my head.' She sniffled and ran a finger under her nose before wiping the moisture on the side of the mattress. 'I was leaving the duck pond at UNM' – her breathing turned into short, gasping pants, and her hushed words fell out more quickly – 'I heard someone following me' – she drew her legs in and wrapped her arms around her knees, shaking back and forth – 'and then someone attacked me from behind.' Wild eyes flickered between the others before shifting to the stairs and staying. 'Something jabbed me in the neck... I remember a hotel, I think, and a car trunk before waking up here.'

The meager contents of Rachel's stomach threatened a reappearance, and she had to swallow several times before she trusted herself to speak. 'My friend Anna wanted me to go with her to a frat party.'

'Is that the friend you asked about when you were brought in?' Becca asked.

Tendrils of fear and pain wrapped around Rachel's insides, and she nodded. 'Yes. I wouldn't even be here if I'd stayed home like I wanted.' She closed her eyes, afraid to see shame on the others' faces at her admission. 'I feel really bad blaming her because I don't know where she is or what happened to her. I'm pretty sure someone drugged my drink at the party, so I went to find Anna so we could go. When I fell asleep, she was lying right next to me. And now here I am.'

Becca shared her story next. 'A girl I didn't know but who seemed familiar asked to borrow my phone because she'd left hers at school. I said sure, and the next thing I knew, I was waking up in this cell with Cheyenne and Meghan staring at me.'

Almost too quiet to hear, Katelyn spoke next. 'I was on my way home when a girl approached me and asked me to help find her phone.' She gripped the edges of her hunter green robe, bunching the material into her fists. 'My mom and dad

will be looking for me – I know it. They're going to find me.'
It was like she was miles away as her eyes shifted to the window,
repeating the same thing over and over.

A sickening feeling in the pit of Rachel's stomach began to
bloom. So far, it sounded as if they'd all been drugged. And at
least in Becca and Katelyn's case, by a female. But how could
one girl do this to another?

For several seconds, Jersey watched Katelyn, and then she
fixed her eyes on the wall, uttering in a flat, monotone voice,
'My dad is currently off in another country with his girlfriend
who's my age, so he probably doesn't even know I'm missing.'
A humorless laugh pushed past her lips. 'My mom's horrible
in a crisis. There's always my cousin, Sophie, but she's probably
still mad at me.' Suddenly, she sat up straighter. 'But my friend,
Holly – her mom's a detective.' Her hands shook, and her voice
trembled as she looked around the room. 'Holly's mom – *she'll*
be looking for us!'

The energy changed in the room at Jersey's proclamation.
'How...' Rachel's words were drowned out by what sounded
like dozens of hammers pounding on the walls.

Instantly, the hope of seconds before crashed, replaced once
again by the nauseating fear of the unknown.

'What do you think they're doing up there?' Jersey asked the
one dreaded question none of them wanted to ask, much less
receive an answer to.

As usual, it was Faye who cut to the chase, shattering anyone
who was foolish enough to dream they'd escape unscathed from
whatever was taking place upstairs. 'It doesn't matter how any
of us ended up here, just like it doesn't do us a damn bit of
good to wonder what's happening because whether we want to
or not, we'll find out soon enough.'

Katelyn huddled into the corner of her mattress, shivering,
a low keening moan vibrating from the back of her throat at
Faye's words. Becca moved to the young girl's side, running
her hand over the other girl's hair. Rachel joined her, leaning

her head against Katelyn's. As she wrapped a protective arm around her shoulder, she was struck again with how tiny she was, in everything from her face to her feet.

Unaware she was even doing it, Rachel rocked Katelyn back and forth, a lump forming in her throat as she did, knowing how viciously the innocence would be ripped from her life. 'She's too young. God, she'll never survive this.' Her words began as a murmur, but before long, they tumbled out like a chant.

Under her breath but still audible, Faye muttered, 'God's not listening, or haven't you noticed that yet?'

'We have to do something,' Rachel choked out, at the same time thinking this, too, was new to her: putting someone else's needs above her own. Her brother, Nick, would be proud of her, if only he knew.

Jersey spoke again, but this time her words held a note of urgency, despite the hushed whisper of them. 'The window.' All eyes swiveled upward. 'If we make a pyramid, like in cheerleading, we can try to pry the window open. And then Katelyn can squeeze through. She's tiny enough. She'll fit. And if she escapes, she can run for help for the rest of us.'

Escape was the word that finally brought Katelyn back around. She clutched both hands to her belly, nodding as she croaked out, 'I can do it.'

No one moved, and no one spoke, and Rachel wondered if, like her, the others felt the electric charge in the air around them at the thought of escaping this nightmare. Her eyes moved around the room, touching on everyone before she stared up at the window. For a moment, she allowed herself to imagine life again on the other side of that glass. But even as she let her imagination take over, a persistent voice nudged itself to the forefront of her mind: *If we fail, we'll be extremely lucky if they grant us a quick death.* With fresh determination, she shut the voice down because, despite the fear, something else had begun to bloom in her chest, something she'd lost within hours of being locked in this place.

Hope.

To use one of her brother's sports analogies, if she was going to die, she'd go out swinging.

Chapter Twenty-Five

Thursday morning, Alyssa sat in the kitchen waiting for Isaac to come downstairs so she could drop him off at Trevor's on her way to the precinct. Mrs. Lewis had called last night to suggest leaving today instead of tomorrow in the hopes of beating the traffic, and though it had meant the family would miss his eighth-grade promotion ceremony, Alyssa had been unable to say no to her son's pleading eyes. Brock would've taken him, but he had a meeting with some of the subcontractors he'd hired for construction on the hospital wing bid he'd won while she'd been hunting Evan Bishop. It was so hard to believe her baby would be going into high school in just a few months. It seemed like just last week she'd been helping him take those first steps on his wobbly infant legs.

Her smile slipped as she thought about the fact that Meghan Jessup's parents would no longer have any more firsts with their daughter. Her gut insisted Beau Cambridge was the boy they'd described seeing their daughter with. Not to mention the undeniable fact that Cambridge was exactly the kind of player capable of trying to date a beautiful fourteen-year-old girl, if for no other reason than to stroke his monstrous ego.

Yesterday afternoon, she and Cord had driven over to Beau's house to talk to him about a possible connection with Meghan, but he wasn't home, and his mother hadn't known where he was or when he'd return. Throughout their questioning, Mrs. Cambridge had steadfastly refused to look at them, choosing instead to focus her gaze over their shoulders.

'Do you know if Beau has traveled to Santa Fe in the last couple of months?' Alyssa had asked.

'I don't keep tabs on my son's comings and goings, Detective. It angers both him and my husband. If they wish for me to know, or if it's important, they'll tell me.'

'Does that mean you also don't know which gym Beau and your husband use to work out?' Alyssa asked because, as of last night, Hal still hadn't found any links regarding a possible financial connection between the families.

Mrs. Cambridge's face registered surprise and though she still kept her eyes carefully averted, she said, 'They have a personal gym on the patio in the back.'

The gym was another brick wall. None of the families attended the same church services as they all belonged to different religious organizations. None of them utilized the same bank or served on the same boards. And now none of the families worked out at the same place.

Alyssa had known the financial link was tenuous, but she'd had to follow the thread to the end to be certain. Which led her back to Meghan Jessup. If she could locate the mysterious senior Meghan had been seeing, whether it was Beau or someone else, they might find the one piece of the puzzle that tied all these girls together.

Upstairs, Isaac stirred as he got ready for his Memorial Day weekend with his best friend's family, and Alyssa decided that she'd make the most of the time she had with him and push the cases to the back of her mind, concentrating instead on how this getaway would be a healing steppingstone for Isaac. Even though he'd still be surrounded by woods, Red River was three hours north from the Sandias where he'd been held captive in April.

Isaac's bedroom door opened and slammed loudly. 'Sorry. Accident,' he shouted as he came bouncing down the stairs.

In the kitchen, the wide grin and the one-armed hug he bestowed on her after he dropped his knapsack on the floor in the corner wiped out any further reservations she had about him leaving too soon after all he'd been through. But Holly was right: if they hovered, if they treated him like he'd never be okay, his healing process would take even longer.

He popped in two strawberry Pop-Tarts, lobbing the wrapper into the trash can, whooping out, 'Slam dunk,' as it bounced off the rim and into the bag. Humming off-key, he moved to the refrigerator and took out the milk, uncapping it and drinking straight from the jug.

'Isaac Wyatt! You aren't a caveman – yet. Get a cup, for God's sake.'

With a milk mustache still rimming his lips, he opened the cupboard and grabbed a glass, filled it to the brim, and then chugged it down before pouring himself another. As he moved about the kitchen, he rambled on about hanging out, fishing, and hiking. 'But s'mores, Mom. S'mores. Mrs. L always brings those campfire marshmallows, and if heaven has a taste, that's it right there.'

Alyssa erupted in laughter, a lightness in her chest, as she witnessed the pure joy that lit up her son's face when talking about the popular sugary campfire treat. 'Try to save some for the rest of the family, if you can.'

'Hey, no promises. Mrs. L knows me, so she knows what she got herself into when she asked me to tag along,' he said, finally plopping down at the kitchen table so he could eat his 'breakfast of champions,' as he liked to call it.

His eyes swept over the table, landing on her case files, and if she hadn't been looking directly at him, she would've missed the slight tightening at the corner of his mouth. When he caught her staring, he recovered quickly. 'I'm okay, Mom. I'm just worried about Holly and Sophie, but if anyone can find Jersey and these other girls, you can.'

To hide the tears that had sprung to her eyes, Alyssa grabbed her dishes and carried them to the dishwasher. If only it was as easy as Isaac made it sound.

On her way to the refrigerator to put the milk away that Isaac had left on the counter, she couldn't resist reaching out and rubbing her hand over his wavy brown hair, so much like his father's. And despite the one-armed hug earlier, he behaved like any typical fourteen-year-old by ducking his head and shrugging her hand away, adding a scowl for good measure. With every bit of normalcy Isaac added back into his daily routine, her heart soared with hope and happiness. She checked the time on the microwave.

'Trevor said he wanted you there by quarter to seven, right?'

Isaac glanced at his phone. 'Yeah, but you can drop me earlier if you want. That way I can help load up the truck and camper.'

'Which reminds me, Dad put your tent in the back of my car.'

'Cool, thanks.' He stood, scraping his chair back and dumping his crumbs in the sink before placing his plate in the dishwasher. Alyssa chuckled on the inside because *that* particular act wasn't normal at all. Then, after he gulped down the remainder of his milk, rinsed the glass, and set that inside, too, he closed the door and bounced on the balls of his feet.

'Whenever you're ready.'

'All right, then, grab your things, and let's hit the road.' At the garage door, she paused. 'You did pack a toothbrush and toothpaste, right?'

He shook his head and rolled his eyes in a highly exaggerated manner. 'No, Mom. And I didn't bring clean underwear, either. In fact, I didn't bring clothes at all. Or deodorant. I figure it's better that way. Keeps the bears away.'

Alyssa swung her hand into his stomach as she laughed. 'Well, at least you're thinking ahead, I suppose.'

Whatever comeback he had was thwarted by a text message notification stealing his attention away. His fingers flew over his keyboard as he answered whoever it was. Then he tucked his phone into his pocket and said, 'Grandma telling me to have a fun weekend.'

Regardless of their past history of contention and barely tolerating each other, the one thing Alyssa could never argue was that Mabel Wyatt adored the ground her grandchildren walked on.

At the Lewises, she chatted a few minutes with Trevor's parents and cooed over his new baby brother, Ryan. It made her arms ache to hold her own babies again. And as soon as that thought whipped through her head, she knew it was time to go. Despite the embarrassment to her son, she kissed the top of his head, told him to have a great time, and climbed back into her car, where she found herself checking the mirror until the Lewis' house was no longer in sight.

And then she pushed all her insecurities about Isaac's camping trip aside and focused her concentration where it needed to be in this moment – finding Meghan Jessup's killer and locating Rachel, Jersey, and Katelyn before they met the same fate as Meghan.

—

When Alyssa arrived at the precinct later that morning, she headed straight to the conference room where printouts of the call and text logs for Rachel, Jersey, Katelyn, and Meghan spanning back to March waited for her. Immediately, she began poring over each page, hoping to find one common number amongst the four girls. And if she was being really honest, she knew she was hoping it would belong to Beau Cambridge, cementing the theory that he was somehow involved in all this.

So far, however, all she'd succeeded in doing was giving herself a throbbing headache and blurry vision. All she needed was one thread to pull. Just one. Was that asking too much of the universe? Because she didn't think so.

She was rubbing circles into her temple when Ruby appeared in the doorway. 'Detective, there's someone here who says it's urgent he speak to you right now.'

'Who is it?'

'Nick Otis.'

Forgetting her burgeoning headache, Alyssa shoved back from the table and hurried to the front where Rachel's twin rapped the counter with his knuckles, drawing attention from irritated officers.

'Nick?'

He swung around, causing his hair to droop into his eyes. Absently, he brushed it off his forehead only to have it lapse right back to where it had been when he rushed over, meeting her part-way.

'Someone answered Rachel's phone.' His words spilled out in a fountain of energy, and it took several seconds for Alyssa's mind to make sense of what he was saying. When it did, she latched onto his arm and guided him toward the conference room before changing her mind and ushering him to the office she shared with Cord instead.

Once inside, she demanded an explanation. 'Talk. What do you mean, someone answered Rachel's phone? When was this?'

Nick tunneled his fingers into his hair, tugging lightly at the ends. 'So, I've been calling Rach's phone ever since I found out she was missing because' – he swallowed – 'because I was hoping…'

Because he was hoping she'd answer, or if someone else did, that they'd tell him where his sister was. Alyssa understood, and she waved her hand in the air for him to continue.

'Like I told you Monday at my parents' house, the first day, her phone went straight to voicemail every time I called. The next day was more of the same.' As he spoke, he barely took a breath, his words firing rapidly. 'I knew it was probably useless to keep calling, but I couldn't stop. I had to try.' Pressing his hand to his chest, he rocked back and forth on his heels. 'If you pull her phone records, my number will be the one that looks like she's got a stalker.' He swung his gaze down to meet hers, unapologetic. 'I called once an hour Monday and Tuesday, and then every few hours yesterday and today. This morning at 8:42 exactly, some guy answered.'

Alyssa's eye flickered to the digital clock on the wall behind Nick. 9:02. Her heart rate took off at a sprint, yet, somehow, she still managed to keep her voice level. 'Why didn't you call me immediately? Why did you waste time driving over here? Did this guy give a name?' She lobbed the questions in quick succession.

'I was afraid you'd be busy, so I thought it might be easier to interrupt if I came here in person. And no, the guy wouldn't tell me his name. All he said was that one of his roommates found the phone – and no, he didn't say where, claimed he didn't even know when I asked – anyway, the friend found it, decided to keep it, and when it rang, this guy decided to answer in case it was Rachel – he said "the owner." When I told him "the owner" had disappeared from a frat party, the guy freaked out, said he didn't know anything about that, and then hung up.' Nick's nostrils flared, and he spoke through clenched teeth. 'I called right back, but it went straight to voicemail again, so he must've powered it off.'

No longer able to stand still, Nick paced in the only available space in the tiny office – in front of Alyssa's and Cord's desks. Four steps to one wall, four steps back. Repeat. 'What if this person has Rachel? What if my calling makes him do something to her? What if—?'

Alyssa planted herself in his path and pointed to a chair. 'Sit. I'm going to get someone to see what we can do to find out what tower that call bounced off. Don't go anywhere, do you hear me?' As soon as she was certain he wasn't going to jump up and follow her, she went in search of Hal, wishing in vain that Cord hadn't needed to take the morning off so he could attend a doctor's appointment with Sara.

She found Hal in the breakroom grabbing a piece of birthday cake someone had left behind a day or two ago. She didn't bother with a greeting. 'Someone answered Rachel Otis's phone this morning. Can you get ahold of Judge Rosario and obtain a ping warrant. I need to know immediately what tower was used when that call was answered. Tell her it's not only relevant to an ongoing criminal investigation, but the lives of three girls may be on the line.'

Hal abandoned the uneaten cake and whirled his chair around, rolling past her. 'Where can I find you after she gives the go-ahead?'

'I'll be in my office or in the conference room. Find me the second you get the approval.'

'Consider it done.'

A minute later, she was back with Nick. 'Okay, we're obtaining what is called a ping warrant right now so we can locate that tower.'

She pulled up short at the sight of Nick. Both hands cupped his head, and his shoulders were shaking violently. When he heard her enter, he jerked up, and using his knuckles, he brushed away the evidence of his tears.

'Can you still do that if the guy shut the phone off?' Crying had changed the tone of his voice into a guttural growl.

'In a nutshell, yes.' Alyssa leaned over to Cord's desk and swiped a tissue, handing it to Rachel's brother. 'Turning a phone off stops it from communicating with nearby towers, but it can still be traced to whatever location it was in when it was powered down.'

Nick graciously accepted the tissue, wiped his nose, and sagged against the back of the chair. 'Thank God for that.' Then he sat up straight again. 'If you need me to, I think I'd recognize the voice of the guy who answered.'

'That's good. If it comes to that, I'll let you know. Now, have you told your parents about any of this?'

Nick actually snorted. 'No. What would be the point? They're still in denial she's missing. It might interfere with their social engagements if they had to take an active concern in their daughter's well-being.'

Alyssa wasn't surprised by his response, but she was saddened. She couldn't imagine not worrying about Holly or Isaac if they hadn't been seen or heard from in days. Hell, she'd nearly lost her mind the second she'd realized Isaac was gone – and that was before she discovered he'd been kidnapped.

She shook the memory away. Her children were safe; this was about Rachel. Plus, something else was bothering her. 'Nick, you already said you didn't know much about this new friend of Rachel's...'

Nick's head snapped up. 'Anna? The one she went to the party with? Have you found her? Does she know something?'

Alyssa held her palm out to halt his barrage of questions. 'No, we've been unsuccessful so far in locating this mysterious Anna. No one at the party seems to know her.' Nor had anyone by that name been reported missing, which could mean any number of things. Should they also be searching for Rachel's friend, or had the girl simply vanished into thin air, never knowing her friend had disappeared? After all, Rachel's roommate had claimed the girl's visits were sporadic at best, with gaps of time between each.

But while the mysterious Anna was important, there was another question burning in Alyssa's mind that she hoped Nick could answer. 'You also said your sister didn't talk about the guys she liked, but did you happen to meet any of the guys she hung out with, even if it was just friends?' *Like maybe a tall, linebacker guy with a chauvinistic, misogynistic attitude?*

'Sure, I met a few of them, but they were more pals than flirtations, and I rarely saw her with the same guys more than once or twice.' He smiled at some memory. 'And even though she was definitely one of the popular girls all throughout school, she avoided athletes like they had the plague.' Then he cocked his head and asked a question of his own. 'Why do you ask? Do you have a suspect?'

Alyssa chose her next words carefully. 'I have a possible person of interest I'm trying to either rule out or prove involvement.' If it was true Rachel avoided athletes, and if she *had* encountered Beau and rejected his advances, Alyssa could easily envision the anger he'd feel at being thwarted, especially with that overinflated ego of his.

Nick's posture went ramrod straight. 'Who?' he demanded.

The flash of anger in Nick's eyes reminded Alyssa of Callie McCormick's husband, Rafe, and the thought that Rachel's brother could easily turn into another vigilante crossed her mind. 'I'm sorry, but I'm not at liberty to share that information with you. At least not yet.'

–

A few minutes later, after promising to call with any news, Alyssa ushered Nick out and went in search of Hal. She'd barely made it as far as the front desk when he rolled out of the conference room, flagging her down.

'Got it!'

'Hal, you're the best! Let's find out where that phone is.' Alyssa was positive that if anyone looked, they'd see evidence of her heart trying to pound straight through her chest right now.

Chapter Twenty-Six

Thursday, May 23

A few minutes after ten, Holly parked outside the precinct. She and Sophie were hoping to catch her mom. They'd just finished their daily walk through the mostly deserted UNM campus where they stopped random people to show them Jersey's picture, asking if they'd seen her. Of course, no one had, unless it was on the news or in the flyers they'd seen.

It wasn't that she didn't trust her mom to do her job; it was just that she and Sophie couldn't sit still, or they'd lose even more of their minds. They *had* to do something. They'd already posted flyers all over Albuquerque, and several times a day they scoured Jersey's social media accounts for anything that seemed off. And still, they heard nothing but crickets.

Since the precinct was just a few miles down the road from the university, the girls decided to drop in. While Holly drove, she instructed Sophie to send her mom a message to see if she had a couple of minutes to meet with them.

As she shifted her car into park, a tall, lean, good-looking guy about her age exited the precinct. Holly followed him with her eyes until her phone chimed, alerting her to a text.

'It's your mom.' Sophie grabbed Holly's phone from the center console and handed it to her.

> Hi sweetie. Got your message. I'm right in the middle of things, so I won't be able to see you girls right now. Sorry. I'll call you when I get a chance. Love you.

Holly dropped her head back against the headrest, closing her eyes against tears that appeared out of nowhere, and released a heavy sigh. 'Mom's busy, so guess we're going to have to catch up with her later. I don't know what else we can do.'

Sophie swallowed, bent at the waist, and lowered her face into her hands. 'Hol, what if we never hear from Jersey again? What if she's… God, I can't even…' Each word wobbled on the precipice of a cliff neither girl wanted to go over.

Even though her best friend didn't say *dead*, Holly knew that was what she was thinking. 'Neither can I.' She did the only thing she could think to do – she reached over, squeezing when Sophie's hand gripped her own. She was glad they had each other.

'I *hate* him, Holly. And I can't help but think that Beau *knows something.*'

Holly twisted in her seat so she was facing Sophie. Her friend's face was red and splotchy – something she'd learned over the years meant Sophie had surpassed upset and sailed into full-on anger. 'If Beau is somehow involved, my mom will find out, and he'll pay the price. You know my mom's the best at her job.'

'I know.' Sophie leaned forward and opened the glovebox where Holly kept the tissues. She pulled one from the box and blew her nose. 'What if he *did* do something to her? God, Holly, I know I complained about all her theatrics, but I'd give *anything* right now if she would just waltz up and regale us with dramatic tales of her adventure of the last few days. *Anything.*' Her voice cracked. 'If anything has happened to her, it'll be my fault…'

'Stop. First, we don't know yet if anything bad has happened to her.' She ignored the voice shouting in her head that they did know; what they didn't know was what exactly that bad thing was. 'Second, no matter what, none of this is your fault. We both could've – and probably should've – been more understanding and compassionate of everything she was going through.'

'Remind me why I was always such a bitch to her? I mean, really, what would it have cost me to actually be patient once in a while?' She brought her fingernails up to her teeth, chewing at the jagged edges, the cuticles red from where she'd already gnawed them. She turned her neck to stare out the passenger window. 'I'm still pissed at Leigh Ann for yesterday, but I kind of wish she was here.' Grudgingly, she added, 'She's been a far better friend to Jersey than I've been a cousin.'

'Damn it! Damn it! Damn. It!'

Both Holly and Sophie jumped, startled by the loud cursing coming from behind Holly's car. A glance in her rearview mirror reflected the same guy who'd been heading down the steps of the precinct when they'd arrived. Now, he paced back and forth in front of a car, his face almost as red as Sophie's had been a moment earlier.

'Damn it!' The guy kicked at one of his tires.

'Should we ask if he's okay?' Sophie flipped down the vanity mirror on the sun visor so she, too, could watch the guy behind them. 'Why am I whispering? It's not like he can hear us.'

Holly hesitated. 'We don't really know him.' Even as she said it, she and Sophie found themselves opening their doors and climbing out. Together they approached him. 'I sure hope that's your car you're taking your anger out on.'

The guy swung around, phone in one hand. 'What?'

'Um, are you okay?'

He waved in the direction of the convertible in front of him. 'Not really. I got a parking ticket.' He fluttered the slip of paper in the air, disgusted. 'And if that wasn't irritating enough, I have a flat tire, and now I have to call Triple A to get them to come change it.'

'Why do you have to call Triple A? Don't you know how to change a flat? Or do you not have a spare?' She knew she sounded shocked, and maybe even a little judgmental, but she couldn't help it.

A whole new level of bright red suffused the guy's face, and Holly had a feeling it had nothing to do with the heat or his anger. 'Nope, don't know the first thing about changing a tire.' His brown-eyed gaze bounced between Holly and Sophie while a crooked smile lifted one corner of his mouth. 'Don't suppose you know, do you?' The tone of his voice implied he was joking.

'Actually, yes, we do. Would you like us to help?'

Sophie's neck snapped in her direction, and from the corner of her eye, Holly could see her friend's mouth hanging open. She had an urge to recite one of her grandma's favorite sayings: *better shut that before the flies get in and nest.*

The word '*oh*' formed on the guy's lips, but no sound emerged. 'I, uh, was joking when I asked that.' He cocked his head to the side and cleared his throat. 'But, really, *you* know how to change a tire? *Both* of you?'

Whether it was the incredulous, doubtful tone of his voice, or the fact she was a little insulted at the implication that she was lying, Holly responded by arching one brow and placing her hands on her hips. 'What? Because we're girls, and girls can't change tires?'

Realizing the insult for what it was, the guy backpedaled. 'I'm sorry. That was… of course, I didn't mean… I mean why wouldn't you…'

'Yes, *we* know how to change a tire.' She moved her thumb back and forth in the air between Sophie and herself. 'My dad made us learn before he'd let us drive.'

'Well, my dad believes it's easier to pay someone to do things like that.'

Holly didn't know him and couldn't be sure, of course, but the way he mumbled the words made it sound like he was embarrassed by the admission. She reached out a hand. 'I'm Holly, by the way. This is my best friend, Sophie.' She turned slightly, angling her body so that she was almost facing the precinct. 'My mom's a detective here, and we dropped by to visit her for a bit.'

A cloud dropped over the guy's face as he lifted his eyes to the tinted windows of the police station, but then he shook his head and dropped his gaze back to Holly, extending his hand first to her and then to Sophie.

'Nick Otis.'

Otis. Their smiles fell away, and Sophie and Holly exchanged a look. Could Nick Otis be related to the missing girl, Rachel? Now that she knew his name, she could see the resemblance between him and the image of the girl she'd seen on the television. She wondered if he was the girl's brother.

'So, Nick, do you want us to help?'

A brilliant white-toothed smile took over his tan face, replacing the darkness that had temporarily shrouded his eyes. 'I'd love it.'

Fifteen minutes later, his spare was on, and Holly accepted Nick's hand as he pulled her to her feet. As she brushed the knees of her capris, she noticed the large grin on his face.

'I just changed my first tire,' he said proudly.

'*Helped* change,' Holly corrected, unable to fight off her own grin. It was contagious. She'd made him remove the lug nuts, as well as replace them, showing him how to make sure they were on snugly so he wouldn't lose the tire driving down the road. She'd planned on making him jack up the car, too, but when he'd almost collapsed it twice, she was afraid he'd crush himself or that they'd be there until the stars came out.

'Helped,' he agreed. 'So, can I take you two to grab a bite to eat to show my thanks?' The unmistakable gleam of hope sparkling in his eyes made it difficult to decline.

Holly shifted her eyes over to Sophie, who'd gone to sit on the curb after moving the flat tire out of their way so she and

Nick could put the spare in place. She glanced at her watch, and then gave a curt shake of her head. 'Thanks, but we need to be going.'

'Well, then, do you mind if I get your number so I can text you sometime? I'd really like to take you to breakfast or lunch or something. You know, to thank you.' Though he addressed both of them, his eyes stayed trained on Holly.

'Um, sure. I guess.' She held out her hand for his phone, and after he unlocked the screen and handed it over, she typed both their numbers into his contacts before handing it back. 'I put both our numbers in there.'

'Thanks.' Nick glanced at the screen, a wide smile crinkling the corners of his eyes as he pushed the phone into his front pocket. 'You know, getting a parking ticket and a flat tire in the same day was kind of worth it, now that I think about it.'

'Well, as pick-up lines go, it's at least unique,' Sophie dead-panned. 'But only "kind of"? Dude, you need to work on your game.'

Holly's face heated as she and Sophie moved back to her car. Fingers hovering over the handle, she pointed with one hand to the back of his convertible. 'Don't forget to have that spare replaced with a real tire. You don't want to drive around too long on that.'

The second her door closed, Sophie said, 'I give him less than three hours before he bounces you a message asking you out. Before the weekend's over, he's gonna be calling you his bae on Instagram. So, I guess this wasn't a wasted trip after all.'

The second the words fell from her mouth, reality slammed back in with the force of a sledgehammer. Holly tried to shake the blanket of guilt that she'd enjoyed a brief moment where she'd forgotten that Jersey was missing, and she knew by the heavy silence and the way Sophie's fingers flew to her mouth that her thoughts were currently traveling the same path as her own.

'Your mom is going to find Jersey.' Sophie's voice was hushed with weak conviction. 'And when she does, we'll charm my cousin into forgiving us. We'll be so clingy and understanding, she'll be the one who gets sick of us, right?'

Holly started the engine and turned off the air-conditioner as a cold chill raced over her skin. 'Right.' She tried not to imagine what would happen if her mom didn't find Jersey in time.

Chapter Twenty-Seven

Thursday, May 23

Tears clogging her throat, and her heart knocking inside her chest, Jersey stared at the blood seeping through Rachel's robe. Whereas her own back was a collection of colorful bruises, Rachel's was a canvas of crisscrossed slashes and welts that were breaking open from their attempts at building a pyramid that would enable Katelyn to reach the window. 'Maybe Rachel and I should trade places?'

Rachel gritted her teeth. 'I can do this.' Despite the conviction in her voice, her words were cloaked in a cloud of intense pain. Still, they'd tried again. But the second Jersey had placed her knee on Rachel's back in an effort to complete the center of their pyramid, Rachel's trembling arms had given out, and she'd collapsed to the ground, panting and gasping for air. After a few moments, she pushed herself to her knees. 'Again,' she'd insisted.

And they had – with the same results.

So now Jersey knelt before Rachel, grasping her hands tightly between her own. 'It might be a little lopsided since I'm so much smaller than you, but let's just try.'

Rachel bit her quivering bottom lip as her shimmering eyes strayed from Jersey's concerned face to the others' and then up to the window. 'I can do this. *This* pain is only temporary, right?'

'Are you sure?' Jersey asked.

Rachel nodded. 'This may be our only chance.'

'Okay, let's do this.' Faye's voice was full of urgency.

Determined, and ignoring the cries of their weak, battered bodies, they all nodded as Becca, Faye, and Rachel once again positioned themselves against the wall beneath the window, darting nervous looks to the door at the top of the stairs. The hammering from above continued, giving them hope that those sounds would mask any noise the window might make when Katelyn pried it open.

'Here I go,' Cheyenne whispered as she carefully planted one knee on Becca's back. Time seemed to stand still as she waited for Becca to control her trembling arms.

'Hurry.' Becca pushed the words past clenched teeth.

Cheyenne settled her other knee onto Faye's back and then steadied herself by gripping their shoulders.

Just as she had with their first two attempts, Faye squeezed her eyes shut, her lips pursed as her face twisted in pain. Her nostrils flared as she sucked in air through clenched teeth.

It was Jersey's turn. Sweat beaded on Rachel's lips as she locked her arms into place, waiting for Jersey to get into position.

She wanted to apologize for the pain, but instead Jersey said, 'Nod when you're ready.'

Rachel sucked in a deep breath and dropped her head forward. Jersey moved into place, balancing herself on Faye's and Rachel's backs, holding her breath as Rachel's body trembled beneath her. This time, however, Rachel's arms held as she managed to keep herself from collapsing to the floor.

'Katelyn, hurry,' Jersey urged.

Quickly, Katelyn shuffled over to the pyramid and, apologizing for every gasp of pain, she carefully climbed her way to the top. Balancing herself, she whispered excitedly, 'I can reach it.'

Jersey closed her eyes to block out the pain, breathing in and out through her nose. The seconds ticked by as she waited for Katelyn to find the latch that would send her to the outside to find help to free them all.

Suddenly, Katelyn wailed something undecipherable, and her movements became jerky, causing the pyramid to become more unsteady. And then she was banging on the window, over and over, ignoring the others as they pleaded with her to stop, to tell them what was wrong. But she didn't stop, and before Jersey could process what was happening, they were all tumbling to the ground, their arms and legs flailing, muffled groans, sharp gasps, and whimpers bouncing off the walls around them.

Tremors shook Katelyn's body as she sobbed, crawling away and burrowing into a corner. Her words, when they finally came, were a combination of disbelief, helplessness, and fear. 'The glass is too thick to break, and the window's nailed shut.'

Stunned silence filled the room as they came to terms with the realization that their fleeting hope of escape was nothing more than an impossible fantasy. Then one by one, everyone moved back to their mattresses, their surge of courageousness flying through the bars of the cell and abandoning them to the truth.

This sense of hopelessness was almost worse than before they'd even tried. Jersey watched as Katelyn rocked her quaking body back and forth, and felt the weight of failure on her own shoulders at the knowledge that, no matter how much they all wanted to, none of them could save the young girl, shield her from the nightmare that was to come.

Chapter Twenty-Eight

Alyssa paced as she listened to Hal's end of the conversation. The second he'd mentioned the phrases 'matter of life or death' and 'search warrant,' the person who'd answered the phone had handed him off to a manager who was pulling up the cell tower information as quickly as he could, which, in Alyssa's estimation was ten times slower than it should be.

She was seriously considering jerking the phone away and demanding the information herself when Hal suddenly reached out and grabbed a piece of paper, flipped it over, and scribbled something on the back, and then recited his email address. 'I'll check my inbox right now and let you know when I get it. Do you mind holding? Great.'

His fingers flew over his laptop keyboard, and a few seconds later, he shouted out, 'Bingo! Thanks for your help. APD surely appreciates it. Yes, your direct line would be great. Okay, got it. We'll be in touch if we need anything else.'

Alyssa moved in behind Hal as he clicked on the map and zeroed in on the image the cell tower had tracked Rachel's phone to. It took her only a second to recognize the general location as the university area and another to realize... 'Fraternity Row,' she breathed out. 'Get Tony and Joe on the phone and have them meet me there!' She whirled around and smacked into Cord. 'I didn't hear you come in. When did you get here?'

He ignored her question in favor of one of his own. 'Meet you where?'

'Never mind about Tony and Joe.' She rushed through the door, expecting her partner would follow. 'Nick Otis called his sister's phone this morning, and someone answered. When he told the person who answered that Rachel was missing, the guy powered the phone off. Judge Rosario issued a ping warrant, and the location tracked back to Fraternity Row.' By the time she hit the precinct doors, she was running.

And a few minutes later, she was stuck in construction traffic on Central, cursing and banging on her steering wheel, just barely managing not to lay on her horn. 'Who in the hell ever thought it was a good idea to narrow Central down to one lane when it was already a traffic nightmare? Oh, that's right, the mayor.'

'You realize breaking your steering wheel off in your impatient frustration isn't really going to get you any further any faster?'

The withering look she shot him would have had most men – and women – cowering in a corner. Not Cord, though. He was used to it and knew her anger wasn't really directed at him anyway. Taking several deep breaths – in through the nose, out through the mouth – Alyssa tried to calm her nerves. When that didn't work, she asked Cord about Sara. 'It's not like you to go with Sara to a doctor's appointment, seeing as how she's a nurse and all. Is everything okay?'

To her surprise, he cut his eyes away from her and out the passenger window. 'Yes, everything's fine. Looks like traffic's finally moving.'

His observation was clearly a dismissal, but as he was also correct, Alyssa dropped the subject and hit the gas, taking the first right turn she could so that, even though it was a longer route, it would still take less time because they wouldn't be fighting construction. As she weaved in and out of slow-moving cars, shooting down the road at fifteen miles per hour over the posted speed limit, she wondered if she needed to be worried about Sara. About Cord.

She shook her head, pushing the concern to the back of her mind. At this moment, neither Cord's health, nor Sara's, was her primary focus. Seven minutes later, she jerked to a stop at the curb in front of the frat house, located a block away from the university. She didn't wait to see if Cord was behind her before she leaped out and raced up the front steps where she proceeded to pound on the door until it was jerked open by a young man with disheveled hair and wearing nothing but boxer briefs, as if she'd just pulled him from bed.

'What the hell's your problem, lady?'

She flashed her badge in his face, aware of Cord's presence beside her now as he did the same. 'Detective Wyatt, Detective Roberts with APD. What's your name?'

'Marcus Lawrence. What's this about?' His face paled, and he stumbled back a step as he tossed a look over his shoulder, his earlier irritation replaced with something else – fear, maybe?

She ignored his question. 'Who else is here with you, Marcus?'

'What, you mean like now, or who lives here?'

'Both.'

'There's only a few of us living here right now since it's summer, and I don't know who else is home right now. I was in bed until you pulled me from it with your pounding.'

'How many is a few?'

'Three of us.' Color rushed to his cheeks, and Alyssa raised her eyebrows, waiting. 'Four of us. My girlfriend is staying here with me through the summer, even though, technically, she's not supposed to.' He cocked his head to the side, adopting a look of arrogance. 'I don't see how it matters since she's paying rent, and she'll be out before the fall semester starts.'

Alyssa couldn't care less where the girl lived; she had far more urgent concerns. 'What's your girlfriend's name, Marcus?'

'Elizabeth Mortley. Now, what's—'

'Babe, what's going on? Who's here?' A young girl with straw-colored hair cascading down her back appeared in the doorway behind Marcus. When she saw Alyssa and Cord, their badges once again held up for identification, her mouth dropped open. 'Oh. Um, is something wrong?' Her gaze shot up towards her boyfriend, but all he did was shrug.

'Miss Mortley?' Alyssa asked.

'Yes. I'm Elizabeth.'

'Elizabeth, do you know who else might be here besides you and Marcus?'

'Sure. I just passed Griffin Parker a second ago. He was heading back to his room. Should I go get him for you? Is he in trouble?'

Alyssa exchanged a look with Cord. Griffin Parker was the first witness to claim Calvin McDougal had gotten quite angry after being rebuffed by Rachel. 'You know what, Elizabeth? I think my partner and I would just like to get him ourselves. Do you mind showing us to his room?' She didn't wait for her to agree before stepping into the frat house, rotating her neck left and right as she checked the area around her. Beside her, Cord did the same.

Aside from discarded soda and beer cans, tipped-over trash buckets, and the general disarray of a place that was used to hosting parties, nothing looked any different than it had on Monday when they'd conducted interviews regarding Rachel's disappearance. Not that she'd really expected a giant neon arrow with a 'Rachel, Jersey, Katelyn This Way,' but still…

'Um, if you follow me, Griffin's this way.'

Elizabeth led the way upstairs to the third room on the right where the booming bass from a stereo rattled the door and instantly grated on Alyssa's nerves.

'Do you need me for anything else? Because I need to get ready for work, if that's okay.'

Alyssa pulled her phone out and tapped on Rachel's image. 'Before you go, have you seen this girl?'

Elizabeth tipped her head to the side as she studied the picture. Finally, she shook her head. 'No, I don't think so.' She lifted her eyes to Alyssa and then to Cord. 'Should I have seen her?'

Instead of answering, Alyssa thumbed over to images of Jersey and Katelyn. 'What about these two?'

This time she pointed a manicured finger toward Jersey's picture. 'I've seen the "Missing" flyers posted all around campus and the restaurants in the area, but I haven't seen the other one. I'm sorry.' Worry had inched into her voice, and she darted a nervous glance at Griffin's door.

Not that she expected a different response, but Alyssa decided to show her Meghan's picture, too. 'One more.' She flipped her phone around and received the same answer. 'Thanks, Elizabeth. That's all for now.' She waited until the girl disappeared back downstairs before nodding to Cord. After he moved into position, she rapped her knuckles on the bedroom door.

Almost immediately, the music cut off, and a second later, the door was jerked open. If Griffin Parker's face paled any further, he would've been invisible. He didn't even wait for Alyssa to tell him why they were there. He simply bounced into an explanation. 'I swear to God I didn't know it was Rachel's phone, and I haven't had it! I told that guy who called, the one who said he was her brother, that Calvin found it, and I just happened to answer it when I heard it ring in case it was the owner calling.'

By the time he was finished, sweat had popped out onto his forehead, and one trembling hand reached up to wipe the moisture away. 'I swear,' he said again, with more emphasis.

'When did Calvin find it?'

Griffin's eyes dilated until they were nothing more than black orbs with a little white around them. 'I'm not sure. I assume he found it last night because that's when he showed me. It was a nice phone, so he was planning on charging it and factory-resetting it.'

It didn't escape Alyssa's notice that Parker sure had no qualms about throwing his fraternity brother under the bus. 'Where was the phone when he found it?'

Parker lifted shaky hands to his hair, tunneling his fingers through. 'His room? I don't— I don't really know. He just said he found it under one of the beds, but he didn't say which one.'

'Where is Calvin's room?' Cord asked.

Rachel had last been seen with Anna and Chance in one of the last bedrooms down the hall. If it turned out that that was Calvin's...

But Griffin's hand shot out, pointing downstairs. 'He's in one of the downstairs rooms. The east wing, closest to the bathroom.'

'Where is Calvin right now?'

'He went camping for Memorial Day weekend with some of the brothers. He won't be back until Tuesday.'

'Where did they go?'

Griffin's left hand pulled at the lobe of his ear. 'I don't know.'

'A group of your frat brothers went camping for several days, and you don't know where they were headed?' Alyssa didn't bother to keep the skepticism out of her voice.

'No. Camping's not my deal, and the guys know it, so it was never a thing I thought to ask about, and they didn't bother sharing.'

Something in his tone made Alyssa believe him. 'Where's the phone now?'

This time, instead of losing color, all the blood rushed back into Griffin's face. He closed his eyes. 'It's in here.' He opened his door wider and pointed to a small computer desk. Next to a stack of books and car magazines was a red, glitter-encased phone.

'We're going to need to take that with us,' Alyssa said.

'Yes, ma'am. Let me get it.'

'Actually, I'll get it.' Cord pushed past Griffin. After making sure the phone on the desk was Rachel's, he donned a pair of gloves and dropped the phone into a plastic evidence bag.

Alyssa asked Griffin to lead them to Calvin's room, which he did, but when she asked him to open the door so she could take a look, he hesitated. 'Look, I'm not trying to be difficult or anything, but are you allowed to go through his room without a search warrant?'

'We're not going to go through his room, Griffin. We're not even going to go into his room unless there's something we see that would tell us where three missing girls might be. All I want to do is peek inside. Now, if it'll make you feel better, I can certainly send Detective Roberts out to get a search warrant, and maybe even add in the need to search the rest of the frat house. Should I have him do that?' She was only kind of bluffing, but she was banking on the fact that Griffin Parker wasn't going to want a bunch of cops poking through the place, especially as she was positive there was more than merely evidence of underage drinking going on. She'd bet half her retirement that there were illegal drugs littered throughout the frat house, as well.

'No, ma'am.' He twisted the knob and shoved inward, causing the door to bang against the dresser that was behind it.

The room was surprisingly neat. Books were arranged alphabetically on a bookshelf, model cars lined a mantel above the computer desk, and pens and pencils were arranged by color in neat little cups. On the walls were various posters of half-nude girls and sports stars. Above the bed was a giant neon marijuana leaf, currently unplugged, the cord draped over the headboard.

Her eyes swept the room, and then she turned to Cord who shook his head, telling her he saw nothing that would warrant a further search. In other words, all they had was Rachel's phone, but they were no closer to locating her or the others.

It was more than they'd had, she reminded herself a few minutes later as she and Cord climbed back into her Tahoe and headed back to the precinct.

Chapter Twenty-Nine

Thursday, May 23

As soon as Alyssa and Cord passed the front desk, Hal rolled out of the conference room and waved them over. 'You'll never believe who I discovered lives in the same vicinity as Jersey Andrews and Katelyn Phillipson.'

Still frustrated that they hadn't been able to speak to Beau Cambridge, Alyssa did something she rarely did; she lashed out at one of her favorite people. 'Three girls' lives are hanging in the balance, Hal; we don't really have time for guessing games, so why don't you just tell me?'

If he was taken aback by her attitude, he didn't show it. 'I was searching through the records for registered sex offenders like you asked, as well as checking property records to see if any sex offenders – past or current – popped up, and I came across the name Abraham Flandreau who lives on San Diego. Mr. Flandreau happens to be Mr. Jessup's stepfather, Meghan Jessup's step-grandfather. And not only that, but Meghan apparently spends every spring break with him. That would've been mid-March.'

A surge of adrenaline raced through Alyssa's veins. If Hal's information was accurate, then it was completely conceivable that Beau Cambridge had seen both Meghan and Katelyn at various times while visiting Jersey. Her gaze swung to Cord. His back was ramrod straight.

But then something else Hal said sank in. 'Wait, he's a sex offender, and the Jessups allow their daughter to spend spring break with him?' Horror didn't even come close to the neighborhood of how she felt about that. They didn't seem like the type who would even allow their daughter to be around someone like that, much less encourage lengthy stay-over visits.

Hal corrected the misunderstanding. 'No, no. I should've been clearer. His name came up in the property search, not on the sex offender registry. The deed is registered to Abraham Dreschel Flandreau and Martha Jessup Flandreau – now deceased. A quick cross-check showed that Martha was married to Mr. Jessup's father until his death in eighty-five. She chose to hyphenate the name when she remarried.'

Alyssa was ready to head back out the door to bring Beau in for questioning when Ruby once again appeared in the doorway. 'Detective.'

'What?' she growled. To Ruby's credit, she didn't even bother to wince at Alyssa's tone. 'Sorry. What?'

The other woman waved off the apology as if it were nothing more than a mosquito buzzing around her head. 'You have another visitor demanding to speak to you and you alone.' She stepped further into the room, peeking over her shoulder as she did. 'You might want to hurry because it looks like she might bolt any second.'

Alyssa glanced over to Cord but addressed her question to Hal. 'We need to bring Beau in now. Where are Tony and Joe?' If nothing else, one of them could accompany her partner to the Cambridge residence.

'The owner of That Tattoo Place called right after you left, said he might have something on his security footage regarding the mystery car Naomi Kenney saw just before Meghan's body was found. They're checking it out.'

A buzzing filled Alyssa's mind. They might finally be getting somewhere. 'Let me know when they get back, especially if they have something.' Then she turned and followed Ruby to the front. Even though there were half a dozen people inside the small space waiting to speak to someone, she knew instantly who had requested to see her specifically.

A young woman, anywhere from eighteen to twenty, sat on the very edge of one of the cold, uncomfortable chairs intended for visitors. Her legs were bouncing so hard, the seat was actually inching away from the wall, emitting a horrible squealing sound that had numerous stares and glares shooting her way, all of which she ignored as she gnawed furiously at the fingernails of one hand as the other picked steadily at the frayed edges of the hole in the knee of her pants. Her eyes darted nervously toward the outer door as if she expected someone to walk through it and bust her there.

The second she spotted Alyssa, the woman dropped her hand from her mouth and wiped it on her jeans, leaping up to meet her part-way, checking behind her several times as she did.

Partly to calm her and partly to distract her, Alyssa reached out a hand and introduced herself, trying not to be squeamish that the same hand which had been gnawing at her fingers would be the same hand the woman shook with. 'I'm Detective Wyatt.' She was careful to speak gently yet firmly so the girl would know she was safe. 'How can I—?'

'Is there somewhere we can speak in private?' the woman interrupted, speaking to Alyssa even as she stared over her shoulder. Her voice trembled as if she might burst into tears at the slightest provocation. 'I can't... I need...' Finally, she turned around and faced her, eyes wide enough to show white all around the irises.

'Come with me.' Alyssa led the woman to one of the smaller interview rooms, ushering her in and closing the door behind her, leaning against it in a silent effort to show the still unnamed woman she was safe. 'Now, how can I help you?'

Instead of answering, the woman's gaze swung between the door and the three chairs in the room before she finally settled on grabbing one of the chairs and pushing it back into the farthest corner. That way, if someone opened the door, they wouldn't spot her immediately.

It was a full minute before she visibly relaxed even a modicum, though her legs still bounced rapidly. Alyssa waited, though she felt impatience building. She had a trio of missing girls she needed to find before they met the same fate as Meghan Jessup.

'I'm sorry. I know I must seem like a case to you.' Red burned up her neck and into her cheeks. 'I don't even know where to start. And maybe I don't...'

'Why don't you begin by telling me your name?' Alyssa pushed off the door and dragged a chair over, angling it so that she was sitting close while still giving enough distance that the woman wasn't boxed in.

The fingers went back to her teeth, and after a few seconds of gnawing at the quick, she dropped her hand back to her lap. 'Lorna Price,' she said, her neck twisted to the side as she kept her gaze trained on the door.

'Lorna. Can I get you anything to drink? Coffee, tea, water?' Expecting a simple yes or no, Alyssa was more than a little surprised when the woman leapt to her feet, forcing the chair she'd vacated to slam against the block wall.

'No!' Blinking rapidly, she lowered her voice. 'I'm sorry. No, thank you. I'd rather you not leave me in here alone,' she admitted.

'Okay, no beverage.'

'Listen, I'm afraid I may totally be wasting your time. I mean, what if I'm wrong or something?'

'Why don't you just start and let me be the judge of that? How does that sound?' Alyssa turned her body just enough to make sure the red light on the digital camera mounted in the corner was on and recording the entire encounter. As soon as she saw that it was on, she informed the frightened woman in front of her. 'Ms. Price, I need to let you know this conversation is being recorded.'

Lorna's eyes widened, and her fingers returned to picking at the edges of the holes in her jeans. 'What if what I tell you ends up being wrong information? Can you use that recording to send me to jail?'

187

If Alyssa wasn't intrigued before, she definitely was now. At the same time, however, she needed to bring Beau Cambridge in, and she didn't need this woman whiling away precious minutes. She forced herself to speak calmly. 'Not if you're disclosing information in a non-malicious manner.' At the woman's blank stare, she explained. 'If you're not purposely misleading the authorities with the information you're providing, then no, it won't be used to send you to jail.'

Instead of making her feel better, Alyssa's reassurance seemed to have the opposite effect, as Lorna's brows furrowed in confusion, and this time, Alyssa felt her patience begin to slide. 'If what you're about to tell me is told in good faith because of something you or someone close to you has witnessed, or if what you're about to tell me involves something that has happened to you directly, then, no, you won't be charged with making a false report. However, if your purpose is to mislead me for some reason, then yes.'

Lorna nodded. 'Okay.' Then she laughed, a sound made from nerves and not amusement. 'I'm sorry for all this.' She waved her hand around the room. 'But I've never done this before, and if I can be honest, it's *nothing* like it's portrayed on television or in the movies.'

'It rarely is,' Alyssa agreed. 'Though it would be nice if we could always solve crimes in the allotted hour of time.' Carefully, she adjusted her body so that she blocked the little red dot that showed the recording was active. 'Okay, Lorna, why don't we begin with something easy? Where do you work?'

The question may have been simple, but Lorna's body went taut. 'I work at Hotel Camino behind that old shopping center they're remodeling near the freeway. You know the one?'

'I know it.' It was an old, seedy hotel situated next to several newer ones going up in the area in the city's efforts to refurbish and revitalize certain neighborhoods. Currently, it was a popular hangout for drug users, peddlers, and prostitutes, especially as it had a 'pay by the hour' option.

Before Lorna continued, she once again glanced at the door as if she was afraid there was someone on the outside of it, just waiting for her to disclose her reason for being there. And when she lowered her voice to a whisper, chewing at the tip of her finger, muffling her words even more, Alyssa had to lean in to hear. 'That girl on the news? The one who went missing after school?'

Outwardly, Alyssa maintained her composure, kept her posture relaxed so she wouldn't startle Lorna. On the inside, however, all her senses went on hyper alert, causing pinballs to ricochet throughout her nerve endings. 'Do you mean Katelyn Phillipson?'

Lorna nodded, biting harder at her fingertip.

'Do you know something that could help us locate her?'

'Not exactly,' Lorna admitted. 'But I have seen her. Actually, I've seen two of them, I think. That Jane Doe that was on the news the other night? She kind of looked familiar, too.'

The words buzzed in Alyssa's head. Apparently, Lorna hadn't seen the news reports that "Jane Doe" had been identified as Meghan Jessup. 'Where have you seen them?'

Lorna held her breath for a second before expelling it in a huge rush. She muttered something under her breath that sounded a lot like, 'This is why you came here. Don't back out now.'

Alyssa leaned in as close as she could get without actually scooting her chair closer. 'Lorna, if you know something about Katelyn's disappearance, I need you to tell me now. It could be the difference between saving her life or finding her dead.' She hoped the urgency in her tone conveyed to Lorna the importance of sharing whatever information she had. 'Now, where have you seen these girls?'

Lorna's voice wavered, as if she were beginning to doubt the intelligence of coming here. 'At the hotel where I work?' She posed her answer as a question of its own.

Alyssa's spine stiffened. 'Did you see them with someone else, or were they alone?'

Lorna's head bobbed up and down, and she swallowed once, twice, three times.

Whatever or whomever Lorna Price had seen, one thing remained clear: she was spooked. It wasn't a question of *whether* she had seen something, but *what* she had seen. Alyssa needed to know what that was. She inched her chair over to the phone sitting on the corner of the table. 'I'd like you to look at some pictures so I know for sure which girls you say you saw, okay?' Alyssa waited for Lorna to nod, and then she dialed Ruby's extension. 'Could you please bring me two waters and my files from the conference room?' she asked as soon as Ruby picked up.

Shortly after Alyssa requested the items, a knock came on the door, and then Ruby walked in carting two water bottles and a stack of folders, setting everything down at the end of the table and leaving without uttering a word.

Alyssa stretched one arm out and pulled the items to her, nudging one of the bottles in front of Lorna. Then she dragged the folders in front of her, flipping them open, and pulling out a picture of Katelyn Phillipson, one of Meghan Jessup that Sergeant Boudreaux had given her, and adding images of Jersey Andrews and Rachel Otis. 'Ms. Price, for the record, could you please point to the images of the girls you say you recognized?'

Lorna glanced down for only a split second before her face paled. Somewhat confused, she whispered, 'All of them.' And then her gaze shot away as she stared at the door.

Alyssa's nerves felt like two hot wires touching each other. 'Are you absolutely certain you've seen all of them?'

Lorna gnawed at her bottom lip as her head bobbed emphatically.

'At Hotel Camino where you work?' Alyssa clarified for the record.

'Yeah, but not like all at the same time or anything.'

'When did you see them?'

'I don't really remember what days they were. Except for that one.' Her finger pointed to Katelyn's photo. 'I saw her Tuesday night, and she stood out because she was so young, and the man she left with was so much older, and he was such a big guy compared to her petite size.'

Blood pulsed in Alyssa's ears. 'Describe this big guy for me.'

'Um, he was built, you know, kind of like a weightlifter. He had brown hair and big bushy eyebrows.'

'How tall was this man?'

'About my brother's height, so probably about five-eleven maybe?'

Because she was expecting to hear something over six feet, it took Alyssa a second to realize Lorna wasn't describing Beau Cambridge. Nor did the description fit Chance Williams, Griffin Parker, or Calvin McDougal. She resisted the urge to sag into the chair. This was still valuable information. 'What time was this, and when Katelyn left, did she go willingly, or did she seem frightened?'

Lorna's eyes fluttered and her hands twisted together, every once in a while twisting an invisible ring on her finger, turning the area a burning red. 'I don't remember what time it was. All I can say is that it was beginning to get dark. And I don't know if she or any of them went willingly or not. Like, they all seemed totally drugged up, you know. And they were always escorted out by two guys, always the same ones.'

'Two guys?'

'Yes. The other guy was a little bit shorter than the other one. He had blond hair, still pretty muscular, but not as much as his friend.' Pink suffused Lorna's face when she admitted, 'I just thought all the girls were maybe hookers, you know…'

Something in the way she said *all the girls* struck Alyssa as odd, so she asked, 'You said "all the girls." Do you mean these four, or were there more?'

Lorna seemed surprised by the question. 'Oh, lots more. That's why I thought they were just working girls.'

Like a boulder sinking to the bottom of the lake, so did Alyssa's stomach. If what she suspected was accurate, having sex was involved, but she didn't think the girls had been given a choice in the matter. On the heels of that thought came another: *If it's a sex trafficking ring, Rachel, Jersey, and Katelyn could still be alive. And while their lives would never be the same, with the right help, they could find a way through their abuse – whereas there would be no coming back from being dead.*

'Lorna, why didn't you come to the police as soon as you realized you recognized at least two of the girls?'

Eyes glowing with moisture, Lorna shifted her chin down and stared intently at the frayed edges of her jeans. 'I was too scared. Am I going to jail now?'

It was clear the girl was terrified and probably with good reason. 'What do you do at the hotel?'

'I work the night shift at the hotel desk.' Her voice quivered with fear that she'd be arrested for not coming forward sooner.

Alyssa risked placing a hand on the frightened woman's shoulder. 'Lorna, I'm not going to take you into custody for waiting. I understand you're scared, but right now, I need you to focus so you can help me find these girls. Can you do that?'

A commotion outside the door drew Alyssa's attention just before there was a knock and then Tony poked his head in, Joe directly behind him.

Her palm covering her mouth to suppress a scream, Lorna shot out of her seat, grabbing her chair and putting it, as well as the table, in front of her. Tony's hands shot up to show he was safe even as he accurately read the situation and backed out again. Maintaining eye contact with Lorna, he directed his words to Alyssa. 'Hal said to let you know we were back. Come hunt me down when you're finished here.' And then he and Joe were gone.

But the damage was done. Alyssa groaned inwardly, both at the disruption and Tony's unfortunate word choice in *hunt*. Already Lorna was moving as if to leave. In an attempt to keep her there, Alyssa tried to reassure the woman that she was still safe, reminding her that the lives of three girls could be on the line. 'Lorna, you could help me save the lives of these other girls, save them from the same fate as Meghan Jessup.' She watched Lorna's eyes follow her finger to the image of Meghan.

Despite that, as soon as Lorna got her breathing back under control, she shuffled to the door, hand hovering. 'I'm sorry. That's all I know. I've seen them at the hotel, and nothing else.' Her mouth opened as if she wanted to say more, but then she snapped it closed and pulled open the door.

'Lorna,' Alyssa stopped her and waited for the young woman to turn back around. 'What or who are you afraid of?'

Lorna sucked her bottom lip between her teeth and glanced behind her, as if she was afraid someone would see her take the business card Alyssa held out. When she turned back, her voice was hushed. 'What if they find out I've come here? What if they know I'm calling?'

'We'll protect you. And even more, you could help us save these girls.'

'I'm sorry. I don't know anything else.'

Alyssa released a frustrated sigh and pushed her card into Lorna's hand. 'If you think of anything else, or if you see these individuals again, call me. It doesn't matter what time, day or night. Please call me.'

Lorna tucked the card into her front pocket. 'Okay.' And then she was gone.

Chapter Thirty

Thursday, May 23

After Lorna left, Alyssa hurried to the conference room, all the while planning the speech she would need to convince Hammond of okaying the cost of setting up surveillance outside Hotel Camino. Not that she expected to have to try too hard because the captain wanted this case solved as much as her team did.

'What did you find out?' she asked as soon as she walked through the conference room door.

Instead of answering, Tony apologized. 'Hal and Cord said you wanted to know as soon as Joe and I were back. I didn't know I'd be spooking someone when I walked in. Sorry about that. Hope I didn't mess things up.'

Hal projected something onto the wall across the room. 'Here we go.'

'Girl was easily spooked, and I'll tell you what I found out as soon as I see this.' She turned her attention to the black and white grainy footage projected onto the wall. As she watched, she spotted who she assumed was Naomi Kenney appear in the top right corner, moving briskly along the sidewalk, head jerking from side to side, clearly alert and on edge in her surroundings. 'Why are we just now finding out about this security camera? Didn't you ask the businesses around there when we discovered Meghan's body?'

It was Joe who answered. 'Owner was closed down for the past couple weeks. Said business was too slow with all the construction and decided to take some time to go fishing up at Navajo Lake. He just got back, saw the news reports, checked his footage, and called right away.'

A minute later, a fancy sports car swerved around the corner, speeding into sight on the camera. Five seconds after that, the driver jerked to a halt, as if he'd only decided at the last minute to stop in that spot. Then the driver popped his trunk and climbed out, a dark hooded sweatshirt covering his face – not a rumpled business suit like Naomi had claimed.

Tony pointed. 'She's still standing there behind that dumpster, out of sight of the man in the vehicle, but not out of sight of the camera. I think she knew by the way the guy pulled up, he was up to no good, and her instincts made her hide.'

'What kind of car is that?' Alyssa asked. 'It looks fancy.'

'Dodge Viper,' Hal, Cord, and Tony all answered at once, their voices varying in degrees of lust and envy. Alyssa shook her head.

At the back of the Viper, the man swiveled his head back and forth before hefting something out of the trunk and heaving it over his shoulder. Clearly, the something was a body bound up in a sheet. With one hand wrapped securely around the legs Alyssa believed belonged to Meghan Jessup, the man stepped onto the sidewalk and into the area where the young girl had been discovered.

Four minutes, fifty-two seconds after entering the building, the man returned, sheet wadded up under his arm. At the car, his eyes darted all around him as he spun around in one quick circle, slammed his trunk closed, and hurried over to the driver's side, climbing in. Though there was no sound, it was obvious the man had squealed away because there was a wisp of tire smoke as he peeled away from the curb.

In the video, Naomi Kenney stepped out of her hiding spot, head moving first in the direction the car had taken off, then back towards the building. According to the timer running in the corner of the screen, the woman debated for a full six minutes before she hurriedly crossed the road and moved out of sight of the camera.

'Too bad there was a license plate cover,' Alyssa said, speaking more to herself than to her team. And then to Hal, she said, 'Can you run a DMV search of individuals in the area who own a Dodge Viper?'

'Already started, but I have to say a quicker, more efficient method would be releasing this footage to the media and sending out a plea for anyone knowing someone who owns a car like this to contact the police.'

'Good idea.' And then she filled everyone in on Lorna Price. 'I'm going to talk to Hammond about getting surveillance set up at Hotel Camino. If what Price said is right, our girls aren't the only ones who've been run through there. I think we need to consider that we're looking at a sex trafficking ring. Hal, I need you to run a search of the missing person's database. Start with central and northern New Mexico, and then expand outward to include the entire state. We're searching for girls aged thirteen to twenty-one, just to be safe.

'And I want someone digging into Beau Cambridge *and* his father's background. I want cell phone records. Go over the missing person report Sergeant Bordeaux emailed and see if any of the witness statements include a description of persons in the area matching Beau Cambridge. If he was there when Meghan Jessup disappeared, we'll have probable cause for a search.' Her eyes caught and held Cord's whose jaw had tightened at the mention of Jersey's boyfriend. 'Because Beau Cambridge *is* somehow involved,' Alyssa continued. 'It can't just be coincidental that he was tied to two of our missing girls.'

Tony cleared his throat. '*Allegedly* tied to two,' he corrected. 'Technically speaking, we only know for certain he's connected to Jersey Andrews. While his general description fits that of the boy Meghan Jessup was secretly hooking up with, he's not the only one who does, and we need to keep in mind that Santa Fe is fifty miles away...' He let his voice trail off.

'You're right, and I promise I'm keeping an open mind,' Alyssa assured everyone, 'but my gut is telling me he's involved. And if he is, we need to bring him in sooner rather than later. Because even if he is part of it, he's not the one in charge – he's not smart enough to pull off something this sophisticated. He's answering to someone else.' She jerked her thumb to the wall where the camera footage was still running. 'Let's find out who that someone is.'

Chapter Thirty-One

It was close to seven on Thursday night, and Alyssa, Cord, and Hal were still in the conference room. Captain Hammond had gone home after approving the surveillance for Hotel Camino, as well as overtime for Joe and Tony, who were right this minute posted outside the hotel.

A throbbing headache bloomed behind Alyssa's eyes as images of Katelyn, Jersey, Rachel, and Meghan's battered body flashed through her mind. Each second that passed was another second these girls were in danger. She refused to accept that they could already be dead.

'I think we found that Dodge Viper.' Officer Hermosa, one of the responding officers who'd arrived at her house when Isaac had been kidnapped, came rushing in. Bent at the waist, hands on his knees, he panted for breath as if he'd just run a half marathon.

Hal wheeled his chair around, Cord shoved back from the table, and Alyssa jolted out of her chair, a loud pop echoing throughout the room as her spine cracked back into place. 'What?' she demanded.

'Dispatch got a call. Sounds like a group of high school kids were off-roading in the mesa when they spotted a fancy red sports car across one of the ravines. They were impressed a car like that would be out there, so they decided to wind their way back around to check it out. They'd been backtracking less than five minutes when they heard a huge *Boom* and saw a plume of dirt explode out of the ravine. So, they turned around again, and headed back. They had to hike over to the edge of the ravine, but when they did, they saw the Viper on its side at the bottom. They were worried someone might still be in there, so they called nine-one-one right away. One of the guys drove back to the road to guide searchers in.'

Alyssa was already grabbing her phone and keys. 'Where was this?'

'At the end of Rainbow in Rio Rancho.'

'I know where that is. That's where Trevor's dad takes the boys to go dirt-biking.' Before heading out, she asked Hal to contact Hammond. In the car, Cord called the Rio Rancho PD to let them know they were on their way.

Because rush hour traffic was over and Alyssa ignored the speed limit, it took less than thirty minutes to hit Rainbow, another five to convince the rookie cop they needed to be allowed to pass, and another fifteen to bump along the trails to the ravine where they hiked the rest of the way in because the area was clogged with police and rescue workers.

Rushing over to one of the officers she recognized, she said, 'Manny, what have they found?'

Manny Hernandez swung around and greeted both her and Cord. 'I heard you were on your way. Saw this car on the news. Looks like someone else did, too, and they decided to dump it.'

'So, there's no one inside it?' She nodded her head to indicate the rescue team now working their way back up the steep, sandy ravine, avoiding the risk of dislodging one of the dozens of other abandoned cars – or the ones that thieves had dumped after stripping them of what they needed.

'Nope.'

'Your guys got the VIN, right?' Cord asked. 'Because I'm betting our guy wasn't kind enough to leave his insurance and registration behind.'

Manny laughed. 'Dude's dumb enough to dump that beauty, so I wouldn't put it past him to overlook something minor like leaving an arrow to where he lives. But no. My guys recovered nothing but dirt, fiber, and shattered glass.'

'We're going to need to get a tow truck out here to drag it up,' Alyssa said, observing the workers scaling the ravine. 'We need to inspect that trunk.'

Manny nodded. 'So, that's why my boys reported such a strong smell of ammonia coming from that area.' Still watching the crew work, he said, 'I don't think you're going to find much. My guess is your suspect scraped that car clean before dumping it. And just so you know, there's not a tow truck company out there who's gonna have a lift big enough, long enough, or strong enough to drag that thing out of there. It'll topple over on top of it if it even tried.'

'Yeah, that's what I thought. But it never hurts to ask, right?'

'Never hurts,' Manny agreed.

A few minutes later, several officers and rescue workers strolled their way, their faces streaked with sweat and grime and red from the exertion of climbing out of the ravine. One of the guys reached into his pocket and pulled out a scrap of paper. 'Here's the VIN.'

Manny took it and handed it over to Alyssa. 'We'll want a copy of that, but I think your department needs this more than we do right now.'

'Thanks, Manny.' She walked back over to her Tahoe while Cord stayed and talked to Manny. When she was far enough away from the commotion to hear, she dialed Hal and read off the vehicle identification number, feeling like she'd hit the motherlode. With this, they could learn everything about the car: the year, make, model. But more importantly, it would reveal the car's ownership history, including whoever it was currently registered to.

Her fingers and scalp tingled in anticipation as Hal typed the information in, mumbling to himself as he did, and then, with something close to reverence, shared what he discovered. 'The 2017 Dodge Viper is registered to none other than Rosenfelt Holdings and Finance.'

'Wait, Rosenfelt Holdings? As in, billionaire Bartholomew Rosenfelt, one of New Mexico's largest land moguls? Doesn't he live in New York or New Hampshire or Delaware or some-where on the East Coast now?' She knew he hailed from the Land of Enchantment, but despite his land holdings, which counted in the upper hundreds of thousands of acres scattered all around the state, the man himself hadn't lived in New Mexico for a number of years.

'Connecticut, and yes, that would be to whom I'm refer-ring,' Hal confirmed. 'And before you ask, yes, he's currently there, not in our great state, and how do I know? Because, as luck would have it, guess who's flying into Double Eagle II tomorrow morning? Let me just tell you: One Bart himself. It's been all over the news for a week now.'

'I don't suppose you have a way of contacting this Rosenfelt fellow now, do you?' Alyssa felt her excitement sink a little at the prospect of having to wait.

'Why, Alyssa, I can't believe you underestimate my abilities. I actually have his personal cell phone number right in front of me – and no, I won't tell you how I acquired it. That's my secret. I'll text it to you now.'

'Hal, you really are the bomb. Do kids still say that?'

'Sure, let's say they do. And… it's sent.'

Alyssa's phone chimed, and she hung up and hurried back to Cord. 'Let's go. We've got a name.' To Manny, she said, 'Thanks for this! We owe you one.'

'By now you probably owe me more than one, but who's really keeping score, right?'

Alyssa laughed, and she and Cord rushed back to her Tahoe. As she performed a three-point turn, she said, 'I'm glad this is a four-wheel drive. I'm amazed that Viper was able to make it through some of this rocky terrain.'

'Maybe because of its lack of clearance, but you never even shifted out of two-wheel drive,' Cord pointed out. 'So, you going to tell me who the car is registered to, or am I just supposed to figure it out by reading your mind?'

'Rosenfelt Holdings and Finance.'

Instead of the excitement she'd expected to see, Alyssa watched as Cord cupped the back of his neck and rotated. 'Bartholomew Rosenfelt is one of the richest men in the country... any country.'

'Yeah, so? That doesn't mean he's above the law, does it? If he's somehow involved in this, well, the same punishment applies to him as it does to anyone else.'

'I'm not saying it doesn't. I'm just predicting a media hail-storm, not to mention the political fallout from the implication of the possibility of his involvement in a fourteen-year-old girl's brutal rape and murder.' She actually heard Cord's teeth grinding at the words.

She risked a glance at him before turning her attention back to the road. 'Not just rape and murder, Cord, a possible sex trafficking ring.' Keeping one hand on the wheel, she handed him her phone. 'Thanks to him working magic the way only Hal can, I've got the guy's personal number, so why don't we just call and see what he has to say?'

'Isn't he arriving in Albuquerque tomorrow anyway?'

'Am I the only one who didn't know this?'

'I just heard about it today while Sara and I were waiting for the doctor. We've been kind of busy with finding out what happened to Rachel, Jersey, and Katelyn, not to mention finding out who killed Meghan. Watching the entertainment news hasn't exactly been high on our list of priorities.'

That reminded her: she wanted to know what was wrong with Sara, and why he'd chosen to go to the doctor with his wife, who was a registered nurse.

Chapter Thirty-Two

Friday, May 24

As it turned out, they had to wait anyway since repeated attempts at reaching Bartholomew Rosenfelt failed – as had her efforts in reaching anyone within his company who may have been able to tell her who drove the Dodge Viper. Alyssa left several messages expressing the urgency of returning her calls, all to no avail. And that was why, just before eight on Friday morning, Alyssa and Cord found themselves sitting in the tiny restaurant located at Double Eagle II Airport listening to the news blasting from the tiny television mounted high on the wall in the corner while watching the privately owned planes take off and land.

'Checking your watch every thirty seconds isn't going to get his plane here any quicker, you do know that, don't you?' Cord asked as Alyssa peeked at the time – again.

'I'm not wearing a watch,' she retorted, then sighed. 'I'm just impatient.'

Her partner's jaw dropped open. 'No. You? Impatient? Wait, wait, let me work on my shocked face. Oh yeah, there it is. How's that?'

Alyssa wadded up her napkin and tossed it at Cord's face, earning her a narrow-eyed glare from the lone woman working the diner who happened to be wiping down the table right next to them. Alyssa didn't take it personally since the facial tattoos the woman wore apparently weren't the only permanent things on her; so was the scowl she'd bestowed on every customer in the place. When she stalked away to help a pilot who walked up to the counter, Alyssa whispered, 'She could *almost* give Ruby a run for her money, don't you think?'

Cord's head bobbed in agreement. 'I'd still place my bet on Ruby any day of the week and twice on Saturdays. You know, I'm not entirely unconvinced she wasn't a pitbull in her past life.'

'I'd pay good money to see her reaction to that comment.'

Eyes widening comically, her partner shook his head back and forth, his hair falling into his eyes as he did. 'I'd kick it into gear and leave the country before she could find me.'

Alyssa chuckled. 'All the gold and silver in the world couldn't take you far enough away to hide you from Ruby's wrath.'

Cord's eyes widened, and his fork clattered to the plate. 'Gold,' he whispered.

Baffled by his reaction, Alyssa stopped smiling. And then she jerked upright, her spine stiffening as what she said clicked. 'The symbol branded into Meghan Jessup's hip – it's the hermetic symbol for gold! The same *gear* that's on the Rosenfelt Holdings logo!' The second she said it, she knew they were finally closing in on more answers than questions.

Cord wiped one hand down his face as he slumped back against his chair. 'Holy...' And then he slammed his fist against the table, rattling the plates, the napkin holder, the salt and pepper shakers, and their half-empty cups of coffee. 'Damn it! It's been right there in front of us this entire time. Jesus! How could we miss that?'

A shadow fell across the window, and they both twisted in their seats in time to witness Rosenfelt's sleek Gulfstream – clearly the priciest one here – hit the tarmac with barely a bounce, showcasing the pilot's expertise. Due to Hal's research, she now knew this private luxury liner held up to fourteen passengers, had a private executive suite, a bedroom, and an extensive bar. And whenever Rosenfelt entertained guests, everyone from bartenders to toddlers was required to sign a nondisclosure agreement that would result in a massive lawsuit if said agreement was breached. In Alyssa's professional opinion, that amount of secrecy was usually only warranted when shady dealings were taking place.

Say, for instance, dabbling in the sex trafficking trade, a lucrative business for the heartless.

Alyssa took a final swallow of lukewarm coffee before heading outside to wait for one of the world's wealthiest men to disembark. At almost nine in the morning, the temperature had already soared into the low eighties, and there wasn't a single cloud in the blue sky or even a hint of a breeze to break up the heat, so when five, ten, then fifteen minutes elapsed with the plane not moving, and no one exiting the aircraft, waiting in the hot sun ate away at Alyssa's patience.

'What in the hell is he doing in there?'

'I don't know, but you need to hold onto your temper. Otherwise, we risk him clamming up immediately when he sees us.' The tightening in Cord's jaw belied his own impatience, and she wondered if he was thinking of his sister, Shelley. If she was, it stood to reason there was a good chance so was he.

When the door to the plane finally opened a couple of minutes later, the stairs whirred their way to the ground, and Bartholomew Rosenfelt descended from inside the cabin, dressed in pressed khakis and a hunter green silk shirt that even from a distance looked like it cost more than Alyssa made in two months. At the top of the steps, Rosenfelt paused, one hand still holding onto the door, surveying his surroundings, and to Alyssa, it appeared he was expecting an orchestra to announce his arrival.

She disliked him on sight.

Standing just behind Rosenfelt was Vincent Yates. According to Hal's research, Yates had been the billionaire's private pilot for close to twenty-five years. While his attire wasn't quite as snazzy as his boss's, he still sported clothes that would've taken more than one of Alyssa's paychecks to purchase. And if anyone would know about Rosenfelt's comings and goings, he would be the one, so she had every intention of cornering him, too. Before descending the steps, both men whipped out aviator sunglasses and placed them over their eyes.

Tired of being patient – well, tired of waiting, anyway – Alyssa approached the land mogul billionaire, hand outstretched to introduce herself only to have him ignore it as he removed his sunglasses and stared down at the badge sitting at her hip. After craning his neck to check that Cord also wore a badge, he popped his shades back into place.

'Albuquerque Police Department?' Rosenfelt drawled. 'Has something occurred with one of my properties that I've been as of yet uninformed?' Barely shifting his chin to the side, it was clear he was expecting a response from his pilot as well as the detectives.

'None that I'm aware of, sir.' Vincent Yates's voice was high-pitched and squeaky, not at all befitting of the man's physique.

'Detectives Wyatt and Roberts. We have some questions we'd like to ask you. Why don't we head inside where it's not so hot?'

His expression guarded, Rosenfelt lowered his glasses to the bridge of his nose and peered over them at Alyssa. 'Do I need my attorney present, Detective? As he's not traveling with me at the moment, this conversation will need to wait. If his presence is necessary, that is.'

'I can't answer that for you, Mr. Rosenfelt. You're not under arrest; we're merely hoping you can provide some answers for us. However, if you feel you can't answer those questions without an attorney present, then I suppose that's entirely up to you. Do you have something you wish to hide from us?'

Bartholomew Rosenfelt threw his head back and laughed, a deep, throaty sound. 'I think I might like you, Detective. But if I do indeed have things to hide, then I most likely wouldn't want to inform you of that fact, now would I?' He turned to his pilot. 'After she gets sprayed down, go ahead and put her in the hangar and wait for me there.'

Yates nodded and took off in the opposite direction, presumably to get one of the service attendants who worked at the small airport.

'Shall we?' Rosenfelt moved past the detectives as he led the way off the tarmac and into the lobby, strutting through as if he owned the place, proving how much clout he truly did have. Without slowing his stride in the slightest, he passed the receptionist's desk, throwing over his shoulder, 'Jenny, my usual conference room is available, I presume?'

Star-struck, eyes shining bright and fluttering her eyelashes in a movie-like caricature of a love-sick creature, Jenny rushed to assure him. 'Yes, of course. As soon as we were informed you were arriving, we made sure to have it ready in case you required it.'

Tottering on ridiculously high stilettos, she moved from behind her counter to follow him but stopped when Rosenfelt waved a hand in the air with the command, 'Be sure we're not interrupted, Jenny.'

Alyssa and Cord exchanged looks. Rosenfelt was a man who was used to being in charge and expected people to obey. Well, he was in for a surprise because she was also used to being in charge, and she was going to get answers from the man, no matter what it took.

Rosenfelt stopped at a large, ornately designed wooden door, which opened into a spacious conference room. He stepped inside and ushered Alyssa and Cord in before closing the door, crossing to a linen-covered table and pouring a glass of ice water from the pitcher perched in the middle. 'Anything for you?'

'No, thank you. I'd actually like to get down to business, if you don't mind.'

He gave a curt nod. 'Certainly. Why don't you start by telling me what this is about?' He made a show of checking the expensive Rolex on his wrist.

Alyssa didn't bother to ease into things because she wanted to see his first reaction before his mind had time to conjure up excuses. 'What can you tell me about the rape and murder of Meghan Jessup?'

One eyebrow shot up, and he frowned. 'Come again?'

'I said…'

'I know what you said, Detective. I have no idea what you're talking about. As I'm in Albuquerque, and you're with the Albuquerque Police Department, I'm going to put two and two together and assume this Meghan woman is also from here. Since I haven't been in New Mexico for more than a year, much less Albuquerque, I'm not sure why you'd think I'd have anything to do with anyone's rape and murder. And I don't mind telling you I'm a little insulted that you would assume I do.'

'Mr. Rosenfelt, Meghan Jessup was fourteen years old. And not only was she raped and murdered, she was discovered with your company's logo branded into her hip. How do you explain that?'

His hands dropped to his side, and he shook his head as if he hadn't heard correctly. 'Excuse me? When was this?'

Of course, it was possible Rosenfelt was a great actor, but to Alyssa, his shocked reaction seemed genuine. Still, she pushed. 'Tuesday, the twenty-first. Is it coming back to you?'

This time, Rosenfelt narrowed his eyes. His jaw clenched as he leveled his gaze on her. 'Detective, I assure you I had nothing to do with this young girl's rape and murder, and while I want to help you, I won't be bullied or harassed, and if you intend to continue pointing your finger at me, I'll be forced to contact my attorney which in turn will force you to wait to get answers. If that's what you want, then proceed with your barely cloaked accusations. But before you do, I want you to understand that I can either be an ally or an enemy, and it's really up to you which I am.'

Cord spoke before Alyssa could. 'Mr. Rosenfelt, security cameras spotted someone driving a 2017 red Dodge Viper removing Meghan Jessup's body from the trunk and tossing her inside an abandoned restaurant. Last night we discovered that same Viper driven off a cliff out in Rio Rancho. That Viper, sir, is registered to Rosenfelt Holdings and Finance.'

'Are you asking me a question, Detective?'

'Why would someone driving a 2017 Dodge Viper registered to your company be dumping a dead body – branded with your company logo – if you don't know anything about it?'

Fixing them both with a steady look, he said, 'I'm reaching into my pocket to grab my phone, Detectives, so I'd appreciate it if you didn't jump the gun so to speak and shoot me because you're afraid I'm reaching for a weapon.'

Despite his words, Alyssa and Cord both shifted so their hands hovered over their service pistols, relaxing them only when they saw the phone.

Rosenfelt punched in a number and brought the phone to his ear. From where she was standing, Alyssa heard the woman on the other end answer.

'Kimberly, drop whatever you're doing. I need to know who's driving the 2017 Dodge Viper in Albuquerque, and I need to know now.' His hand tapped impatiently on his sweating glass of ice water as he waited for his secretary to supply an answer. When she came back on the line, his eyes cut over to Alyssa. 'Steven Yarmini. You sure about that? Yes, I want his address and phone number. And Kimberly, this conversation is not to be discussed when I hang up. Not with anyone. Am I clear?'

Eye contact unwavering, voice firm, and a decisive nod later, he shared the information. 'Steve Yarmini is in charge of my Albuquerque holdings. His responsibilities include meeting with investors as well as scouting out acreage I may be interested in purchasing. He's been with my company for approximately four years, and to my knowledge has never given me cause to suspect him of any wrongdoing, much less something of this heinous nature. That being said, you claim to have seen the car he drives at the scene of the crime and later discovered it at the bottom of a cliff. And while I may be many unsavory things to certain people in this world, and my methods may not always be met with approval, one thing I will not be accused of is rape and murder. And if someone in my employ is guilty, I, along with my company, will do what it takes to bring that person to justice. On the other hand, I assure you, if my employee proves to be innocent, in the wrong place at the wrong time, I, along with my company, will provide counsel and fight the charges.'

Alyssa heard everything he said, but what had her mind buzzing was that Steven Yarmini was responsible for scouting out acreage. If Rachel, Jersey and, Katelyn – and others, if Lorna Price was correct – were being held somewhere, he might know where. A wave of urgency gave emphasis to her words. 'I appreciate that, Mr. Rosenfelt' – her gaze flickered to Cord and back – 'but if Yarmini *is* involved, he may be in deeper than rape and murder. He may be involved in a sex trafficking ring.'

All color blanched from Rosenfelt's face as he set his jaw. 'Then why are you still standing here, Detective? Why aren't you out there finding him?'

–

The forty-minute drive from Double Eagle II Airport to the foothills of Albuquerque took Alyssa just under half the time because she ran her lights and siren, turning them off only as she neared the neighborhood. Still, Joe and Tony had already arrived by the time she finally rolled to a stop in front of a house that was concealed behind two massive boulders and tucked up a long, hidden driveway. But before she and Cord could climb out of the car, her phone rang. A quick glance showed her it was Joe. She hit the speaker on her Bluetooth screen.

'We just pulled up, Joe. What's happening?'

A frustrated sigh filled the air before Joe answered. 'It appears we're too late. Yarmini's already cleared out.'

'What?'

'When no one answered the door, Tony and I took a peek inside one of the windows. The place is dark, but there was still enough light to see that it was in disarray, like someone left in a hurry.'

Alyssa pounded one fist on her steering wheel as she cursed. 'Damn it, damn it, damn it! Okay, I'll see you in a second.' She didn't wait for a response before she ended the call and shot a quick glance over to Cord. The tight lines around his mouth told her he was as infuriated as she was with the news. Together, they climbed out of the car, and when she closed her door, it was with more force than was necessary.

If she hadn't already been convinced that Bartholomew Rosenfelt's employee was somehow involved, she was now. She yanked her phone from her pocket and dialed Hal. 'I need another search warrant,' Alyssa said as soon as he answered. Then after rattling off the address, she and Cord met up with Joe and Tony and then waited until the evidence technicians arrived so they could go through and process the house.

Chapter Thirty-Three

The pungent odor of her own vomit assaulted Rachel's senses as she gripped the sides of the toilet bowl and emptied the contents of her stomach. Just outside the door, Becca and Faye whispered, but what they said escaped her because all she could hear in her mind were the words of the man who'd delivered their food this morning.

He'd come downstairs, whistling, an ear-to-ear smile stretching across his face, his soulless eyes gleaming with his news. 'Well, girls,' he'd said, 'you'd better enjoy the next few hours because tonight or tomorrow, you'll be back to work in The Toybox. And from what I hear, we've had some pretty impatient clients.' And then he'd laughed, rubbing his fingers against his thumb in the universal sign of 'money, money, money.'

And then he'd unlocked the cell, set the tray of cheese, crackers, and water inside, relocked the door, and headed back upstairs, this time laughing as he sang the lines to, 'Don't Worry, Be Happy.' And that was when Rachel had leapt up and raced to the bathroom.

Too weak to move, she chose to lie on the cold tile floor instead of trying to crawl back to her mattress. A fine sheen of sweat broke out on her skin, and she shivered.

She couldn't survive another trip to The Toybox, the twisted den with a childlike name that held nothing but a horrific menagerie of cruel instruments all neatly organized in The

Toolbox. She didn't want to survive. Tears leaked from the corners of her eyes, and then she was gasping for air as sobs shook her entire body.

How long she lay there, howling in frustration and helplessness, she wasn't sure, but she finally allowed Becca and Faye to help her up and guide her back to her mattress where they covered her in a sheet before settling themselves next to her. Even as they comforted her, Rachel noticed how Jersey and Cheyenne cocooned themselves around Katelyn as the younger girl sat with her back against the wall, her arms wrapped around her knees as she rocked back and forth, her eyes closed tightly.

Rachel wished she could go to her, help comfort her, but how did any of them go about protecting her from what was to come? They couldn't escape this nightmare, and they couldn't save Katelyn from the grips of the evil that awaited her.

So, no one spoke. Even as the shadows in the cell darkened, they remained silent, lost in their own fears. What was left to say?

Instead, they listened, jumping at every unexpected noise, their hearts pounding at the prolonged periods of quiet. And they watched the door at the top of the stairs, willing it to stay closed a little longer and wondering how any of them had allowed themselves to foolishly hope they'd be spared further torture.

Chapter Thirty-Four

By the time Alyssa and Cord made it back to the precinct, she was in a full rage at having not only hit the proverbial brick wall, but completely crashing into it. Steve Yarmini was on the run, and right now, she was putting the blame squarely on Bartholomew Rosenfelt's shoulders because if he had answered her calls, had they obtained Yarmini's address last night, they may have gotten to him in time. Instead, she'd had to rely on obtaining a search warrant to go through Yarmini's home, only to come out empty-handed there, as well.

From the obvious disarray of the man's house, the way clothes were strewn about his room as if he'd grabbed whatever he could, and anything that fell was left behind, it was clear he'd left in a hurry. There was a chance he might've slipped through their grasp anyway, but she didn't know that, and so she chose to blame the man's boss.

Not to mention that the surveillance team outside Hotel Camino had reported nothing but the usual one-hour comings and goings of the clientele they were known for. No young girls had been brought in and stolen out, drugged or otherwise.

Her expression thunderous, Alyssa's path to the conference room was clear as Cord followed in her wake. She was disappointed the door was already open because she really wanted to slam it against something. Instead, she settled for tossing her phone onto the table, feeling both better and worse when it slid off and landed on the floor.

Hal had something projected on the screen, and before Alyssa could ask, he told her what it was. 'Here's that list of missing persons ranging from thirteen to twenty-one you asked for earlier. There were 183 females reported missing in New Mexico this year. Roughly one-third of those were under the age of fifteen and taken by a parent; approximately two-thirds of those left are runaways. Of the remaining individuals on the list, more than half fell outside the age limit parameters you requested or were already located, leaving the number that we're going to need to look into at around fourteen.'

'God, why can't Liz be back now? We could use all the help we can get.'

'Well,' Hal said, 'I can't help with that, but what I have done is divide the fourteen girls into sections of the state from where they went missing, and I've already started cross-referencing data from this list to that of Meghan Jessup, Rachel Otis, Jersey Andrews, and Katelyn Phillipson.'

'Any luck so far?'

'Not yet.'

'There has to be something. We need to find it.' She was interrupted by her phone ringing, and it took her a second to realize it was still on the floor. Cord bent over and retrieved it, passing it her way before going back to help Hal.

Alyssa glanced down and saw Leigh Ann's name flashing on her screen. Why would her daughter's friend be calling her? All the blood rushed from her face as the thought that something had happened to Holly filled her head.

'Leigh Ann? What's going on? Has something happened with Holly?'

Cord's head snapped in her direction, his eyes boring into hers as he waited.

'Holly? No, not that I know of. Why?'

A rush of air escaped Alyssa's lungs, and as the fear lifted, she felt almost weightless. 'What can I help you with then?' The tension visibly fell away when Cord heard that Holly – who he knew had a very well-known 'secret' crush on him – wasn't in danger.

A nervous titter escaped Leigh Ann. 'Um, I have something important to tell you, and I think I'm going to be in trouble, and I don't want to go to jail...'

Alyssa waited... and waited some more. Then biting back her frustration, she employed her *mom-detective* voice. 'Leigh Ann, I can't help you unless you tell me.'

'I didn't do... do... anything. Well, I kind of did. But.' Alyssa heard Leigh Ann suck in a deep breath before blurting out her purpose for calling. 'I was at the same frat party where that girl went missing? Rachel Otis?'

Of all the things she could've guessed might fall from the lips of her daughter's friend, this was nowhere on the list, and Alyssa went still, blinking several times to make sure she'd heard correctly. 'What were you doing at a frat party?'

'I was trying to see where I'd fit in when classes start this fall, and I know I shouldn't have been there. Please, please don't tell my mom,' she implored.

Somehow, through the red haze that filled her mind at the fact that her daughter's friend was just now coming forward with this information, Alyssa was able to temper her voice... for now. 'Did you see something, Leigh Ann, that night? Something that would help us locate Rachel?'

'I don't know,' she whispered. 'But I can't keep his secret anymore. It's just not right.'

The words were spoken low, as if they weren't meant for Alyssa to hear. 'Whose secrets, Leigh Ann? Who are you keeping secrets for?'

'Jersey's boyfriend.'

Alyssa stiffened. 'You're keeping secrets for Beau Cambridge?' Again, Cord's head snapped up, his face freezing into a mask of hardness as he abandoned any pretense of assisting Hal and openly listened to Alyssa's end of the conversation.

'Yes, ma'am. I mean, no, not really *for* him. I mean, I don't even think he knows I know.'

'Then what secrets did you mean you've been keeping?' Alyssa was finding it harder to keep the anger and impatience out of her voice. The lives of at least three girls, and probably more, hung in the balance. If Leigh Ann knew something, if Beau Cambridge was involved, she needed to know right now. Actually, she needed to know five days ago.

'He was there that night, too.'

Alyssa's pulse doubled in speed. 'You weren't there together?'

'What? No! No, of course not. I'd *never* do that to Jersey. Never! I told you I don't even think he knows I was there.' Leigh Ann blew her nose before continuing. 'I don't remember what time it was, but I was starting to feel uncomfortable and guilty for being there, and so I was about to leave. And that was when I saw him. He was in the kitchen talking to Rachel. Actually, she didn't really look like she wanted to be talking to him, you know. To be honest, she kind of looked frightened of him.

'I mean, not at first. The truth is, I watched them for a while. I mean, I was shocked to see Jersey's boyfriend there at all, especially with another girl, you know. I was going to snap a picture to have proof, but I was afraid he'd see me.

'Anyway, she – Rachel – seemed annoyed. And then she kind of put her hands up between them, like she was pushing him away, but he just leaned in. I thought he was going to kiss her or something, and then someone bumped into his back, and that's when Rachel escaped. And then I left before Beau saw me.'

'Why didn't you tell me this days ago, Leigh Ann?' This time, her anger did seep through.

'I was afraid of getting into trouble myself, and then when Jersey went missing, I knew Holly and Sophie would be so mad… and I was just afraid.'

'What did Beau do when Rachel walked away?'

'What do you mean?'

'I mean, what did he do? Did he go after her? Did he get angry? Grab at her?'

'Well, um, he watched her, I guess. And yeah, he seemed a bit pissed, but he didn't follow her or anything. Not that I know of anyway. Like I said, I left right after that.' Leigh Ann swallowed audibly. 'Am I in trouble for withholding evidence? Do you have to tell Holly?'

'I don't tell my family about my ongoing investigations, Leigh Ann. But my advice to you is that you need to come clean with both Holly and Sophie because when they find out you knew and withheld this information – and they will find out somehow, I'm sure – they're going to be understandably upset and hurt. You need to try to fix the damage now. It'll only get worse the longer you wait.'

'I know. You're right. It's just they're going to be so mad at me. I guess I deserve it though.'

Alyssa didn't have time to reassure the girl, especially when she was pretty pissed herself. 'Is that everything you wanted to tell me, Leigh Ann?'

After a brief pause, Leigh Ann admitted, 'There *is* one more thing. So, the other day, when Beau came over to your house – I'm sure Holly told you about that – the reason I invited him in was because I wanted to see if he was truly distraught over Jersey's disappearance or just pretending.' She snorted. 'Like I'm some kind of detective or something, right?'

Alyssa clenched her teeth, unclenching them only when a burning pain radiated through her lower jaw. She was still upset that Beau had been at her house with Holly and her friends while she and Cord had been trying to locate him in order to question him about his possible connection with Meghan Jessup.

She pushed her anger aside for the moment. 'Leigh Ann, listen to me. I want you to stay away from Beau. I wish you'd told me all this sooner, but at least you're telling me now.' What

Alyssa really wanted to say was *If Beau is involved, and we could've saved these girls that much sooner, it's on you.*

'I know you're disappointed and even mad at me for not coming forward earlier, but I was afraid, you know.'

At some point, Cord had begun pacing, stopping only when Alyssa said goodbye.

'What's going on?' His voice was tight, controlled.

'I'll tell you on the way, but right now, it's time we bring Beau in for questioning.'

It took them less than twenty minutes to reach Beau Cambridge's house, and only when they'd pulled into the drive, blocking his Jeep in, did Alyssa consider whether or not it was a good idea for Cord to have come along. Maybe it would've been wiser to have Joe or Tony meet her here.

But it was too late now, so together they climbed out of the Tahoe and approached the house, ignoring the doorbell in favor of pounding on the front door.

Chapter Thirty-Five

Friday, May 24

Ninety minutes later, Beau Cambridge sat in the chair across the table from Alyssa and Cord in the smallest interrogation room they had. It wasn't the room Alyssa would've chosen – especially given her concerns about Cord's potential volatility – but it was what was available, and the closet-like atmosphere seemed to intimidate Jersey's boyfriend far more than the detectives did. She was okay with that. Whatever worked.

Sweat dripped down his forehead, splashing into his eyes, and every few seconds, he reached up to wipe it off. Though his posture indicated he was cool, calm, and collected, the physical evidence pouring off him stated otherwise.

Alyssa scooted her chair in closer, purposely crowding into Beau's space. As she did, she saw Cord's fists clenched in his lap, but aside from the ticcing in his jaw that told her he was holding onto his temper by a fine thread, his face remained impassive. 'So, Beau, let's play a game, shall we?'

He blinked but otherwise remained quiet, so Alyssa continued. 'Let's say you're at a frat party, and…'

Beau's face paled at *frat party*. 'I won't be hitting college until August, so what would I be doing attending a frat party?'

'That's a great question. What *would* you be doing at a frat party? Yet, I have witnesses who not only put you at one, they put you at *the* one. You know the one where a girl went missing. You might've heard her name. Rachel Otis?'

Looking smug, he crossed his arms over his chest. 'You're lying. No one there knew me, and I didn't even know I was going. I was just cruising the area when I saw the party and decided to crash it.'

Alyssa remained silent and stared, waiting for Beau to catch his own blunder. It took him about ten seconds.

Immediately, he began squirming in his seat, his head snapping back and forth until he realized what he was doing. 'Who saw me?' he asked weakly.

She almost told him to gauge his reaction, but it was clear he hadn't seen Leigh Ann. 'So, for the record, you're admitting you were at the frat party, Saturday, May 18?'

The way his eyes darted all over the room, Alyssa knew the wheels were spinning as he tried to decide the ramifications of copping to the truth. 'Okay, listen, I was there, but I swear I don't know anything about a missing girl. I don't even know anyone by that name you said.'

'Rachel Otis disappeared from a party you attended a day before your own girlfriend went missing near the same area. Pretty coincidental, don't you think?'

Beau again wiggled in his chair. His left eye twitched, and his head jerked toward the door as if he was making sure no one else was listening. 'Like I said the other day, I don't know where Jersey is. I swear to God.' Right hand up, he lifted two fingers in the traditional Boy Scout oath. As if he were the epitome of a Boy Scout. Fingers still in the air, he added, 'Hell, maybe the two are off together. Has anyone thought of that?'

'Funny you should mention that, Beau, because not only have we thought of that, we happen to think the same thing. It's where they are that we'd like to know.'

Perspiration beaded on Beau's lips as his eyes widened. 'Wait just a second. That was a joke, lady. I was kidding.'

Despite the temper brewing just below the surface, Cord's next words were posed in a calm manner. 'See, here's the thing, Beau; like Detective Wyatt said, witnesses place you at this party. More importantly, they say you were talking to Rachel, who suddenly dropped off the face of the planet after that party.

According to these witnesses, you put the moves on Rachel, and she turned you down flat. Now, I'm thinking to myself: a big, handsome guy like you doesn't like to get rejected, especially in front of a group of people. You get pissed. You decide to do something about it. And then the next day, your girlfriend does the same thing, rejects your kinky fantasy, and now that's two rejections in a couple days, and you snap. Decide to make Jersey pay...'

Beau jerked upright in his chair, palms out to stop Cord from continuing. 'Whoa, whoa, whoa. Yes, I admitted to being at the party. I even admit to talking to some girl – whose name I never found out by the way – but when she walked away, that was that. I moved on. I swear to God I didn't do anything to her. Or Jersey.' Sweat trickled down the side of his face, and he reached up to wipe it off.

'You can see why we're finding it a little bit difficult to see how it's just coincidental that you happened to have direct contact with two missing girls, both within a day of each other, right?' Again, Alyssa scooted her chair an inch closer.

His face sheet-white, Beau's eyes cut to the door and back, and one leg bounced up and down. Alyssa pressed harder. 'How often do you travel to Santa Fe?'

Blinking rapidly, he said, 'What?'

'Were you dating Meghan Jessup from Santa Fe? You know she was only fourteen?' Before he had time to process that, she dropped another bomb. 'I think there's a name for that.' She peered over at Cord. 'Statutory rape, right? Punishable by up to eighteen months and a $5000 fine?'

Cord's eyes remained steady on Beau until the kid looked away, blanching at Cord's response. 'Sounds right. Unless it was forced. Then, you know, we're talking a lot more prison time.'

Beau's hands dropped to hang at his side as his head swiveled between Cord and Alyssa. Then he pressed his palms onto his knees as if he was attempting to keep them steady. 'Am I under arrest here? Do I need a lawyer?'

It was Alyssa's turn to shrug. 'You're not under arrest. Yet. And have you done something that would require an attorney?'

Instant red flushed his face as he banged one fist on the table. 'No. I didn't do anything! How many times do I have to tell you that? Yeah, sure, I was at the party.'

Alyssa remained quiet in the hopes that she'd given him enough rope to hang himself.

'And yeah, I talked to that girl, Rachel, but I had nothing to do with her going missing. Nothing! Lots of guys were there that night, and a hot girl like her could've hooked up with any of them. And just because I spent a few minutes passing conversation with her doesn't mean I did something to her.'

'If you'd heard she went missing, why didn't you contact us? Maybe you could've cleared up a few questions and saved yourself the trouble of having to come down here. Surely you knew we'd eventually figure out that you not only had a connection with two, but three missing girls. One of whom is now dead.'

'Wait a minute, I never said I knew that other girl!' A cross between anger and disbelief etched across the features of Beau's face. 'Wait! Am I suspect in murder now? And if I am, why aren't you arresting me, and why did you say I didn't need a lawyer?'

'I didn't say you didn't need a lawyer, Beau,' Alyssa corrected. 'I asked if *you* thought you needed one.' She hoped the reminder wouldn't encourage him to use what limited brain cells he had and require that attorney, but she had a feeling this interrogation was about to come to a screeching halt before they got any real answers.

And she was right. Beau swallowed, nodded once, and then lawyered up. 'I'm not saying anything else until I talk to my lawyer. I didn't do anything, and if you guys really want to know what happened to these girls, you need to stop wasting your time harassing me.' He stood. 'Am I free to go or am I under arrest?'

Alyssa really wanted to say he was under arrest, but unfortunately, they didn't have enough to hold him. She, too, rose to her feet. 'You're free to go. But don't stray from Albuquerque, Beau, in case we need to ask you more questions.' At the door, she paused before opening it. 'And if you happen to think of anything you might've forgotten to tell us, you might want to make sure you give us a call before someone else tells us. Otherwise, we might consider that obstruction to justice.' She opened the door, just in time to see Mr. Cambridge storming their way.

'What the hell is going on here?' he roared, his words coming out with a mouthful of spray.

'Our job is what's going on. We had some questions for your son, so he agreed to come down to the precinct so we could formally ask those questions.'

'He already told you where he was when that slut went missing!'

'Which "slut" would that be, Mr. Cambridge? Jersey Andrews? Or Rachel Otis? In case you're keeping count, that's *at least* two girls.' Alyssa held up two fingers, watching his reaction to the news. 'At least two girls your son has "coincidentally" been in contact with shortly before they disappeared.'

The color in his face surpassed red and stormed into purple. His voice surprisingly controlled and even, Mr. Cambridge said, 'The next time you want to talk to my son for any reason, you better have an arrest warrant in hand. And even if you don't, we demand his attorney be present.' Before stalking away, he reached out and squeezed his son's arm, shoving him in front of him. As he stormed off, Alyssa heard him berate Beau. 'Are you stupid? Where the hell is your head?' The remainder of his words were lost as he rounded the corner, but she had a pretty fair idea of how that conversation would play anyway.

Chapter Thirty-Six

Friday, May 24

Late Friday night, Holly studied herself in the full-length mirror in the corner of her room. The pants that fit her nicely just last week now hung a little looser on her hips, held up by a belt she'd had to tighten by notching it an extra space over. Her cheekbones were sharper and more pronounced, and even though, on a normal summer break, she'd already be sporting a nice sun-kissed tan, right now her skin had taken on the pallor of someone who'd never gotten a dose of external Vitamin D.

Her rapid weight loss wasn't only a result of her stress over Jersey disappearing; she'd also made up her mind *not* to attend Cornell University when August rolled around. And the thought of telling her parents zapped any remaining appetite she might've had.

Ultimately, it was her decision to make, but the nerves in her stomach spasmed at the very idea of disappointing her dad, who she knew was going to take the news like a physical blow to the gut. Everyone in her family, of course, had been thrilled when she'd received her acceptance letter to the Ivy League school, but her dad? He'd been *so* proud – no, not just proud – boastful was a more apt description. He bragged unselfconsciously about her accomplishments to his friends, his colleagues, his subcontractors, even the servers at their favorite restaurants. Honestly, it was all a bit embarrassing, not to mention the amount of pressure she'd felt at anticipating having to succeed at every single point in her college career – but she hadn't had the heart to ask her dad to stop. After all, she was only going to be home for a few more months.

Until that first tiny whisper of a thought had nudged her while she slept. And when she woke, the nudge had grown into a push and then into a full-out shove.

And sure, her mom would be concerned about Holly's choice, and she would most certainly fall into what Holly liked to describe as *mom-detective* mode in that she'd question every minute detail as to how Holly had come to this decision, but she was prepared with her answers. And just like her mom, once her teeth sank into something, she was superglued to it, and it would take a Herculean amount of force to change her mind. So, she knew that once her mom understood not only why she'd made such a momentous change to her future plans (without first discussing it with her family) but that she'd truly thought through every angle, her mom would become her biggest champion.

More importantly, she would plow through anyone else's disgruntled attitudes about it. And by everyone else, she meant Grandma and Dad.

Which was a good thing because once her mind had been firmly set on the new course, she'd placed a call to the admissions office and set a meeting date with the registrar of the University of New Mexico. Instead of becoming a Big Red Bear of Ithaca, New York, she'd be a howling Lobo in Albuquerque, New Mexico.

Not only would this allow her to remain close to home with her family at only a twenty-minute drive away from the dorms, she'd also get to hang out with Sophie as opposed to Skyping or viewing each other's Instagram posts.

Thinking of needing to be there for Sophie deflated Holly. *Jersey*. Moisture pooled in the corners of her eyes, making it difficult to see as the tears spilled over, streaking her carefully applied make-up. If someone had told her even a week ago she'd *ever* miss – crave, even – her friend's drama-filled, angst-ridden personality, she would've laughed in that person's face, maybe even accused her of being on some serious mind-altering drugs.

Yet, here she stood, praying she could turn around to find Jersey curled up on the futon nestled under Holly's window bawling about all the things Jersey liked to cry over. Even if that was Beau.

Beau. Asshat of a boyfriend. Armpit of humanity.

Like a light switch had been flicked, Holly's tears were replaced with blinding anger, and the face staring back at her in the mirror was now suffused with a red so deep, she appeared to be on the verge of a stroke.

Late that afternoon, Leigh Ann had sent her and Sophie a text claiming she needed to tell them something, but she was afraid. Sophie, still holding a grudge that Leigh Ann had fallen into the trap of feeling sorry for Beau, had snapped off a less than friendly, far from encouraging, response.

> **SOPHIE**
> Why would you be afraid to tell us something... unless you're about to admit to banging one of your supposedly best friend's boyfriends while she's missing?

Ouch. Holly's own response had been less scathing and combatant.

> **HOLLY**
> Whatever it is, you can tell us.

It was five minutes before Leigh Ann responded, her admission robbing breath from Holly's lungs.

You know that girl Rachel who went missing from the frat party? Well, I was there that night, too... long story... I'll tell you why later if you're still talking to me... Anyway, I saw Beau hitting on her before I left. I'm sorry I kept it a secret, but I was afraid to tell you. I told Holly's mom today what I saw. I hope you two can forgive me.

Ten seconds later, Holly's phone rang. Where she'd been left speechless, Sophie was in a full rage.

'What the actual HELL does she mean "if we're still talking to her"? What if he did something to Jersey *and* that Rachel girl? What if this nightmare could've been over days ago if she'd just told your mom right away? If she'd told us! And what the hell was she doing at a frat party to begin with? Was she *with* Beau? Maybe they're both involved! What if—'

Holly cut her best friend off. 'Sophie, come on. We might be mad at her right now, but really, Leigh Ann and Beau? She's the patient one among us. Do you really think she'd do that to Jersey?'

Sophie snorted. 'I didn't think she'd withhold information that might help us find Jersey. And why is she telling your mom now? Unless she thinks Beau's involved somehow? And if she's afraid Beau's involved, why would she *invite him into your house?*' By the end of her rant, she was screaming, forcing Holly to hold the phone away from her ear.

Tears of frustration sprang to her eyes. Sophie was right. 'I don't know,' she whispered.

'Well, I don't know about you, but I'm done with her. Done. This goes beyond a simple betrayal. I mean, what if she really is protecting him?'

If Leigh Ann knew something more, would she really have held it in this long? Holly wanted to say no, but after this bombshell, she didn't know what to believe anymore.

An image of the third girl flashed in her mind, and she gasped. 'Oh my gosh, Sophie, the thirteen-year-old who just went missing. She lived near Jersey, right?' Was Beau another Evan Bishop? Was he capable of something that evil? The blood drained from her face so fast, dizziness slammed into her, forcing her to sink onto her bed before she fell.

Sophie's gasp mimicked her own. 'Do you think your mom knows? What am I saying? Of course, she does. What does all this mean?' Her best friend's voice wobbled. 'What if she really is…?' She couldn't finish the word neither of them wanted to think.

'I wish my mom could tell me what's going on, beyond what's on the news already.'

'Me, too. Listen, my mom is at Aunt Natalia's again, and I'm going to head over there for a while. Do you want me to swing by and pick you up and we can go together?'

For a brief second, Holly toyed with the idea, but decided not to. 'Thanks, but I think I'm going to tell Mom and Dad tonight about my decision to attend UNM instead of Cornell.'

'Wow. Do you want me to come over there instead, give you moral support? I can go to Aunt Natalia's after.'

'Thanks, but I think I need to do this on my own. I'll call you later and let you know how it goes. Hug your mom and aunt for me.' After they ended their conversation, Holly's thoughts returned to Jersey and Beau.

Had Jersey contacted him that night like Holly, Sophie, and Leigh Ann suspected she would? Had Beau picked her up? Had he tried to force her to give in to his demands and they'd fought again? Had things gotten so out of hand he'd…

Holly's stomach twisted itself into a pretzel, but she forced herself to concentrate, to think like her mom might, which was what she'd been doing, up until about half an hour ago.

Downstairs, the door from the garage to the house banged open followed by her mom's tired voice as she greeted her dad. Inhaling deeply, Holly decided that, despite the late hour and the fact that her mother was just now getting home from a long day at work, now was as good a time as any to drop the bombshell that studying criminology was exactly what she was supposed to do with her life.

She took one last look in the mirror, whispered, 'You can do this,' to her image and then headed down to break the news. Entering the kitchen quietly, she pressed her back into the counter and rubbed her neck nervously. When she realized she was bouncing on the balls of her feet and that her mom was now staring at her from the corner of her eye, she tried to stop. And when her mom turned her way, that knowing, steady stare of hers drilling in, Holly did her best to avoid direct eye contact.

Her mom shot one quick glance her dad's way and then focused once more on Holly.

'I'm guessing whatever it is you're trying to work up the nerve to say, neither your father nor I are going to like. So, you may as well spill it and get it over with. Like ripping off a Band-Aid.'

Holly intertwined her fingers to avoid wringing her hands. Avoiding her father's eyes, she finally blurted it out. 'I'm not going to Cornell.' Her gaze bounced from her father's open-mouthed reaction before settling on her mother's more startled, but less crushed face. She steam-plowed forward. 'I already spoke to the admissions officer at UNM, and she doesn't think there's any reason I won't be able to start in the fall with all the other freshmen.'

Her dad just barely managed to lift his chin from the floor even as the color faded from his face. 'Baby, you worked awfully hard to get into Cornell. Why would you toss this opportunity out the window like that?'

'Is this because of your brother?' her mom asked.

Holly tipped her head forward and shrugged her shoulders. Then, realizing that seemed like she was still unsure of her decision, she straightened up. 'Yes, partly. Well, not *because of* Isaac. But, yeah, because of what happened. But that's not the only reason.

'It's also due, in part, to Jersey's disappearance.' She focused her attention on her mom, knowing the hurt in her dad's eyes could easily derail her. 'I've been trying to look at this from several different angles, like you would. And maybe Beau is as innocent as he proclaims. Maybe he's not. Leigh Ann sent Sophie and me a text this afternoon, by the way, telling us what she told you.' The tightening around her mother's mouth was the only indication that she was affected by what Holly said.

'The bottom line is,' she continued, 'I want to study criminology. And before you ask, yes, I'm sure. In fact, I'm more certain about this than any other career choice I've ever considered in the past.' This time she turned pleading eyes her father's way. She *needed* him to understand, to support her decision, to *not* be absolutely crushed by her choice.

'I've already picked out my course of study. And I know you're both probably very disappointed, especially you, Dad, because I know how proud of me you are. But I hope you can understand *this* is where I belong. Not New York.' An impish grin tilted up one corner of her mouth. 'Besides, you should be happy I chose a school where I don't have to buy a whole new wardrobe to match the school colors. UNM and Cornell both wear red.'

'Cherry,' her dad automatically corrected. 'Lobos wear cherry.'

Though he hadn't said it in as many words, Holly knew her father had accepted her decision. Her shoulders sagged down, the tension releasing as the weight of telling her parents lifted.

Even though he couldn't completely hide his disappointment, her dad said, 'It's hard to argue against my baby girl staying close to home where I can see her far more easily and often.' Then he cocked his head and narrowed his gaze. 'You *are* planning on coming around more than just holidays, right?'

Holly laughed, the sound light. 'Of course, Dad. I'll be around so much you'll wonder if I even left for college at all.' It was a lie, and they all knew it, but it did the trick as her dad wrapped her in a hug and kissed the top of her head.

231

Her mom, however, wasn't quite finished. 'I may not like it, but I'll honor your choice. I can tell you've already considered what a huge commitment this will be, and your decision to stay here and attend UNM will have lifelong consequences, whether negative, positive, or a combination of both. So, if you've truly considered all the options and come to this conclusion as your path in life for now, Dad and I will support that choice and do what we can to help.'

Holly practically flew into her mom's arms. 'Thanks, Mom.'

'You're welcome. Besides, it's kind of nice knowing that my very bright, courageous, beautiful, strong-willed daughter is going to follow in her mother's footsteps.'

As Holly stepped back, she saw there was no hint of worry in her mom's face. Instead, it was filled with a glow she hadn't seen in a long time – or at least not since April when Isaac had been kidnapped.

Seeing that, Holly was suffused with warmth, like she'd been out in a sub-zero freeze and was now standing in front of a toasty, blazing fire.

'But you tell Grandma,' her mom and dad said at the same time, laughing when they realized they'd been holding onto the same thought.

Chapter Thirty-Seven

Saturday, May 25

At two-thirty in the morning, Alyssa's phone woke her. Groggy, she fumbled blindly for it until she groped it with her hand, pulling it to her head which still rested on her pillow. 'Hello?' Raspiness made her sound like she was catching a cold.

'Detective Wyatt?'

All Alyssa could tell from the tremulous voice on the other end of the line was that it was female, and she jerked up, fully awake as she crawled out of bed. 'Yes, this is she. Who is this?'

'This is Lorna Price from Hotel Camino. I came to see—'

'I remember. Are the men you mentioned there right now?' Even as she spoke, she tugged off the t-shirt she'd fallen asleep in and replaced it with a fresh one from the closet. With the phone secured between her ear and her shoulder, she dragged on the first pair of jeans her hands touched. From her dresser, she pulled out a pair of socks, not caring what kind or color. She debated waking Brock to let him know she was heading out, but found he was already awake, watching her carefully as she moved quickly around their bedroom. She lifted a hand, mouthed, 'Gotta run. Love you,' and then raced down the stairs.

'Not exactly,' Lorna answered. 'But there's another guy here. I forgot about him, but I'm pretty sure he was with that girl who was killed.' If it was possible for her to speak any lower, she managed. 'I saw him trying to get into one of the rooms even though he's not a guest. I pretended I was taking out the trash, and I took a picture in case it helps.'

Alyssa felt her heart drop to her stomach. 'Lorna, listen to me. I want you to lock the front door.' She waited until she heard a click. 'Now, can you still see him from where you are?'

'Yes, but now he's just looking around.'

'What's he's driving? Can you see that?' Alyssa climbed into her Tahoe and backed out of the garage.

'No. The only cars in the parking lot are the ones that were here when I got to work. Should I go out—'

'No! No, stay where you are. I want you to stay on the phone with me and tell me what you see but stay where you are. Okay?'

This time Lorna's voice was filled with panic. 'He's coming to the door. What do I do?'

Alyssa pressed the accelerator. 'Get inside the office and lock it. I'll be there as quickly as I can.'

'He's rattling the door. What if he gets in?'

Where was the surveillance team that was supposed to be posted outside? Alyssa's heart rate tripled, but somehow she managed to keep her voice calm. 'Lorna, listen to me. You have an office phone, right?'

'Yes.'

'Don't hang up now, but I want you to use that other phone and dial nine-one-one, tell them you've got me on the line, but you need a unit sent to Hotel Camino immediately. Tell them I told you to request no lights or sirens. Do that now.'

She listened as Lorna spoke to Dispatch, and when she said, 'I don't see him at the door anymore. I don't see him anywhere,' Alyssa didn't know if Lorna was informing her or the dispatcher. Either way, she had a feeling she was too late.

Twelve minutes later, she pulled into the parking lot of Hotel Camino and parked next to one of the squad cars, ending the call with Lorna after telling her to stay inside. The lights in the office were blazing, and despite several broken streetlamps, the parking area was well-lit, making it easy to see there was no one there. 'Damn it.' She climbed out of the car at the same time as one of the officers, and together they approached a second officer.

'I just checked the perimeter. Saw a couple homeless gals asleep behind that dumpster back there, but that's it. No sign of anyone else. He must've been spooked when he saw our cars.'

'Thanks. I'm going to head inside and talk to the receptionist.' She dialed Lorna back. 'This is Detective Wyatt. Can you unlock the door for me?'

'Is he out there? What if he sees me and figures out I'm the one who called the police?'

Angry not only at the fact that the mystery man had slipped through her fingers, but that the surveillance Hammond had approved was nowhere to be found, Alyssa wanted to snap that the young woman couldn't hide in the office forever. But not only was it not her fault, she'd called Alyssa immediately when she spotted someone suspicious. She'd done exactly as Alyssa had asked, even though she'd clearly been frightened already. It wasn't Lorna's fault someone on the police force had failed in his or her job.

'You'll be okay. I'll make sure a couple of officers stay behind until you're off your shift, okay?' Even as she said it, Alyssa vowed that someone's head was going to roll for this blunder.

A minute later, the same terrified look on her face as the one she'd worn the day she'd shown up at the precinct, Lorna unlocked the door and stepped back for Alyssa to join her. Scurrying back behind the counter as if it provided more safety, the woman retrieved the phone she'd set down, tapped a few buttons, and handed it to Alyssa.

It was the photo she'd snapped. The image wasn't as dark as Alyssa had suspected it would be, but it was grainy because Lorna had zoomed in and taken it from a distance. Still, there was enough detail there to show that the man, dressed in gym shorts, was probably thirty-something. Something about him seemed familiar, and it took a second for her to figure out what it was.

The man in the photograph shared the same height and physique as the one who'd removed Meghan Jessup from the trunk of a sporty 2017 Dodge Viper and tossed her body in an abandoned restaurant. She was getting a better look at Steve Yarmini, and he'd slipped through her fingers for the second time in less than twenty-four hours.

'Detective?' A man's voice came up from behind her, and Alyssa turned to see a plainclothes officer she'd seen around the precinct from time to time. Though she couldn't recall his name, she knew immediately who he was.

Bullets were slower than the anger that erupted from her. Through clenched teeth, she said, 'Weren't you supposed to be surveilling this hotel?'

The smile fell from the officer's face. 'Yes, ma'am. But I had to use the restroom, and since nothing was going on…'

'The *nothing that was going on*,' she exploded, 'was that the man we believe is responsible for dumping and possibly murdering a fourteen-year-old girl was not only here, in this parking lot, but doing his best at attempting to break into one of the rooms, not to mention trying to get into the front office. No thanks to you, I was able to convince the receptionist to lock the door and secure herself in the office. And now our suspect is gone. And do you know *why* he's gone?' Each word brought her closer to the officer who somehow managed to stand his ground without backing up. Her finger jabbed at his chest, coming close but not quite making physical contact. 'He's gone because you weren't doing your job!

'And where was your partner? Huh? Why didn't you have back-up?'

His face red from the dressing-down he was receiving, he admitted the truth. 'He called in sick. I didn't think it was necessary for someone to take his place.'

'Clearly, you thought wrong!' Alyssa was shouting, and she didn't care. 'I expect to see you in Captain Hammond's office at the end of your shift.' And then she dismissed him by turning her back on him.

'Lorna, I need to see the room this man was attempting to break into. Can you get me a key?' She tried to ignore the wide-eyed look of fear on the woman's face, probably at Alyssa's loss of temper as much as the events of the early morning hours.

'Sure, sure.'

A few minutes and a phone call to Cord later, Alyssa was inside the hotel room. Though she didn't expect to find much, she wondered what Yarmini could've possibly been searching for. After checking the shelves and opening both water-stained nightstand drawers, she found nothing but the relics of an old, seedy hotel room. Still, she planned on sealing off this room until she could get a team of technicians in to comb it. Worst case scenario, she found nothing. Best case, there was something here she'd overlooked that would lead them to the missing girls.

Chapter Thirty-Eight

It was almost eight-thirty on Saturday morning before Alyssa and Cord finished at Hotel Camino and strolled into the precinct. Ever since he'd squealed into the parking lot of the hotel shortly after three, Cord's usual poised self-control had been slowly splintering. Maybe not so much that others would notice, but enough that she definitely did.

Hal, Tony, and Joe were already in the conference room when she and Cord walked in, all of them more than willing to come in on a Saturday. On the drive over, Hammond had called to inform her that both the officers who were supposed to be surveilling the hotel were being pulled from that particular duty and disciplined, though he declined to say what that punishment entailed. It didn't matter; she'd hear it through the grapevine eventually, and right now, she had other things to deal with.

They settled themselves around the table, and Alyssa filled everyone in on last night's events. When she was finished, she pointed to Joe and Tony. 'You two canvass the businesses around Hotel Camino, see if any of them have security systems in place that might've caught Yarmini, what he's driving now, which direction he went when he took off – whatever you can find. Hal, I need you to dig into Yarmini's financials. See if he's had any big or unusual deposits that stand out. We—'

Alyssa's phone rang, and she glanced down, the number familiar, but not one she readily recognized. 'Detective Wyatt speaking.'

'Detective, this is Bartholomew Rosenfelt. Do you have a few minutes? I have something that might be of interest to you and your investigation.'

'And what is that?'

'You know, I'm sure my attorney would reprimand me for contacting you like this. In fact, I'd wager he'd go so far as to call me a complete idiot. Not to my face, mind you. After all, he gets paid a hefty retainer and he wouldn't want to risk getting fired.'

Her patience splintered once again, Alyssa cut him off. 'Mr. Rosenfelt, I'm a bit embroiled in locating three missing girls and solving a murder, so if you have something to share with me regarding my cases, please just tell me.'

Immediately, Rosenfelt adopted a more serious demeanor, his voice more matter-of-fact. 'Forgive me. You're right. I shouldn't be making lighthearted conversation in light of what my employee is suspected of. What I'm about to share with you is not something my employees are aware of, nor is it something I generally have need to remember, which is why I didn't think of it when you and your partner intercepted me at the airfield.'

She knew it was rude, but the fear in Lorna Price's eyes last night when Steve Yarmini showed up at the hotel, coupled with the fact that she'd been so close to catching him, forced her tolerance to a new level of low. 'Are you going to get to your point soon?'

He took her attitude in stride. 'All the vehicles purchased by and for Rosenfelt Holdings are equipped with GPS trackers. It's a system designed and set into place after I discovered certain discrepancies in my ledgers, and it became prudent for me to find a way to keep track of my more distant employees. However, it's been several years since I've last had a reason to track the comings and goings of any of the hundreds of people in my employ.'

Alyssa went on full alert. 'Mr. Rosenfelt, are you trying to tell me there was a tracker on the 2017 Dodge Viper Steve Yarmini was driving?'

'I'm not trying; I'm telling you straight out there was a tracker on the car Steve Yarmini was driving. From what I understand, the system only keeps a log of the last thirty days before self-deleting. I've taken the liberty of having my receptionist contact the company in charge of retaining that data.'

'How soon do you expect to hear back?'

'I already have. And I've asked that the information be emailed directly to you. It should already be in your inbox.'

Keeping him on the line, she pointed to Hal's laptop. 'I need that.' She waited while he shut down whatever program he'd been in and slid the computer over.

Alyssa didn't want to come across as ungrateful, but she was curious – and a bit suspicious – as to why one of the world's richest men would go out of his way to be so helpful. 'Mr. Rosenfelt, I appreciate this, but *why* are you doing it – sharing this information with me?' There was a brief pause before Rosenfelt spoke. 'Despite your personal opinion of me, Detective, or what advice my attorney would give, I'm not in the habit of hindering police investigations, especially when they involve one of my employees being a suspect in the rape and murder of a young girl, and who, apparently, has taken off.'

Alyssa's head snapped back in surprise. 'How did you hear that?'

'I have my ways. Suffice it to say that it doesn't look too good for Mr. Yarmini, does it?'

Her fingers flew across the keyboard as she logged into her email where she found a new message from Advanced Technology Securities. She opened the message and clicked on the link before pushing the laptop over to Hal. 'Can you project this onto the wall?'

A few quick taps later, the information was displayed across the room for everyone to see. And then suddenly GPS coordinates scrolled down the page, dates and times stamped beside each. She pointed to Joe. 'Start with May 20, and confirm that those coordinates match the location of Hotel Camino.

'Hal, figure out which of these coincide with Yarmini's residence in the foothills.' Scanning the screen, she tapped one of the coordinates and said, 'Start with this one since it seems to show up more frequently than any others. Cord, Tony, go back to the earliest date and start jotting down all the locations. If anything seems "remote," flag it. That could be where the girls are.'

She'd forgotten Rosenfelt was still on the phone that was pressed to her ear until he said, 'Detective, I'm not sure what else I can do, so I'm going to hang up now. If you need me for anything else, you have my number. In the meantime, I'm staying at Hotel Parq Central.'

Absently, Alyssa thanked the multi-billionaire, trying her best not to let frustration build as she waited for the coordinates to produce anything that might tell her where the girls were. Several minutes after Rosenfelt hung up, Cord said, 'None of the data from the April dates show that the Dodge Viper made a trip into Santa Fe where Meghan was kidnapped – which could mean that he wasn't involved with her kidnapping, or simply that he used another car.'

'Or that she wasn't in Santa Fe when she was taken. Does anything place the Viper near the area around her step-grandfather's house?'

Suddenly, Joe piped up, excitement in his voice. 'Pay dirt! On Monday, May 20, at three minutes before midnight, the Dodge Viper was at Hotel Camino. Ninety-eight minutes later, he stopped at Central and Louisiana where Meghan Jessup's body was discarded. Thursday, May 23, at 5:43 p.m., the tracker places the vehicle at the end of Rainbow in Rio Rancho.' He looked up from his phone. 'And the tracking ends there.'

Instead of her frustration and impatience leveling off, Alyssa was more aggravated. 'That doesn't tell us where Meghan Jessup has been all this time. It tells us where she was just before her body was dumped...' She spoke out loud, but she was talking mainly to herself as she tried to work out the puzzle.

Cord cleared his throat before speaking, and all eyes cut his way. 'None of this explains why Meghan Jessup would have the Rosenfelt Holdings logo branded on her body – unless Bartholomew Rosenfelt is somehow involved and trying to throw us off by pretending to help?'

The same thought had crossed Alyssa's mind. 'On the other hand, if he *is* involved, do you really think he's stupid enough to have Yarmini dump Meghan's body in the center of town when his logo was branded into her hip? I mean, if I had that much expendable income at my disposal, I'd make sure her body wasn't discovered at all.'

'Maybe he's not as smart as you're clearly giving him credit for,' Cord bit out, causing Joe, Tony, and Hal to stare at him, mouths gaping open.

'And maybe you're not thinking clearly, and you're letting your judgment be clouded by biases,' Alyssa retorted. She would never embarrass him by revealing what those biases were, but nor would she allow them to derail this investigation.

When he didn't respond, she said, 'Let's dig into Steve Yarmini's past. I'd like to find out if he has any connections to Beau Cambridge or his father.'

When her phone chimed, she glanced down to see a text message from Bartholomew Rosenfelt.

> Just emailed you a link to Steve Yarmini's cell phone records. And before you ask, that is a business expense that Rosenfelt Holdings reimburses for. As to how I was able to get them so quickly, let's just say money goes a long way. I hope they help.

She read the message aloud and asked Hal to open the link to the records since he already had her email open. The first thing she did was run a quick scan to see if Beau or Hugh Cambridge's phone numbers popped up on the list.

Of course, they didn't. That would've made her life a little too simple. Tension tightened the muscles in Alyssa's back and neck, and she rolled her shoulders in an effort to release the tautness. There were still a lot more numbers to go through, and she had a feeling one of them would lead to the girls. 'We need to find out which cell towers were pinged when these calls were made.'

'I'll ring Judge Rosario and ask her to issue us another ping warrant and let her know it's for the same case. I don't think we'll have any problems getting a green light on this,' Hal said.

Alyssa nodded. 'In the meantime, let's start at the top and begin calling those numbers, see who answers. Maybe we'll get lucky.' She could always hope.

Chapter Thirty-Nine

At noon, Alyssa was alone in the conference room. Cord had offered to go pick up lunch and bring it back, Joe and Tony were checking out the local GPS coordinates, and she wasn't sure what Hal was up to. The last she'd seen him, a new officer had knocked and asked to speak to him privately. She wasn't surprised. He'd always been the go-to guy for rookies and veterans alike.

Sprawled in front of her were printouts of call and text logs from Rachel, Jersey, and Katelyn's phones. The pages didn't give her as much as a subpoenaed record might, but at least meant she could check for common numbers. As it turned out, there was one that both Rachel and Jersey had called or texted, and she highlighted it.

Just as she was about to dial the number, Lynn Sharp called, skipping the pleasantries and diving right in, the kind of direct approach Alyssa appreciated. 'I told you we found fibers in the abrasions on Meghan Jessup's body. Some of them match the fibers found in the carpets of the rooms at Hotel Camino. Good call on getting someone over there this morning. I've already sent them off to the same lab, and put a priority rush on it, explaining we have the lives of three young ladies on the line, possibly more. I have to say the technician wasn't overly impressed with my plea, saying everyone's items were urgent. But don't worry. I called in a favor. I'm going to text you a contact name and number. If you don't hear something soon, Tyler said you could call him directly.'

'That was fast.'

'Like I said, three lives on the line.'

'How does this Tyler person owe you a favor? If you don't mind my asking.'

Lynn laughed. 'Truthfully?'

Why did people always ask that? 'No, lie to me. Of course, I want the truth.'

'Tyler and I met at a medical conference in Oregon a few years back. One of my cousins lives there, and she met me at the hotel for lunch. He saw her, fell head over heels in lust, and begged me to set up a date. I did. They've been happily married for a year now.'

A few minutes after they ended the call, Lynn sent her the text containing Tyler's contact information while also telling her she'd forgotten to mention that the lab *could* already have the results from the fibers discovered on Meghan Jessup. Immediately, Alyssa placed a call to Lynn's cousin by marriage.

'Tyler Rhodes.'

'Tyler, this is Detective Alyssa Wyatt with the Albuquerque Police Department. I believe Lynn told you to expect a call from me.'

'Detective, yes, she did. Give me just a second while I pull up that file.' After a series of clicks, Tyler was back. 'Here it is. Okay, it appears the fiber that came from Meghan Jessup's wounds were from a rug, but not from your run of the mill rug or carpet. In fact, there's only one manufacturer here in the United States that creates them, and each rug is custom ordered right down to the dye, shape, and length.'

Alyssa stretched across the table to grab a pen and a blank piece of paper, ready to take down the information.

'Royal Empire Textiles out of Connecticut is the manufacturer. Believe it or not, I was able to email them the specifics and scan in a copy of the fiber discovered, and they said that's all they'd need to be able to tell us who purchased it, when, and where it was delivered. They said to give them at least twenty-four hours, and I sent that early yesterday morning. If you're ready, I can give you the contact information. And I already checked: someone is always there on Saturdays.'

Alyssa's heart picked up speed. 'Just to be clear – what you're telling me is that we now have carpet fibers from two different locations? One is from Hotel Camino and one came from this manufacturer out of Connecticut. Is that correct?'

'Correct.'

There was no way a place like Hotel Camino could afford the type of textiles that came custom-made, right down to the smallest detail. 'Thanks, Tyler. Can you run that number by me one more time so I can make sure I jotted it down right?'

'Sure thing.'

A minute later, Alyssa thanked him again and hung up.

Her pulse fluttering because she knew they were getting closer, she entered the digits for Royal Empire Textiles, glancing up when Cord walked in, holding two take-out bags from Taco Cabana. She pulled the phone away from her ear and placed it on speaker, propping it in the silver tray of the whiteboard, amplifying the sound. Just when she was positive she was going to have to leave a message, a disembodied, nasally, and alto-gether bored voice answered.

'Royal Empire Textiles. Raleigh speaking.'

Raleigh? 'Raleigh, this is Detective Alyssa Wyatt from Albu-querque, New Mexico, and I'm trying to reach Andie Kirkland. Is he available? This is somewhat of an urgent matter.'

An impatient and irritated sound echoed around the room as Raleigh huffed out her breath. 'Andie,' she said slowly, as if she was speaking to someone she'd had to explain the same concept to fifteen times already, 'is in a meeting right now, and *she* won't be available again until Tuesday.'

Before Alyssa could suggest interrupting the meeting, another voice, loud but indistinguishable, could be heard. For sixty seconds, she and Cord listened to the garbled sounds of two people arguing before a series of clicks echoed into the room.

Then, 'Hello? Detective Wyatt? This is Andie Kirkland. I wasn't in a meeting. I was heading out when I overheard Raleigh tell you I was unavailable.' The woman on the other end of the line laughed lightly, a throaty whisper of sound. 'I don't know how much you heard, but Raleigh doesn't like to be contradicted. As she's the owner's niece, she often feels a bit *entitled*, shall we say, and she's yet to accept that she's been relegated to such lowliness as being someone *else's* secretary.' This time, Andie's laugh was full of glee. 'While I would've preferred her being assigned to pretty much anyone else, it does my heart good to see the girl not have everything handed to her on the proverbial silver platter. But enough of that. Your urgent matter has nothing to do with our spoiled Raleigh, so, how can I help you?'

Alyssa had a feeling she'd like this Andie Kirkland. 'I understand Tyler Rhodes emailed you with the specifics of a piece of fiber we discovered on the body of a young girl, and I was hoping you could help me out by giving me the name of the purchaser of that particular rug or carpet.'

'He didn't speak to me, but he was given my name by the person who forwarded the email to my inbox. Give me just a second to bring it up... Okay, here it is. Are you ready?'

'Fire away.'

'It would appear that particular rug was ordered in 2015 by someone named Tatiana Salazar. The cost was $463,000 and was paid in full as is our policy before we begin any piece. When the order was complete, it was shipped to the Royal Gorge Hotel in Taos, New Mexico.'

Cord whistled low at the price.

'Is there anything else I can help you with?'

'Not at this moment. Thanks for taking my call, Andie.'

As soon as the call ended, both Cord and Alyssa were up and moving. 'Who do you know in New Mexico who has been living in Connecticut and that could afford that price tag on a rug?'

'Bartholomew Rosenfelt,' he said.

Their lunch was left abandoned on the table as they sped over to Hotel Parq Central.

–

Sixteen minutes later, Alyssa pounded on the door of Bartholomew Rosenfelt's room. She held her badge to the peephole, assuming he'd check it before opening. When he did, she didn't give him a chance to speak first. 'Royal Empire Textiles ring a bell for you?'

'Manners dictate I invite you inside, but common sense prevents me from doing so.'

'You know one of the best things about forensic science, Mr. Rosenfelt? You can glean almost anything from the tiniest fiber. Now, Royal Empire Textiles?'

'Yes, I've heard of them. One of my personal decorators has purchased a number of items from them for various houses I own, and not just in New Mexico. And before I answer any more questions, I need to know if I need to contact my lawyer. My assistance only goes so far before self-preservation kicks in.'

'Right now, we just need you to answer some questions.'

'Then please come in, as we seem to be drawing an audience.' He stepped back and swept his arm to usher them into a suite that was easily three times larger than the average hotel room.

'This decorator... Is she still in your employ?'

'Tatiana Salazar, and yes, she is, though she's taken a brief leave of absence for the past four months as she deals with family issues.'

'Family issues?'

'I don't know much, but what I do know is that Ms. Salazar was going through quite a nasty divorce after she discovered her husband was having an affair with one of her acquaintances. This came on the heels of her father dying and discovering the fortune she'd always thought she'd receive had been spent by her husband and his mistress. Mrs. Salazar's husband was her father's financial advisor, which is how they met.'

'Fibers discovered on Meghan Jessup's body were traced back to a rug priced at $463 grand and shipped to one Tatiana Salazar at the Royal Gorge Hotel in Taos.'

As soon as the words left her mouth, Rosenfelt stumbled backwards, the back of his knees hitting the leather sofa which he sank onto. 'Steve Yarmini and Tatiana often work together, as she spends most of her time in New Mexico since she's originally from here. That rug was ordered for one of my properties, but not in Taos. It was a place I purchased in 2015 – and sold to her when she expressed an interest in it. I allowed her to keep the rug as a housewarming gift.'

A new sense of urgency kicked Alyssa's pulse into overdrive, and she and Cord exchanged a look. 'I need to know right now where that house is located.' Somehow she knew this was the place they were looking for.

'Placitas. Let me call Kimberly so she can get me the exact address.'

As she waited for him to place the call, Alyssa's mind swung back to another time in April when she'd discovered where Isaac had been held. That same sensation swarmed her, and her nerves demanded she move.

A couple minutes later, Bartholomew hung up and handed her a piece of paper. 'God, I hope this doesn't mean what I think it means, Detectives.'

Neither she nor Cord responded to that, but what she did say was, 'Stay where we can contact you, Mr. Rosenfelt.'

They rushed to the car where Cord called Hammond to request the telephonic search warrant and a chopper. While he was doing that, Alyssa called Hal and had him contact the chief of police in Placitas, who to no one's surprise, Hal knew from 'back in the day.'

Chapter Forty

Never in Rachel's nineteen years had she ever been so desperate to change something, *do* something, *help* someone else. The desperation was a physical hum that raced through her nerve endings, setting them on fire as she hung suspended in the contraption.

And though her back burned from the slashes sliced into her from the whip, though her hands were raw from gripping the rope dangling to the side of each handcuff, those things faded when the men disappeared, only to reappear moments later with Katelyn. Despite knowing it was unrealistic, she'd still hoped the young girl would somehow be spared this deviant torture.

She'd watched helplessly as the men had dragged Katelyn into the room, her feverish, over-bright eyes spotting Rachel, naked and suspended from the contraption. She'd collapsed to the ground, hand clutched to her throat, her breaths coming in short bursts as she tried to get enough air into her lungs. And then she was crawling to the door, clawing her fingernails down it as the blond muscled guy laughed and dragged her back.

Bile burned its way up from Rachel's stomach and into the back of her throat as she forced her lungs to breathe in steadily, willing Katelyn to stay strong.

And then, before she could process the change in the men's positions, one of them had pulled up the long leather strap lying across the foot of the bed and moved in behind her while the other man gripped Katelyn by the chin, holding her face immobile. Even as she screamed out at the searing agony, she saw the man holding Katelyn lean down, an evil, malicious smile decorating his face as he whispered something in her ear.

Trying to dislodge the man's grip, tears streaked the young girl's pale face, her mouth opened in a terrified scream drowned out by Rachel's.

And then a thunderous boom that reminded Rachel of the time Nick had stolen their father's Hummer and crashed it through their block wall when he'd taken the corner too fast reverberated throughout the entire house, shaking it on its foundation. She hoped it was a nuclear bomb that would kill them all because she would rather die than watch Katelyn try to survive the nightmare that awaited her.

Muscle Guy shoved himself away from Katelyn as he jerked his head towards the closed door. Where a second ago a solid wall of chest had pressed into Rachel while strong hands gripped her forearms, there was suddenly nothing as she was jolted forward, her upper body twisting, the bindings at her wrist tearing through flesh.

When another explosion rocked the house, both men scrambled, ripping their pants off the floor, tripping over each other in their frenzy to get dressed. Not bothering to put on their shirts, they yanked open the door and bolted down the hall.

With the door ajar, Rachel watched shadows slice across the hallway as individuals shouted and ran in different directions. Someone, maybe Muscle Guy, shouted, 'Leave them!' when someone inquired what to do with the girls.

Another noise, this one outside and more distant, penetrated through the heavy fog and pain in her brain – a helicopter whirring overhead. She didn't know what it meant, couldn't bother to care. After all, she'd already learned – they all had – that hope was for fools.

The sound of more pounding footsteps, shouted orders, and frantic demands trickled down the hall, and then suddenly, several uniformed officers stormed the room, led by a short female with auburn hair. Mortified at being naked in front of all these people and suddenly terrified that she was only dreaming, she closed her eyes, her unleashed tears streaming as the lady commanded someone to get her down before rushing over to Katelyn, who'd drawn her knees up into the fetal position in the middle of the bed, her face and nose red, eyes bulging, lips and chin trembling.

Two officers worked the bindings on Rachel's wrists to free her as a third stood behind her, ready to catch her when she was released. And as her body gave way to gravity, a voice in her ear whispered, 'I've got you. You're okay. You're safe now.' The sweetest words, even if they weren't true. But she let them utter the lies, and when they tried to wrap the silk robe around her, a howl of agony tore from her throat. As much as the pain was like molten lava spreading across her raw back, and as much as she wanted to shrug the robe off, to never have the sensation of silk against her skin again, she wanted to be covered up more and so she allowed it to stay on.

'*Anna?*' Her throat was on fire, and what emerged was nothing more than a raspy whisper of sound that no one seemed to understand, but she suddenly needed to know what had happened to her friend.

She wanted to ask again, but her neck could no longer hold her head up, and it fell forward onto her chest; in that moment, nothing mattered more than escaping this place. Seconds later, the auburn-haired officer was yelling for the paramedics. And then she felt herself being wheeled out into the hall, down the corridor, and into the front room where she'd first met the men who'd abused her. A crashing crescendo of commotion and noise and fear surrounded her, and it took several tries before she realized the woman was urgently asking her where the others were. 'We need to find them so we can help them. Where are they?'

Before her mind went blank, Rachel pointed toward the door hidden behind the new built-in, moveable bookshelves that weren't there until a few days ago, and then she allowed herself to collapse into nothingness.

Chapter Forty-One

Saturday, May 25

Alyssa pressed harder on the gas pedal, ignoring the way the dirt road jostled her bones because right now, her main focus was on reaching the girls, praying they were there... and alive. They'd deal with the rest later. The police chopper flying overhead and the rumble of vehicles in front of and behind her almost drowned out the cackle of the mic at her shoulder.

Not wanting to risk anyone slipping through the closing net, Alyssa had requested that Placitas send in several officers to set up both an inside and outside perimeter until her team could arrive, and it was one of them reporting in.

'We count four vehicles, three parked in the driveway and one in the four-car garage.'

'I'm less than a minute out.'

As the trees, rocks, and bushes blurred past her window, she forced back the memory of a similar operation when her team had surrounded Evan Bishop's lair only to have him escape and resurface at her house, where he'd gleefully shared with her the tortures he had planned for her and her family. *My family is safe* she reminded herself as she skidded to a halt outside the grand residence.

Unlike then, this time a squirrel would be lucky to slip through the perimeter they'd set up. No one in that house was getting away.

She barely had the car in park before she and Cord jumped out to the sound of slamming doors and thunderous shouts. A man wearing a bullet-proof vest and a police cap hurried over, grabbing her by the arm. 'This way,' he ordered. Then, when they were standing next to an unmarked white van, he said, 'We have two snipers in place in case we need them. How do you want this to go down?'

Alyssa explained her tactics, and shortly after that, the three of them approached the house. Pounding on the door, Alyssa shouted, 'Albuquerque and Placitas police departments. We have the house surrounded. Open up and come out with your hands raised.' Inside, booming footsteps sounded as the occupants scrambled. She stepped back, turned to the side, and gave the order: 'Knock it in.'

It took three tries before the battering ram did the trick, but once the door exploded off its hinges, officers rushed in. The first thing Alyssa saw was two muscular, shirtless men, their belts undone and their pants draped open, running for a back door. She directed Joe and Tony their way as she headed down the hallway from where they'd come. On her way, she grabbed three female officers she didn't recognize. 'I need you with me.' She didn't know what they were going to find, but she felt deep inside that whatever they encountered, it would be far less intimidating and frightening with women officers.

Or at least she hoped so.

The hallway was dimly lit, with three sets of closed doors on either side, but the one at the end stood ajar. Strangled sobs poured out into the corridor from inside the room, and Alyssa ran the rest of the way, hesitating only long enough to make sure the room was clear of any threats before rushing forward to the young girl on the bed who she recognized immediately as Katelyn Phillipson.

'Get her down!' She ordered the officers flowing in behind her to assist the female suspended nude in some kind of contraption. All around her came the sound of whispered reassurances of safety, and Alyssa knew it would be a long time, if ever, before these girls would be able to believe them.

Careful not to further terrify either girl, she turned to the one the officers were frantically trying to get down.

'Rachel Otis?'

Tears rushed down the girl's cheeks as she confirmed her identity with a weak nod. Alyssa addressed both girls. 'We're going to get you help now, but we need to know if there are any other girls here. Can you tell me that?'

Mewling noises continued from Katelyn's throat, but Rachel either nodded or her neck could no longer support her head as it flopped forward. At the same time, her knees buckled, and Alyssa yelled down the hall for someone to get the paramedics inside to help move the girls out of the room. She didn't want them in there a second longer. Images of a battered and beaten Callie McCormick pushed their way into her mind, but she shoved them back. She might've been too late to save Callie, but she was determined these girls would live.

Four minutes later, the girls were being wheeled down the hall on stretchers. In the front room, amid the hustle of officers rushing around, she caught Cord's eye, and the pale look on his face was replaced with one of fury as he spotted the girls.

Before the paramedics could take them outside, Alyssa approached Rachel, her voice filled with urgency. 'Rachel, where are the others? We need to find them so we can help them. Where are they?'

Rachel pointed to a wall lined with shelves of books, but when her eyes landed on two of the men the officers had rounded up, they rolled to the back of her head, and she fainted.

One of the paramedics pushed Alyssa aside. 'I'm sorry, ma'am. We need to get her to the hospital,' and then they rushed her out.

At the same time, another hand, surprisingly strong in its grip, clutched at her wrist, jagged fingernails slicing lines into Alyssa's skin. Katelyn Phillipson's petite frame shuddered violently, and her teeth rattled as she tried to explain what Rachel had been pointing at. Throat hoarse and raspy from screaming, tears streaming down her pale face, she whispered, 'The shelf moves. When we came upstairs, that wall of books was over there.' Her eyes followed the paramedics carting Rachel outside. 'The others are down there.'

'How many, Katelyn? How many others?'

Her answer nearly shredded what was left of Alyssa's self-control. 'Four.'

A commotion near the wall stole Alyssa's attention, and when she twisted around, Cord had located the switch that rolled the bookshelf out of the way, but the door behind it was locked. Cord didn't hesitate, kicking it in and leading the charge down the steps. She heard him yell, 'Clear' before several booming footsteps rushed down after him.

Anger heated Alyssa from the inside out even while her heart broke at the sight that greeted them.

Four girls, one of them Jersey Andrews, huddled together onto one mattress, their arms around each other, their faces streaked with tears. One of the girls sat slightly forward of the others as if she alone could protect them from whatever was happening. Each of them wore silk robes matching the ones discarded in the room where Rachel and Katelyn were discovered. Of all the houses of horrors she'd encountered in her career, this had to be one of the worst.

Alyssa approached the cell door. 'Jersey?'

Holly's petite friend lifted her head from where she'd been hiding her face in the crook of one of the other girl's necks, and when she saw who was calling her name, she cried out, collapsing twice as she struggled to stand and move to the metal bars separating her from safety.

'Oh my God. Mrs. Wyatt?' And then she sank to her knees, the top of her head pressed into the bars as a torrent of anguished cries escaped.

Trying her hardest not to react to the bruises covering Jersey's face, Alyssa reached through the bars and touched her hair, gently rubbing a hand through the strands. Twisting only her upper body, she turned and pointed to the officer closest to the stairs. 'Find the damned keys! Now!' she roared when he didn't move fast enough to suit her.

Upstairs, the whines of men protesting their innocence filtered down to her, and a red haze clouded her vision. She sensed movement beside her, and she lifted her head to find Cord pacing as he waited for the man to return with the keys. 'Tatiana Salazar?'

'No. According to one of the guys up there, she stepped out about an hour before we arrived, and she's not expected back before tomorrow. And they all claim to know nothing about her whereabouts.'

'Damn it,' she swore. 'Where are those keys?'

Finally, the officer bounded back down, a set of keys jangling in his fingers. 'Found them on one of the muscles up there.'

Alyssa moved her hand from the top of Jersey's head and pushed herself to her feet so she could meet him partway, but she was too slow because Cord's stride was longer, and he'd already snatched the keys away so quickly that it elicited an *ouch* from the officer when the metal teeth scratched across his hand. And then Alyssa was stepping back out of the way as Cord fitted first one key then another until he found the correct one. The second the cell opened, Alyssa rushed forward, catching Jersey, as once again, she collapsed to her knees.

Several officers and three paramedics moved inside the small enclosure to assist the other girls while crime scene technicians snapped photographs and documented evidence.

A young paramedic with light brown hair and soft blue eyes squatted down so she could address Jersey, but Jersey burrowed her head further into Alyssa's shoulders, her sobs crushing Alyssa's heart as her tears soaked through her shirt.

'Jersey, sweetie, you need to let the paramedics check you out so we can transport you to the hospital.' Holly's friend tightened her grip, her cries changing to low moans. 'I'm going to be right here with you, I promise. No one else is going to hurt you. You trust me, don't you?'

Alyssa didn't take it personally when Jersey hesitated. She couldn't blame her. How would she ever trust again? Slowly, gently, she coaxed Jersey's arms away from her and into the waiting arms of the kind paramedic. But as the paramedic tried to guide her away, Jersey struggled, her eyes wide with fear, and Alyssa stepped so that she was back in Jersey's line of vision. 'Jersey.' Her voice was gentle but firm. Jersey stopped squirming and stared at Alyssa, her lower lip quivering. 'We need to get you to the hospital where you can get checked out. Can you be brave just a little longer?'

Jersey's gaze clouded over. 'Brave?' The word was nothing more than a whisper of sound.

Alyssa cupped Jersey's cheek and tilted her face up. Holding her gaze, she repeated, 'Brave. You and the others have been very brave. And we need you to do that a little longer. Don't quit on me now. Can you do that for me?'

Slowly, Jersey nodded, her mouth once more forming the word *brave* as she allowed the paramedics to assist her upstairs and out to the ambulance. Alyssa hated that the girls would have to pass by the men who'd tormented them, but she also trusted that the professionals here would shield the girls as much as possible as they escorted them out.

After a quick glance to make sure evidence was being preserved, Alyssa climbed the stairs and headed outside. As each girl was loaded onto a gurney, she asked her name, age, and who they could contact to let them know they were safe. She knew it would be a long time before they believed that word ever again, but still she used it. They needed to hear it as often as possible.

The second she had the information, the ambulance doors closed, and then they were gone in a caravan of urgency. When the last one disappeared down the road, she tugged at Cord's arm and indicated he should follow her back inside. She spotted Joe and Tony and motioned for them to join her.

'Before we do anything else, before they hear it on the news, I want the families notified.' They divvied up the task with Alyssa contacting Jersey's mom, Katelyn's parents, and even though it was against protocol, she opted to call Rachel's brother instead of her parents.

As the first call was placed, she watched the scene unfolding in front of her, watched four men hauled outside in cuffs, protesting their innocence the entire way. Her hand squeezed the phone, hurting her fingers, but she didn't ease her grip because the pain was helping her to focus on the task at hand instead of the burning compulsion to go outside and confront the men herself.

'Hello?' A woman's choked voice answered on the second ring.

'Natalia? This is Alyssa Wyatt, Holly's mom…'

'Oh my God, have you found Jersey?'

Alyssa swallowed past the lump in her throat. 'We've found her, but she's in rough shape. She's on her way right now to the Trauma Center at UNMH. If you leave right away, you'll probably beat her there. Mrs. Andrews, if you give me your husband's number, I'll be happy to call him for you to give him the news as well.'

'Would you? Thank you.' Ten seconds later, Alyssa was armed with Mr. Andrews's number, but she chose to call him after she'd contacted Mrs. Phillipson and Nick.

Next, she dialed Mary Phillipson who answered so quickly, it was almost as if her finger had been hovering over the phone.

In a whispered hush, she breathed out Alyssa's name. 'Detective Wyatt?'

'Mrs. Phillipson, is your husband with you?'

A garbled cry escaped, and Alyssa heard Mr. Phillipson's muffled voice before he took the phone from his wife. 'Katelyn?'

'We found her. She's…'

'Is she… is she…'

'She's alive, and she's going to need you to be strong for her. I'm not going to sugarcoat it; your daughter's been through a lifetime of horror in the past few days.' Like she had with Jersey's mom, she informed Mary and Jason where Katelyn was being taken, and then, after promising to meet up with them later to answer their questions, she dialed Nick's number.

'We've got her. We found Rachel,' she said as soon as he answered.

'Where? What? How is she? Is she okay? What happened to her?'

'She's got a long road of recovery ahead of her, but right now she's on her way to UNMH.' She paused. 'I haven't contacted your parents yet. I'll do that next.'

'I'll do it. Thank you, Detective. I can't...' Nick's voice broke on a sob. 'Thank you. Um, there's someone here who wants to talk to you.'

A second later, the last voice she would've expected to hear came on the line. 'Mom? Was Jersey with Rachel? Did you find her?'

'What are you doing with Nick Otis?'

'Later, Mom. I promise. Now – Hold on, my phone's ringing. It's Sophie. Mom, I'll call you back.'

And then she was gone, and Nick was on the line. 'Detective, I have questions. Will I be able to find you later?'

Alyssa pushed aside the confusion of hearing Holly with Nick. 'As soon as I can leave here, I'll be heading to the hospital, though it might be late.'

'I'll look for you.' And then he, too, was gone.

Mr. Andrews, the last person on her list... Alyssa steeled herself because as of yet, the man couldn't have shown any less interest in the fact that his daughter had disappeared. Like Mr. and Mrs. Otis, it was too much of an inconvenience to his social life to take it seriously. She dialed the number and listened to it ring. On the fourth one, a gruff voice answered.

'Hello?'

'Mr. Andrews?'

'Yes. Who's calling?'

'Mr. Andrews, this is Detective Wyatt with the Albuquerque Police Department. As you're aware, your daughter has been missing for the past six days.' She intentionally changed her tone to sound more accusatory. 'I just wanted to inform you she's been found and has been taken to UNMH's Trauma Center. Mr. Andrews, your daughter has been through a traumatic experience, and she's going to need the support of *both* her parents. When can I expect you'll arrive?'

Jersey's dad cleared his throat, and Alyssa knew right away that he wouldn't be returning for his daughter, and she was suddenly quite glad the man was an ocean away because as it was, she wanted to reach her hand through the phone and throttle him.

'Well, I'm relieved she's been found. Please tell her and her mother I'll see them in two weeks when I return home.'

'No.'

'Excuse me?'

'I said, no, Mr. Andrews, I will *not* be your messenger girl. I don't think you understand the extent of your daughter's injuries, the hell she's endured the past six days. Torture—'

'Detective, there's nothing I could do to help her heal any faster if I were there, so I really don't see how my being there now or in two weeks will make much of a difference.' His next words were muffled, which Alyssa assumed meant he'd covered the mouthpiece to speak to his new girlfriend. Her anger grew exponentially with every tick of the clock.

When he came back on the line, she cut him off before he could infuriate her any further. 'Mr. Andrews, your *being* here, Jersey knowing you *care enough* to cut short a vacation to be here for *her*, that *she* is more important... those are the things that will be instrumental in assisting with your daughter's healing.'

Several heartbeats of silence passed, and Alyssa began to hope she'd finally gotten through, only to be slammed back into reality once again.

'I hardly see how my pacing and watching her heal will do anything other than make Jersey more nervous. No, I think it's better if I follow my instincts here.'

'You mean your selfishness. That's fine, you do that, Mr. Andrews, but let me tell you something: you're an even bigger ass than I expected you to be. I hope destroying that last bit of hope in your daughter that you care is worth whatever you're doing.'

And then she jabbed her finger into the screen of her phone over and over as she ended the call.

When she was sure she wouldn't take her anger out on undeserving individuals, Alyssa headed down the hall where she'd watched Cord disappear after finishing his calls. She found him standing in the doorway of the room labeled *The Toybox*, face ashen as the technicians moved about, measuring and cataloguing evidence. She knew him well enough to know he wasn't just seeing the stomach-churning contents of the items openly displayed or the ones in the wardrobe that she couldn't even fathom a use for.

With a firm hand on his arm, she pulled him away. 'I think the team downstairs could use your help.'

Without a word, he dragged his gaze from the blood stains on the mattress and stared down at her hand before lifting his eyes to meet hers. Coldness replaced whatever memories his brain had forced upon him, and after a quick nod, he walked away, leaving her to oversee the rest.

–

By the time the forensics team had combed every inch of the house and collected all the evidence, it was dark out, with the only light slicing through the darkness coming from the headlights on the vehicles as they drove away. The car said it was close to ten; still, instead of heading home, Alyssa and Cord were headed to the hospital. There was a good chance they'd have to wait until tomorrow to interview the girls, but even if that were the case, she wanted to check in, see them for herself. If she didn't, sleep would elude her until she did.

Finally turning onto the main road, Alyssa blindly reached out her hand and touched Cord lightly on the arm to get his attention. From her peripheral vision, she saw his head tilt her way. 'That had to be hard to see, for more reasons than one. How are you doing? And don't try to BS me.'

Cord's fingers tightened into a fist in his lap, and he tipped his head back. She heard his teeth grind against each other before he exhaled in such a rush of air, it was almost as if he'd been holding his breath for the past hour. 'I wanted to shoot every one of those bastards.'

She took her eyes off the road long enough to catch him watching for her reaction at his admission. 'It would be unnatural if you didn't feel that way. In fact, I'd be *more* worried if you didn't. Thank you for telling me the truth.'

A mirthless sound slipped past his lips. 'Like you wouldn't have been able to tell otherwise.'

'True. Still, you could've tried. I can drop you off at the precinct to get your car, or I can take you home and pick you up in the morning if you don't want—'

He cut her off with a wave of his hand, his voice firm. 'I'm going to the hospital with you. Don't treat me like I can't be objective, like I'm incapable of doing my job.'

'I didn't mean to do that. I'm sorry if it sounded that way.' The rest of the drive to University of New Mexico Hospital was made in silence.

Chapter Forty-Two

Saturday, May 25

A steady beeping penetrated Rachel's fog-filled sleep, and she forced her eyes open to locate the source, only to discover her brother's face looming over her. An unpleasant sensation of being trampled by elephants replaced her confusion as awareness inched its way in.

A deep inhalation sent shards of pain through her ribcage as if she'd swallowed shattered glass, and she gasped, then cried out when the movement seemed to rip the skin off her back. Something pulled at her arm when she struggled to sit up, and her head snapped down to see an IV poking out her arm, the drip suspended from a metal hook resting beside her bed. Next to it was a monitor flashing her vital signs.

'Easy there, sport,' Nick said as he gently pushed her shoulder until she was fully reclined again. Then he eased himself onto the side of her bed, careful not to make contact with anything but the hand he gently grasped in his own. 'You don't want to rip out your stitches. Welcome back, lazy bones.' His lips may have formed a smile, but the sadness that filled his eyes was something Rachel had only witnessed once before – the day their mother had taken their new puppy to be put down after it had chewed the leg of one of her chairs.

'Mom and Dad?' Her voice was scratchy, and her throat was on fire. 'Water?'

Nick leaned over and dragged a table on wheels closer to the bed, and then he reached behind and above her head and pushed a button that slowly elevated her bed until she was no longer lying flat. Only then did he hold a cup for her, placing the straw in her mouth. 'Only a little,' he whispered. 'You don't want to get sick.'

Even if she'd wanted more, the pain of swallowing prevented her from having any. Still, the coolness of the water felt good on her raw throat. After another careful sip, she turned her head so the straw would fall out. The bed shifted as her brother replaced the cup on the table before settling back down beside her, as if he was afraid to allow more than a breath of space between the two of them.

'Mom and Dad?'

His silence spoke louder than his words.

'They were here a while ago, but they left when the doctors said you needed your rest.'

When Nick lied, one eye twitched, and he always stared off to the left, like he was doing now.

The fissure in her heart widened. How much more could she take before she broke completely? 'It's okay, Nicholas. You don't have to lie.'

Moisture pooled before one lone tear escaped down his cheek. 'I'm sorry, sis.'

'No, don't be. You're here. That's what matters the most.'

A sudden sharp pain hammered at Rachel's head, and she sucked in a breath at the excruciating sensation, her eyes closing of their own accord. When the throbbing subsided, she reopened her eyes, catching the fury etched across the lines of Nick's face before he could smooth out his features.

It was her undoing, and she began to cry softly.

Startled, Nick eased himself off the bed so as not to jostle her. 'I'm going to get the doctor. He can give you something.'

Rachel shook her head. 'Don't leave me.'

His pained stare bounced from her face to the door and back again. 'Please, Rach, the doctor can give you pain medicine to help.'

While escaping from everything, including the pain, had never sounded so appealing, she knew she couldn't risk slipping into a nightmare, one in which the drugs would trap her. As it was, the nightmares would shadow her for the rest of her life. 'No, no drugs.'

He tried again, this time weakly, as if he understood her need not to be medicated. 'It might help you relax.'

'No drugs,' she repeated. 'Will you sit with me?' Only when he rested beside her again, her hand once more engulfed in his, did she allow the weight of weariness and exhaustion to drag her under, to lull her back into sleep, trusting Nick would still be here when she woke… or if her nightmares returned.

Chapter Forty-Three

It was after midnight before Alyssa and Cord left the hospital. She'd been right in that they hadn't been able talk with the girls since they'd been asleep – or at least resting – but they had commandeered a conference room where she and Cord met with the families. Nick had come in briefly before dismissing himself in fear that Rachel would wake to find him gone. Becca Marshall and Faye Harrison's parents were still on the road driving in from out of state, but they'd been able to join them on the phone. The questions they asked were as difficult as the answers Alyssa and Cord had to give.

This morning, when she arrived back at the hospital, she'd been mildly surprised to see Mr. and Mrs. Otis, who had been glaringly absent last night. No matter how angry or annoyed at their daughter, Alyssa simply couldn't fathom them not wanting to be here, especially when they *knew* what had happened to her. The same could be said for Jersey's dad.

Whatever their reason for not being here last night, at least The Otises were here now. However, within moments of spotting them in the waiting room, Alyssa realized they were in a heated argument with their son. Or to be more accurate, Mrs. Otis was involved in the confrontation with Nick; Mr. Otis stood slightly off to the side, arms crossed over his chest, his head swiveling back and forth as if he were embarrassed to be in the middle of this. Alyssa wondered if it was because he knew some of the doctors and nurses around here, or if it was something more than that.

They still hadn't noticed her approach when Mrs. Otis's hissed exclamation reached her ears. 'She has done this to herself, Nicholas! How are we expected to feel sorry for her when she dresses like she does and attends these parties like some kind of trollop? Her actions are an embarrassment to your father and me! What do we tell our friends?'

The color that suffused Nick's face was not one Alyssa could describe, and if he wasn't careful, she thought the vein would explode from his temple. Danger leaked from his pores as he clenched his teeth and leaned down to address his mother. 'You are the most vile person I know, and as much as I *loathe* the very idea of you being in the same room as Rachel, this isn't about what *I* need or what *you* want. It's about Rachel. So, I'm going to tell you what you're going to do, and you're going to do it because if you don't, you can't imagine the type of embarrassment that'll rain down on your head. I will personally see to it that I ruin you in front of all your so-called friends.'

Mrs. Otis pressed her hand to her chest and took a small step back.

'You and Dad are going to go into that room, and you're going to put on the best acting hat you've ever worn, and you are going to pretend like you're relieved your daughter is finally safe. You're going to become the most loving mother this hospital has ever seen. And you will do this every' – jab – 'damn' – jab – 'day'– jab – 'until she is released. Do you understand me, Mother?'

'Nicho—'

'Go ahead and call my bluff, Mother, and you'll see how very nasty I can play. After all, I learned from the best, didn't I?'

Mrs. Otis paled under her son's threats, and to Alyssa's surprise, when the woman turned to her husband for support, he merely shook his head, his jaw tight, and said, 'You heard him, Nina. Do what you're best at. Act.'

Maybe the man had a backbone after all.

Mr. Otis faced his son. 'Is she awake? I'd like to see her, and not because I'm being forced to, because I need to.'

Nina Otis stood speechless as her husband and son turned their backs on her. But when she saw that Alyssa had witnessed her humiliation, she pretended nothing was amiss as she hurried to catch up. At the doorway, Nick stopped to talk to Alyssa.

'Detective, I know you want to talk to Rachel, but first, my... parents... need to see her. They won't be long, and then I'll come get you. I know you need some answers.'

Alyssa didn't miss the hesitation when he uttered the word *parents*. 'Thank you. I appreciate it.' Before he walked off, she pulled Nick to the side. 'I overheard what you said. Do you think it's wise to have your mother in there with your sister right now?'

'Rachel was crushed last night every time she woke up and realized they still hadn't come. Even if it's a lie, she needs to know they're here for her.'

Nodding, Alyssa let him go. As the Otises walked through the double doors, a breaking news report caught her attention, and she turned toward the television mounted in the corner.

Channel 7 News has learned that several arrests were made last night after the shocking discovery of a sex trafficking ring. Albuquerque and Placitas police departments worked together to rescue six girls from a house previously owned by multi-billionaire Bartholomew Rosenfelt. An undisclosed source told us that Rosenfelt sold that particular property to his personal decorator, Tatiana Salazar, in 2015. Salazar, however, was not at home at the time of the raid, and police are looking for her at this time.

Among those arrested were Daryl Wainwright, a day trader who lives in Los Alamos; Martin Mendez, a hedge fund manager from Santa Fe; Carl Morton and Charles Harper, both landscapers for Salazar. Morton and Harper have lengthy criminal records, and both have spent a good amount of time in prison. In fact, Harper was released as recently as 2018 for his part in an armed robbery. Attorneys for all four men claim their clients are innocent and look forward to clearing them of these charges.

In the meantime, police are still searching for thirty-four-year-old Steven Yarmini, pictured here on the screen. Yarmini is suspected of raping and murdering fourteen-year-old Meghan Jessup who went missing from Santa Fe in April and who is believed to be one of the girls trafficked from the Placitas location.

If anyone knows the whereabouts of either Yarmini or Salazar, they are urged to contact the police right away. And now, we're going to go live to watch Captain Guthrie Hammond of APD as he addresses the media in a press release.

Alyssa shook her head, her lip curling at the men's proclamation of innocence. It was all they'd gotten out of them last night, too. She pulled her phone from her pocket and sent a text to Cord.

> Are you on your way?

> In the stairwell. Elevator was too crowded. Be there in thirty seconds.

In half that time, a loud clang rang through the room as the door to the stairwell banged open, announcing Cord's arrival.

Except the man coming toward her was not the partner she'd known for the past five years. Instead of his usual long strides and his confident persona, he now held his elbows tightly against his sides as his eyes darted from Alyssa to the metal doors behind her which housed the girls. The way he approached made him appear taller than his six-foot-two height.

She didn't even get a chance to say hello before he grabbed hold of her and pulled her around a corner where they could talk more privately. 'I just want to get this out there in the open. Yes, Shelley is in the back of my mind, but I can stay objective. Now, I stood by you when you discovered Evan Bishop was really Timmy, and so I need you to afford me the same courtesy and stand by me like we agreed.'

Alyssa took two steps back, tilted her head back, and crossed her arms over her chest. 'Have I somehow given you the

271

impression that I wouldn't? That I somehow suddenly find you incapable of doing your job?'

Cord rotated his neck on his shoulders and rubbed one hand over his hair, sending it into disarray as he did. 'No.'

'Then afford *me* the courtesy of believing I would've stood by you without the lecture. And on that note, we have some survivors we need to interview. We'll start with Jersey, unless you have somewhere else you'd like to begin?'

Her partner had the grace to blush. 'Jersey's fine. And I'm sorry. I guess I'm more sensitive than I thought.'

'Of course, you are. Just like I was.' She twisted so she could jostle him with her elbow. 'Now, if you're finished being melodramatic, let's go.'

Cord laughed. 'Lead the way.'

But when they reached Jersey's room, she was still sleeping, despite the bevy of nurses and assistants flurrying around as they poked and prodded. Alyssa nodded to Natalia Andrews who sat on the edge of her seat as she sat vigil over her daughter. The remnants of a sleepless night were evident in her puffy, red eyes and tear-streaked make-up.

Alyssa backed out of the door, heading instead to Cheyenne Jones's room. Just as they reached that door, the girl's mother rushed past them and into the visitor's restroom, emerging a few minutes later, her eyes bloodshot, her face waxy. The tiny veins on her nose stood out in sharp contrast to the rest of her skin. She skidded to a stop in front of Alyssa and Cord.

'Cheyenne woke hysterical about an hour ago, and they were forced to give her a sedative.' Her voice cracked. 'They wanted to secure her arms and legs because she keeps thrashing so hard, they're afraid she'll break the railings and fall off the bed. I refused to allow them to tie her up. Hasn't she been through enough? And what are you doing to capture these sick, twisted perverts that were on the news this morning? Why aren't you out there searching for them before they can destroy another girl's life?'

Alyssa knew the woman's anger wasn't really directed at her, and she allowed Mrs. Jones to wear herself down before answering. 'We do have officers searching for them as we speak. We anticipate several more arrests before this is over.

'But my partner and I need to talk to the girls, find out what they can tell us. We need every bit of information we *can* get so we can prevent this from ever happening again.' She retrieved a card from her pocket and handed it over. 'This is my number. Would you mind calling or texting when Cheyenne's awake?'

Mrs. Jones's fingers toyed with the card, her tears dotting the center. 'What if she can't talk about it? What will you do?'

Alyssa's hand went to Mrs. Jones's arm. 'Let us worry about that, okay?'

Mrs. Jones nodded. 'My husband is in there by himself.' With that, she walked away.

At the same time, the Otises walked out of Rachel's room. Where Mrs. Otis continued walking toward the door, Mr. Otis and Nick remained just outside where they conversed, their voices low. Then, after a quick nod and an awkward one-arm embrace, Mr. Otis followed his wife, turning back twice, as if he wasn't quite ready to leave his daughter's side.

'He'll be back later,' Nick said, coming up to them. 'Rachel's awake if you want to come in. But I'm telling you, if it gets to be too much, I'm going to have to ask you to go. I'm sure you understand.'

Chapter Forty-Four

Desperate to stop pretending, Rachel was relieved to see her parents, especially her mother, leave her room. Though her father had remained quiet throughout the visit, the way his hands had shaken as they'd clasped hers, his eyes shimmering with tears, she knew his concern for her was genuine. However, it didn't matter how large a smile she pasted on, her mother wanted to be anywhere but in a hospital room with her only daughter. Rachel tried to tell her heart it didn't matter. Even if it did.

Not once in her life had Nina Otis flitted about, plumping pillows, feeling her forehead, and straightening her covers – not when she'd had the chicken pox in first grade or when she'd had the swine flu in seventh. Her mother preferred to leave the actual mothering to whatever maid was on hand. Yet hover, fluff, and smooth was exactly what she did for thirty minutes before Rachel claimed she was exhausted and needed to sleep, even going so far as to close her eyes until they left.

She reopened them when the door swooshed open. Expecting Nick, she was surprised to see the auburn-haired officer who'd rescued her and beside her, a man who was head and shoulders taller. Shame that this woman had seen her suspended naked from the contraption washed through her, even though, in the back of her mind, she knew she had nothing to be ashamed of.

But it was the sight of the gun resting at the man's hip that triggered her panic. Rachel ripped and pulled at the tape holding the IV in place as she tried to yank it from her arm. She knew nothing except that she had to get away, get out. She swung her feet over the side of her hospital bed, ignoring the wave of dizziness. She had to get to the window. She'd leap from it before she allowed herself to be taken back to that place.

'Rachel! Rach! It's okay, you're okay. You're safe. No one's going to hurt you, not ever again.' The pain and urgency in her brother's voice penetrated the overwhelming terror streaking through her, and as it did, she became keenly aware of a high-pitched wail, realizing it was her own only when Nick spoke softly as he gently lifted her legs back to the bed. 'Breathe, Rach. You need to take a steady breath. Come on. With me. In, out. In, out. There you go. Let's do it again.'

She forced herself to focus on nothing but the soothing tone of his voice. And when she was finally back in the hospital room, not in *The Toybox*, she blinked and concentrated on inhaling and exhaling, the whole while squeezing Nick's hand as if it were her lifeline.

It was only minutes, not the hours it felt like, before the female detective stepped forward, introducing herself. 'Hi, Rachel. I'm Detective Alyssa Wyatt. Do you remember me?'

Rachel's chin dropped forward, but she didn't trust herself to speak. Not yet.

'Good.' Without taking her eyes from Rachel, she pointed behind her to the man who still stood in the doorway, an odd expression on his face. 'This is my partner, Detective Cord Roberts. We're both here to help you, to try to find out what happened, what you remember. But if it's easier for you, my partner can step out of the room. Would that make you feel better? Don't be afraid to tell the truth.'

Rachel opened her mouth to speak, though she wasn't sure what she wanted to say. Nick cupped her chin and turned her face so she was focused on him. 'You're safe. These two, along with a lot of other people, have been searching nonstop for you. They won't hurt you. Neither of them.'

She trusted Nick. She didn't trust the man. She tried to nod, to say the man could stay. But then the man's mouth was moving, and she was sure he was speaking, but her mind couldn't make sense of his words. And then he was outside, and just like that, her heart rate slowed, and things came back into focus. 'Nick?'

'I'm still here. I'll be with you the entire time. I promise.'

Her brother was the calm in her storm, so she focused on his grip as she turned to the detective, who took three careful steps closer to the bed. Her voice was kind when she spoke.

'Okay, Rachel, I know the questions I'm about to ask are going to be tough and personal, and I know you've suffered through a terrible ordeal, so if at any point you need to stop and take a break, you just say the word, all right?'

'I'll try.' Her voice was scratchy, and she shifted towards Nick. 'Water, please.'

Before he could release her grip, the detective handed him the cup. 'Thank you,' he said as he placed the straw at Rachel's mouth. Mindful of her raw throat, she took several small sips before twisting her head to the side.

'Enough?'

'Yes.' Her skin went clammy as she waited for the detective to ask her questions.

'Rachel, why don't you begin by telling me what you remember. Can you do that?'

'Remember?'

'Let's start with when you went missing. You were at a frat party, right? Tell me about that night. Who did you go with? Did you leave with that person or someone else? Or no one?'

An image floated in Rachel's mind, and her stomach clenched, a tangle of insects in her gut, but then it was gone. 'I went with a friend. Anna. She was with a guy, and I tried to get her to leave, but then I fell asleep. And when I woke up... I don't know where Anna is.' Her heart galloped, and her blood pressure shot up so quickly, the alarms on her monitor blared, and within seconds, two nurses rushed in.

Rachel spent the next several minutes trying to keep track of Nick as a nurse with dishwater-blonde hair mumbled incoherently above her. It was only when the words 'sedative' and 'calm her' trickled down that she was able to speak again. 'No. No drugs.'

At the same time, Nick stepped in front of the nurse, 'My sister doesn't want any drugs.'

Much to Rachel's surprise, the nurse gave one curt nod of her head and then smiled down at her with gentle eyes. 'The medicine can help, so if, at any time, you change your mind, you let one of us know. We can even start off with a half-dose, if you'd like.'

'No drugs,' Rachel repeated.

'Okay, no drugs.'

It seemed forever before the medical staff left with a warning to the detective. And then she was back in Rachel's line of vision. 'Rachel, I know this is scary, and I wish I didn't have to ask you to replay any of it. But it's the only way we're going to be able to catch all the people who are responsible for doing this to you.'

The detective was right; she didn't want to replay this. But then Katelyn's terrified face flashed in her mind, and she knew she had to. She spoke slowly, telling her nightmare, sobs shaking her as she told the detective about the men, the whips, the clips. The pain. The degradation. The desire to die. Losing the will to live. She turned away, embarrassed and ashamed that Nick had to hear of her humiliation, but she knew she couldn't bear to have him leave her side, either. Tears trickled down the side of her face, splashing onto the fist that clutched the sheet tightly under her chin.

A smooth hand touched hers. 'Rachel, I want to remind you that you're in a safe place right now, and you have nothing to be ashamed of. You need to remember that none of this is your fault. Nothing you did caused this.' Rachel listened to Detective Wyatt's kind voice, trying to believe her.

'Rachel, can you look at me?' Reluctantly, Rachel moved her gaze back to Alyssa, careful to avoid eye contact with her brother. 'Are you ready to continue, or do you need a few minutes?'

Inside, she shouted, *I just want it all to go away, to never have happened at all.* 'I can continue.'

'Did you know Meghan Jessup?' the detective asked.

'Briefly. She disappeared shortly after I got there. Did you find her? Is she okay?'

When the detective flipped her phone around to show her a picture of a man, Rachel knew Meghan hadn't survived, and her stomach spasmed.

'Is this one of the men you saw at that house?'

Rachel studied the picture for several minutes, though it really wasn't necessary. She'd never be able to get them out of her head. Finally, she shook her head. 'No, I never saw him.'

'Are you sure?'

'Yes.'

She tapped on her screen and pulled up another image before turning her phone toward Rachel once more. 'What about her? Do you recognize this woman?'

Staring back at her from the detective's phone was the lady who'd dispassionately stood in the doorway after the very first time Rachel had been violated, the woman they'd all believed to be in charge because everyone obeyed her commands. The memory of the pain and degradation was so real, so intense that, before she knew what was happening, she was retching, barely conscious of her brother moving to hold her hair back as the detective placed a bucket beneath her mouth.

After her stomach was empty, dry heaves took over, and then finally, blessedly, it was over, and she allowed Nick to ease her back onto the pillow as she cried.

'I'm so sorry, Rachel. I'm going to let you get some rest now, and I'll be back later today, if that's okay.'

Something was different in the detective's voice, and Rachel turned her head toward her, surprised to see such pain in her face, the kind her own mother should have had.

'None of us knew the woman's name; no one ever spoke it out loud, at least not around us. But we always believed she was in charge because everyone followed her commands and deferred to her.'

The detective smiled and reached out one hand, allowing it to hover over Rachel's, giving her the choice to accept it or not. Her right hand still encased in her brother's grip, she lifted her fingers to allow the detective to take hold of her left.

'Thank you. You've been very courageous, both in surviving this ordeal and for sharing it with me now. I know that wasn't easy, and I promise we're going to do everything we can to catch everyone involved.' Then, speaking to both Nick and her, she said, 'If the staff haven't talked to you about it yet, you might want to mention having a victim advocate here. They can help.'

Rachel didn't know what a victim advocate was, but she knew she didn't want another stranger around that she had to divulge her secrets to.

Chapter Forty-Five

Sunday, May 26

In the waiting room, Holly sat next to Sophie, who sat next to her parents while Jersey's mom was in the room with her. Her phone dinged, and she grabbed it off the seat and flipped it over so she could read the text. It was from Nick.

> Your mom just left the room. How are you holding up?

Holly's eyes flickered to the silver metal doors separating the waiting area from the patients' rooms then to the television in the corner. The girls' rescue had been on the news all day.

> I'm holding up as well as can be expected, I guess. You?

> As good as can be expected, I guess.

Holly stared at the screen, her fingers poised above the keyboard as she bit her cheek, then she puffed the air out and typed.

> How's your sister? I mean, besides the obvious.

> I don't know how to answer that. How's your friend?

> I don't know how to answer that.

She waited another minute, but when there was no reply, she set her phone aside, and studied Sophie's profile. Her cheeks were splotchy, but not from tears, from anger. Holly tugged gently on her friend's hand, pulling her up. 'Come on. My mom and Cord are back there, so it's probably going to be awhile yet. Let's go grab some drinks and snacks.'

After only a brief hesitation, Sophie climbed to her feet, then swiveled around to check the same metal doors Holly had been searching only a moment ago. Pressing the heels of both hands against her eyes, she nodded, but before following Holly, she leaned down to kiss her mom and dad on the cheek. 'Do you want us to bring you anything?'

Sophie's mom smiled sadly up at her daughter. 'Nothing for me, darling. Thank you.'

'Are you sure? You need to eat something. When's the last time you ate?'

Mrs. Quill tipped her head, a sad smile lifting up one corner of her mouth. 'When's the last time you did?'

Sophie merely stared, waiting. Her mom sighed. 'I know, but right now I can't. I'll wait for Aunt Natalia to come out, and then we'll go eat together. I promise. But you two go ahead. You were here until late last night and got here early this morning. You need a break.'

'Daddy?'

'No, thank you. I'll go with Mom and Aunt Natalia, make sure they both get a warm bite inside when you and Holly return. But take your time.' His gaze was on his daughter, but his words were directed at her best friend.

At the elevator, Sophie reached out and jabbed the down arrow several times, hard enough that Holly was a little afraid she'd actually break it. When the doors opened, the two girls stepped aside to allow a family of five to disembark before climbing in themselves, grateful that no one else had been waiting for the car.

Once the doors closed, Holly pressed the button for the cafeteria. Leaning her head back against the stainless steel of the elevator wall, she breathed deeply, a million thoughts racing through her mind, when Sophie spoke.

'I know it's her daughter, and she has every right to be in there with Jersey, but we're worried, too. We should've been allowed to see her.' She swallowed loudly before admitting what was really bothering her. 'What if she doesn't want to see us? What if she told her mom that, and Aunt Natalia just hasn't found a way to tell us yet?'

Holly stepped closer to her best friend and draped an arm over her shoulder, pulling her in closer to her, and reaching up to draw Sophie's head onto her shoulder. 'That's not what's going on, Sophie. We're going to see her, I promise. It's hard, I know, but we need to be patient just a little longer.' And though she knew she shouldn't, she brought up Jersey's dad. 'I still can't believe what he told my mom.' When her mom had pulled Natalia aside last night to inform her of her soon-to-be ex-husband's response to returning, Natalia had nearly disintegrated, and likely would've, if it hadn't been for Sophie's mom.

Sophie's jaw tightened. '"Tell her I'll see her when I get home in two weeks." What a prick.' Tears spilled over until she wiped them angrily away. 'Whatever. He's a bigger ass than we already knew he was.'

There was nothing left to say after that, so they remained quiet until the elevator doors opened on the main floor where the cafeteria was located. As they stepped out, they practically bumped into Beau Cambridge, and Sophie stumbled back.

'What the actual *hell* are you doing here?' she spat, heedless of the curious stares she received as people stopped and gawked.

Beau crossed his arms over his chest and sneered. 'I heard they found Jersey, so I'm here to see my girlfriend.' He tried to step into the elevator, but Sophie was faster, blocking his path.

'Like hell.'

'And you think you can stop me?' He moved in closer to Sophie, towering over her much smaller frame in an effort to intimidate her, but she didn't budge.

Eyes narrowed into slits, she spoke through her teeth. 'Maybe I can't physically bar you from trying, but if I start screaming, I bet I can get those security guards over there – the ones who are right now, as we speak, keeping a careful watch on this situation – to come over here, and I bet I can put on a very convincing act about how you've been abusive to me, and I'm so scared, and ask them to please just make you go.'

As she spoke, Sophie's gaze flickered to the guards who were indeed studying the situation, and then, raising her voice, she said, 'Please, Beau, you need to go. You're scaring me.'

His nostrils flared, and the veins at his temples bulged as his face flamed crimson. Eyes blazing, he took a menacing step forward, forcing Sophie against the wall when a tanned hand stopped him. Automatically, his fist swung up and out, but the security guard blocked the punch. A brief scuffle later, the two security guards dragged Beau away.

Before he was escorted outside, he twisted his upper body around and shouted back. 'You better watch your back, you stupid cow.'

Holly and Sophie watched him shrug off the two guards and stomp off. But before they could turn around and head into the cafeteria for some food, the automatic double doors opened again, and Leigh Ann rushed in, panting, her face red from exertion. Slightly out of breath, she hurried over as soon as she spotted them.

'I heard it on the news. How is she? Is she awake? What happened? Was that Beau I just saw leaving?'

At the mention of Beau's name, both Holly and Sophie tensed, and in Sophie's case, her face fell into a careful mask. In a monotone voice, she said, 'She's stable, we don't know, we don't have all the answers yet, and yes.'

'How about you? Are you doing okay? Is there anything I can get you, do for you?'

Sophie stared at Leigh Ann like she'd grown a second head. 'Are you serious right now? What you can do for me is leave me the hell alone.'

Leigh Ann's gaze flickered between Sophie and Holly. Her shoulders sagged. 'I get it. You're still mad because I waited to tell Holly's mom about the frat party. I guess that's why neither of you sent a text. How many times do I have to say I'm sorry before you forgive me?'

A twinge of guilt ate at Holly's conscience because Leigh Ann was right, and now that she saw her friend's face, she knew one of them should've been a big enough person to tell her Jersey had been rescued.

'Um, has she said what happened exactly?' Leigh Ann stared out the window as she asked the question.

'We actually haven't seen her yet.' It was clear by the tone of her voice that Sophie hadn't wanted to admit that.

Leigh Ann nodded. 'Do you want me to leave?'

Sophie sighed. 'Yes, but that's what *I* want, not what Jersey might need. Even if she doesn't want to see any of us, I know it'll help her knowing we're *all* here.'

'Thank you,' Leigh Ann whispered.

Half an hour later, the girls headed back after stopping to buy three hot chocolates, a bag of chips, and a peanut butter cookie – none of which they planned to touch. They rode the car up in silence, and as they climbed off the elevator, Holly ran into her mom and Cord.

Chapter Forty-Six

Sunday, May 26

After leaving Rachel's room, Alyssa found Cord near a vending machine. 'How are you holding up?'

Cord shifted his gaze from the window to his partner. 'Me?'

'Yes, you. I'm sure seeing Rachel reminded you of Shelley's ordeal. So, I repeat: are you holding up okay?' She watched as he shoved both hands into his front pockets, his head tilting toward the ceiling.

'You're right. All of this reminds me of her. But I'm not worried about me right now.' He swallowed, then leveled a steady stare at her. 'I just don't want any of those girls to end up feeling so hopeless that they do what Shelley did.'

Alyssa placed her palm on Cord's arm. 'We'll do all that we can to ensure that doesn't happen. Now, you ready to hear what I found out?'

'I wish I didn't have to be, but yes, I am.'

She shared what she'd learned, and then together, they went to visit Jersey. From her daughter's friend, she learned much the same as she had from Rachel, except that Jersey gave her a very detailed description of one of the men who'd abused her, one who Jersey hadn't seen at the scene when they were rescued. She didn't recognize Yarmini, but she did recognize Tatiana Salazar, although she couldn't tell them what her name was.

And then, in excruciating detail, stopping every few minutes to get her breathing back under control, she described the torture she'd gone through.

Jersey's words and listening to her struggle as she mentally relived her torturous ordeal tore at Alyssa's heartstrings. This was her daughter's friend and someone who had slept over at her house. More than once, she had listened to Holly, Sophie, and Jersey giggle all night long over silly things. She'd watched them give each other pedicures and French-braid each other's hair. She'd overheard them whisper about secret crushes and worry about whether or not a boy liked them back. And because of that, Alyssa found herself hiding her hands inside her jacket pockets so no one could witness the way they shook or how they clenched in anger at what had happened.

Jersey stared across the room at the blank screen of the television as she described what had happened just before she found herself in the cell. 'The last thing I remember was leaving the duck pond, hearing footsteps, and then someone tackled me.' A flicker passed over her face. 'Whoever it was whispered "nighty-night," and I thought I recognized the voice, but now I'm not so sure.'

Jersey's mom stiffened.

'I need you to think, Jersey,' Alyssa said. 'Was it a male or female voice?'

Jersey closed her eyes, and when she opened them, tears formed in her lower lids. 'I don't know,' she whispered. 'Why can't I remember?'

Alyssa removed her hand from her pocket and placed it over Jersey's. She chose her words carefully. 'Sometimes, when a person experiences a traumatic event such as you and the others have had, they experience a form of amnesia. I'm not a medical expert, but I've been told it's a way for the brain to protect itself. You'll remember when you're ready.' She gave Jersey's fingers a light squeeze. 'And I'll be here when you do.'

Sobs shook Jersey's body, and her chest heaved in and out as she sucked in great gulping breaths of air. 'Wh—What if I never remember and he gets away because of it?'

Alyssa didn't have an answer for that, so she said the only thing she could. 'We're going to do everything we can to

286

make sure we arrest every person involved — even if you can't remember.'

Before she could leave, Jersey stopped her. 'Mrs. Wyatt? Could you please tell Holly, Sophie, and Leigh Ann I want to see them?'

'Of course.'

Next, they tried Becca Marshall. Alyssa knocked, and when Becca's mother answered, she invited them in and, after explaining that Becca's younger sister would be up later that evening, introduced them to Becca's father and two brothers, one younger, one older. Each one of them looked as if they wanted to punch something. Alyssa understood the feeling, but she also knew that, although it might make them feel better now, in the long run, it would do nothing to help Becca. And in fact, a show of violence might actually hurt.

To Alyssa's surprise, Becca didn't mind having her brothers in the room as she recounted what happened. 'I was in the park, just kind of enjoying the sunshine when a girl walked up to me — she looked like she was in high school — and asked if she could use my phone. She said she'd left hers at school and needed to ask a friend who was still there if she could get it for her.' One hand reached up to rub at her neck, her blank stare indicating she'd returned to that day. 'I remember she looked familiar to me, but I couldn't figure out from where I'd seen her. I handed her my phone, and when I did, she jabbed something into my neck, and then I woke in the cell. Meghan and Cheyenne were already there. Faye came next, then Rachel, then Jersey, then Katelyn.'

Alyssa and Cord exchanged a glance. 'Can you describe this girl who asked to borrow your phone?' she asked.

Becca blinked several times, as if she'd forgotten she was speaking to them. 'I'm sorry. I can't really remember,' she whispered.

'That's okay. I'll leave my number so if it comes to you, all you have to do is call, alright?'

'Okay.'

'Becca, you said Meghan was there when you arrived. Do you recall what she was wearing that day?'

'A silk robe. That's all any of us were ever allowed to wear. Our clothes were taken as soon as we arrived.'

Keeping her expression neutral, Alyssa glanced over in time to see Cord's hand tighten on the pen as he scribbled down notes.

'Do you know what happened to your clothes?'

'No, ma'am. I never saw mine again.'

'Okay, we're almost finished here, but first, I'd like to show you a couple of pictures and see if you recognize the people in them. Do you think you're up for that?'

Becca's hand moved from her neck to burrow under the sheet covering her bruised and battered body. Her legs began trembling, causing the bed railings to rattle. One of her brothers jumped up and moved over to clasp her hand in his. The other members of her family wore masks of rage, frustration, and helplessness.

'We're right here with you.' Becca's brother's voice was gruff and husky with emotion.

The corners of Becca's lips tipped up slightly as she tried to smile. Then she took a deep breath and turned to face Alyssa. 'I can do this.'

Once again, Alyssa was struck by the strength of these girls. Maybe, eventually, they would really be okay. From the front pocket of the notebook he was holding, Cord pulled out the photos of Yarmini and Salazar and handed them to her, and she turned them for Becca to see.

Instead of the definite no she'd expected, Becca couldn't say for sure if she'd seen Yarmini or not, claiming he seemed familiar, but she verified what the others said about Salazar. It was looking more and more like she was the mastermind. Then Becca, too, gave a description of one of her abusers.

'And you didn't see this man when you were brought upstairs?'

'No, ma'am.' She turned so that she couldn't see her family. 'I only saw him twice at the beginning.' Her voice trembled as she held Alyssa's gaze. 'Detective Wyatt, thank you for finding us. Jersey told us you'd be looking, that you'd save us, but I don't think any of us believed it would happen. So, thank you for not giving up.'

Alyssa reached down and squeezed Becca's hand, hoping the dim lighting in the room hid the shimmer in her eyes. 'Thank *you* for being so courageous and strong. Now, you rest, and we'll stop by and see you again.'

Out in the corridor, Alyssa inhaled deeply, releasing a quivering breath, but before she could say what was on her mind, Cord beat her to it.

'These are some pretty incredible girls. Courageous, heroic. Resilient.'

'That they are.'

–

Faye and Cheyenne were still under heavy sedation, so Alyssa and Cord tried Katelyn next. Opening the door when they knocked, Mr. Phillipson, with his pale face, wrinkled clothing, and bloodshot eyes, invited them in.

Hovering next to Katelyn's bed stood Mary. Her face was devoid of make-up, and dark bags circled her eyes, making them appear bruised. One hand brushed over the top of her daughter's head even as she glanced up to see who had entered the room. 'The detectives are here to speak to you, sweetheart.'

Katelyn's eyes clouded over when she turned her head to Alyssa and Cord, and she reached up and covered her face with her hands, her chest heaving as great gulping sobs escaped.

Cord hung back by the door while Alyssa moved forward, opening her mouth to speak, but finding the words stuck in her throat, and realizing she was too emotional to say a word.

A minute passed before she could. 'Katelyn, I'm Detective Wyatt. Do you remember me?' She asked the same question she'd asked Rachel Otis.

Katelyn nodded, and though her hands had moved from her face, her gaze remained fixed on the window to her right. 'I couldn't get it open.' Her words came out quietly, strangled.

'Couldn't get what open, Katelyn?'

Fat tears rolled down her cheeks, and her body quivered, along with her voice. 'The window. I couldn't get it open. It was too thick, and it was nailed shut, but I tried. I tried so hard, but the pyramid collapsed, and we couldn't get out because I failed. And they were doing it for me, to protect me, even though it hurt them so bad, but I couldn't protect them because I couldn't get it open, and I failed, I failed, I—' A moan escaped, growing louder and sharper in volume.

Alyssa swayed slightly on her feet as she realized what Katelyn was saying. She'd known these girls were courageous, but this went beyond her imaginings. She turned back to look at Cord. He'd moved further into the room but had stayed back so as not to frighten Katelyn. He blinked rapidly before finally reaching up to wipe the tears away from his red-rimmed eyes.

Mary's comforting tone had finally soothed Katelyn's panic, and so Alyssa focused her attention back where it belonged.

'Katelyn, you didn't fail anyone, sweetie. What you did – trying like that – was risky, but you did it anyway. That was so brave of you. All of you.' As she spoke, Katelyn's chest heaved less, and her tears slowed, though they still fell. And then finally, she turned to Alyssa.

'But I couldn't get it open.'

Alyssa engulfed this sprite of a girl's hand in her own and gave it a gentle squeeze. Speaking softly, she said, 'Maybe not, but you tried. For the others and for yourself. Even though it meant risking your own life. Can you see how brave that is?'

'They wanted to protect me,' she repeated.

A sad but proud smile lifted the corners of Alyssa's mouth. 'Of course, they did. Just like you wanted to protect them. You didn't fail. Now, are you ready to talk to us about what you remember?'

'I didn't fail?' Katelyn whispered.

'No, you were unbelievably *brave*,' Alyssa promised.

'Can my mom and dad stay here while I talk?'

'Of course, they can.'

Katelyn's eyes found first her mother's, then her father's before returning her attention to Alyssa. 'I was on my way home when a girl came up to me and told me she'd lost her phone. She wondered if I'd seen it. I turned to look where she pointed, and when I did, I felt something stick me in the neck. My vision got blurry, and then my legs started to shake—'

Gasping for air, Katelyn's hands flew to her throat, eyes wide as she concentrated on her mother who had settled herself on the bed. 'You're okay. You're safe. We're right here.' Mary repeated the words over and over until her daughter's breathing was back under control.

'Katelyn, do you need a few minutes?' Alyssa asked.

The young girl shook her head. 'The girl tossed my backpack into the tree. And then I woke in the cell with the others surrounding me.' A fresh round of tears fell down her face. 'They were already trying to protect me.'

Pride for these girls filled Alyssa's heart and gave her hope that, someday, they might actually be okay again. 'Can you describe the girl who approached you?'

Confusion clouded Katelyn's eyes. 'I think I'd seen her hanging out in the park before. She had shoulder-length hair and was taller than me. I'm four-eleven.'

After several more minutes, Alyssa showed Katelyn the same pictures she had of Yarmini and Salazar, but unlike the others, she recognized neither.

Alyssa thanked Katelyn and turned to go when Mary stopped them. 'Detectives, do you mind if I speak to you for a moment out in the hall?' At her daughter's panicked look, she said, 'I'll be just a moment, sweetheart, and Dad will still be right here. Okay?'

Hesitantly, Katelyn tipped her head forward in agreement.

Out in the corridor, Mary gripped both Alyssa's and Cord's hands. 'Jason and I can't thank you enough for finding our girl. Kate said you saved her before they could—' Her voice wobbled, and then releasing a steady breath, she said, 'Stephanie's mother is planning on bringing her by today. Despite how close they are, it worries me a little.'

Remembering how Trevor had played such an important role in Isaac's healing, Alyssa said, 'I think it could be good for both of them.'

Mary nodded and turned to go back in the room. Her hand gripping the doorknob, she whispered her plea, 'Please, detectives, hurry and find the rest of the monsters who did this to my baby.' And then she was gone.

Quietly, Alyssa and Cord left the patient wing and headed to the waiting room where she spotted Holly, Sophie, and Leigh Ann exiting the elevators. As soon as her daughter spotted her, Holly rushed over.

Alyssa caught her and wrapped her in a hug. 'Jersey asked for the three of you just before we left her room. But before you go see her, I need to prepare you for what to expect. She and the others have been through quite an ordeal, so of course, she's emotionally fragile. But it's her physical state that might take you aback. She's been badly beaten, and she doesn't resemble the Jersey of a week ago. Don't pretend it's not there but try not to overreact. Right now, what she needs is for you all to be strong for her.'

'Thanks, Mom.'

When Holly leaned down for another hug, Alyssa said, 'I love you,' squeezing tighter when her daughter whispered the words back.

Chapter Forty-Seven

Sunday, May 26

Leigh Ann shuffled behind Sophie and Holly, her shoes scratching along the floor and causing goosebumps to pop up all over Holly's skin. Feet from Jersey's room, and just when Holly thought her head would explode if she had to hear that sound another second, Leigh Ann stopped.

Darting nervous glances at the door, she brushed both hands down the front of her capris, leaving a streak of moisture as if she'd forgotten to dry her hands. 'Maybe you should just tell her I couldn't come,' she whispered so quietly Holly had to lean closer so she could hear over the noise and bustle of the nurses' station.

Sophie, however, wasn't nearly as hushed, but still spoke low enough that Jersey wouldn't be able to overhear through the heavy door. 'I'm not lying to Jersey for you.'

A tear trickled down Leigh Ann's cheek, and she shifted her gaze to the side in order to avoid eye contact. 'I'm sorry. I just don't think I'm ready for this.' Without another word, she swung around and headed back out the double doors.

Neither Sophie nor Holly said anything for several minutes, and then finally Holly sucked in a gulp of air and linked her arm through her best friend's. 'Are *you* ready?'

A myriad of emotions crossed Sophie's face as she hovered on a mental ledge. 'As ready as I'm going to be.' Her gaze shifted up. 'I'm scared.' Her words were soaked in trepidation.

'Me, too. Um, so do you want to go in alone first? I mean since she's actually your family and all?'

'What?' Sophie jerked back as if she'd been electrocuted and gripped onto Holly's wrist tight enough that Holly winced. 'No way do I want to do this alone. First, *you're* my family, too. Just because we don't share a blood bond... Second, she likes you better. And third, *I* need you with me. I mean, what am I supposed to *say* to her? Besides, she asked for all of us, and Leigh Ann already bailed, so...'

Holly gently pried her friend's fingers from around her wrist and then removed the tiny seashell bracelet that had left its mark embedded in her skin. 'You're right. I just wanted to make sure.' They faced the door and then, palms gripped tightly together, the two girls pushed it open.

Aunt Natalia's head snapped up when they entered, and to be honest, if it hadn't been for Jersey's mom hovering over the gaunt and battered figure in the bed, Holly would've thought they were in the wrong room.

Sophie's hand squeezed so tightly, Holly's fingers tingled.

Natalia offered them a watery smile then bent and kissed the top of Jersey's head. 'Look who's here to see you. I'm going to leave you to talk, but I'll be back as soon as they leave again, okay?'

'Thanks, Mom.'

Natalia gathered her purse, phone, and the book she had with her, and gave Jersey one more quick kiss before moving to the door where she hesitated again, afraid to let her daughter out of her sight. 'I'll be in the waiting room. Come find me when you leave,' she told Holly and Sophie. And then she was gone.

Careful to keep her expression neutral, Holly stepped closer to the bed, bringing Sophie with her. She tried not to flinch at the marks marring her friend's once perfect features. And then without any warning, a dam opened, releasing all the emotion she'd held inside from the moment Jersey went missing to the moment she'd heard she'd been found alive. She yanked her hand from Sophie's and grappled for a tissue. 'I'm sorry. I didn't mean... you don't need...'

Something flashed in Jersey's eyes, but then she turned away and stared out the window. 'It's okay.'

Sophie moved into her cousin's line of vision. 'I'm so sorry, Jersey. I should've been more understanding about what you were going through,' she choked.

'It's nothing.' Jersey's voice was flat. 'Trust me.'

'Do you want to talk about what happened yet?' Nerves jumbled into a tight ball in Holly's stomach the second the question fell out, but she reminded herself they had to be strong for their friend, and so she steeled herself for whatever came next.

Despite her emotionless, monotone voice, it was clear by the way Jersey's fingers curled into fists as she tightened her grip on the blanket, shifting it further up her body and securing it beneath her chin – as if the blanket alone could keep her safe as long as she was cocooned within its embrace – that her mind was replaying the horror she'd lived for the past week. 'No, not really.' She lifted her head from the pillow and peered behind them. 'Where's Leigh Ann? Didn't she come?' It was clear she was hurt that one of her best friends hadn't come by to visit her.

Holly fought to keep her eyes steady on Jersey's. 'She was... she said she'd be by later after you'd had a chance to rest more.' Even to her own ears, the lie was weak.

'Of course.' Jersey pursed her lips and nodded before turning to her cousin. 'Mom said Dad was doing his best to get back to the States as soon as he could. She's lying, isn't she? He's with his bimbo and can't be bothered to make sure his own daughter is okay, right?' Hurt clouded her eyes, only to be replaced by anger seconds later.

Sophie averted her eyes, taking a sudden interest in her torn cuticles. 'Aunt Natalia knows you need to concentrate on healing, and she doesn't want anything or anyone to get in the way of that.'

'You know your non-answer was an answer, right?' Jersey's eyes drifted closed. 'Could you just sit with me until I fall asleep? I'm so tired, and I don't want to be alone.'

'Of course.'

Nearly an hour later, Jersey's eyes flitted nervously behind her closed lids even as her chest lifted and fell in a steady rhythm. Quietly, so as not to disturb her, Holly and Sophie tiptoed to the door, turning back to check she was still asleep before they headed out into the corridor. When they were far enough away from Jersey's room, Sophie stopped and leaned her head back against the wall, hand against her throat.

'That was even worse than I thought it was going to be,' she choked.

The image of seeing Isaac that first time after his escape flashed into Holly's mind. As if she were there all over again, she could feel the crippling fear of seeing his body covered in bruises. When would the people she loved stop being kidnapped? Trailing that thought was the sensation of being the common denominator, like she was bad luck to be around.

After checking in with Sophie's parents and Aunt Natalia, assuring them Jersey was asleep, she and Sophie left the hospital to grab some food. It wasn't easy leaving, but they knew they needed to clear their heads in order to be any good to Jersey. On the way to her car, Holly found herself searching for Nick, knowing he was likely still with his sister. She hadn't realized she'd been half-hoping to see him inside.

Chapter Forty-Eight

Two blocks from the precinct and stopped at a light, Alyssa took a call from Hal. 'Tell me you've located Tatiana Salazar.'

Hal cleared his throat. 'Sorry. Not yet, but we'll find her. Also, as we expected, all the men brought in yesterday are still squawking about it all being a great big misunderstanding that'll get cleared up in the light of day.'

'Of course, it's a big misunderstanding. Isn't it always?' Cord's jaw looked like it might crack if he clenched his teeth any tighter.

'Usually,' Hal agreed, 'but that's not why I'm calling. Like you asked, we've been tracking Steve Yarmini's credit cards.'

Alyssa shifted in the driver's seat, unintentionally pressing the accelerator and jolting the car forward. She hit the brake inches from tapping the car in front of her.

'We just received a credit card alert that Steve Yarmini just purchased a one-way plane ticket to Nepal. Flight leaves at 1:16 from United heading into Dallas.'

Alyssa glanced at the clock displayed on the dash. 11:18. 'Is he trying to throw us off, or is he really that thick?' Though she muttered the question more to herself than to Hal, he answered as if she'd asked him directly.

'Not that thick, Alyssa. It's my understanding, after all, that Nepal has a no extradition treaty with the United States.'

'Thanks, Hal. Can you update Hammond for me?'

'Sure thing. Anything else?'

'I'll let you know.' At the intersection, she flipped the car around and sped toward the freeway. Cord was already on the phone with Joe.

'You and Tony get to the airport and get in place. We'll be there as soon as we can. That plane isn't taking off with Yarmini onboard.'

The second she hit I25, she hit the accelerator, the speed on her Tahoe steadily climbing to seventy-five, eighty, ninety as she hurried to intercept Steve Yarmini. Thankfully, it was before noon on a Sunday and traffic was still fairly light, so less than ten minutes later, the car barreled onto airport property.

Inside the terminal, they stopped at the large display for departures, noting what gate they needed, and then took the escalator two at a time. At security, they flashed their badges, and one of the guys ushered them through. Maneuvering around the cleaning crew, Alyssa and Cord sprinted down the corridor to Gate B. The crowd was sparse, and they picked out Yarmini right away. His head was in a magazine, but he darted nervous glances out the window every few seconds. It was during one of these that he spotted them, and he leaped to his feet, his head jerking left and right as he spun around in a circle, desperately searching for an escape route.

Apparently the guy wasn't used to going on the lam, considering he'd used his own credit card and hadn't scoped out possible escape routes before they'd arrived. It was a rookie mistake that would cost him. Alyssa and Cord shared a look, then Cord moved off to the left while Alyssa continued straight down the aisle. 'Mr. Yarmini, we've been searching for you, and here you were, planning on leaving without saying goodbye? That was quite rude, and I admit I'm a little hurt by that. But you can make it up to me by coming with me peacefully.'

It was the way his eyes flickered to his right that alerted her he was really going to make a run for it. And she wasn't wrong. She adjusted her approach as he darted around the chairs, heading for one of the doors leading into nothing but a steep fall to the tarmac. When he tripped over his bag, she actually shook her head. Not the sharpest criminal in the class.

Two minutes later, with the small crowd waiting for the plane watching, Alyssa had Yarmini on the ground and cuffed. Yanking him to his feet, she read him his rights as Cord latched onto his other elbow.

Yarmini continued his futile struggles, his face turning bright red from the exertion. 'You're making a huge mistake here.'

'You're the one who made the mistakes, and now you're going to pay for them,' Alyssa promised as they escorted him outside to Joe and Tony who were waiting by the curb to drive him to the police station.

–

Half an hour later, just after noon, Alyssa and Cord rushed past Ruby and headed straight to the interrogation room where Joe had taken Yarmini.

As soon as he saw them coming, Joe uncrossed his arms and stepped away from the door. 'All yours. I'll be writing up my report if you need me for anything.'

'Thanks, Joe.'

Alyssa unlocked the door to a pacing Steve Yarmini, interrupting him mid-rant. Closing the door behind him, Cord moved into the corner while Alyssa pulled out a chair and offered a smile that wasn't meant to be the least bit friendly.

'Why don't you take a seat and get comfortable? We're going to be here a while.'

Dark smudges stained the bags under the brown eyes that glowered back at her, but he dragged back one of the chairs and plopped into it like a sullen teenager. 'Can't say I'm sorry I interrupted your travel plans, Mr. Yarmini. What's in Nepal anyway?'

Steve Yarmini did his best to look intimidating as he crossed his arms and narrowed his gaze at her, but his shaky voice and the sweat popping out on his lip belied his confidence. 'I was heading there on vacation.'

Cord's posture was relaxed, though Alyssa knew him well enough to know he was anything but. 'Do you happen to drive a 2017 Dodge Viper, Mr. Yarmini?' He mirrored Yarmini's stance – crossing his arms over his chest.

'What?'

'Dodge Viper? Sporty little number? Sound familiar?' Cord's tone suggested he wasn't buying into Yarmini's act.

Yarmini's eyes flickered around the room. 'Yeah, but it was stolen a few days ago.'

Cord feigned shock. 'Stolen? Really? If it was stolen, why didn't you report it?'

Manic energy radiated off Yarmini. 'What?'

'Why. Didn't. You. Report. It? I mean, hot little number like that, I'd be on the phone to the police immediately.'

Alyssa skewered Yarmini with her glare, not giving him time to answer Cord's question. 'Was it stolen, or did you dump it like you did Meghan Jessup after you raped and murdered her?'

Like a spring-loaded trap, Yarmini bolted out of his chair and pressed his back against the wall. 'I don't know what you're talking about. I don't know—' His eyes widened into near-perfect circles.

Alyssa cut him off. 'Do you know what's great about science these days, Mr. Yarmini? We can determine assailants from the tiniest little things. Say for instance, bodily fluids discovered in a fourteen-year-old rape victim.' The results from the lab hadn't yet come back, but Yarmini didn't need to know that.

Steve Yarmini paled at her announcement. 'You're lying,' he sputtered, specks of spittle spraying outward and landing on the table.

'Am I?'

Defeated, Yarmini sank back into his chair. 'I demand to speak to my attorney before I say anything else.'

Alyssa stood and Cord pushed off the wall. 'Of course. That is your right. In the meantime, you'll be a guest of the

Metropolitan Detention Center.' At the door, her hand hovered above the handle as she twisted around, her smile stretched tight. 'I do hope you're aware that while prisoners are guilty of many things, they still hold grudges against child rapists and murderers.' She had the satisfaction of watching all color drain from Yarmini's face as she pulled open the door and walked out in search of someone to escort him to a holding cell.

Chapter Forty-Nine

Sunday, May 26

An unfamiliar perfume drifted in the air. Someone was in Rachel's room, someone who wasn't her brother. Her muscles turned into hot liquid, and she couldn't get any of them to obey. She needed to be quiet, needed them not to know she was awake. Still, a whimper escaped.

'Good morning.' A voice like polished silver came from near the side of her bed, and Rachel's eyes flew open. A nurse wearing camel-colored scrubs stood with a dry erase marker in one hand, eraser in the other. 'I didn't mean to startle you. You were sleeping so well, I didn't want to disturb you. I'm Bethany. I'll be your nurse today. I was jotting my name and extension on your board over there in case you needed me for anything when you woke.' The smile she wore was soft and kind, but it was the gentleness and understanding in her demeanor that made Rachel want to cry.

'Where's my brother? Can I have some water, please?' She wondered if her voice would ever again sound like her own.

'I think he stepped out to get a bite to eat, but he said if you woke to tell you he'd be right back.' Bethany scooted the table nearer to the bed before picking up the water and wrinkling her nose. 'Let me go get you some fresh stuff, okay? This looks like it might've been sitting here all night. I'll be right back.'

A few minutes later, Bethany returned with a fresh pitcher of water and a cup of ice. 'Here you go, hon. Now, you just lay back and relax while I take your blood pressure.' She secured the cuff around Rachel's arm and squeezed the bulb, watching the needle and keeping her rambling monologue going.

A fine sheen of cold sweat broke out on Rachel's skin, and so she concentrated on breathing, reminding herself this was a blood pressure cuff, she was in the hospital, and this was a nurse. She wasn't in the contraption in *The Toybox* with her torturers.

'You and your brother seem close. Blood pressure is 120/74. Excellent.' Bethany removed the cuff from Rachel's arm, folded it, and shoved it into a very large pocket on the front of her scrubs. 'I know most nurses prefer the mechanical cuffs, but I like my old-fashioned one. It hasn't failed me yet, anyway.' After she ran the thermometer across Rachel's forehead and jotted down her temperature, Bethany turned serious.

'Okay, let's find out how you're doing today. On a scale of one to ten, where does your pain or discomfort fall? And be honest because we can't help you if we don't know.'

'Four, five. It's a little better today.'

'I can get you something to help with the pain, if you'd like.'

'I'm okay with acetaminophen or ibuprofen.'

Bethany nodded. 'If that's what you prefer, we can work with that. Now, the doctor prescribed an antibiotic to help stave off any possible infections from those lacerations on your back. That's the extra bag you see hanging there.' Despite her efforts to remain matter-of-fact, Rachel could see the pity in the nurse's eyes. Then she tucked the call button remote closer to Rachel, patted her hand, and said, 'I'll be in again in just a bit to check on you.'

Just as Bethany reached the door, Rachel stopped her. She had a question, but she'd been afraid to ask Nick. 'Did anyone… did they do a rape kit on me?'

The nurse crossed back over and gripped Rachel's hand gently in her own. 'Yes, they did. You probably don't remember because you were in and out of consciousness when they brought you in yesterday. They needed to collect whatever evidence they could to help convict the men who did this to you.'

Tears trailed from the corners of Rachel's eyes as she nodded. How could she admit she was glad she hadn't been alert enough to know what they were doing? Mentally, she knew it was done to help. Psychologically, she felt as if she'd been violated all over again.

No sooner had Bethany exited than Nick entered carrying a take-out bag from Blake's Lotaburger, the scent of French fries drifting toward Rachel's nose. 'You're awake. Just got off the phone with Dad. They'll be by this evening to see you. In the meantime, you have another visitor.'

She twisted her head toward the open door. Anna. Rachel struggled to sit, a sob breaking through as her friend moved hesitantly from behind Nick and further into the room. And then Nick was by her side in an instant, squeezing her hand, reminding her he was there, and she realized she'd been on the verge of hyperventilating.

'Anna?'

Her friend moved cautiously closer to the bed where she shoved her hands deep into her pockets and then swayed back and forth on the balls of her feet. 'I'd heard you were here. I'm so sorry I haven't come to see you before now. I just, I felt so bad because…'

'I didn't know what had happened to you. When I woke up, and you weren't with me, I didn't know if they'd taken you or killed you or…' Rachel gripped her brother's hand, reminding her to stay anchored in the moment, not to return to the house of horrors.

'I'm the one who convinced you to go to the party that night. This is all my fault. I shouldn't have left you alone. I forgot my purse, and when I came back, you were already gone. I just thought you'd gotten tired of waiting or that you were mad at me. And then you didn't answer any of my texts, so…'

What was Anna talking about? When had she forgotten her purse? The last thing she remembered was sinking into the mattress…

Nick released Rachel's hand long enough to set the take-out bag on the chair by the window and then crossed back over to Rachel, taking her hand in his again and clasping it between both of his before directing his question to Anna. 'Why didn't you go to the police when you realized my sister had disappeared?'

To a stranger, Nick probably sounded curious, but to Rachel, she heard the underlying tension in his voice. Plus, there had been a subtle tightening of his fingers around hers.

Anna averted her gaze, her shoulders drooping. 'I went to visit my father in Kentucky, so I didn't know. I got back late last night and saw it on the news. I'm so sorry.'

'None of this is your fault.' Even as Rachel said it, a tiny voice inside her screamed, *Yes, it is! If you hadn't insisted I go with you to that stupid party, none of this ever would've happened.*

'Um, I have to go, but I'll be back tomorrow. If that's okay?'

Rachel didn't have a chance to answer because Nick did. 'I'll give you my number. Why don't you text me before you come, and I'll let you know if she's up to visitors?' He may have been smiling, but his voice contained a dark hint of distrust. Or blame.

After Anna left, something shifted inside Rachel, leaving her mind murky and confused. And even while Nick tried to coax her into replacing her hospital food with the fries he'd bought, she couldn't shake the feeling that she was forgetting something, something urgent.

Chapter Fifty

Monday, May 27

Five-thirty on Monday morning, Alyssa was showered and ready to go. Just before she'd drifted off to sleep late last night, something had tickled at the back of her mind, but she'd nodded off before she could fully pull on that thread.

'You know you're not going to do anyone any good if you drive yourself into the ground, Lys. The girls are safe and surrounded by hospital staff and security. Take a day and refresh.' Brock, hair tousled, rested on his elbows, eyes still heavy with sleep.

A cocktail of guilt and frustration burned through her because she'd been trying so hard to find these girls that she'd been neglecting her husband. And she was about to do it again. 'I can't, honey. There's something I'm missing, and I'm close to figuring out what that is. Plus, not only are we still looking for at least three more men, but we're also trying to hunt down Tatiana Salazar, not to mention this mysterious girl Becca and Katelyn remembered approaching them about a phone just before they were drugged.' Her eyes begged him to be patient and understanding a little longer. 'Let me wrap this case up, and I promise I'll make it up to you.'

'There's nothing to make up, babe. You're doing your job. I'm worried about you is all. When's the last time you actually ate a decent meal? Notice I said *decent*, not fast food.'

'I don't know,' she mumbled.

'At least let me make you an omelet before you go.' He'd already swung his feet out of the bed and pulled on a pair of shorts, so even though she was itching to get out the door, Alyssa capitulated.

'I'll meet you downstairs.' Lost in the elusive link she was missing, she didn't notice someone was in the kitchen until she practically knocked into Holly, who was apparently one step ahead of her father in that she was already assembling all the ingredients for an omelet. 'Morning, sweetie. What's got you up so early?'

Holly continued chopping green chile. 'Wanted to feed, see, and talk to you.'

Alyssa chuckled as she poured herself a cup of coffee. 'You and your father seem to be on the same wavelength this morning. He'll be down any minute to make me an omelet, too.'

'Great minds and all.'

Something in her response made Alyssa feel like Holly was mentally miles away. She snagged a knife from the butcher block on the counter and proceeded to help chop vegetables. 'Should I be worried?'

Holly stopped chopping. The knife in her hand wobbled. 'What do you mean?'

'Whatever you've got on your mind this morning. Should I be worried?'

Holly resumed chopping, the motion of the knife going fast enough that Alyssa was a little afraid her daughter was going to slice her fingers off. 'Will the other girls be okay?' There was the slightest waver in her voice, and Alyssa wanted to do nothing more than grab her daughter up and promise her everything would be all right.

Instead, she was honest.

'Physically? I hope so. Emotionally? It depends on the support and therapy they receive. I guess only time will tell.'

'Sophie called last night.' Holly set the knife aside and turned around, leaning her back against the counter and wrapping her arms around her middle. 'Jersey's nightmares are so horrible, they had to give her a heavy sedative. Sophie said Aunt Natalia freaked out because Jersey was thrashing around like she was trying to get loose and screaming, "I thought you were…"' Holly's voice cracked, and Alyssa guided her to a chair before sitting beside her. Tears falling freely now, Holly asked, 'What are we supposed to do? Whenever Natalia tries to ask Jersey about her nightmare, Jersey has another anxiety attack, and they have to sedate her again.'

There was that elusive thread again. Alyssa reached across the table and grabbed a tissue, handing it to Holly. Then she put one finger beneath her daughter's chin and tipped it up so she could look at her. 'What Jersey and these girls went through is nothing short of horrendous and appalling. They're bound to have nightmares for years to come. Even Isaac still has night terrors from his ordeal – not that I'm comparing the two. I'm just saying it's going to take time.'

Holly shifted in her seat and shot a watery smile Alyssa's way. 'Thanks, Mom. I know you're right; it's just hard seeing her like this.' Then a smile transformed her face. 'Speaking of Isaac, he gets back today. I can't wait to hear how things went.'

'I think I'll just be glad he's back home with us.' Alyssa knew that was one of the other reasons she'd kept so busy. She didn't want to have any time to fret about Isaac being off in the woods. Besides, Trevor's mom had promised to call if anything happened.

Holly cleared her throat, dragging Alyssa back and reminding her of her suspicion that her daughter had another motive for making her an omelet this morning. 'Um, there's something else I wanted to talk to you about… I went on a date with Nick Otis. It was only once, well, kind of twice.'

And there it was. 'I gathered as much. I have to tell you I'm glad you already let Dad and me know that you weren't attending Cornell in the fall, or I would've been concerned you were doing it for a guy.'

Holly frowned. 'Please. I thought you knew me better than that. Besides, like I said, it was one – and a half – dates. We're not picking out furniture and drapes, you know. He might not even want to see me again after...' Instead of finishing that thought, she asked a question. 'Is it going to bother you if I date him? I mean, will it affect your case at all?'

'No, it won't affect my case. If you like him, and he treats you well, then that's what matters. How did you two meet, anyway?'

Holly chuckled. 'You know that day Sophie and I wanted to stop by and see you?'

'Yeah.' Alyssa drew the one-syllable word into two.

'Well, we saw him coming out of the precinct, and long story short, he had a flat tire, so we helped him change it.' This time the laughter hit her eyes. 'He didn't have a clue; couldn't even find the jack.'

Alyssa snickered. 'Oh, your dad will love that.'

'Your dad will love what?' Brock said, rounding the corner into the kitchen and dropping a kiss on the top of Holly's head. 'My two favorite girls.' He waved his hand toward the counter. 'Great minds, huh? I'll just take over from here.'

'Thanks, Dad. And I helped a guy change a tire.'

Even though her daughter played it off, Alyssa knew from the smug look on her face that, internally, she must be feeling the tiniest bit superior.

'Hmm. Your mom's right: Dad does love that.'

The conversation died out while Brock made the omelets, slid them onto plates and set them on the table. The three of them ate in companionable silence, and when they finished, Alyssa carried her dishes to the dishwasher. 'Thanks for breakfast, but I really need to get going.' After she grabbed her gun from the safe, she paused in the doorway to the garage. 'When are you going to see Jersey today?'

'I'm going to swing by Sophie's around eight so we can go together.' She bit her bottom lip.

'What's wrong?'

Holly sighed. 'I'm not looking forward to telling Sophie that Leigh Ann sent me a text around midnight saying she was sorry and she was ready to visit Jersey.'

Alyssa's forehead furrowed in confusion. 'What do you mean? Didn't she visit her yesterday with you?'

'Nope. Said she wasn't ready yet. Plus, to be honest, Soph and I were still pretty pissed at her for waiting so long to tell you about Beau being at the frat party.' A mask dropped into place, so she was clearly not over it yet. 'Her reason for waiting – she was afraid of getting in trouble – just makes me want to scream. Especially since Beau apparently knew both Rachel and Jersey, and both of them disappeared after being with him.' She huffed out a breath of air. 'But how *I* feel about her right now doesn't matter. Jersey was obviously upset when Leigh Ann wasn't with us, so Sophie and I are just going to have to deal with it.'

'You're a good friend, Holly Wyatt,' Alyssa said before heading out, that tickle in the back of her mind returning full force.

Chapter Fifty-One

Monday, May 27

Alyssa was focused on trying to locate the common link between the seven girls when Cord walked into the conference room a couple of hours after her. She shot him a startled glance. 'What are you doing here?'

'Same as you, I imagine.' He tipped his head to the white-board where she had written the names of every player, real or suspected, and the girls. Then she'd drawn a line connecting the ones who went together. A red line traced from Beau Cambridge to Jersey and Rachel, and a dotted line from Meghan and Katelyn, and yet another to Chance Williams. 'Want to talk it out, see if I can help connect the dots?'

Before she could answer, Hal rolled in. 'Still no activity on Tatiana Salazar's credit cards, so she's obviously laying low. I took the liberty of contacting Bartholomew Rosenfelt to see if he had any idea as to where she may go if she was trying to stay hidden, but aside from the Placitas property, he couldn't help. So, I put out an APB for her and her Porsche Carrera as well as alerting border patrol in case she tries to hop over into Mexico.'

Alyssa hadn't asked any of them to come in today, knowing they needed to get the same rest her husband claimed she did, yet here they were. Damn, she had the best team.

'A Porsche Carrera is an awfully noticeable car.' Cord twisted his phone end over end on the table. 'Do you really think she'd be dumb enough to be driving it? She's gotta know we're searching for it.'

'I'm going to resign and work for Rosenfelt. Everyone around him seems to have a fancy car,' Joe said around a yawn as he strolled in with Tony trailing behind.

She really did work with the best, and she was about to say so when her phone rang. She didn't recognize the number. 'Detective Wyatt.'

'Detective, this is Spencer McKay. I'll be representing Steven Yarmini. He wants to talk, but we want some assurances first.'

'What kind of assurances?'

'Well, he wants immunity.'

'You know we can't offer that.'

'I do know that. That's why I said *he* wants that. I've already told him it's more likely he'll be the next man on the moon. That aside, I want it to go on record that my client came to you, willing to cooperate. So, when it comes time to offer a plea deal, we'd like your cooperation when we go to the district attorney.'

'It depends on what your client offers up, and whether or not it helps us. When do you want to meet up?'

'How's now?'

'We'll meet you over there.'

Twenty minutes later, Alyssa and Cord sat across from Steve Yarmini garbed in an orange jumpsuit that gave him a washed-out pallor. Beside him sat his attorney, tan and dressed in a crisp, expensive-looking suit. The contrast between them couldn't have been more pronounced.

And the fact that McKay was here on Memorial Day when most families were home barbecuing... whew, that had to be costing a pretty penny.

Urgently trying to fit the missing piece into the puzzle, Alyssa dived in. 'Tell us what you've got, Steve.'

'I want immunity.' Yarmini steepled his fingers together and propped them under his nose as if he was holding it up.

Alyssa shook her head. 'As your attorney has already shared with you, we can't promise that. What we can promise is to tell the DA that you cooperated. And trust me, our district attorney is a real bulldog, so you're going to want to rack up as many brownie points as you can.'

He glanced at his attorney then back at Alyssa and Cord, his gaze bouncing back and forth between them. Then he closed his eyes and began. 'I didn't mean to kill her,' he uttered. 'My job was to take her to the hotel where her buyer would pick her up and transport her to her new location.' He spoke so quietly, it was difficult to understand him, but Alyssa knew the recorder would still pick up every word.

'To whom are you referring, Mr. Yarmini, when you say you didn't mean to kill her?'

His eyes flickered open only to study the ceiling tiles. 'That girl that you found at the abandoned restaurant on Central. Meghan Jessup.'

'Transported where and why?' Cord asked.

Yarmini's Adam's apple bobbed up and down. 'She'd run her course.' Finally, he brought his gaze down, though his focus skirted everywhere except on the detectives. 'The girls there don't last long. It's a, uh, highly... specialized... sex ring. The clientele there are into certain... violent kinks. And because of that, the price is quite steep, and those guys you picked up at the house? They were regulars.

'Anyway, once the girls can no longer perform to their satisfaction, they're moved out to another buyer where they' – he swallowed – 'they're sold into prostitution. I guess one of the clients became a bit... rough... and possibly overdid it when he was getting his freak on. When he finished, she was unresponsive at first. That's when Tatiana – she's the one in charge – called me up. She even joked about how much money someone might pay for a brain-dead bitch.' From his face down to his neck, Yarmini flushed crimson. 'Then she laughed and asked how soon I could get there for pick-up.' The more he spoke, the quieter his words became, and the more his body vibrated in his seat.

The omelet Alyssa had eaten earlier threatened to make a reappearance. She really hoped there was a special place in hell reserved for people like Yarmini, the men who'd paid to torture the girls, and Tatiana Salazar, too. She shot a quick glance at Cord, knowing he had to be thinking about Shelley. Despite the way his fingers clenched into fists, he maintained his composure.

'What about that brand on Meghan's hip?' Cord asked.

'Tatiana wanted buyers to remember the girls came from her, so she chose the Rosenfelt logo since we both work for Rosenfelt Holdings. She found it amusing.' His cheeks burned, and he dropped his chin to his chest. 'She has a twisted sense of humor.'

'Yeah, that's some sort of humor. Kidnapping girls and collecting large sums of money so men can torture and rape them? Excuse me for failing to see the humor in any of that.'

The lines around Spencer McKay's mouth tightened as he focused his laser stare on Alyssa. 'Careful there, Detective. Remember, my client is choosing to cooperate. That could always end. Now, for the record, he never stated that this situation was funny; he simply theorized about this Tatiana's personality.'

Alyssa matched McKay's glare then continued with the interrogation. 'So, you get the call that Meghan is no longer *useful* to this organization' – her lip curled into a sneer – 'you arrive at the designated place to pick her up, and then you transport her to the hotel. What happened after that?' The underlying tremble in her voice hinted at the anger bubbling just below the surface.

Yarmini angled his body away from the three other occupants of the room and punched his fists against his thighs. He spoke barely above a whisper when he finally answered. 'I just figured she was already, you know, and so I asked her if it was okay. I mean, I didn't think it was rape if she agreed to it.' His arms pressed tighter into his sides even as he continued pummeling his thighs.

Cord's teeth gnashed together. 'You didn't think it was rape if you took advantage of a fourteen-year-old girl who'd already been raped and tortured, and in your own words, was "used goods"? In what universe would that be considered anything but rape?'

One of Yarmini's hands reached up and pulled at his hair. 'She said yeah,' he said weakly.

'She said yeah? Just like that? You sure about that?' Alyssa watched Cord's face flush crimson and the tendons in his neck tighten as he tried to rein in his temper.

Yarmini used the sleeve of his jumpsuit to wipe the sweat beading on his brows. 'Well, not exactly. She just kind of nodded and rolled over.' His gaze was still averted from the other occupants of the room.

'She nodded and rolled over, and you took that as *assent*?' Blood pounded in Alyssa's ears. The man in front of her wasn't just sick and twisted, but apparently stupid as well. A sharp pain in her palm ricocheted up her arm, and she realized she'd been squeezing her fists so tightly that her fingernails had sliced tiny crescent-shaped figures into her hand. She wiped the light line of blood off on her pants.

'I don't know what happened. I got—' Yarmini shook his head back and forth, not finishing his sentence. 'And then she suddenly stopped breathing, and she never started again. I panicked and dropped her off downtown. And then I dumped my car.' His upper body hunched forward, and his arms crawled around his middle.

Alyssa found it difficult – if not impossible – to feel anything but anger and disgust toward him. 'When we discovered Meghan's body, she was wearing clothes that didn't belong to her. Explain that.'

Yarmini's legs bounced, and he rubbed his hands up and down his thighs as his gaze flew around the room. 'Tatiana kept all the clothes from her first operation. And before you ask, I don't know why. I just grabbed something from the box I thought would look sexy and dressed her in that.'

Alyssa was aware that one of the evidence technicians had uncovered a cardboard box containing clothing in one of the rooms when they'd searched the Placitas property but believed the clothes belonged to the girls in the house. Those items had been sent to the lab for testing in hopes they'd uncover a link to one or several of the men involved.

Alyssa's pulse quickened. 'What do you mean by "her first operation"?'

Yarmini's face paled even more, and he dropped his head into his hands. Alyssa suspected it was because he thought they'd already known.

About ten seconds later, he raised his head, glanced once at the door, then at the red blinking light on the recorder. His shoulders drooped as he spoke. 'The Placitas property was the second, more high-end operation. About a year ago, Tatiana ran a trafficking ring out of southern New Mexico for about six months. She mostly targeted prostitutes and undocumented immigrants because their disappearances would be less likely to send up any red flags to the authorities.'

'What changed?' Alyssa was holding on to her fraying temper by a fine thread, and one glance at Cord convinced her he was, too.

'Tatiana and I were having drinks one night late November, and after a few shots of tequila, she told me how her ex had frittered away her father's funds – apparently legally – and she wanted to make more money, faster.' He shifted in his chair. 'She told me she was thinking of turning her operation into a more 'high-end, specialized' one, but we'd need 'cleaner' girls. And she thought her property in Placitas was classy enough and far enough back from prying eyes.'

Cord piped in, anger and disgust evident in the tone of his voice. 'And how about you, Mr. Yarmini? For Tatiana Salazar, it was about money. What was in it for you? The thrill of degrading and abusing women?'

To Alyssa's surprise, Steve didn't shy away from Cord's angry glare. 'I'd gone deep into debt over my gambling addiction – I owed a loan shark a hundred grand at an interest rate of thirty percent. I got scared and told Tatiana about it. A week later, she approached me with her idea. I wasn't sold on it right away. Then she offered seven percent of profits, and all I had to do was transport the girls she no longer needed out. I wouldn't have to be involved with finding or getting the girls. She said she'd find someone else for that.' He spoke nonstop, his voice never altering from the monotonous tone of someone who knew he'd sold whatever soul he had to the devil. 'Money from the first operation was good, so when she dropped the idea of making more while being able to stay closer to home, I jumped at it.'

Alyssa brought the questioning back around to something that had bothered her since she'd realized the picture on Lorna Price's phone was that of Steve Yarmini.

'You'd already cleared out of your house by the time we discovered the Viper, so tell me, what brought you back to Hotel Camino in the early hours of Saturday morning?'

One arm dropped and hung loosely at his side while the other rose to hold his head in his hand. 'I thought I'd lost my watch. It was a gift from my mother, and it had my name etched on the back. I was afraid.'

To Alyssa's knowledge, no watch had been discovered.

A self-deprecating laugh escaped. 'It turned out it was in the bottom of my suitcase.'

'Tell us something, Mr. Yarmini. What made you decide to cooperate today? Aside from hoping to cop a plea deal?'

His breath hitched. 'I know you won't believe this, but… maybe I can't make it right, what I did, but I can try to help stop it from happening again.'

Even though something in the way he said it made Alyssa believe him, she felt zero sympathy for the man in front of her.

'Who picked you up after you tumbled your car over the cliff?'

'I don't know.'

'You don't know?'

'No, some guy saw me walking and asked if I wanted a ride. I said yes, gave him twenty bucks, and had him drop me off about a mile from my house.'

'We need names of all the individuals involved,' Cord said. 'Aside from the men we arrested at the house, you, and this Tatiana. Who else are we looking for?'

Yarmini's eyes flickered to the door. 'Tatiana hired a recruiter to get the girls. She targets the mark, incapacitates her, then transports her to Hotel Camino – where Tatiana sends in her men to pick up "the package." Sometimes it's a few hours; sometimes it's overnight.'

'She?' Cord leaned back and crossed his arms over his chest again. 'She had to be pretty strong to get these girls into her vehicle by herself and then into the hotel.' His tone implied his skepticism.

'If she had help with that, I don't know anything about it.'

'What's this girl's name?' That same itch she'd been having was back, and Alyssa's pulse fluttered as she waited for Yarmini's answer.

'I only knew her first name. Anna.'

It was Alyssa's turn to pale as the connections all flashed before her, finally linking together. 'Can you describe this Anna?'

'I only saw her once, and it was dark. But she was about five-feet-four with a weird scar on her right cheek near her ear. She had what I guess you'd call strawberry-blonde hair…'

Doing the best to control the trembling in her hands, Alyssa tapped on her phone and scrolled until she found what she was looking for, then flipped it around. 'Is this the girl you recognize as Anna?'

'Yeah, that's her.'

In a move that startled everyone in the room, Alyssa shoved back from the table and rushed to the door. 'This interview is over. Have Joe escort Mr. Yarmini back to his cell.'

Chapter Fifty-Two

Monday, May 27

With a hand on her forearm, Cord halted Alyssa before she barged through the double doors heading into the patient wing of the hospital. 'Stop. Let's make sure the rest of the team is in place before you go barreling in there half-cocked. We don't want to mess up this chance.'

A clap of thunder from the random, freak rainstorm distracted Alyssa long enough to bring her back to her senses and heed Cord's warning. Despite the urgency of the situation, it wasn't lost on her that he was the one reminding her she needed to be in control when it should've been her calming him after he'd sat through that painful interview, knowing he was probably reliving the nightmare his family had gone through with Shelley.

Pulse pounding, nerves shaky, she waited while Cord confirmed that Joe and Tony were ready. The second they radioed back that they were in place, Alyssa shifted her focus to the doors in front of her. Taking a deep breath in an effort to calm the bees swarming her insides, she hit the button on the wall and waited only long enough for her to squeeze herself through the door, aware that Cord was right behind her.

Her head pivoted left and right as they moved along the hall. At the first nurses' station, she flashed her badge and ordered one of the attendants to stop any more visitors from coming through and to keep others in whatever rooms they were in. It took one look at her face for the nurses to grasp the gravity of the situation, and several staff members scattered in different directions to do as directed.

Just as they turned the final corner of the patient wing, Alyssa watched the girl known as Anna enter Jersey's room. Her breath caught in her throat as time slowed almost to a standstill. Holly was in that room.

In the next second, commotion erupted everywhere. Something that sounded like someone gasping for air reverberated out into the hall from Jersey's room, someone yelled for a nurse... no, not someone, Holly... and then two nurses raced from behind the counter and headed straight for Jersey's room, ignoring Alyssa's shouted commands to stop.

Even as she rushed forward, her mind processed things in slow motion. Nick Otis exited his sister's room, his head swiveling down the hall, his brows arched high, forehead wrinkled in concern. And then Anna was there, backing out of Jersey's room slowly, apologizing as she turned to leave.

Only to pull up short as she spotted Alyssa and Cord. 'Mrs. Wyatt?' Leigh Ann said. 'If you're here to talk to Jersey, you might have to wait.' She whipped her head toward her friend's door. 'She's having a bit of an episode, I'm afraid.'

Holly poked her head out the door, and her wide-eyed, scared gaze landed on Alyssa and Cord before she swung it back to Leigh Ann. The hair on the back of Alyssa's nape lifted, and she had to bite the urge to snap at Holly to get back inside. A tear trailed down Holly's cheek as she tipped her head forward in what Alyssa recognized as defeat, and then eyes boring into her mother's, she slowly backed into Jersey's room, closing the door softly behind her.

Alyssa released the breath she'd sucked in when Holly had poked her head out, secure in the knowledge that, for the moment, she was safe. Careful not to shift her eyes away from the person in front of her, she took two small steps forward. 'Hello, Leigh Ann. I'm glad to see you here.' In her peripheral vision, she noticed Cord slowly inching his way between Leigh

Ann and Jersey's room. As soon as he was in place, the elephant sitting on Alyssa's chest moved, and her smile turned more feral. 'I'm sorry – should I have addressed you as Anna instead?'

Leigh Ann adopted a puzzled expression, and she laughed a little, as if she was aware a mistake had been made, and she was uncomfortable pointing it out. 'I'm sorry. No. Why would you call me Anna?'

'I'm sorry. Maybe that's just what Tatiana Salazar calls you.'

In a matter of seconds, Leigh Ann's face contorted from an expression of innocence to a cold sneer. Even the shadows in her eyes darkened, as if she'd pulled a shade down. 'I'm sure you don't know what you're talking about.'

Mindful of the growing interest of the staff and various onlookers, Alyssa shifted just slightly in order to place herself between Leigh Ann and as many innocent bystanders as she could. 'Oh, I know full well what I'm talking about. You target and incapacitate girls for Tatiana Salazar's sex trafficking ring, isn't that right?'

Leigh Ann's eyes flickered to the side, telegraphing her intent to flee.

And then Nick Otis, still standing outside his sister's room, took one small step forward. 'Anna? Is everything okay?'

Leigh Ann's head snapped around, and Cord took advantage of her distraction by closing in and jerking her arm behind her back before shoving her against the wall.

Above the howls of Leigh Ann's rage, Cord read her the Miranda Rights, and Alyssa spared a quick look in Nick's direction. A rage she fully understood brewed in his eyes, and she knew then that he'd correctly interpreted the situation and purposely distracted the person responsible for kidnapping his sister.

His fingers clenched into fists as Cord pushed Leigh Ann toward the exit, and when she was directly in front of him, Nick stepped back inside Rachel's room without uttering a word and closed the door in Leigh Ann's face.

Alyssa wasn't sure whether, in his shoes, at his age, she'd have been quite as in control.

Chapter Fifty-Three

Monday, May 27

Cord leaned his back against the door of the interrogation room while Alyssa pulled out a chair and sat across from Leigh Ann. She flipped open a manila folder and began to read from it.

> My daughter has been troubled most of her life. We'd hoped a fresh start in Albuquerque would be what she needed, and for a while, I thought it was working.

She lifted her head to gauge Leigh Ann's reaction, but the girl's face remained impassive. Alyssa lowered her head and continued reading from the interview Hal had conducted while she and the rest of her team had raced to the hospital. As soon as Leigh Ann's mother received the call about what her daughter was suspected of, she had readily come in, bringing with her folders of past psychiatric evaluations for the detectives' use.

> After some troubling incidents in school when she was twelve, and then again in our neighborhood when she was thirteen, my now ex-husband and I forced our daughter into counseling where she was soon diagnosed with a narcissistic sociopathic personality – a social predator who plays with people's feelings and emotions. My daughter is the perfect chameleon; she can fit in anywhere and make anyone like her. She can and does become

whoever she needs to be to gain whatever it is that
she wants. Picture if you will, a cat with a mouse
before it finally destroys it. Do you have any idea
what that's like for a mother to hear? It's not easy.

The narrow-eyed glare Leigh Ann shot her way was the only
indication she'd heard any of it. Alyssa closed the folder and
leaned back, crossing her arms over her chest, letting the silence
grow heavier as the girl she'd believed to be Holly's friend
absorbed the things her own mother had shared about her.

Finally, Alyssa spoke. 'Aren't you curious as to how I figured
it out?' The air inside the room dropped ten degrees from the
icy gaze Leigh Ann drilled into her. *How had she ever missed the
cold emptiness in those eyes?*

'See, I remember when you moved here from Artesia a few
years ago, and Holly brought you over to our house. I was
passing by her room, and I overheard you refer to yourself as
Anna when you told Sophie and Holly about your mother
yelling at you. But that didn't click right away. It was only when
I started shifting pieces of the puzzle around that the picture
started to become clearer.

'Faye Harrison moved to Albuquerque for a career change
just over a year ago. When I saw that she was also from Artesia,
things started to open up for me. The two of you attended the
same middle school, but you weren't friends since she was two
years ahead of you.' Alyssa didn't expect a response and didn't
receive one. 'Becca Marshall is from Hobbs, which is pretty
close to Artesia, but it's not so close you would automatically
run in the same circles. So, we dug a little deeper, and you
know what we discovered?' Leigh Ann's face remained a cold,
emotionless mask. 'Becca used to visit her sister in a treatment
facility – you might be familiar with it since you were there at
the same time.'

Leigh Ann maintained her stony silence, but each word
tightened the skin across her face. If there was going to be a

reaction, Alyssa wanted it to be to the next bit of news, so she straightened in her seat and leaned in until she was mere inches from Leigh Ann's face. 'Meghan Jessup used to visit her grandfather every spring break. Oddly enough, Jersey's house is located near Meghan's grandfather.'

Face and neck flushing red, nostrils flaring, Leigh Ann opened her mouth just enough to bare her teeth, giving her the appearance of a rabid animal. Alyssa pressed on. 'Beau Cambridge saw Meghan one day and decided he liked her, despite already having a girlfriend. And that made you jealous and sent you into a rage.' Of course, she didn't know any of that to be true, but it made sense as to why Leigh Ann would've targeted Meghan and even Jersey. 'How could he notice a fourteen-year-old child when you were right there in front of him? It was nothing personal against Meghan; she was just someone who was in the way of you getting what you wanted. And you wanted Beau. Is that why you ended up targeting Rachel, too? You saw him hitting on her at the frat party?'

When Leigh Ann's reaction came, it was far from what Alyssa was expecting. Leigh Ann's neck flung back as a high-pitched cackle exploded from her throat. When she finally brought her gaze back, merriment beamed from her eyes as she shook her head. 'Here I was beginning to think you were so smart, maybe even a match for my intelligence, and then you go and blow it with some stupid, amateur observation. Allow me to correct your erroneous *assumption*.

'If Beau Cambridge was on fire, I wouldn't let a stray dog piss on him. The only purpose that oversized buffoon had was that he was the perfect scapegoat. Clueless and arrogant, the perfect cocktail. I saw an opportunity, and I took it. Except he was too stupid to even do that right. I mean, really, how perfect was it that he could be tied to *three* of the missing girls? And then I saw Katelyn walking near Jersey's and Meghan's neighborhood, and oh damn, it was like a calling. And I *knew* Beau was so convinced of his own god-like status that he wouldn't be able to stop from being himself when you finally connected those dots.'

Alyssa cocked her head to the side and arched her brows. She looked over at Cord, shook her head, and sighed before turning her attention back to the girl across from her.

'What? You don't believe me? You actually think I love that moron? You're far dumber than I thought. Poor Holly will be so disappointed to learn that.' Leigh Ann twisted her head away to stare at the wall as if she didn't have time for such idiocy.

Alyssa's muscles stiffened at Holly's name emerging from the monster in front of her. 'So, all the girls you chose were a matter of convenience and nothing more?'

Leigh Ann shifted in her seat. Once started, she couldn't seem to stop from spouting about her own brilliance. Over the years, Alyssa had seen this often – where a perpetrator had to show everyone how much more intelligent he or she was than everyone around them. The girl in front of her was no different.

'Look, Jersey and Meghan are nothing more than rich, over-dramatic drama queens who got on my nerves and deserved a reality check anyway.' One shoulder lifted in a blasé shrug. 'They needed to see their lives weren't nearly as atrocious as they thought. I hated Faye from the first moment I laid eyes on her. Becca's sister did nothing but blather on and on about how sickly devoted her older sister was. Cheyenne was nothing more than convenient.' She laughed, an evil sound that made the hairs on the back of Alyssa's neck stand up. 'God, what a thrill it was watching all you idiots scrambling to figure out the truth when I was right there under your nose' – she lowered her voice to an excited whisper – 'in your *house* – the entire time.'

The glee in Leigh Ann's face as she recounted how she'd chosen each girl was reminiscent of a child at Christmas who sees the present she's been waiting for all year. It sent a chill racing down Alyssa's spine, leaving her cold all over.

But when Leigh Ann scooted forward, propping her elbows on the table, her eyes lit with joy as she dropped her next bombshell, the subzero temperature of her heart all but flashed on her chest. 'Rachel… Rachel is nothing more than a spoiled little rich bitch who needed to be taken down a peg. But she had nothing to do with me. Rachel was purely payback for someone who took something of Tatiana's.'

Beside the door, Cord stiffened.

'Tatiana Salazar?' Alyssa clarified.

Leigh Ann's chin jutted out, and she smirked. 'Oh, I know something you don't,' she taunted in a sing-song voice.

Careful not to let her emotions show, Alyssa feigned boredom, checked the time on her watch, and twisted her upper body to face Cord. 'Are you hungry? I'm hungry.'

Cord immediately caught on to Alyssa's cue and played along. 'I'm thinking a burrito. What about you?'

Leigh Ann tapped her foot.

'A burrito sounds good. Golden Pride?'

Leigh Ann clenched and unclenched her fist. 'Don't pretend you're not curious.'

Alyssa kept her body angled toward her partner but twisted her head around to face Leigh Ann. 'Curious about what? If you really knew something, you'd have told us, if for no other reason than to prove your superiority.' She lifted her shoulders and let them drop back down.

Leigh Ann snorted, but when Alyssa once again turned away, she broke, and Alyssa had to bite back a smile.

'Rachel Otis's mother had an affair with Tatiana's husband. Rachel was Tatiana's way of getting back at her.'

More pieces of the puzzle began to click into place, but Alyssa was still careful to school her expression. 'And how is it that you came to know Tatiana Salazar anyway?'

'Well, *Detective*' – Leigh Ann rolled her eyes – 'if you'd dug a little deeper, you would've known Ms. Salazar and I became friendly when we were in Red Valley Treatment Center together. She was there under court order after she shattered all the windows on her husband's car, and you know what people say: like minds attract. There we were, sitting in forced group therapy, listening to some gal cry on and on about how her daddy pimped her out to his friend for drug money.' She chuckled. 'Let's just say we discovered a way of making sick money, and we stayed in touch.'

Sick money was exactly right. 'You know, I heard that Tatiana and Steve Yarmini came up with this plan. Maybe you're not as bright as you thought?'

Leigh Ann brushed off the insult. 'Another scapegoat to take the fall. I mean, seriously, who's going to believe two females would be responsible for being innovative leaders of a sex ring? Please.' This time, it was her turn to lean in toward Alyssa as she lowered her voice, a taunting grin spreading across her face as she dropped her biggest bombshell. 'You know, Holly was next on the list. She was just so holier-than-thou, so, "*Oh, my mom is so great; she'll find Jersey and the others and swoop in and save the day*." She really needed to be knocked off that freaking pedestal. You both did.'

Blood pulsed in Alyssa's ears as she struggled to keep her fury under control. 'Yet here we are. The girls are safe, and you're under arrest.'

Her words were met with more disdain. 'You couldn't save poor little Meghan, though, could you?'

Alyssa was glad she was sitting as the lights flashed in front of her eyes. She was still trying to regain her composure when Cord asked the obvious question. 'What stopped you from going after Holly?'

Leigh Ann's smile was filled with hate as she drilled a glare into Alyssa's eyes. 'Who says I've stopped?'

Chapter Fifty-Four

Monday, May 27

Late Monday afternoon, Alyssa and Cord found themselves back at UNMH, this time outside Rachel's door. She'd tried reaching the Otises, but after several unanswered calls, she opted to try Nick to see if he knew where they were. He'd surprised her by telling her they'd just arrived at the hospital.

'Oh good. I just have a few questions I need to ask, so Detective Roberts and I will stop by shortly.'

'Okay, but Rachel's resting right now.' He chuckled, but the sound wasn't entirely merry. 'Or at least she's pretending to.'

'Actually, it's your parents I want to speak to, so if Rachel's still *resting* when we arrive, we'll just let her be.'

Due to a massive pile-up caused by a wreck on the freeway, the journey had taken longer than she'd expected, so she was relieved to see that Mr. and Mrs. Otis were still there when they entered Rachel's room.

Rachel lay in the bed, her eyes closed, her chest rising and falling in a steady rhythm. The bruises on her face were still a brilliant shade of colors but fading. If only her nightmares would fade as easily. And with that thought, Alyssa swung her gaze to Mrs. Otis, who looked like she'd rather be picking weeds from her garden than sitting beside her daughter's bed.

'Mrs. Otis, could you please step out into the corridor. We have a few questions we're hoping you can clear up.'

Alyssa saw Rachel's fingers twitch, and Nick moved to settle his hand over hers.

'Whatever kind of questions would you have that I could clear up for you?'

'I'll be happy to answer that for you as soon as you follow me.' The threat implicit in her words blanched the color from Nina's face, and it brought a great deal of satisfaction to Alyssa that she was the one responsible for it.

Maintaining her regal posture, Mrs. Otis stood and clutched her bag to her chest. 'Very well, let's speak outside. We wouldn't want to disturb Rachel. After all, she does need her rest.'

Nick's eyes nearly rolled to the back of his head, and then he bent low as if he were going to kiss his sister's forehead, but Alyssa heard him whisper, 'I promise I'll be right back. I'll just be outside the door if you need me.'

Alyssa thought it might be better if Nick stayed with Rachel, but it was his choice to make, not hers. After all, it wasn't like he wouldn't discover the truth soon enough. She held the door open as Cord stepped out, followed by Nick, then Mr. and Mrs. Otis.

As soon as the door closed behind Alyssa, Mrs. Otis turned her disdain up full blast. 'Now, Detective, what is so important that you felt it necessary to interrupt my visit with my daughter?'

As if she really wanted to be there. Alyssa leveled her gaze on Mrs. Otis. 'You were once an interior decorator, is that correct?'

Clearly thrown by the question, Nina Otis scowled her displeasure. 'Yes, though I don't see how that has to be any business of yours.'

'And you traveled often to conferences and such where you met other interior decorators?'

'What in the world does my career path have to do with my daughter? Or are you just trying to waste my time?'

'No, ma'am.' From her back pocket, she retrieved a photo and held it up for Mrs. Otis. 'Do you recognize this woman?'

A barely discernible wobble swayed Rachel's mom. She chewed her bottom lip before realizing she was doing it and stopped abruptly. 'Yes, that's Tatiana Salazar. I've met her a handful of times.'

'And have you heard her name on the news lately?'

Mrs. Otis waved her hand in the air, clearly implying the question was ludicrous. 'I don't have time for such frivolity as watching news reports. If I need to know something, I can look it up.'

'I see. What about Tatiana's husband? How many times did you meet him?'

Nick stiffened and snapped his neck toward his mother. Mr. Otis, on the other hand, showed no emotion whatsoever, aside from a mere curiosity.

Mrs. Otis swallowed. 'A few.'

'And during these meetings, did you perhaps have an affair with him?'

'What? Of course not! I demand you leave this instant!' Mrs. Otis's shaking hands and mock outrage exposed her crumbling composure.

Though his face remained unreadable, Mr. Otis asked a question of his own. 'Detective, may I ask why this is important?'

'Because Tatiana Salazar is our prime suspect. We believe she ran the sex trafficking ring that your daughter was forced into, and it has come to our attention that Rachel was targeted because of your wife's infidelity with Ms. Salazar's husband. Furthermore, we believe your wife can help us locate Ms. Salazar.'

'I told you—' Mrs. Otis began before her husband interrupted.

'Shut up, Nina. Just shut up.' His voice was hard and clipped even as sadness and shame seemed to make him shrink before their eyes. 'Nina did have an affair.'

His wife gasped, but he ignored her.

'Clearly, she didn't realize I knew. But she wasn't very smart about it. Now, I can verify that, but as for where Ms. Salazar is' – he turned toward his wife, eyes full of rage – 'if you do know where this woman is, you will tell these detectives now, or I promise you'll regret it for the rest of your days.'

A single tear trailed down Nina's cheek, leaving a streak in her perfect make-up.

Nick swung around as if making certain Rachel hadn't appeared in the doorway, and when he turned his gaze back to his mother, he stepped closer and lowered his voice into a hiss. 'You can't manage to find one shred of decent humanity within yourself when it comes to your own daughter being raped and tortured, but *your* sins come to light, and now you're a sniveling idiot? You disgust me. Not only am I done with you, but you will not come near Rachel ever again. Do you understand me?'

One shaky hand lifted. 'Nicholas,' her voice wobbled, 'don't say that. You don't mean it.'

'Actually, Mother, I've never meant anything more in my life.' He turned his back on her and placed his hand on the door, but before opening it, he asked his father if he'd make sure to say goodbye to Rachel before leaving. The only evidence of the hurt he must have been feeling came from his crackling voice. His father assured him he'd be in soon, and then Nick returned to his sister's side.

And Nina shared what she knew. 'Tatiana and Warren – her husband – shared a cabin near the Fourth of July Picnic Grounds. It's where he and I would meet.' She swallowed, her eyes imploring Alyssa and Cord to believe her. 'I swear I didn't know anything about Tatiana and a sex trafficking ring.' She choked on a sob. 'Warren told me they were divorcing. I didn't know…'

The woman's tears did nothing to move Alyssa, and from the cold expression her husband still wore, neither was he affected. 'Where exactly is this cabin? I want the address.'

Alyssa didn't think she could be shocked any further, but she was proven wrong when Nina pulled out her phone and supplied the address.

As soon as they had the location of the cabin, Alyssa and Cord rushed to her Tahoe. She was on the verge of contacting the state police to send a unit out just in case Salazar was there, but before she could, her phone rang. *Damn it!* 'What!' she snapped at the person on the other end before knowing who it was.

'Uh, Alyssa?'

'What is it, Joe? We have a lead on Tatiana Salazar.'

'Oh.' He sounded surprised. 'That's why I was calling. I didn't know you already knew.'

Now Alyssa was confused. And irritated. 'Thought I already knew what, Joe? Spit it out. Time's wasting.'

'We just got a call from the Greyhound station on 1st Street. Salazar came in to purchase a one-way ticket to Tucson. She's chopped off and dyed her hair completely gray, but when you wave around the amount of cash she apparently flashed, people pay closer attention. Someone recognized her.'

Once again, Alyssa found herself flipping a U-turn and heading the opposite direction. 'What time does that bus leave?'

'Twenty-seven minutes. And Tony and I are already headed that way. If you're still at UNMH, we'll make it there before you. Transit officers are aware of the situation, and they're keeping track of her whereabouts until we arrive.'

'No sirens. Go in silent. I don't want her to catch on that we're aware of her movements. Cord and I will be right behind you. And, Joe? Needless to say, we can't let her board that bus. We can't risk putting that many people in danger if she feels cornered.'

'You got it. See you there.'

Thirteen minutes later, Alyssa and Cord parked the Tahoe in the Alvarado station parking lot, radioed Joe that they were there, and took off at a sprint, noting the long line of buses with even longer queues of people waiting to board.

Alyssa thumbed her mic. 'Joe, Tony, do you have eyes on her?'

'Affirmative. She's wearing a yellow visor and carrying a burgundy tote. She's near the middle of the line, third bus from the front. Holding position until you tell us otherwise.'

Adrenaline caused Alyssa's heart rate to triple as she surveyed her surroundings. There were too many options for escape, and they didn't have much time. 'Okay, Joe, Tony, you approach from behind, but wait until you see me. Cord will come in from the right. I'm coming in from the left. Be careful not to let her see your uniforms. I don't want her to spook.'

'Okay, we're moving in behind.'

What probably only took a minute felt like forever as Alyssa waited for the signal that everyone was in place. And just as she thought things might actually go their way, a little kid, maybe three years old, spotted Joe or Tony and began jumping up and down as he tugged at his father's shirt, and squealed with excitement.

'Daddy, daddy, peece off-cer!' His little finger jabbed at the air, pointing. 'Peece off-cer! Hi, peece off-cer! Bang bang!' He clutched his chest, pretending to be shot as he collapsed to the ground.

Everyone – including Tatiana Salazar – turned to stare at the kid before looking to see where he pointed. Her eyes strayed from Joe to Tony before spotting Cord moving in closer to her, and then finally landing on Alyssa as she, too, approached.

Pandemonium erupted when Salazar reached into her bag and pulled out a gun. She waved it wildly in the air before grabbing the person nearest her – a teenage boy with braces and a face full of freckles. The boy's mother screamed as she reached out to clutch at her son only to have the gun pressed harder into her son's head. Some passengers scattered onto the buses while those behind Salazar skittered out of the terminal. Those closest to her were frozen to their spots, afraid movement would draw attention to them, causing them to be shot. Mothers and fathers still out in the open carefully tucked their children behind them.

Alyssa tuned out the horrified wail of the teenager's mother, her laser-like focus on Tatiana's hand. From the corner of her eye, she noticed the two transit officers join Cord, but they stopped when she gave a barely discernible shake of her head.

A wild-eyed Tatiana now had the boy gripped around his neck as she dragged him in front of her, stopping to point the gun at the boy's mother. 'Shut. Up. Or I'll drop him in front of you, and then I'll shoot you in the mouth just for the hell of it.'

Alyssa, now less than twenty feet away, ignored the frightened cries and whispers of the people still outside the buses. She raised her voice to pull Tatiana's attention away from the terrified mother as much as to distract her from the woman dressed in military fatigues who had exited the bathroom and crept in closer to Salazar. 'Tatiana, it doesn't have to go down like this. We just want to talk to you. That's all.'

The sound that erupted from Tatiana's throat was the sound of pure evil. 'Talk. Right. Well, all *I* want is to get out of this god-forsaken state. Now, let's check our situation, shall we? I've got a gun. Your people have guns. And sure, if you all rushed me at once, you could probably take me down, but can you do that before I begin shooting? No. How many casualties are worth my capture, Detective? One, five, more? How many lives are worth my one?'

Without warning, she jerked her hand to the side and shot. A man cried out as he fell to the ground clutching his leg. 'Oops.' Her cold glare met Alyssa's steady gaze. 'The next will be right in the head.' She bumped her chin against the teenage boy in her arms as she brushed her gun along his cheekbone. Then she leaned down to whisper something in his ear. Something that made the boy whimper.

'We need to get that man medical help,' Alyssa said, more to distract Tatiana from the movement behind her than because she truly believed Tatiana cared what happened to the guy she'd shot for no reason other than because he'd been there.

As she suspected, Tatiana laughed. And pointed the gun at yet another innocent bystander. But this time, before she could pull the trigger, the woman in military fatigues dove low, knocking into Tatiana's legs and throwing her off-balance, which forced her to loosen her grip on the teenage boy, who dropped and rolled away.

And then Cord was there, pressing down on the wrist still gripping the gun until Tony could pry it from her fingers. While Joe and the two transit officers raced over to the man who'd been shot, Alyssa joined the Army private as together they wrestled Tatiana Salazar over. By the time they got her flipped over onto her stomach, Alyssa's vision was hazy from anger, and she pressed her knee harder into the woman's back as she struggled against their restraints.

It took all four of them to subdue her long enough to slap the cuffs on her. It was Cord who yanked on the manacles and dragged her off the ground. Tatiana stopped shouting obscenities long enough to spit at both Cord and the private. And then Cord was in her face, and though Alyssa couldn't hear what he said, it was enough to shut Salazar up, though the murderous glare she bestowed on him would've felled most men.

Chapter Fifty-Five

'I just don't understand,' Holly said for the third time as she and Sophie clasped each other's hands. 'It doesn't make sense.'

Sophie stared out the window, traces of the tears she'd cried earlier streaking her make-up and leaving a jagged line down her cheek. 'I think we chose not to see it,' she finally said. 'When Leigh Ann moved here our freshman year, do you remember her first day of school, the way she walked in like she was the most important body to ever grace the halls, like she was a *gift* to the student population?'

Holly did remember it because it was one of the few times she and her best friend had fought. She'd thought Sophie was being mean and irrational, and frankly, a snob. 'Do you have any idea how difficult it is to move somewhere now in *high school?*' she'd asked.

To which Sophie had replied quite snippily, 'No, and neither do you.'

'Exactly. So, why don't we be the ones to give her a chance, give her a group to belong to?'

As the memory flooded back, Holly placed her head in her hands. *She'd* been the one to invite the monster into their inner circle. If she had only listened to Sophie at the time, maybe all of this could've been prevented. Or at least the part with Jersey.

'Stop it!' Sophie released her grip on Holly's hand to smack her own down on the nightstand, rattling the lamp, but she succeeded in getting her friend's attention. 'Neither of us is

337

responsible for Leigh Ann Wolfe's actions,' she said with a heavy emphasis on *neither*.

In her heart, she knew her best friend was right. Her head, however, wasn't convinced. She wasn't sure she ever would be.

'She's right,' Isaac said, appearing in his sister's open doorway. His skin was tanned a dark brown, and his hair had sun-kissed golden streaks running through it in a look some of Holly's friends would've paid hundreds of dollars to achieve. The camping trip with Trevor appeared to have done more to help her brother than his weekly therapy sessions. Ever since he'd returned, she'd seen more glimpses of the brother she remembered before he'd been kidnapped, though every once in a while, such as now, the memories that haunted him darkened his eyes.

'It's not your fault or anyone else's. Just like it's not Mom's fault Timmy was kidnapped, not her fault that she didn't somehow magically know her little brother was still alive. Just like it's not anyone's fault that Evan Bishop... did to me what he did to get to Mom. Some people are just bad, and the unlucky ones who cross their paths pay the price.'

The way he poured his whole heart into those words turned Holly into a blubbering mess of tears. She shoved herself off her bed and crossed the room to wrap her brother into a tight hug, surprised when his hold tightened around her as he consoled her.

When they finally stepped back from each other, Holly smiled up at her 'little' brother. 'After that speech, how am I supposed to call you my dumb kid brother?'

'Guess you'll just have to start telling the truth, introducing me as your hot, smart, younger brother.'

Sophie threw her head back and laughed. Wiping her eyes, she said, 'I needed that.'

Holly couldn't decide if the expression on Isaac's face was one of insult or relief, and then Sophie's phone rang.

After checking the screen, she yanked her phone up and answered. 'Hey, Jersey… No, that's fine… Of course, we'll come pick you up. When are they discharging you?'

Not that Holly minded picking Jersey up, but she wondered why her mother wasn't. And then her phone chimed with a text. It was from Nick.

> Rachel's being discharged today. I'd love to see you again sometime, but right now I need to focus on my sister. A lot has happened in the past few days. I hope you don't think that's a blow-off. I genuinely like you…

Holly bit her cheek as she wrestled with how to respond.

> I understand. Concentrate on being there for your sister. And text me when you're ready.

Isaac backed out of her room, throwing his hand up in a salute as he did. 'I'm gonna bounce.' He disappeared around the corner but popped his head back in a second later. 'Hey, Hol?' Holly twisted around to see unshed tears in her brother's eyes. 'Jersey'll be okay. She has you two. Talk to you later.' And then he was gone again, the sound of his bedroom door closing behind him.

She watched him go, her heart turning into a liquid puddle of mush, before turning back to Sophie. 'Not that I mind, but why isn't your Aunt Natalia taking Jersey home?'

'She told her mom there was something she needed to do, and she thought it would be easier with us.'

'Did she say what?'

'Said she'd tell us when we got there.' The fingernail on Sophie's index finger went into her mouth, muffling her words as she spoke around it. 'Do you think that's because she knows we're not going to want her to do whatever it is either, and she doesn't want to give us time to think of a way to talk her out of it?'

'I don't know.' But Holly had wondered the exact same thing. 'Let's go, so we can find out.'

–

Nearly three hours later, the nurse finally delivered Jersey's care instructions, a list of names and numbers for counselors to assist her in dealing with her ordeal, and instructions on how to keep her wounds clean and safe from infection.

Before they left, Jersey excused herself to go to the restroom, and Aunt Natalia took the opportunity to speak to Holly and Sophie. Her knees bounced, and her eyes darted to the closed door as she lowered her voice. 'I'm not sure where Jersey wants you girls to take her, but please use common sense. And watch out for her.'

Sophie squeezed her aunt's hand. 'We promise. And we'll send a message when we're on our way to your house.'

'Thank you.'

When Jersey reappeared a moment later, her watery eyes caught her mother's and then her friends' worried gazes. 'I think I'm as ready as I can be.' Tremulous words gave evidence of her fear of what was beyond her hospital room door.

Holly and Sophie each linked an arm with Jersey as Aunt Natalia walked behind her.

'Are you sure you won't let them get you a wheelchair, sweetheart?'

Jersey kept her focus straight ahead as she answered. 'I'm okay, Mom. I'm just a little weak, still. Walking will do me good.'

Outside, Holly heard someone call her name. Ten feet away stood Nick. He waved his hand for her to hold up, then said something to his sister. When she turned, her eyes widened, and then she nodded, and Nick tenderly led his sister over to their group.

340

'Hi. This is…' but before he could make the introductions, Jersey and Rachel stepped into each other, wrapping their arms gently around the other, careful not to hurt the wounds on their backs, and sobbed together.

Helpless to do more than watch, that's what they all did, allowing the two girls to embrace and bond over their shared horrifying experience. When they stepped back, they didn't release each other; they simply moved so they gripped each other's hands.

'I'm so sorry. I heard about your—' Rachel began.

'I'm so sorry. I heard about your—' Jersey said at the same time.

Neither finished their thought, but once again, they clung to each other, their words and shared nightmare connecting them.

'Can we keep in touch?' Jersey whispered. 'If you'd rather not, if it's too much of a reminder, it's okay.'

Her eyes still full of tears, Rachel said, 'Everything will be a reminder, at least for the time being. And yes, I think we can help each other. Did Becca and Faye stop by to see you before they left?'

Jersey shook her head, then looked over Rachel's shoulder toward the parking garage. 'No. But they had to sedate me a few times, so maybe they tried.'

'I'm sure they did. They said they would. They gave me their numbers and made me promise I'd call whenever I… if I ever felt like giving up.' Rachel turned to her brother. 'Will you hand me my phone so I can type Jersey's digits in?' As Nick did as he was told, Rachel continued. 'I wish we could've gotten Katelyn and Cheyenne's information, too, but I guess their parents had them transferred to a different hospital.'

They talked for another minute, then Nick officially introduced Holly to his sister and Sophie. 'And these are the gals I told you about, the ones who helped me change my tire.'

Rachel tilted her head to the side, her eyes appraising what she saw. 'Thank you for helping my brother. And for being there for him lately. He needs someone, too.'

'Anytime. I hope he knows that.'

Jersey waited until they were in Holly's car before she spoke again. 'So, you and Rachel's brother, huh?'

Holly blushed. 'That obvious, huh?'

'Girl, it's written all over both your faces.'

Holly chewed her cheek before angling her body toward Jersey. 'It was only one date...'

'Technically, it was one and a half,' Sophie chimed in from the backseat.

'One and a half. Does that bother you?'

'Why would it bother me?'

'Because I met him when... when...'

Jersey's smile was soft but sad. 'You met because of the circumstances. I'm not upset. I promise.'

Holly searched her friend's eyes for any hint of dishonesty, but saw none, and a sigh of relief escaped her. She turned the key in the ignition and shifted into reverse as she backed out of her space. At the light, she asked, 'Where to?'

A knot formed in Holly's stomach at Jersey's answer, but her friend stared straight ahead, refusing to look at her. 'Jersey, are you sure?'

'Yes.'

Hands unsteady on the wheel, Holly headed east.

Half an hour later, she and Sophie stood silently back but close enough for Jersey to know they were there to support her as their friend and cousin explained to Beau Cambridge that under no circumstances should he ever contact her again; that he should lose her phone number altogether.

Then, her posture almost regal, she turned and walked away without a backward glance. It was only once they were back in Holly's car and around the block that she asked Holly to pull over somewhere. As soon as she could safely do so, Holly obeyed. Then Jersey unbuckled herself and after shoving the door open, she practically fell outside into the parking lot.

Doubling over, she fell to the ground, her body vibrating as she howled, releasing more of the hurt and pain inside her.

Mindless of rubberneckers, Holly and Sophie dropped to the ground on either side of Jersey and wrapped their arms around her, holding her tightly, holding her together, promising they'd always be there for her, every step of the way.

Holly wasn't sure how much time passed before Jersey's tears were depleted, but the sun had definitely changed positions in the sky. When she was able to stand, they helped her back into the car, and as promised, Sophie sent a message to Aunt Natalia letting her know they were bringing Jersey home.

Chapter Fifty-Six

Wednesday morning, Alyssa met Cord in the parking lot outside the precinct when they both pulled in at the same time. She rounded the hood of her car, staring when he stayed by his driver's door. 'Morning. You okay?'

A smile broke out on her partner's face. 'Morning.' He tipped his head toward the precinct. 'Got a sec before we head in? I have some news.'

She ignored the nerves in her stomach. 'Oh-kay.'

'Sara's pregnant. We're going to be parents! Me, a daddy!'

Alyssa couldn't stop the silly grin that spread from ear to ear, and she reached in and hugged her partner. 'That is great news, Cord!' She pushed away from him. 'Wait, is *that* why you went to the doctor with Sara?'

Cord's head looked like it might topple from his neck as it nodded up and down. 'Yep.'

'Well, congratulations. I have some news myself. Want to hear it?'

Cord's elbow jostled her in the side. 'You pregnant, too?'

Her own elbow hit him back. Hard. In the stomach. 'God, no. Bite your tongue.'

'Then what?'

'Holly's not going to Cornell after all.'

Cord stopped moving, and when she turned to look back at him, his mouth hung open. 'What? And why are you smiling about it? What did Brock say?'

Even if she had wanted to rein in her pride, she couldn't. 'Brock is disappointed but also excited. And I'm smiling because Holly will be staying home to study criminology so she can follow in her mama's footsteps.'

'What did Mabel say?' This time Alyssa threw her head back and laughed at the way her partner checked all around him as if he was afraid Mabel was eavesdropping.

'Surprisingly, after she grilled Holly for several hours over two days, she came around, and is in fact, quite excited that she'll still get to see Holly on more than just long weekends and holidays.'

'Well, then, I'm happy for her.'

Two officers walked out, and since one of them stopped to hold the door, Alyssa and Cord jogged up the steps and inside where they bumped into Lynn Sharp.

'Oh, just who I was coming to see. Detectives, do you have a minute?'

'Of course. What can we do for you?' Alyssa's feet moved automatically in the direction of the conference room, but she stopped at Lynn's next words.

'It's more what I can do for you.' The medical examiner inhaled through her nose and released her breath slowly through her mouth. 'We received some of the results already from the DNA swabs taken from the men you arrested in Placitas. As you're fully aware, the hospital performed rape kits on all the girls, and the DNA discovered in Rachel Otis's kit match both Daryl Wainwright and Martin Mendez. As soon as the rest of the results come in, I'll let you know, but I wanted to come tell you that first, and since I was going to be here anyway...'

'Thanks, Lynn. We appreciate it.'

Instead of leaving to attend to her other business, Lynn's head swiveled, her gaze landing on a dirt-streaked man cursing at an officer. And then softly, she said, 'You know I'm an agnostic, but it's moments like this that I really hope there's a fiery hell where men like them will go straight to, do not pass go.'

Alyssa understood and agreed with the sentiment. 'Me, too, Lynn. Me, too.'

Ten minutes later, she sat around the table in the conference room with her team, which included Liz Waterson who'd returned yesterday from visiting her parents in North Carolina.

'Before we get started, Lynn Sharp stopped Cord and me a few minutes ago to inform us that the DNA samples taken from two of the men match the DNA taken from the rape kits performed on the girls. Wainwright and Mendez.'

'Well,' Tony said, 'this is good news. It's sick and sad, but it's just one more nail in their proverbial coffin.'

A kerosene-soaked wooden coffin that's headed straight to the hottest flames of Hades. The vehemence of the thought was so forceful and startling that Alyssa was almost afraid she'd uttered it aloud.

Liz twirled a red pen around on the table. There was a hard edge to her voice when she finally spoke. 'It is insane what people will do for the almighty buck. I mean, good heavens, even without the bundle of money Salazar would've had if her husband hadn't swiped her father's money, she was still an extremely wealthy woman in her own right.'

'You're not wrong,' Alyssa agreed. 'But I think it was more than that. Her husband's affairs and the financial aspect were just her excuses to release the evil person she already was inside. And since everyone's here, I thought I'd let you all know that the DA called this morning. The judge refused bail for Tatiana and Leigh Ann, claiming they were flight risks, and agreeing that a monitoring bracelet wouldn't be much of a deterrent.' A chorus of relieved sighs floated around the room. 'As for Wainwright, Morton, Harper, and Mendez, bail was set at ten million each, cash only.'

'What about Steve Yarmini?' Joe asked, but before Alyssa could answer, Hammond appeared in the doorway and stepped inside, closing it behind him as he did.

That was never a good sign.

'Guards found Yarmini in his cell around six this morning. He hanged himself with his bedsheet.'

Alyssa and Cord shared a look, but it was Cord who asked, 'How did he manage that when he'd been removed from the general population over death threats and was on suicide watch?'

Hammond shrugged and glanced around the room at the others. 'We'll be launching an investigation into that matter.'

Ruby poked her head in. 'Alyssa, there's a Spencer McKay on line one for you. He said it's urgent and that he tried your cell, but it went to voicemail.'

Alyssa glanced down at her phone. A blinking red light in the corner showed she'd missed a call. Huh. She wondered why she hadn't heard it. 'Thanks, Ruby.'

She felt everyone's eyes on her as she picked up the extension. 'Mr. McKay, I heard about your client.'

'Yes, well, heads should roll. But that's not why I'm calling you. Last night, Yarmini left a message on my phone. I got it this morning. He gave me a list of names you're going to want to take down. Tell me when you're ready.'

'Hold on. I'm going to put you on speaker. My captain and team are with me.'

Hammond's eyebrows arched high, but he remained where he was.

'Okay, go ahead.'

'As I was saying, my client left a message on my phone giving me a list of players you might be interested in and asked if I'd pass the information on to you. Taylor Adamson is a manager at the Builder's Depot near the canyon. He was one of Salazar's first clients. Yarmini met him because Salazar asked if Yarmini would show the man how to get to the house in Placitas. He didn't indicate how Salazar knew Adamson.'

Alyssa's team began to shift in their seats as tensions grew.

'Aaron Anderson is the president of Wellington Power Company near Lovington and was what Yarmini referred to as a "frequent flyer." You may have heard of Harold Devigne. He's a United States health official who lives near Show Low, Arizona. The final name he gave me is Doctor Darren Coen from Tucson.'

Joe and Tony exchanged swift glances with each other before shifting their eyes to Alyssa and Cord as they all wondered if Coen was the reason Tatiana had purchased a bus ticket to Southern Arizona.

McKay cleared his throat. 'There's more. Two of the men, Daryl Wainwright and Martin Mendez, you already have in custody, but Yarmini mentioned that the two men generally operated together. According to my client, during one of Tatiana's drunken tirades, she let loose that Wainwright and Mendez met through the dark web when they were part of a snuff film. He didn't mention how she came across them.'

Blood rushed from Alyssa's face, making the room spin. Had that been their plan all along? Had their evil rampage been stopped before they could complete that final act? Her stomach roiled as the image of Rachel suspended from the contraption and Katelyn curled into herself on the mattress flashed into her memory and stayed there.

'Detective, I'll need to go through the proper channels, but I'll have a copy of this recording to you by day's end. Good luck and goodbye.'

Silence filled the room for several seconds after Alyssa settled the receiver back in its cradle. Liz was the first to break it.

'Why do you think he did it? Yarmini, I mean? Give up the names and take his own life?'

Cord's voice was gruff, and his face flushed with anger. 'Maybe he was afraid, or maybe he did it because he really felt crushing guilt for what he did. Maybe he felt like death is what he deserved – and it is. But one thing remains clear: he robbed Meghan Jessup's family of justice, of seeing him in a courtroom answering for his crimes, of the *opportunity* to confront him, to show him their faces and to demand he tell them *why*.'

Alyssa watched the way her partner's jaw tightened, how the muscle ticced above his left eye, how every word was punctuated with both grief and rage, and she knew he was thinking about Shelley as much as Meghan Jessup and the others.

She pushed herself to her feet. 'Cord's right. However' – she tipped her head to the list of names in front of her – 'while we can't undo Yarmini's choice, what we can do is find these guys and round them up before they can hurt anyone else or before they get a chance to skip town.'

Hammond jerked his head forward in a brief nod. 'Keep me apprised; let me know if you need me to intervene with anything.' He left the door ajar behind him. 'I'll contact the local and state police in Arizona and make them aware of the situation.'

'I'll notify Lovington police,' Joe offered.

'And Cord and I will head out to Builder's Depot. Liz, can you round up Adamson's residential address for us? Tony, I need you to contact Judge Rosario and get telephonic arrest and search warrants secured.'

They were already moving. 'On it.'

–

Ten o'clock that night, Alyssa sat in her living room with Brock, Holly, Isaac, and Mabel watching the news.

Channel 7 was there when police moved in and arrested Taylor Adamson in connection with the sex trafficking ring organized and run by Tatiana Salazar, previously employed by land mogul multi-billionaire Bartholomew Rosenfelt. Another employee of Mr. Rosenfelt's, Steve Yarmini, committed suicide in the county jail sometime between the hours of midnight last night and six this morning. We tried to reach Mr. Rosenfelt for comment, but he has yet to return our call.

The cameraman panned over to Alyssa and Cord ignoring shouted questions from reporters as they escorted Adamson, his head down, face shielded by his shirt, into the detention center before moving over to footage from the search warrant served upon his home. Just out of camera range, in the shadow of a window, Alyssa knew, stood a teenager watching police raiding her family's home and taking her father's belongings. Alyssa didn't think she'd ever forget the look of horror on the girl's face at what her father was being accused of. Beside her daughter was Adamson's wife. A film of moisture covered her eyes, but no tears fell. Instead, she blinked repeatedly, as if she could stop her life from unraveling by doing so.

Police aren't speaking, but as this horrifying story unfolds, we caught footage of officers removing Adamson's vehicle along with several computers and discs from his home. What appears to be a bag of clothing was also taken.

Holly's form was stiff beside her, and Alyssa wrapped her arm around her daughter's shoulder, encouraging her to lean into her. When she did, Alyssa alternated between rubbing circles on her back and running her hand over her hair. Every once in a while, Holly would sniffle and reach up to wipe her nose with a tissue and erase the tears with her fingers.

Isaac and Mabel both split their attention between watching the news report and staring at Holly, ready to catch her if she broke.

'You don't have to watch this, sweetie,' Alyssa whispered into her daughter's ear.

Holly's chin fell toward her chest. 'I do,' she answered back, voice breaking.

Also arrested in today's round-up were Aaron Anderson, president of Wellington Power Company in Lovington. In Arizona, authorities worked with our local police department to round up United States health official Harold Devigne of Show Low, as well as Doctor Darren Coen of Tucson.

As you can see for yourself, these are some high-profile names, and Captain Guthrie Hammond of APD has promised a press conference tomorrow at seven a.m. Of course, Channel 7 will be there to bring you the latest on this shocking and disturbing crime.

Brock pointed the remote at the television and shut it off. Holly stayed nestled by Alyssa's side while Mabel secured Isaac to hers. Alyssa rested her head into the crook of Brock's neck, and he kissed the top of her head. Tomorrow would be another busy day, and she knew she should go to bed and grab what sleep she could, but for now, Alyssa wanted to bask in the warmth of the knowledge that her family was physically safe and together in her home.

A Letter From Charly

More than a century ago, Loren Eiseley wrote "The Star Thrower" – a story many of us are more familiar with in one of its many variations. In one of these variations, the narrator tells us of a man walking along the beach, tossing one starfish after another back into the ocean. When someone approaches him and ponders why the man is doing such a thing since there are so many starfish to save, he couldn't possibly make a difference, the man tosses a starfish into the ocean, saying, "It made a difference to that one."

Research for *The Toybox* had me delving into eye-opening and oftentimes brutal stories. Sadly, the global, world-wide reach of human and sex trafficking grows exponentially every day. And despite what people believe, victims come in all ages, ethnicities, and from all cultures and financial circles. To fight and stop this epidemic, to protect these individuals, we have to educate ourselves and be brave enough to SPEAK UP. Unfortunately, too many people want to look the other way, afraid to get involved – or be wrong. But if we suspect someone is a victim of trafficking, and we're too afraid to reach out on their behalf, imagine how frightened that person is of the life they're being forced to live. Often, these victims are under strict control of others, and they may be scared to reach out on their own because of personal threats against them or their families. They don't know who they can trust, which is why it's imperative we reach out for them.

For signs on what to look for and who to contact in case of suspected sex trafficking, please click on the following links.

353

And remember, your choice to speak up could save more than one life.

https://www.modernslaveryhelpline.org/about/
spot-the-signs

https://www.acf.hhs.gov/otip/victim-assistance/
national-human-trafficking-hotline

https://humantraffickinghotline.org/

Thank you to all the readers out there. If you'd like to reach out and say hello or follow me on social media, you can find me at the links below.

Until next time...

Charly Cox

Charly Cox Author Website: https://www.clcox-author.com/

Twitter: @charlylynncox

Facebook: @charlycoxauthor

Goodreads: https://www.goodreads.com/author/
show/19490745.Charly_Cox

BookBub: https://www.bookbub.com/profile/charly-cox

Acknowledgments

Writing can sometimes be a daunting journey, but I have a bevy of people who encourage me along the way (or sometimes nudge, push... shove) and keep me putting pen to paper (or fingers to keypad). So, I'd like to take the time to thank some of those very important people – without whom, I'd be lost.

First and foremost, I want to thank Keshini Naidoo (and not just because you have one of the coolest names ever), one half of the amazing Hera Books team. Thank you not only for your endless hard work, but for trusting in me, my writing, and my characters from the very beginning... and then finding a way to pull all the various threads to help make everything a thousand times better. My world of characters would definitely not be the same without you, and I will forever be in awe of your ability to see through the most mundane words and scenes and extract exactly what is needed to make them shine. I treasure you, your advice, suggestions, and wisdom. Thank you for always taking the time to allay my fears and concerns and answering all my questions. The support you have lent me is worth its weight in gold.

Thanks also goes to Lindsey Mooney, the other half of Hera Books, for your extensive efforts in getting my work out there in front of readers, for cheering with me through all of it. Thank you for explaining things and helping me stay calm as my words go out into the world. I can't even imagine what goes on behind the scenes as you work your magic, but I'm hugging you for all of it!

For Melissa Naatz – Where do I even start? You have been such an incredible friend, cheerleader, support, guidepost, shoulder to cry on, advocate... Thank you for those phone calls when you sense I'm stepping too close to the ledge and then knowing exactly what to say to talk me down. You make me laugh, you make me think, and you let me cry. You stay on the phone with me for hours at a time and wade through plot points with me until things fall into place. And after that, you still patiently read the same words over and over and over... and give me your honest, insightful feedback every time. But mostly, thank you for all those nudges that put me back on track and in the right frame of mind and for reminding me what readers want to see. I can't believe we haven't been a part of each other's lives forever, but that doesn't matter because you're stuck with me now. And I can't wait to celebrate with you (at low altitude, of course) when badass Devin meets the world of readers. My cheers will be heard all the way into space.

For my sister Kim – From the time we were little girls living with Grandma and Grandpa to the time we moved out and started our own lives, we banded together and weathered the kind of storms that made us stronger and made us who we are; we always listened to each other's secrets, rants, fears, hopes, and dreams, and helped to wipe each other's tears... even during whatever sisterly fights we might've had going on. And even though years and nearly two thousand miles separate us from those times, there are three things that will forever bond us: unity, love, and above all, friendship. Thank you for believing in my dreams with me. And telling others to believe, too! And for always telling me (and others) how proud of me you are. As the recent gift you gave me says: I may not always be there *with* you, but I will always be there *for* you.

For Kerrie and Victoria. Being an aunt is such an amazing gift, but being an aunt to people you love, respect, admire, and call your friend is something that goes beyond special. You are such incredible women! And Kerrie, when I picture amazing, selfless, kickass mothers, you're the person I see. Victoria, from the moment you crawled into my lap so I could read to you to today where I get to watch you bravely sing and perform in front of strangers, you have awed me. Thank you both for standing not just *by me*, but *with me* and for reminding me of who I am and *who* and *what* matters. For someone who writes words for a living, I fall short of being able to express exactly how much I love you and how important you are in my life. But I hope you know it anyway. Thank you… for you… for *everything!*

For Susan – When I first moved to Albuquerque, you gave me a family to belong to. And ever since then, you have been there to watch me grow and to chase my dreams. You've been there to cheer me on and congratulate me through all my many milestones. We just maybe shouldn't attend football games together anymore – at least not when the Giants and Broncos are playing each other.

Thanks, once again, to my cousin, Bud Wolfenbarger – first, for sending me the most thoughtful, amazing, unexpected gift when *All His Pretty Girls* debuted. Your quest to find Booberry cereal and candy cigarettes was one of the coolest things ever… I still can't get over the entire package. Thank you also for continuing to answer my multitude of law enforcement questions, and then walking me through what criminal investigations look like so I can at least try to get them right. (I think this is where I remind readers that any and all errors in my story come from me – not from your explanations.) You are still and will forever be my favorite law enforcement person.

For my son Timothee who laughs at me and makes me laugh at myself… Every time I falter, you're there to make sure I don't fall. You let me talk storylines and plot holes and then give me ideas to make those things better. I am so happy I get to be your mom. Plus, you give the best hugs ever.

For my husband Kevin: You are so fiercely protective and proud of me, and I absolutely cannot imagine traveling this journey without you. Thank you for never giving up on my dream and for never letting me. You believe in me when I forget to believe in myself. You are the most amazing man, husband, and friend. I love you.

For all those who have always stood with me, either in person or online: Tam, Tracy, Ang, Annette, Ro, Kevin and Theresa, Drew and Deb, Mary McAfee, Trudy Randour, Stephanie Schlitz, Jodi Lew-Smith, and Hallie Tassin. No matter how often I say it, I could never thank you enough.

And finally: to all the readers out there who gave *All His Pretty Girls* and me a chance. Your emails, your messages, your reviews, your kindness have blown my mind time and time again! YOU have made it possible for me to keep going. So, a billion thanks to all of you.

I hope you enjoyed reading *The Toybox*, as well. If you did, please drop me a line and let me know. I'd also love it if you'd leave a review and tell your friends about it!